A LAI ⌐⌐⌐⌐

Felicity George is a writer and teacher from Toronto, where she lives with her husband, her two teenage children, a large cat, and a tiny dog. A lifelong devotee of Jane Austen and Georgette Heyer, Felicity adores a happily-ever-after. *A Lady's Risk* is her first novel.

Connect with Felicity:

🐦 Felicity George @ElizabethWelke
📘 Felicity George, Author @
FelicityGeorgeRegencyRomance

A LADY'S RISK

Felicity George

First published in Great Britain in 2022 by Orion Dash,
an imprint of The Orion Publishing Group Ltd,
Carmelite House, 50 Victoria Embankment
London EC4Y 0DZ

An Hachette UK company

1   3   5   7   9   10   8   6   4   2

ISBN (Mass Market Paperback) 978 1 3987 1414 4
ISBN (eBook) 978 1 3987 1 0450

Typeset by Born Group

To Jessica R and Julie,
who inspire me.

I

September 1812

Lady Margaret Fairchild, on her knees in the grass in an entirely undignified manner for a lady of one-and-twenty years, plucked one last blackberry from the brambles between Berksleigh Hall's parkland and the road from Warwick. She plopped it into the basket clasped in her little sister Sophy's berry-stained hands. 'Are you still counting, Harry?' she asked her seven-year-old brother, the newly made Earl of Berksleigh.

Little Lord Berksleigh rubbed his snub nose with a grubby paw. 'I lost precise count, but I think that makes one thousand, Meggy.'

Meggy stood and shook her wrinkled skirts in a futile attempt to clean the dirt from her faded yellow frock and red apron. 'Do you suppose we've picked enough, my loves?' she asked, waving her hand towards the baskets of fragrant fruit filling their pony cart. There were far more than one thousand berries, and Meggy had picked most of them whilst Harry and Sophy chattered and skipped about like two playful squirrels, their spaniel Copper dashing in circles around their feet.

'Not nearly,' nine-year-old Sophy said. 'Cook needs ever so many for jam.' A tear trickled down one pink cheek and dropped into the blonde curls spilling over the child's shoulder. 'Although I don't suppose it matters, as *we* shan't be here. The strangers leasing Berksleigh Hall will eat the jam instead.'

Harry kicked at the dirt with his scuffed boot. 'I wish I were a man. Then we needn't leave our home to live with someone we've never met. I'd go to sea and make the Fairchild fortune back in prize money.'

Meggy embraced her brother, leaning down to inhale the sun-warmed scent of his thick brown curls. She understood the dear boy's sentiments more than he'd ever know. If Meggy had been born male, she'd be the Earl of Berksleigh now. Then she could find *some* way to care for the children without relying on aid from the dreadful stranger their recently deceased half-brother Edwin had appointed as joint guardian to Harry and Sophy.

'You cannot go to sea, Harry.' Her stomach lurched at the thought of her beloved little brother slipping beyond her protection. 'Who then would care for Sophy and me?' Harry squirmed, but Meggy kissed his forehead before he wriggled out of her hug.

Sophy nestled into his abandoned spot, with the basket still in her hands. 'We might bring jam with us when Lord Holbrook takes us to Alton Park.'

Harry's blue eyes darkened under drawn brows. '*If* he takes us, Sophy. I think Lord Holbrook might be as scaly a rascal as Edwin was. Wasn't he meant to arrive a fortnight ago?'

'Yes,' Meggy said, holding her sister close. 'And he'll be here before the tenants arrive in two days.' She spoke with false conviction for the sake of the children, for the Marquess of Holbrook had a notorious reputation. He'd likely forgotten about them – holed up in London with whores and gamblers, no doubt. 'I'm afraid the jam must be for the tenants, but perhaps, if you're especially good at lessons with Miss Kimberley this afternoon, Cook will bake a tart for tonight.'

She tickled her siblings under their chins. Although the children smiled, no sparkle lit their eyes, and Meggy swallowed back tears. Edwin's rapid ruination of the family had taught her no one was more selfish and irresponsible than a reprobate, and the unknown marquess was proving that yet again.

Meggy tried another tactic to brighten her siblings' spirits. 'Let's return home and have lemonade, loves. The day is scorching, and we haven't any more containers to fill, anyway.'

Harry stuffed his little fists into his trouser pockets. 'Perfect day to be at sea.'

'Perhaps a swim in the pond after lessons,' Meggy said, wiping perspiration from her upper lip. Her words elicited the longed-for joyful squeals from the children. Meggy beamed as she kissed her sister's soft cheek. 'Put your basket with the others, Sophy darling.'

As Sophy complied, a cooling breeze from the nearby Avon blew across the Warwick Road. Meggy arched her aching back whilst a pair of swans glided along the river's serpentine path. The wind livened the willows and rustled the rushes at the water's edge, and the river current danced like rippling satin ribbons, but Meggy muffled a sigh. Berksleigh Hall was home, and the pain of their imminent departure stabbed like a knife.

Her heart leaden, Meggy stuffed her leather work gloves into her apron pocket. 'Harry,' she said, forcing a lilt to her voice, 'please lead Hazel home.'

Harry snapped to attention like a soldier. 'Aye, aye.' He grabbed the pony's reins and led her onto the road.

Sophy tucked sticky fingers into Meggy's hand whilst Meggy whistled to Copper. But as the whistle died on her lips, the cry of an unseen coachman and the hammering hooves of a team of horses roared from the south. Meggy's heartbeat quickened. There was a blind curve in the road, and the rumble of the carriage grew louder every second.

The vehicle was travelling too fast, and Harry stood directly in its path.

Meggy released Sophy's hand and leapt for Hazel's reins, yanking her brother and the cart to safety just as four thundering horses and a black and silver carriage rounded the turn.

Meggy glowered at the liveried coachman. 'Mind your speed, you horrid man!' The hooves upon the hard-packed dirt road swallowed her words, but at that moment, the occupant's head – topped by a tall-crowned black hat – turned in her direction. The sun's glare on the glass obscured most details, but crisp white shirt linen cascaded below the man's powerful jaw.

The carriage slowed at the gates of Berksleigh Hall twenty yards down the road, allowing Meggy her first clear view of the painted coronet topping the crest on the door.

Three strawberry leaves – two in profile – with two pearls between them.

A marquess.

Of course.

Lord Holbrook had proven himself an incapable guardian already by permitting his coachman to gallop horses on a blind curve. Meggy balled her fists, readying herself for battle as the team pulled to a halt and the carriage door opened.

The infamous marquess emerged with his head bowed as he assisted a small dog down the carriage steps. A dark blue tailcoat, tailored like a second skin, covered his broad shoulders, and tight buff trousers displayed muscular thighs before tapering into gleaming black Hessian boots.

Lord Holbrook lifted his head.

Meggy gasped as her fists slackened. Her heart, already racing in anger, now hammered.

Edwin had been forty when he died, but his friend was no more than thirty – and handsome beyond compare. Thick dark curls fell to his forehead from under his hat brim, long sideburns cut a sharp line under his high cheekbones, and black brows arched over clear grey eyes. But his mouth arrested the most attention. He wasn't smiling, and yet his lips curled up tenderly at the edges.

What a gentle, *kind*-looking man.

But as Lord Holbrook walked closer, he lifted his firm chin, threw back his shoulders, and smirked, displaying perfect white teeth whilst a mocking gleam shone in his eyes.

Ah, he was a devil in disguise.

Meggy's hammering heart calmed its nonsense. She knew better than to let a handsome face – even one as magnificent as Lord Holbrook's – sweep her away.

'Excuse me, miss,' the marquess's deep voice rumbled. 'Did my carriage cause you some trouble?'

Meggy blinked. *Miss*? 'Miss' was not the proper address for Lady Margaret Fairchild, daughter of an earl.

Clearly, Lord Holbrook didn't know who *she* was.

The day before, Nicholas Burton, the Marquess of Holbrook, had endured a seven-hour journey from London to Warwick in blazing heat, and he'd amused himself for the duration by cursing his dead friend's name. Bah – not even a friend. The late Lord Berksleigh was an acquaintance at best. In fact, Nicholas had avoided him when possible, for Edwin Fairchild was a distasteful person, oozing debauchery from every pore of his wheezing, shattered body.

But dammit, Edwin had saved Nicholas's life years ago, and he owed him.

'My siblings, Holbrook,' Edwin had during Nicholas's deathbed visit in late July. The wasted, jaundiced earl lay upon a sagging mattress in a sordid flat off Lincoln Inn Fields whilst Nicholas, perched on the edge of a rickety wooden chair, pressed his handkerchief to his nose. Faecal odour from a nearby public boghouse blew into the dank room along with the cries of beggars, the clop of hooves, and the rumble of carriage wheels. A drunken nurse snored in a corner, with a trail of drool dribbling down her chin. 'My half-siblings from my father's second marriage. I need you to provide them a home at one of your estates whilst Berksleigh Hall is let.'

Nicholas coughed into his handkerchief. '*What?*'

Edwin held up a skeletal hand. 'There's more. You must stand as their joint guardian.'

Nicholas stiffened. Memories of his own childhood guardian surfaced, but he repressed them quickly. 'Joint with whom?' he asked through his handkerchief.

'With my half-sister, Margaret. She's past her majority now – she turned one-and-twenty last month. But she is yet unmarried, and I cannot leave Henry and Sophia to her without guidance from a male guardian.'

Nicholas stifled a snort of laughter. 'I'm hardly qualified to guide anyone.' He folded his handkerchief and returned it to his waistcoat pocket. 'You'd best choose someone else.'

'I cannot. Who else would do more for me than spit on my grave?' Edwin knitted his trembling fingers together on the threadbare counterpane. 'I've been a friend to no one, Nicholas. But *you* . . . you owe me your life, and I'm asking you to repay that debt by helping them.'

Nicholas respected few rules, but he must honour a debt, even though, on his gloomiest days, he wished

Edwin had let him die. 'Very well, damn you,' he said. After all, he could pawn the children's daily maintenance off on his sister Rose. 'How old are they?'

'Sophia is nine, and Henry is seven.'

'*Seven*? Fourteen years from his majority?' Even Rose wouldn't want a fourteen-year responsibility to grubby little Fairchilds.

'Yes – and there is another task you must do.'

'Bloody hell, Edwin. Absolutely not.' Nicholas crossed his arms over his chest.

'Ah, but the sooner you do the second thing, the sooner my siblings are entirely off your hands.' Tears welled in Edwin's yellow-tinged eyes. 'They're near destitute. I've left them with nothing. The townhouse in Mayfair is sold, and those proceeds long gone. Of course, I couldn't sell the estate, connected with the title as it is, but it's mortgaged and in poor repair, although Margaret did her best. She was fourteen when our father died, and I was three-and-thirty, and yet I left it all to her – raising the children, managing the estate.' Edwin pulled upon the strands of thin hair clinging to his scabby scalp, his unshaven chin quivering. With a ragged breath, he continued, 'Locate tenants for Berksleigh Hall, and then do your best to find Margaret a good husband – a man of means and honour. Once she's wed, your obligation is complete, for her husband will be joint guardian then. But, promise me, Nicholas – a *good* husband. Someone who will love Henry and Sophia, someone who will be kind to poor Margaret.'

Nicholas twisted his signet ring and sighed. 'Oh, very well. I shall do my goddamn best. That's all I can offer.'

'Thank you. You give me great peace.' A thin smile hovered on the earl's lips. 'One more thing.'

'By God, I shall kill you myself soon.'

Edwin laughed until he wheezed. 'You're not as horrid as you pretend, Nick.'

Nicholas flicked a speck of dust off his coat sleeve. 'You don't know a damned thing about me.'

'I know a bit, and I stand by my opinion. This is the last task, I promise. Care for my dog Caesar once I'm gone.' Edwin lifted the coverlet to expose a fawn pug with a black face and curled tail. 'It'll be hard on him – the poor beast has loved me when no one else could.'

So Caesar accompanied Nicholas in the carriage on his journey to Berksleigh Hall. In fact, the pug accompanied him almost everywhere, for once Caesar had ceased mourning for Edwin, he'd bestowed all his affection upon Nicholas.

After hours on the road, a night spent at an inn in Warwick hadn't improved Nicholas's mood. The charms of a dark-haired chambermaid provided a brief distraction, but she became so annoying – thrusting her breasts in his face as she served his dinner and whimpering, 'My lord, you are the handsomest gentleman that ever lived' – that in the end Nicholas pursued nothing beyond an uninspiring kiss. He closed the door on her sobs and crawled between scratchy sheets in a stifling room with only Caesar for company.

Nicholas arose miserable with half the morning gone, and his mood like a hurricane. During the short ride to Berksleigh Hall, he fumed. Now he must endure a couple more days' travel in the summer heat with two children and an insipid virgin – undoubtedly pasty and plain, as she was Edwin's sister – to transport them to his estate near Ipswich. Then how long must he bear that burden before he found someone willing to marry the destitute sister of foul Edwin Fairchild?

But when his carriage slowed near the gates of Berksleigh Hall, Nicholas's pulse quickened. A delectable village wench stood next to a waggon bursting with blackberries.

He paid little mind to the two children with her, for the doxy was a joy to behold. The high waist of her wheat-coloured summer frock defined her full breasts; a cherry-red apron enhanced her skin's rosy glow, and hints of soft lips, fine eyes, and thick golden-brown curls peeked out from under the brim of her straw bonnet. The girl drew her lovely face into an adorable scowl, quite as if she wished to murder his coachman.

The all too familiar thrill of the chase revived Nicholas's languid spirits. The Fairchild siblings could wait. First, he should make amends for whatever wrong this morsel had suffered. And as he soothed her, he'd discover if she were willing for a tumble with a lord. She was certainly ripe for one.

Nicholas banged his walking stick for his coachman to stop and then emerged from the carriage with Caesar at his heels.

★

When their eyes met, the village girl's lips parted with a gasp, and her cheeks flushed even rosier. She was smitten, and Nicholas's excitement ebbed. A good hunt heightened his pleasure – why did women make it so easy to be caught?

He stepped closer, and his pulse raced again.

She was provincial perfection. As lovely as a summer meadow, with full lips and a round face. Dusky lashes framed her cornflower blue eyes, and a spattering of freckles fell across her small nose.

Nicholas no longer cared if she was easy. She was a tumble-in-the-hay busty beauty, and he wanted her.

He *always* got what he wanted.

Nicholas grinned. 'Excuse me, miss – did my carriage cause you some trouble?'

Her thick lashes fluttered. No doubt she was attempting to recover from the excitement he'd aroused. 'As a matter of fact, yes. Your coachman nearly ran over my brother and our cart.'

Her pronunciation was refined, and Nicholas hesitated. But the girl looked as if she'd been crawling in the dirt, and gentlemen's daughters didn't pick berries by a public road without a maid nearby.

Nicholas returned to the hunt. 'Please accept my apology.' He placed a hand to his heart. 'The fault is entirely mine, for my coachman was acting under my orders to make haste. Allow me to make amends by assisting you home.'

One rounded brow raised, and her lips compressed. Ah, perhaps she wasn't so easy after all. Clever beauty.

Nicholas motioned to his coachman to drive on through the gates.

He turned to her siblings. They resembled her with their blue eyes and copious curls, but the little girl's hair was fair and the boy's was dark.

'Here, lad,' Nicholas said, 'I shall lead your waggon, and you tell me where to go.'

The boy looked at his sister. But before she replied, a cacophony of barking and growling broke out behind them.

Nicholas glanced over his shoulder. Caesar and a spaniel, noses to the ground, were having words over who had the greater claim to some creature's burrow.

He and the beauty dashed for their dogs. It was the work of a moment for Nicholas to kneel and tuck Caesar under one arm. It was the work of one moment more to place his other arm around the kneeling girl, ostensibly to pet her spaniel, but really to embrace her whilst her bottom brushed against his thigh.

Only the brim of her bonnet distanced their faces. Her curls tickled his nose. Her warm skin smelled of berries and fresh air. One of her soft breasts grazed his chest, and Nicholas's loins tightened. 'My dear, I'm afraid Caesar is a terribly behaved beast. Alas, I've been his master only a month, or he'd have *much* better manners.'

She licked her luscious lips with the tip of a pink tongue. 'Indeed, sir? And where would he learn those manners? For clearly *you* have none.'

Her answer delighted Nicholas, but he retained a solemn expression. 'Why! Have I offended you, sweetheart?'

She looked at him as if he were a fool. 'You've done nothing *but* offend me.' She squirmed away from his embrace by pushing against his chest with a determined little shoulder but remained kneeling to restrain her wriggling spaniel. 'Your carriage nearly injured my brother. Your vicious little pug attacked my dog, and you . . . you were *holding* me without my permission.'

Nicholas leaned towards her, and his lips brushed a tawny tendril upon her cheek. 'My most sincere apologies. You're so intoxicatingly beautiful I'm afraid I *am* too forward.'

He formed his features into the hazy-eyed gaze women loved. Despite her protestations, a ghost of a gasp parted her pretty lips. She blushed, and her eyes trailed to his mouth. Yes, she'd melt into his arms in due time, but he should get rid of the children and the livestock first. Then he'd ask her to stroll with him, and he'd locate a shady meadow. He'd untie her dress laces, remove her bonnet, and loosen her hair so those curly tresses spilled over what must be perfect breasts. And then he'd lay her down in the sun-dappled grass.

He was damnably close to an erection, so it was time to act. 'I shall be on my best behaviour now, Miss . . .? Forgive me, sweetheart, I don't know your name.'

She scratched her spaniel behind its floppy ears and glanced at him from the corner of her eyes. 'Yes, I have the advantage over you, *Lord Holbrook*.' A dimple deepened in each cheek as she smiled.

Nicholas raised his eyebrows. 'My heavens, clever puss. How do you know who I am?'

She opened her mouth, but before she responded, her little brother called out. 'Meggy, may we return now? I'm thirsty.'

Nicholas winked. 'Aha, you don't have the advantage anymore, *Meggy*.'

She released her spaniel and stood. 'Yes, Harry and Sophy, let's return. And since Lord Holbrook has kindly offered to lead the pony home to Berksleigh Hall, do hop into the waggon, loves.'

Nicholas still knelt on one knee, holding Caesar, but it was as if she'd knocked the breath from him.

Home to Berksleigh Hall.

Meggy, Sophy, Harry.

Margaret, Sophia, Henry.

Bloody hell.

Meggy offered her little hand. 'Do you need help up, Lord Holbrook? And I *do* think it's best if you call me Lady Margaret. We're not on terms of *familiarity*, sir.' Sunlight fell across her smirking lips, and her eyes flashed in triumph.

Nicholas rose without the help of Meggy's hand and without another glance at her smug countenance. He turned on his heel and took up the pony's reins, seething as the children scrambled into the waggon.

Meggy had every right to gloat. Only a fool sought dalliance with an earl's daughter, for high-born young ladies were untouchable outside a marriage contract.

And marriage was something Nicholas Burton would *never* do again.

With the pony breathing down his arm and his inner hurricane raging, Nicholas followed Meggy towards the gates of Berksleigh Hall.

God *damn* Edwin Fairchild.

2

Meggy silently cursed Edwin as her boots crunched along the elm-lined gravel drive towards the three-storey, flat-roofed limestone manor house where she'd lived all her life. How *dare* Edwin force her into partnership with a rake and a reprobate?

Harry and Sophy's giggles rose over the churn of the waggon wheels behind her. Meggy was grateful the children seemed happier, but she burned with shame. Perhaps her siblings laughed about her interaction with Holbrook. After all, she must've looked a fool nestled in the marquess's arms.

Good God, he'd wanted to ravish her by the roadside. Utterly disgusting.

Except it hadn't been.

Her heart had pounded when he whispered the words *'intoxicatingly beautiful'*. Her cheek had tingled at the brush of his lips. His mouth had mesmerised her. She'd wanted to slip into his silken web and melt under his smouldering heat.

And *that*, Meggy thought as she marched, was exactly how scoundrels ensnare young ladies. It wasn't a trap she could fall into. Edwin had ruined the Fairchilds, and Meggy must restore the family's honour for Sophy and Harry. Just as she'd had to do *everything* for the last seven years since her father's death, when Edwin dismissed the responsibilities of his inheritance in order to squander the family fortune.

Meggy lifted her face to the sky as she strode, allowing the dappled sunlight filtering through the verdant leaves of the elms to clear her mind. Yes, Holbrook's handsomeness upset her good sense for a moment, but only because she'd led a sheltered life at Berksleigh Hall caring for her young siblings and the estate. Now that she'd put the marquess in his place so effectively, she'd have no further difficulty resisting his physical allure.

Meggy led Holbrook around the side of the house and down the path leading towards the stables. To save money, she'd long since expanded the kitchen gardens by converting the side lawn to growing vegetables, and the scent of ripe beans and fennel hung in the air. She stopped at the kitchen entrance – an oak plank door recessed into the stone walls – and pulled upon the wooden latch worn smooth from two centuries of use.

'Harry, Sophy, bid farewell to Lord Holbrook. Then dash inside, have some lemonade, and find Miss Kimberley. You're late for your lessons.'

Harry bowed, Sophy curtsied, and the children scurried away. The two kitchen maids, Ann and Martha, arrived to unload the baskets, and Daniel, the groom, walked from the stables to take charge of the pony and cart.

'Will you stay for dinner, Lord Holbrook?' Meggy asked over her shoulder as she untied her red apron. Dammit, her silly heart fluttered when she addressed him.

There was no reply. Meggy handed her apron to Martha with a quick smile and turned. The marquess stood at the front corner of the house and gazed at Berksleigh Hall with his handsome face drawn as if he'd bitten into a lemon. No doubt he was sneering at the windows blackened to avoid tax, which rendered the house gap-toothed and desolate.

Meggy joined him, holding her chin high. The sorrowful state of the manor didn't represent the honour of the Fairchilds. *Meggy* embodied her ancient family's resilience and dignity – and she guided Sophy and Harry by her strength and example. 'I enquired if you wish to stay for dinner, Lord Holbrook.'

'No, thank you.' His words were terse, and his consonants clipped. 'I shall return to the inn at Warwick as soon as we've discussed our business.'

Meggy nodded. 'Very well. Shall we go inside to speak?'

He shrugged. 'I'm indifferent.'

Meggy thought of the peeling plaster in the drawing room. 'In that case, let's walk.'

'As you wish.' He offered his arm.

Meggy's mouth went dry as she recalled the sensual heat of Holbrook's broad body leaning against hers. She declined the arm with a wave of her hand.

Best not to touch him.

Holbrook's lips twitched, as if in amusement.

Meggy bristled. Did he imagine his good looks affected her? Clearly, she must put him in his place again.

With the dogs wagging their tails as they trotted between them, Meggy walked with Holbrook across the front of the house and into the East Garden, a grassy lawn criss-crossed with low-hedged paths. 'I assume you wish to discuss our removal to Suffolk,' she said, trailing her fingers amongst the bright-green box leaves. 'Or do you want me to point you to the village so you can seduce the tenants' daughters, or whatever you imagined I was?' She cut her gaze to Holbrook with a smirk.

The marquess's grey eyes flashed. 'Sarcasm is less clever than you may think, Lady Margaret. If you'd refrain from it, we could conduct our business more quickly.'

Meggy raised her eyebrow. 'Your manner is certainly less appealing now.' She pushed aside a wave of disappointment. If he intended to be unpleasant, it would make preserving her resolve against him much easier. 'I must say, you fooled me for the briefest of moments by the roadside. I imagined I glimpsed a kind man when you first stepped from your carriage. Fortunately, I saw through the deception and reminded myself that my brother has forced me into a partnership with the most notoriously hard-hearted libertine in Britain.'

Holbrook half smiled, but his eyes glinted. 'Fortuitous, indeed. Yet you weren't entirely averse to my charms.'

Meggy turned her face aside, lest the warmth of her cheeks betray her. 'What charms?' She pointed at the waggling rear of Holbrook's pug. 'You possess as much charm as your beastly little dog.'

Holbrook put a hand to his broad chest and bowed his head; the black beaver fur of his hat glistened in the sun. 'I must thank you for your compliment. Caesar is extraordinarily adorable.'

Meggy narrowed her eyes. 'Your pug is hideous. He pounced on sweet Copper as vilely as you pounced on me. And whilst we're on that subject, answer me a question so I may determine exactly what sort of man my brother placed as guardian over my beloved siblings. What would you have done with me had I been a village girl as you thought?'

'I'm afraid, Lady Margaret,' Holbrook said, swinging his walking stick like a pendulum as he strode, 'I shan't answer such an inappropriate question from a young lady.'

'Never mind,' Meggy said, with as nonchalance as she could muster. 'I know the answer. You would've ravished me.'

The marquess raised his eyebrows almost imperceptibly. 'My goodness. That's quite the accusation. Yet I wonder if you know what that bold word truly means?'

Meggy halted, pivoting her heels in the gravel as she faced Holbrook with her fists clenched. '*You* are the one whose behaviour is inappropriately bold, embracing me where anyone might've seen us. The very least you can do in atonement is answer my questions, so let us try again. Tell me, what would you have done after you ravished me?'

The marquess placed his hands behind his back, his expression intolerably smug. 'Firstly, I wouldn't have ravished you. If you'd chosen to accept my advances, we would've passed a mutually pleasurable hour or so together.' Meggy's cheeks blazed like fire. 'Afterwards, I would've very pleasantly wished you a good day and never looked upon you again, because, invariably, once I have what I want, I don't want it anymore.'

Meggy clapped her hand to her mouth. 'You're not *hard*-hearted,' she gasped. 'You're heart*less*. You're worse than Edwin.' What had her half-brother done, putting Meggy and the children at the mercy of such a vile man? Edwin's last betrayal was cruel, indeed.

Holbrook glanced towards the house. 'I don't know about that. My fortune is intact, and my properties are well maintained. You're fortunate my man of business found tenants willing to take on the expense of repairs to Berksleigh Hall.'

'*Fortunate*?' Meggy crossed her arms under her bosom. 'I don't feel fortunate to leave the only home I've ever known. Especially not if I'm indebted to you.'

Holbrook waved a hand dismissively. 'You and I shall do fine if you remember two things, Lady Margaret. As you've ascertained from your questioning, I'm not a kind man. You must never trust me. However, whilst you live under my roof, I shall make considerable effort to keep you safe – even safe from me. My sister Rose resides at my estate in Suffolk, and you can trust her, which is why I proposed taking you and your siblings to Alton Park. Secondly,' he said, pointing his cane at Meggy, '*you* hold the key to the dissolution of this partnership, as you termed it. All you must do is marry. I don't suppose you have a suitor already?'

Meggy's ears burned beneath her bonnet. 'No.'

'Pity. And rather surprising.' Holbrook stroked his firm chin as he looked her up and down. 'Are the gentlemen in Warwickshire blind?'

Meggy hated the fluttering of her heart. 'I don't have time for suitors,' she snapped, with a toss of the curls that spilled onto her shoulders from under her bonnet. 'Unlike most young ladies of my age and rank, I have, since the age of fourteen, raised two young siblings and managed this estate.'

'Well, you haven't those concerns anymore.' Holbrook kicked at an errant stick on the path with the burnished toe of his boot, and Copper wagged his tail expectantly. 'Berksleigh Hall is let, and Rose and my servants can help with your siblings.'

'I don't need help with my siblings.'

A gold signet ring shone on the little finger of Holbrook's left hand as he leaned down and picked up the stick. As Copper leaped jubilantly, Holbrook stood and threw it in a high arc far past the hedge. Copper vaulted off with his tail held high, sprinting out of the East Garden into the neighbouring grove, where majestic cedars stretched their wide-arching boughs in layers against the cloudless sky and a chorus of song thrushes trilled.

'Yes, you *do*,' Holbrook said, watching Copper, 'because I expect you to apply yourself to your search for a husband.'

Meggy fidgeted with the red bonnet ribbons falling over her breast as Copper located the stick near the knobbly roots of a cedar. Tiresome though it was, finding a suitable husband was her highest priority. Only through a sensible marriage could she save Harry and Sophy from inappropriate guardianship and financial distress.

Copper ran back, carrying his stick proudly.

The marquess threw it again. 'Perhaps we might continue our conversation amongst the cedars? They're magnificent.'

Meggy's chest swelled at the unexpected compliment. 'The first earl planted them in 1623. The largest grows upon the far rise.' She pointed. 'Its girth is six yards, two feet, eleven and three-quarters inches. The children and I measure them every year.' Her hand fell; her spirits accompanied it. How many years would pass before they measured the cedars again?

Holbrook cleared his throat. 'Six yards, two feet, eleven and three-quarters inches? Not . . . seven yards?'

Meggy shook her head. 'Not yet, but maybe soon since it was such a wet summer.' She gazed up at the sky, her thoughts drifting to the too-short grain growing on the home farm. 'This sunshine comes a bit late for a good crop yield, unfortunately, and that may affect the cedars' growth as well.' She turned to Holbrook. 'In '07 they didn't grow at all. Plenty of sunshine, but not a jot of rain. Do you recall?'

'Er . . . naturally,' Holbrook said, drawing his eyebrows together as he studied Meggy.

She returned the favour. Did he groom those perfect dark brows? They were as defined as his tidy sideburns, with the extended, close-clipped lines across his otherwise smooth-shaven cheeks. Lines which drew one's attention to that mesmerising mouth . . .

Meggy's knees weakened; she rested a hand on the hedge. 'Shall we, then?'

Holbrook bowed his head. 'After you.'

Meggy led him into the shady grove, her feet falling softly on the mown grass, and her mind sifting through her confusing fascination with Holbrook's appearance. Likely, she was attracted to him because she was ready for a husband, which was a *good* thing, really.

'Perhaps,' she said, both to amuse herself and because she was genuinely curious, 'since you know so very well what I do and don't need regarding my siblings, you could also explain *how* one searches for a husband? Is it similar to a game of hide-and-seek, where I run about hunting for men, or do I announce my intention to marry, perhaps on the front page of *The Times*, and wait for bachelors to flock to me?'

Holbrook cleared his throat, but if it disguised a laugh, he hid it well, for his expression remained impassive. 'My sister Rose will assist you.' A cedar-perfumed breeze blew through the grove, ruffling his snow-white shirt linen. 'Over the upcoming months, she has agreed to help you acquire a certain *polish*, which Edwin suggested – quite rightly, I think – that you might lack, and then she'll introduce you to eligible suitors. If you're not yet wed by springtime, she'll take you to

London, present you at Court, and lead you through the Season's marriage mart nonsense.'

Meggy placed her hand to her forehead and leaned her head back as if overcome with sentiment. 'How charmingly romantic.'

Holbrook pointed his finger. 'Given your circumstances, you must push ideas of romance from your head.'

'I spoke in jest,' Meggy said, giggling. 'I hoped to delight you with more of the sarcasm you enjoyed so much earlier. In truth, I'm not in the least bit romantic. I'm shockingly practical.'

Holbrook's lips thinned. 'I'm too jaded to fall for your pretence. All young ladies fill their heads with romantic rubbish they glean from novels and poetry. You tuck Byron and Radcliffe under your pillow, no doubt.'

Meggy fluttered her hand over her heart. 'Why, sir! I'm amazed how well you already know me.'

'I infer you are again attempting sarcasm.'

She laughed. 'No, not *attempting*.'

He glared down his perfectly straight nose. 'Apparently you amuse yourself, anyway.'

The ground ascended into the rise, and Meggy lifted the skirt of her yellow gown slightly so as not to trip on her hem. 'I do, yes.'

'Rather than be silly, let us focus, Lady Margaret.' Holbrook brushed his walking stick against the needly branches of a nearby tree. 'My point is that you cannot afford to be choosy. Your half-brother was generally despised, and until the memory of him fades, most *notable* families won't relish a connection with the Fairchilds.'

Although Meggy's temper flared, she couldn't deny the likelihood of the statement. Even amongst those neighbours who'd known Meggy's father, Edwin's actions had tarnished the family reputation.

'The difficulty, of course,' Holbrook continued in the manner of a tutor instructing a child, 'is that you must marry a man of fortune. Your beauty might sway an older man, or an ugly one, *if* you make yourself agreeable to him.'

Meggy snorted in laughter.

With only a small hesitation and the barest hint of a glare, Holbrook continued. 'And you need a useful sort of person to help you raise your brother to handle the responsibilities that will be his one day. A Member of Parliament would be ideal for Henry's sake, or a clever and prosperous tradesman wishing to elevate his connections might do—'

It was too much. Meggy halted halfway up the rise, dropped her skirts, and held up a hand. 'I shall stop you there, Lord Holbrook.' From her elevated position higher on the hill, his face was eye-level with her own. The brim of his hat cast a rounded shadow over his smooth brow as he returned her gaze steadily. 'I understand the complexity of my situation, and I comprehend better than you how urgently I must marry a suitable husband. You won't find me missish on matters such as appearance or age, for I'm a practical person, as I told you, and I know my duty to my siblings and my family honour. I shall accept the first eligible offer I receive, but *I* shall determine what makes an offer eligible.'

'Oh?' He drew up his gorgeous mouth. 'And what do you want in a husband?'

Meggy squared her shoulders. Accustomed to dealing with tenants, attorneys, and neighbouring landowners who initially assumed her to be a foolish child, she could manage Holbrook. 'Someone of financial means, yes, but also someone not controlling.'

Holbrook scoffed. 'You mean, of course, you want a *manageable* husband so you may rule the roost.'

'Yes – and so what if I do?' Wives were at the mercy of their husbands, and Meggy had decided long ago not to accept the hand of a man she couldn't control. 'I've learned to rely solely on myself. More importantly, Sophy and Harry depend on me as well. I would lay down my life to protect my siblings, so why would I place them at the mercy of a guardian I cannot control?'

A line appeared between Holbrook's brows. He studied Meggy with a penetrating gaze.

'Why do you stare at me?' she asked, undaunted.

The marquess's expression softened, rendering his appearance as impossibly gentle as it was when he first stepped from his carriage. 'Forgive me. I was lost in my own thoughts for a moment. I understand your sentiments regarding your siblings, Lady Margaret, but having shouldered great responsibility alone for so long and from such a young age, aren't you eager for a partner who will help you? A husband will want to provide that.'

Meggy blinked, taken aback by the thoughtfulness of his response, but she shook her head. 'I cannot risk interference from someone else.'

Holbrook frowned. 'You'd care nothing for your husband's opinions?'

'I'd care for them if they align with my own,' Meggy replied with a grin.

The marquess narrowed his eyes, evidently unamused. 'So you want a husband to provide the financial means for you to continue to do as you please. Is that it?'

'Precisely.'

'That will make our task rather more difficult,' Holbrook said, his tone icy. 'Spineless rich men being somewhat of a rarity – and unmarried ones more uncommon yet. Those poor sods are the first to be snapped up by women wishing to take advantage, are they not?'

Of course, a man like Holbrook would take a narrow-minded view of the matter. 'But I shan't take advantage of my husband. I shall ensure his comfort, be a help-mate, have children – God willing – and raise them lovingly, as I have done with my siblings. And I'm not particular about other matters. I'm perfectly willing to marry an old man.'

'Men tend to become *less* manageable as they age. Unless you want a decrepit ancient looking for a nursemaid.'

Meggy brushed aside his words with a wave of her hand. 'As long as he is rich, kind and manageable, he could be ninety and toothless, and I'd still marry him.'

Holbrook raised his eyebrows.

Then he erupted into laughter so genuine it was infectious, and despite herself, Meggy joined him. The marquess's mirth was rich, warm and natural; he was like a joyful boy lost in a candid moment.

And more handsome than ever.

'You needn't be so amused,' Meggy said when their laughter subsided. 'I'm perfectly serious.'

Holbrook's grin deepened – so lovely and sweet that Meggy's heart twinged – and his grey eyes sparkled. 'My dear Lady Margaret, that's easy for you to say now, but how will you feel when your husband's toothless gums want to kiss your luscious lips?'

Meggy's breath caught. Lest Holbrook discover the effect of his compliment, she turned her head away, allowing her bonnet brim to shield her face as she climbed the rising ground. 'Perhaps I like toothless men.'

'Perhaps you do. Personally, I consider it a shame for you to surrender your sublime beauty to an old man's weak embrace, but to each his own.'

Meggy increased her pace. Her heart raced from the exercise, not his flattery.

Luscious lips, sublime beauty – what nonsense.

She changed the subject. 'When do we leave for Alton Park, Lord Holbrook?'

'How soon can you be ready?'

Meggy ventured a peek around her bonnet brim. 'We were ready to depart a fortnight ago when we expected your arrival.'

Holbrook received Meggy's chastisement with a bright smile. 'Then I shall arrive to collect you and the scamps at nine o'clock. Be aware it'll be a journey of at least two days. And I assume you've some suitable wizened woman to act as chaperone? A maiden aunt, the village witch – something to that effect?'

Meggy crinkled her nose and laughed. 'Miss Kimberley, the children's governess – my old governess – will accompany us.'

'Excellent. You'll need her. You must never trust me, sweetheart.'

Meggy sobered. 'I already knew not to trust a reprobate. My brother taught me that.' As always, Meggy's heart ached when she thought of Edwin's betrayal. 'Your kind thinks of nothing but yourself.'

'True.' The diabolical glint returned to Holbrook's eyes. A shiver ran down Meggy's spine, but Holbrook's villainous mien vanished when they crested the rise.

The grassy meadow of North Park stretched below them. To the east, the red-brick cottages of the estate village huddled around the pointed steeple of the parish church. Directly ahead, nestled near a grove of oak trees, the swimming pond gleamed silver, with bright white waterlilies dotting the glassy surface.

Holbrook stopped. 'How lovely this is.'

Meggy took a deep breath to control tears that suddenly threatened to come. The marquess's words affected her profoundly, for the pond was one of her favourite spots on the estate. A place where she brought a book in her rare leisure time. A place where she picnicked with the children whilst Harry caught frogs and Sophy chased butterflies with a net. 'Yes,' she said quietly. 'I shall miss this prospect, and I shall miss our pond.'

'Shall we venture down there?' Holbrook asked kindly. 'Perhaps you'd like to say goodbye?'

'I promised the children a swim this afternoon, but a quiet farewell would be lovely.' Meggy bit her bottom lip. For a time, at least, Holbrook would be present in Harry and Sophy's lives. Did he possess playfulness besides teasing Meggy about old men and chaperones? 'I'm afraid there's only one proper way to go down the hill.'

Holbrook frowned as he examined the descent. 'Only one? Then which is it – rolling or running?'

Meggy laughed, delighted he understood. 'For a young lady, it must be running. You see, I'm more polished than you supposed.'

The marquess turned his head to the side. 'No doubt,' he said with a small cough.

Perhaps he laughed at her, but Meggy didn't care. It was the last afternoon at her home, and for once she'd relish the sunshine of a fine day without a thought to her infinite responsibilities. She lifted the long skirt of her faded yellow frock halfway to her knees and ran down the hill with Copper loping at her feet. The wind whipped the tangle of curls that had escaped her bonnet, the overgrown grass brushed her calves, and her heart thumped joyfully.

At the pondside, the water's crisp scent permeated the warm air along with the sounds of croaking frogs and chirping birds. Meggy flopped onto a wrought-iron garden bench. She pressed her palms against her heaving torso, as if pressure could restore her breath.

The relief of being off her feet for the first time in hours washed over her.

Meggy closed her eyes. As a breeze cooled her heated cheeks, her mind returned to duty. Despite what she had said to Holbrook, there was much to be done before they could leave tomorrow. She began compiling a mental list.

A rustle of wool and rush of air, and Holbrook sat beside her. Meggy opened her eyes.

The marquess observed her, and she returned his gaze. Again, his mouth was oh-so-tender, with the gentle curl at the edges.

What was Holbrook's true nature? The reprehensible behaviour by the roadside and at the start of their walk? Or was he as warm and playful as he had seemed in the last quarter of an hour?

Holbrook broke into Meggy's musings. 'You're tired, Lady Margaret,' he said softly. 'Did the scamps help you pick all those berries, or did you do most of the work?'

Meggy smiled. 'They did more eating than helping, but they were amusing.'

He laughed. 'Undoubtedly.'

As they sat, the dogs snuffled amongst the reeds. Copper splashed into the pond whilst Caesar yipped from the bank.

'Your pug doesn't swim?' Meggy asked.

Holbrook shrugged. 'I suppose not. I haven't had him near water before.' He paused. 'He was Edwin's dog – another of your brother's responsibilities I now shoulder.'

Meggy's heart clamped at the unexpected connection to Edwin. She hadn't realised her brother kept a dog. Within the last four years, Edwin had returned to Berksleigh Hall only once: encased in a wooden coffin already nailed shut.

Holbrook continued. 'I thought I'd gift your brother or sister with Caesar, but I'm afraid he's rather attached to me now. I suppose he, unlike you, is fond of a reprobate.'

Meggy knit her fingers in the folds of her skirt. 'Was Edwin your friend?' she asked, tilting her head.

Holbrook pulled a face. 'My *friend*? No, not at all.'

Meggy frowned. 'Then why did you agree to do this for him?'

The marquess leaned against the back of the bench, stretching his long, muscular legs – as graceful as a dancer's in his tight buff trousers – before him. 'I agreed to do this to pay a debt.'

'You owed him money?'

He snorted. 'No, heavens not.'

'Then *what* – if you don't mind my asking?'

'I *do* mind.' He leaned closer, with a half-smile playing at the corner of his mouth. The broadcloth of his coat brushed against Meggy's arm; her bare skin tingled where it touched. It was a fine-woven, well-tailored, masculine cloth: smooth, dark blue wool as soft as silk, warm from Holbrook's body. 'However, your beauty moves me to generosity, so I shall satisfy your curiosity. Edwin saved my life once. I have yet to decide if I'm grateful, but it's a debt all the same.'

'You're uncertain if you're grateful to be alive?' Meggy asked, incredulous. 'Are you so unhappy?'

Holbrook sat back. His eyes slipped over Meggy's face and followed her bonnet's red ribbons where they fell against the curve of her breasts.

Could he see how Meggy's heart pummelled?

When Holbrook met her gaze again, he smiled sweetly. 'It's a fine September day, and there's a beautiful lady at my side. It's impossible to be unhappy at this moment.'

Meggy's chest tightened, depriving her of breath. Holbrook's eyes were as grey as a dove's wing, and Meggy held his gaze longer than she ought. He was remarkably beautiful in the cool shade, with leafy shadows dancing across his chiselled features. 'But sometimes you're unhappy?'

'Don't worry about *my* troubles, Lady Margaret. You have too many of your own. Tomorrow you must leave the only home you've known and throw yourself into the protection of a man you cannot decide if you like or loathe.'

Meggy's hand flew to her mouth.

Holbrook smiled as he continued. 'Furthermore, you have much to do this afternoon, in addition to taking your siblings swimming. And as if that weren't enough trouble already, you're sore from berry picking.'

Meggy's hand fell from her lips and rested on her bosom. In all the years she'd picked berries or weeded the vegetable garden or mucked out stables, no one had ever considered how her body felt afterwards. 'How did you know?'

'I simply suspected. You have a tremendous number of responsibilities for one so young. That is why, right now, you must simply rest for a moment. You came here to bid a quiet farewell to your pond. I shan't intrude upon your reverie.'

Meggy leaned her back against the wrought-iron bench slats, closed her eyes, and attempted to focus on memories of the pond.

Instead, her mind filled with Holbrook's twinkling eyes, beautiful smile and muscular arms. His proximity awakened her senses: his fragrance of bergamot and cloves; his occasional quiet movements; the warmth of his body next to hers.

Surely the marquess wasn't horrid. He was *unhappy*, as he'd hinted. Naturally he was; after all, rumours claimed he'd buried his heart with his wife and stillborn child. Grief must ravage him.

Poor heartbroken Holbrook.

Poor, breathtakingly handsome, theoretically *eligible* Holbrook.

Meggy blinked open her eyes. Good lord, what a surprising thought.

Clearly, the farewell to the pond wasn't working.

She sat up and rolled her shoulders. 'I should return to the house to help the children and Miss Kimberley ready themselves for tomorrow.' For the first time, the thought of spending two days in a carriage with the marquess thrilled Meggy, and she smiled warmly. 'Thank you for an unexpectedly lovely walk, Lord Holbrook.'

Their eyes locked.

Something unreadable flickered across his face.

His expression grew solemn as his gaze fell from her eyes to her lips. 'Please don't go yet, Lady Margaret,' he said, his voice a near-whisper, his eyelids heavy.

Meggy's pulse raced. Did he sense a connection between them, as she had just begun to do? Was he thinking of kissing her? If so, were his intentions honourable now? Surely they were – he was a marquess and she was an earl's daughter. There could be only one interpretation to his intimacy.

Holbrook lifted Meggy's chin with his fingertips. Her breath quickened. She would let him kiss her, she decided. She'd longed for her first kiss for years, and she'd never met anyone as appealing as Holbrook. One kiss and she'd at last know what a man's mouth felt like pressed against hers. It didn't amount to accepting a proposal, after all. She could decide about that later. She'd request time to consider after he asked.

She closed her eyes and lifted her lips to his.

And then a handkerchief rubbed her nose vigorously.

Meggy's eyes flew open. Holbrook examined her with his brows drawn, all traces of intimacy absent. 'What a shame.' His voice was brisk and businesslike. 'I did no good and may have made it worse. Blackberry juice, you understand. It's on the tip of your nose.'

Meggy's jaw dropped.

Holbrook released her chin. 'I hope, Lady Margaret, you didn't think I meant to kiss you? And I certainly hope you didn't intend to accept a kiss from a rake like me?'

Fury rose like a phoenix inside Meggy. 'You . . . you horrid man!' Through a red haze of humiliated rage, Meggy pushed Holbrook's chest with all her might, hoping to shove him off the bench.

It was like pushing a brick wall.

She tried again.

But Holbrook seized both of her wrists in one of his hands. Although Meggy struggled, his grip was secure. With his spare hand, he tucked his handkerchief into his waistcoat pocket. 'For all your bold proclamations,' he said, bringing her close, 'you offered those pretty lips all too easily, even after I told you not to trust me, silly chit.' He flicked his thumb across her cheek. 'Whilst you go about your packing this afternoon, remind yourself of this little lesson.'

When Holbrook released her, Meggy collapsed against the back of the bench.

She trembled from head to foot as Holbrook stood, brushed his fingers over his coat-sleeves, and adjusted the ruffle of his shirt at his cuffs.

He lifted his walking stick from the bench. 'Be ready when I arrive at nine.'

He whistled for his pug and, without another word, strode up the hill with Caesar.

Mortified tears stung Meggy's eyes, and she buried her face in her hands.

Damn Edwin. Damn rakes and reprobates.

But most of all, damn the intolerably smug, impossibly handsome, unbearably horrid Marquess of Holbrook.

3

As soon as Nicholas crested the hill and descended into the cedar grove, he inhaled sharply, threw his hand over his pounding heart, and exhaled.

Dammit, that he must be cruel to such an artless ingénue.

And dammit, dammit, dammit that he couldn't kiss those sweet lips, offered so trustingly.

Lady Margaret Fairchild was *not* what Nicholas had expected.

At times, she was a cursed annoying, sarcastic wench. As bold as a hellcat, admitting she'd emasculate her future husband. No doubt she *would*.

But at other times, she was a darling.

As Nicholas hurried across the grove, he imagined Meggy measuring the massive cedars, her supple, sun-kissed arms stretching a measuring tape around the contorted trunks.

She'd recited the circumference to the *quarter-inch*.

Nicholas shook his head, smiling.

Amusing, clever little thing.

With such magnificent blue eyes.

Nicholas cleared his throat. Edwin had sent a lamb

into a wolf's den, and now Nicholas must resist every urge of his nature.

He passed into the hedged lawn and trailed his walking stick in the box.

Meggy's combination of vivacity, beauty and sweetness was the sort of thing that would draw a man in until, with a snap, the shackle clamped, tightened, and Meggy reigned supreme, for better or worse.

Thank God Nicholas wouldn't be the poor sod who'd succumb to her charms.

But therein lay the difficulty, for Meggy possessed *such* sensual femininity. Those soft, full breasts and lips . . . and the adorable dimples . . . and the way she crinkled her freckled nose when she laughed . . . Nicholas slid a finger under his collar, loosening the fabric's strangling hold.

Shortly after he had laughed with Meggy over the toothless husband, Nicholas realised his danger. Seconds later, he devised a long-term solution for keeping his distance. He'd take her to Suffolk, leave her in Rose's care, and depart Alton Park *immediately*. He'd conduct the business of guardianship from afar, passing the autumn at one of his other estates and spending the winter in town. Meanwhile, Meggy would marry, and Nicholas needn't see her again until her little hand rested upon the arm of her husband.

But first Nicholas must survive the two-day journey to Suffolk without surrendering to temptation.

He'd be on his guard.

The trouble was, he didn't trust his guard.

Nicholas narrowed his eyes as he studied his boots for a dozen steps.

Then he nodded.

He'd simply continue with his improvised plan – derived during their charming walk – to put her on *her* guard. Meggy could do the hard work. He'd make himself unpleasant and enjoy the view. She was adorable when angry.

'Excellent scheme, eh, Caesar?'

The pug cocked his wrinkled face and grinned his approval.

'You concur. Good boy.'

Caesar wagged his curled tail. Nicholas lifted his chin, breathed in the sweet scent of late summer, and with a bounce in his step, whistled a merry tune.

The next morning, he cast his features into lazy-lidded boredom as he stood by the open door of his carriage, waiting to hand up the ladies. He even extracted his pocket watch as if impatient to leave, but no one noticed his masterful performance. Meggy, attired in a black crepe mourning gown, emerged from the house with her sobbing siblings, a wailing white-haired governess, and a cluster of weeping servants. She embraced and comforted the others whilst the children clung to her skirts with fisted hands and wiped their drippy noses on the soft silk. She then walked down the front steps and, without greeting Nicholas, directed the stacking of the trunks on the carriage roof.

Nicholas returned his watch to his fob pocket. Oh well. Might as well appreciate Meggy's beauty instead.

Unlike the day before, she now looked every inch the earl's daughter. A jaunty black silk bonnet perched atop her head. Her golden-brown curls – orderly and tidy now, rather than windswept and wild – were smoothed back except where they framed her forehead. A ruffled fichu of fine white silk surrounded her neck and was tucked into the ebony bodice of her gown.

She acted like an earl's daughter too.

An especially overbearing one.

'No, no,' Meggy said to his footmen, 'that case goes on the bottom, for it contains books. *Really*, can you not feel how heavy it is? And tie the portmanteaux down. No, these smaller ones will ride inside with us. Where's the basket of food? Yes, these are to come inside as well.'

'Good lord,' Nicholas said as the inside of the carriage filled to bursting, and Caesar sought refuge in a corner. 'Do you intend to load the seats with boxes and baskets as well? Shall I ride on the rumble with the footmen?'

Meggy didn't smile at his jest. In fact, she barely acknowledged his presence. 'Children, say good morning to Lord Holbrook.'

Little blonde-haired Sophy, in a pale purple muslin frock, uttered inaudible words into her sister's skirts, but Harry stood up straighter and smoothed the bibbed collar of his blue one-piece suit. 'G-Good morning, my l-lord,' he said as tears spilled from his red-rimmed eyes.

Meggy clasped the children close to her body. 'Oh, my sweet, brave darlings.' She spoke only to them, as if Nicholas weren't there. 'Remember, when we're together, we're home.'

A lump formed in Nicholas's throat, and he turned his head aside to regain his composure. He hadn't expected such a moving maternal display.

'Copper will go in the carriage first, my loves,' Meggy said to her siblings, 'and we shall follow so that he isn't lonely.' The spaniel leapt into the carriage at Meggy's command, and he and Caesar pressed their quivering noses together. 'Now you, Harry – into the carriage like a brave soldier.'

Just as the young earl placed his foot upon the first step, Sophy gasped and tugged at her sister's skirts. 'Meggy, I don't think I packed Dolly.'

'Where is she then, dearest?'

The child's lip trembled. 'I . . . I don't recall. I was holding her this morning, but I . . .'

As Nicholas stood by the carriage door, Meggy organised a search party. She commanded the servants as if she were a general on the battlefield, and everyone returned to the house.

Everyone but the little earl, who still stood upon the carriage steps, gazing at Berksleigh Hall. Harry's tears had ceased, but his cheeks were damp.

Poor boy.

'Grim morning?' Nicholas asked.

Harry sniffed, nodded, and rubbed his nose with the back of his hand. 'Edwin did this to my sisters, and I cannot save them.'

Profoundly affected, Nicholas put his hand to his heart. 'Oh, my boy.'

The child's mouth turned down. 'Is it wrong to be angry at the dead, sir?'

Nicholas considered the boy's question. 'It's not *wrong*. But being angry at the dead is . . . well, it's fruitless.'

Harry's blue eyes flashed. 'I want to plant Edwin a facer.'

'I imagine you do.' Nicholas half smiled, impressed by the child's pluck. Harry reminded him of himself at a certain age, back when he'd been full of plans to right the world's wrongs and defend those he loved.

'But I can't,' Harry sighed. 'So how do I feel better?'

Bitter irony the boy should ask *him* such a question. But the child was a hopeful imp, so Nicholas tried. 'Be better than Edwin was, Henry. *You* are Lord Berksleigh now, the latest in a long line of earls, some of whom used their position for good and some of whom didn't, as is the case with all noble titles.'

'Do you use your position for good, sir?'

Nicholas was many things, but he wasn't a liar. 'I could be better, Henry.'

'I prefer Harry.'

'Harry, then.'

'I shall make Berksleigh Hall grand again one day. Meggy tells me I needn't worry, she'll take care of everything, but *I'm* the head of the family, aren't I? It's *my* responsibility.'

Nicholas's heart clenched. 'You needn't take on the burdens of adulthood quite yet, my boy.'

43

Harry scowled. 'But I want to. I wish I were a man.'

Nicholas recalled his own misery as a child unable to control his circumstances, especially when he was exposed to cruelty. He tried again. 'I know you're immensely frustrated by your current situation, Harry, and so I shan't offer you useless comfort.' The boy tilted his head, attentive to every word, and Nicholas felt a sudden spark of inspiration. 'But you do have an extremely important responsibility.'

'What responsibility?'

'You must spend the next fourteen years growing into the best man you can be. That takes considerable gumption, and although I don't know you well, I can tell you have gumption in abundance.'

Harry's eyes sparkled. 'Oh, I do, sir. I do have gumption.' He put his hand on Nicholas's sleeve. 'Please don't tell Meggy, but I want to be an admiral one day.'

Nicholas raised his eyebrows. 'Indeed?'

Harry nodded vigorously. 'And although I'm now an earl, I think I might yet manage it. What do you think?'

'You wouldn't be the first earl *and* admiral.'

At that moment, the crowd re-emerged from the house with Dolly in Sophy's arms. Harry hopped down from the carriage stairs as the ladies approached. 'Remember, don't tell Meggy, for she says it's too dangerous.'

'I shan't.'

Nicholas offered his hand to assist the governess up the carriage steps. Sophy followed.

Then he extended his hand to Meggy. Although she hadn't cried, she was pale and drawn, and Nicholas felt a tug upon his heart. Her touch warmed his palm when she placed her gloved hand in his. He pressed her fingers gently and stroked his thumb over her knuckles.

She glowered at him as if he were a maggot.

Ah, she remembered not to trust him. That was good. And also not.

The caress had been an impulsive but genuine attempt to comfort her after she'd had to comfort everyone else, but Nicholas suppressed his regret, for it was best if she remained wary.

'Blackberry juice is gone, I see,' he said.

She yanked her hand away and climbed unassisted into the carriage.

Nicholas wasn't prepared for the tightening in his chest.

He clamped his jaw. He must focus. It was essential to maintain an emotional distance since physical separation was impossible until he got Meggy to Suffolk.

Nicholas inhaled deeply, released the breath, and smiled at Harry. 'Your turn, my boy.'

Harry clamoured up the steps and paused in the open doorway. He looked between the forward-facing seat, half occupied by Miss Kimberley, and the bench where Meggy and Sophy sat with their backs to the horses.

Meggy patted the space beside her. 'Sit down so Lord Holbrook can come in, Harry.'

'But . . . I'd like to sit by him, please.'

Nicholas started.

Meggy blinked. 'No, Harry, you must sit by me. There isn't room for you to sit by Lord Holbrook, and Miss Kimberley feels ill if she has her back to the horses.'

The boy's shoulders slumped.

Had the misguided child cast Nicholas as an idol?

Nicholas rubbed the back of his high collar. He'd have to explain to Harry one day why the boy mustn't admire him, but he couldn't disappoint the child now – not on the same morning that Harry must leave his home. 'Harry and I shall sit with our backs to the horses, Lady Margaret,' Nicholas said over Harry's head. 'You and Sophy take the forward seat with Miss Kimberley, please.'

Meggy looked between Harry and Nicholas with pursed lips. But, at last, she shrugged. 'Thank Lord Holbrook, Harry.'

Harry turned on the carriage steps. Eye-level with Nicholas, who still stood upon the drive, the boy threw his arms about Nicholas's neck and squeezed. 'How glad I am to sit with you, sir.'

Harry's soap-scented curls tickled Nicholas's chin as he patted the child's back. 'Yes, well, into the carriage with you.' Nicholas's voice caught. This was something *else* he'd not expected. 'Mustn't keep the horses standing.'

He hoisted the boy up the last step and followed, edging his way around the ladies' legs, the baskets and packages, and the exuberant spaniel. Meggy passed him Caesar, and the pug turned in three circles upon the upholstered seat and relaxed beside Harry, with his panting tongue curled up. Nicholas tied the green velvet curtains back and opened the windows. The outside light and air would make the ride feel less cramped.

He sat and banged his walking stick for the coachman, and the carriage swayed into motion. When they turned from the gates of Berksleigh Hall, the team galloped, their hooves thrumming along the river road north towards Coventry. Nicholas adjusted himself in the seat so that his knees leaned to one side, as there was no space to stretch his long legs.

A little hand pulled at his own as Harry nestled warm fingers into Nicholas's palm. Nicholas suppressed his surprise and smiled at the boy.

Harry's sparkling blue eyes gazed back, and something tugged at Nicholas's heart.

Sophy still sobbed. Copper thumped his tail against the boxes and baskets as he placed his paws on the girl's knees and licked her face until Sophy giggled through her tears. 'Look, Meggy, Copper wants me to be happy.' Sophy kissed Copper's head, and the spaniel jumped down. Tongue lolling and mouth grinning, he bounded about on the crowded carriage floor.

Both children giggled, and the time for tears ended.

Only to be replaced with requests for food, enquiries about which travelling activities Meggy had packed, and a stream of questions about passing landmarks.

Despite her wan face and heavy eyelids, Meggy pared apples, spread creamy goat's cheese on crusty white buns, and exclaimed over cat's cradles and atlas pages – and she did so with the same loving patience Nicholas's sister Rose showed to her three daughters. But Meggy was ten years younger than Rose, and *ought* to have been enjoying her youth rather than mothering siblings since the age of fourteen.

Nicholas's heart twisted – no, it *ached*. He'd disliked Edwin before, but now he sympathised with Harry – it'd be damned satisfying to plant the dead man a facer.

Lady Margaret Fairchild and her cherubic brother and sister needed to be out of his life as soon as possible, but in the meantime, Nicholas would offer sincere help. Not because he was at risk of succumbing to her charms in a *lasting* sort of way. Only because . . . why?

Oh, damn, it didn't matter, did it? Knowing the extent of his selfishness, it was probably because he wanted Meggy to admire him as much as he admired her.

Warm breezes and road dust blew in from the open windows, but with panting dogs and excited children, the carriage was muggy. Meggy's temples thrummed, and each pounding hoof fall intensified her headache.

She'd packed until after midnight and risen before dawn that morning. And in between, her restless dreams had dwelt on Holbrook's handsome face.

After the humiliation by the pond, Meggy had determined to despise the marquess.

With each passing hour in the carriage, her resolve crumbled.

The man holding her little brother's hand was different from the cruel rake who'd mocked her the day before. Harry adored him, and Miss Kimberley was the next to fall under his spell.

Before the first team change, Holbrook solicited the governess's opinion on the best way to encourage children to practise the pianoforte. 'I've frequently offered my nieces various trinkets and treats if they do so – to help my sister Rose, for Elizabeth especially can be quite defiant – but the method doesn't seem effective.'

'Oh, no,' Miss Kimberley said. 'That won't work at all, my lord, for you cannot supply them with treats for the rest of their lives. Motivation must come from *within* to achieve proficiency.'

'Ah, but how does one encourage such motivation?' Holbrook leaned forward with shining eyes as the conversation continued, and soon the governess patted her heart, fluttered her hands, and giggled like a girl in response to the marquess's every word.

Half an hour later, the morning's excitement drained Miss Kimberley, and she fell asleep with her head tilted back on the seat and her mouth agape. Meggy, exhausted herself, leaned against the velvet curtains as Holbrook amused the children with tales of knights and dragons. Sophy clasped Dolly and crawled over the baskets to snuggle on the marquess's other side.

Without Sophy's clammy body pressed against her, Meggy breathed deeper, and breezes blew against both sides of her oppressively warm mourning dress. A little game developed between Holbrook and the children, something involving a few of Harry's tin soldiers rescuing Dolly, who'd been imprisoned in a tower by Pugius Caesar. The children shouted in laughter, and Miss Kimberley gasped in her sleep. Then the governess repositioned her head to lean against the curtains and the snores resumed.

'Hark,' Holbrook said in a falsetto, pointing Dolly's wooden arm in the governess's direction. 'Pugius Caesar placed a dragon to guard me, but the dragon snores.'

Sophy and Harry howled, and Meggy chuckled. When Holbrook's eyes flickered to hers, Meggy stifled her laughter. But her attempt at a scowl was half-hearted, and Holbrook smiled.

'Sir Knight,' the marquess said in Dolly's soprano, 'save me now whilst the dragon sleeps.'

Harry supplied the voice and actions of a tin soldier. 'I shan't save you, for you're likely to fall in love with me if I do.'

Holbrook replied for Dolly. 'Not I, Sir Knight, for I'm a practical lady. Romantic nonsense is tomfoolery, and men are disgusting blighters.'

Meggy bit her bottom lip to repress her smile. Holbrook was like Harry when he played, with an irresistible naughty gleam in his shining eyes, brash attempts to catch Meggy's attention with outrageous statements, a wide grin, and belly laughs at the children's proclamations. Sometimes he amused himself so much he tossed his head back and roared with his hand clamped to his chest. Sophy giggled as she leaned against one of Holbrook's arms, and Harry snickered beside the other. They formed a pyramid of laughter.

Meggy soon gave up pretending she wasn't amused. If not for her increasing headache, she would've joined in the play.

When Miss Kimberley awoke, the governess laughed uproariously at Holbrook and the children.

'Why, 'tis as amusing as a puppet show,' Miss Kimberley said, wiping tears off her wrinkled cheeks. She leaned against Meggy with one hand over her mouth, but her eyes remained on the marquess. 'He's a lovely young gentleman, Meggy. Sitting with his back to the horses, excellent with the children, a caring uncle, and so *extremely* handsome – the reports we heard must be malicious falsehoods. As gossip is, more often than not.'

Meggy's face flamed. Miss Kimberley's whispers were louder than she'd intended, and Holbrook grinned at Meggy. Despite the breathless fluttering his smile aroused, Meggy turned a shoulder to him, for his expression was *too* smug. He was undeniably appealing, but he was also an arrogant cad.

And she wouldn't suffer another humiliation.

Meggy closed her eyes, although she couldn't sleep with her pounding headache.

During their luncheon stop in the bustling small town of Northampton, Holbrook ordered a private dining room at a modern stone inn. The high-ceilinged chamber was cool and airy, with a large central table covered in white linen. An army of servants produced a veritable feast of steaming covered silver dishes, but the vegetables swimming in brown-butter sauce and the boiled beef turned Meggy's stomach.

Holbrook placed down the carving knife after serving Miss Kimberley and the children. 'This food doesn't appeal?' he asked Meggy, who'd refused everything offered.

The proprietor, standing at Holbrook's shoulder, gasped. 'Would her ladyship prefer something else?'

Meggy nodded weakly. 'Some cold chicken, perhaps?'

She withdrew to a spindly mahogany chair by the window, closing her eyes and breathing in the fresh air as she rested her head against the sill.

When the waiter returned, she nibbled at the chicken, sliced cucumber, and buttered bread. The mild, cool food revived her a little.

Holbrook approached and stood beside her.

Meggy peered up. He was hatless for the first time since they'd met. From the crown of his head, thick and luscious dark curls fell forward and lay upon his tanned brow.

He really was shockingly handsome.

Heat smouldered in Meggy's core.

'Are you ill, Lady Margaret?'

'I have a headache.'

'May I ascertain if you have a fever?' he asked, holding out his palm.

She nodded, breathless.

He placed his hand to her forehead, and his touch enflamed her. 'You're warm.'

Meggy turned her head away. 'Only overheated.' She'd never uttered a truer statement.

'Perhaps you need rest,' he said, gently. 'Would you prefer to stop here for the night?'

'No.' Meggy spoke with difficulty. Despite her head-ache, she imagined Holbrook enfolding her in his arms and giving her the kiss he'd denied her by the pond. 'It would delay our journey another day.'

Holbrook lifted his broad shoulders. 'There's no harm in a slight delay. You could sleep.'

Meggy shook her head. 'The children will be awake for hours yet. We might as well continue.' Sleep was the last thing on her mind anyway, although she'd begun to wonder how she and Holbrook might make use of a bed.

'Do you have headache powder?'

'No. I never get headaches.'

'Then I shall fetch some, and I'll take the scamps with me so you may rest here with Miss Kimberley.'

Five minutes later, he left with Sophy clinging to one hand and Harry to the other. 'A hunt,' he declared to the children as they exited. 'A hunt for an apothecary, my scamps.'

Sophy's voice echoed from the corridor, high-pitched and joyful. 'Shall we be explorers, then?'

'Pirates,' Harry said as their footsteps faded.

Meggy exchanged a smile with Miss Kimberley before resting her head against the sill again with her eyes closed.

When they returned, Harry carried a folded square of brown paper, and Sophy a corked flask, which they laid upon the table.

Holbrook opened the paper, sniffed the white powder inside, and shrugged. He stirred the powder into the flask with a thin spoon and grimaced as he handed the concoction to Meggy. 'Angostura bark infusion. Best to pinch the nose and pour it all back at once.'

She did as he instructed, swallowing the tonic before shuddering at the vile bitterness.

The medicine eased Meggy's discomfort during the afternoon's travels, but more soothing yet was Holbrook's deep voice reading from their well-worn *Robinson Crusoe*. She drifted in and out of peaceful sleep, lulled by the marquess's cadences. By the time they arrived for their night's stop in the market town of Huntingdon, Meggy was fully in charity with Holbrook. No man who read aloud for five hours whilst squished between two sweaty children in a hot carriage could be entirely reprehensible.

After dinner at The George, a boisterously busy timber-framed coaching inn, Miss Kimberley clasped Meggy's arm, and the children swung upon Holbrook's for an evening walk. They crossed through the town square, containing a stone church and the shire hall, and strolled past rows of ivy-laden cottages until they reached the River Ouse. Free-ranging herd animals grazed in the waterside meadows. The lanolin smell of woolly sheep and the musky scent of cows mingled with rich earthiness as they rambled through the lush grass dotted with yellow sun-like fleabanes and delicate, pale-blue harebells. The Ouse reflected the clear sky; its calm waters broken only by the wakes of gliding ducks and white-sailed boats.

'What do you think of Huntingdonshire, Lady Margaret?' Holbrook asked later, as Harry ran with the dogs, and Sophy and Miss Kimberley picked wildflowers. 'Not Warwickshire, of course, but still pleasing, I hope?'

The golden evening light on Holbrook's alluring features stole Meggy's breath, but she maintained her calm as they ambled along the riverbank. 'At the moment, I'm primarily grateful my head no longer aches. Thank you for the medicine.' He bowed his head, and Meggy smiled. 'Tomorrow I shall observe the countryside more as we travel. Harry is excited to see the ocean vessels in Ipswich, I know.'

Holbrook glanced at Harry, who threw a stick for Copper. 'I'm afraid I must disappoint the young scamp.' He paused, pursing his lips. 'But only for *now*,' he added suddenly, with surprising forcefulness. He nodded his head. 'Yes, only for now. I shall take Harry and the other children – and you and Rose, of course, should you wish to come – on a day trip to the shipyards soon, but Alton Park is located inland, some fifteen miles to the south-west of Ipswich.' He returned his gaze to Meggy. 'On the Dedham Vale along the River Stour.'

'And what is the Dedham Vale like?' Meggy asked, plucking a single tall stem of devil's bit with its spherical purple-blue bloom. She held the flower to her nose, inhaling its faint honey scent.

Holbrook watched her with his head angled and his eyes soft. Then he grinned his impossibly lovely smile and swept an arm out, indicating the river and the meadow. 'The Dedham Vale is more bucolic beauty, much like this belt of England. Gently rolling meadows, cows and sheep, market towns with stone churches and trim cottages, a picturesque river.' His eyes returned to Meggy. 'But it has one advantage, to *me*, that no other place has, which I think you'll understand. It's *home*.'

Meggy swallowed a sudden tightness in her throat. 'Yes, home has a special beauty.' She dropped her flower into the tall grass. 'The beauty of familiarity.'

Holbrook raised his eyebrows. 'Is *that* what it is? Ha! I wonder I should like it then. No one has ever accused me of finding beauty in the familiar. I'm known for my preference for novelty.'

Meggy laughed, despite herself.

Holbrook picked up the dropped wildflower. 'May I?'

'May you what?' Meggy asked, puzzled.

He broke the stem and nestled the bloom into the crease of his cravat. 'A memory,' he said with a smile.

Meggy put her fingertips to her mouth. Her heart fluttered uncontrollably, and this time, she didn't attempt to reason the sensation away. 'I begin to wonder if you are like your reputation at all, sir.'

A glimmer flashed in Holbrook's eyes. It vanished before Meggy could register its meaning. 'But I told you not to trust me,' he said, his voice oddly flat. 'Perhaps I'm toying with you to re-engage your interest after my utterly reprehensible behaviour by the pond.'

Meggy studied the sunlight dancing along the river's ripples before returning her gaze to the marquess. 'Why *were* you so beastly then and so kind now?'

Holbrook shrugged. 'I'm rather mercurial, I'm afraid.'

Meggy tilted her head. 'And why should you wish to engage my interest?' she asked, purposefully presenting him with the perfect opportunity to declare an intention to court her.

He didn't profess any such thing.

Instead, he grinned like a rogue and waggled his eyebrows. 'Because I'm the weakest of men, sweetheart. I cannot resist a beautiful face, and yours is one of the loveliest I've ever seen.'

Meggy scrunched her nose to hide his words' effect on her heart. For years, Miss Kimberley had instructed Meggy not to demonstrate her feelings for any gentleman until she knew his objective. Meggy suspected she'd mangled this first flirtation so far, but surely, she could still recover her dignity. 'You're attempting to flatter me when you call me beautiful, of course, but sadly for you, it won't work. I'm *not* beautiful, and before you protest with more false compliments, you should know I don't *care* to be beautiful.'

'No, my darling? And why not?'

'I'm strong, I'm intelligent, I'm assiduous – and I value those traits more than beauty.' She paused near a willow, and a gentle breeze rustled the tree's draping leaves. 'And, anyway, besides my dreadful freckles, I'm perfectly content with my appearance. Save your flattery for someone else, for it won't work on me.'

'But *now* I know you are, in fact, the most beautiful lady I've ever seen.'

'You don't learn, do you?'

Holbrook leaned closer with twinkling eyes. '*You* don't understand that self-confidence makes a lady irresistible.'

Meggy's breath caught. 'Well, if that's true,' she said to hide her confusion, 'I cannot say the same for gentlemen. Your self-confidence is repulsive, Lord Holbrook.'

He burst into laughter, and Miss Kimberley looked their way. He stifled his mirth and bowed to the governess, who directed her attention back to Sophy's wildflowers. But Holbrook whispered against Meggy's cheek the moment Miss Kimberley's back turned.

'Please keep your repulsion towards me.' His breath was warm against her skin. 'If I should ever become as irresistible to you as you are to me, we shall perhaps find ourselves in some difficulty.'

Meggy turned her head aside, for her cheeks blazed. Was *that* a declaration?

Her heart hammered.

It must be a declaration.

Holbrook was instructing her, in his customarily teasing manner, to let him know if she returned his interest.

Meggy didn't trust herself to respond, so she feigned fascination with the wavering branches of the willow. She was grateful when Harry claimed Holbrook for frog-catching assistance, for her thoughts were in turmoil.

Whilst Holbrook's handsomeness had entranced Meggy the day before, his behaviour throughout *that* day was, in fact, irresistible.

Later, as Meggy strolled with Sophy and Miss Kimberley, she gazed at the figure crouching by the water's edge with her brother. The shadowy idea of a future husband took on a solid form, at last.

A tall, broad-shouldered, grey-eyed form.

4

Nicholas tucked the bedcovers under a sleeping Harry's chin. After returning from their evening walk, the boy had asked to sleep with him rather than with the ladies, and after considerable effort, Nicholas convinced Meggy he *really* didn't mind. After all, she'd insisted he take the larger of the two bedrooms in their suite, and it made no sense for one bed to sleep four whilst another slept one.

One brown ringlet, still damp from his bath, stuck to Harry's forehead, and Nicholas brushed it back. Harry's dimpled hand curled over Caesar's rotund belly, and the boy's soft, regular breaths mixed with the comical snores of the pug.

As he pulled off his boots, Nicholas recalled the burden of coming into his own title at fourteen. Mourning his adored father, the one source of stability in his life, and facing the disdain of his detested uncle – although he'd not known the extent of the man's malevolence then – Nicholas had been caught between childhood and manhood without a mentor.

Harry needed a mentor. Not Nicholas, but not a ninety-year-old either.

Nicholas removed his tailcoat and picked up his clothes brush. As he cupped the silver handle in his palm and scraped the boar bristles over the dark broadcloth, removing all traces of dust, he considered. He didn't have many acquaintances he considered friends, but there were four men – all still bachelors – whom he respected profoundly. One was a curate and far too poor to take a penniless wife, but any one of the remaining three might do splendidly as a husband for Meggy and as a mentor for Harry. Perhaps Nicholas should promote the chit to his friends, rather than leaving the responsibility of Meggy's marriage entirely to Rose?

After laying his brushed coat carefully over the back of a wing chair, Nicholas extracted Meggy's wildflower from the folds of his cravat and held the bloom between his thumb and forefinger. He'd picked it up impulsively after she discarded it, with some foggy notion of pressing it between the pages of *Childe Harold*, which was nestled in his valise.

He lifted the field-fresh flower to his nose, as Meggy had done as she strolled through the riverside meadow, her complexion glowing and her brilliant blue eyes shining. How simple it would be, if Nicholas were a different man, to slide into a courtship with such an angel. Perhaps, if he'd met Meggy many years ago . . .

Nicholas swallowed.

What nonsense. When he was a wide-eyed innocent himself, Meggy was sewing samplers in her schoolroom.

Nicholas flicked the flower out of the open window.

His courting days had passed. Marriage wasn't for him. Not again.

Not when love led to pain.

A cool dusk breeze swelled into the chamber, billowing the cotton curtains, as Nicholas loosened his cravat and unfastened the high neck of his cotton shirt. He leaned against the sash and slipped his fingers into the pockets of his white silk waistcoat. The inn's court-yard bustled with evening activity. Servants marched about carrying bundles of linen and pails of steaming water, and the ostlers and postillions passed the time until their next deployment by drinking tankards of ale and whistling at women.

A curvaceous blonde maid sashayed across the yard. The men announced their admiration with lewd trib-utes, but she ignored them. Instead, she lifted her chin and gestured up at Nicholas. Even in the twilight, her enquiry was clear.

Good lord.

Nicholas jingled some coins in his waistcoat pocket as he considered. Meggy's beauty aroused him painfully. Perhaps a fervid tumble in a deserted bedchamber of the inn with this buxom maid would expend his lust. He could pretend . . .

But *that* cleared his thoughts. Many years ago, he'd pretended one woman was another, and he'd never repeated the unsatisfying experience. No doubt he could be a callous bastard afterwards, but whilst he was with a woman, he gave *her* his attention.

Before he could indicate a denial, the mistress of the inn entered the courtyard and engaged the maid. Nicholas withdrew, not wanting to be near the window if she repeated her enquiry.

With his boots in hand, Nicholas walked into the private parlour that adjoined the two bedchambers and a bathing room. The close-carpeted sitting room, furnished with upholstered seats and decorated with framed colour-tinted prints hanging on the diamond-patterned wallpaper, was empty, and no sounds emitted from behind any closed doors.

Nicholas crossed the parlour and placed his boots in the corridor outside. Then, with a smile, he fetched Harry's scuffed little half-boots and positioned them beside his own. He fastened the lock on the door, securing their suite, and lit a candle. In its flickering amber light, he poured himself a brandy from a decanter atop a mahogany side table. He relaxed on a small sofa, stretched his long legs, and sipped the pungent drink.

The door from the bathing room opened.

Nicholas froze with his glass inches from his lips.

Meggy hesitated with her hand still on the brass knob, but then she stepped into the parlour and closed the door behind her. The smell of lavender soap clung to her freshly washed rosiness, and a snowy cotton nightdress fell to her ankles. A ribbon threaded through white lace decorated the scooped neckline and was drawn into a bow at her décolletage. An untied peony pink linen dressing gown framed her figure. Her thick curls, bound with a rose-coloured satin ribbon, cascaded down one shoulder, the tips falling beside a nipple barely disguised under the thin cotton.

Nicholas couldn't stand as was proper when a lady entered a room because he was *instantly* as hard as a rock. He shifted his position on the sofa and rested the hand holding his brandy in his lap, with his forearm covering the bulge in his trousers.

Meggy approached. Nicholas remained as still as a statue, not trusting himself in the least.

She stood by his knee. 'I want to thank you.'

With difficulty, Nicholas lifted his eyes to her sweet face without lingering on her unbound breasts. She was an innocent, and he was once an honourable man. He could attempt integrity, at least. 'Thank me for what?'

'For amusing the children all day, and for your attentions to Miss Kimberley and to me. It was . . . unexpected and quite . . . quite *kind*, despite your assertions about your character yesterday.'

Nicholas nudged a rolled armrest pillow over his loins and sipped his brandy. 'I said I'd make an effort to keep you and your siblings safe whilst you're in my care.'

'Keeping us safe is ensuring we're alive and unharmed. Today you showed kindness.' Meggy tilted her head. 'But is that what it is for you – an effort?'

She had no idea how much effort he was exerting now, for matters weren't subsiding in his trousers.

'Yes. It almost killed me.' He raised his glass of brandy, as if toasting her. 'I seek solace from drink, as you see.'

She laughed – dimples deepening, eyes shining. She was adorable beyond words.

'On occasion, I do as well after a strenuous day with the children. But only a small glass of wine, in my case. Drink goes straight to my head.'

'Then I shan't offer you brandy. Your ineffective chaperone would accuse me of nefarious deeds if she found you drunk with me. Where is the dotty bat, anyway?'

'She's asleep. And you're terrible,' Meggy said with a smile, gently smacking his shirt-clad shoulder, which sent an electric jolt straight to his loins. 'She's *not* a dotty bat nor a snoring dragon. She's . . . she's aged recently, and that's been heartbreaking. But she loves me and the children, and I want her to know she is valued, even as she grows old.'

Nicholas's throat thickened. Meggy was beautiful inside and out. His feeble conscience whimpered, although his husky voice hid the plea. 'I told you to bring a witch. What good is a chaperone who allows you to linger with me in the evening dusk?'

She cast down her eyes. 'I suppose I should go.'

'Yes, you should. Leave.' His cock throbbed. 'Leave *now.*'

But she didn't. She twisted a finger in the folds of her pink dressing gown. 'It's just . . .' She smiled hesitatingly. 'I'm not very tired since I slept all afternoon.'

At the best of times, Nicholas's resistance to carnal temptation was minimal.

Alone in the candlelight with a luscious angel in white and pink nightclothes, he could no longer hold back.

Just a kiss . . . just the one tender kiss he'd denied them both yesterday by the pond.

One sweet kiss.

Nicholas placed down his brandy and lifted Meggy's hand, as cool as marble, from the folds of her nightdress. He held it by the tips of her slim fingers. Her nails were pink and white ovals – pretty, feminine – and Nicholas brushed his thumb over her delicate knuckles, as he'd done beside the carriage that morning.

This time, Meggy didn't snatch her hand away.

She gasped, barely audible.

A soft inhalation.

A whisper exhalation.

Nicholas brought his eyes to Meggy's. 'Sit with me?'

She nodded, her blue eyes round, her cheeks flushed, her full red lips parted.

Nicholas gently pulled her down beside him and placed an arm on the back of the sofa, above her shoulders. Her breath hitched, and her breasts rose and fell as she settled next to him with their thighs touching.

Nicholas's cock strained to break from the prison of his trousers.

Calm down, Nicholas told it. *We aren't going there. Only a little fun.*

I hope.

He stroked Meggy's satin-smooth cheek with the backs of two fingers, and as she turned towards his touch, his knuckles brushed the corner of her mouth. His hand trailed down to the tips of her curls. Although he barely grazed the cotton covering her breast, her nipple poked against her nightdress, suddenly erect.

Oh, dear God.

Nicholas's hand slipped around Meggy's waist. It was trim and slender before widening into round hips. He drew her closer, her face inches from his own, and she leaned her cheek against his shoulder.

'I've decided your mother must've been Aphrodite.' Nicholas breathed the words into her sweet-smelling curls. 'I cannot account for your relation to Edwin unless your father's second wife was a goddess.'

Meggy placed a hand on Nicholas's biceps and slid her palm over his shirtsleeve.

Her touch stoked his desire. With his eyelids half closed, he moved to kiss her.

'Edwin was handsome *once*,' Meggy said in a clear voice just before Nicholas's lips touched her own.

'Oh?' Nicholas said, brushing a curl from her forehead. He regretted mentioning Edwin, for he didn't want to think of the late earl. Not now. Not when Edwin's deathbed requests – words about guidance, honour, kindness – nagged Nicholas's conscience.

Nicholas only wanted one kiss . . .

One kiss from those innocent yet oh-so-ripe lips.

He leaned in again.

Meggy spoke before he reached her mouth. 'Edwin was very handsome, indeed. When I was quite young, I thought him the most splendid gentleman in all the world.' She ran her palm up and down Nicholas's arm, smoothing the loose fabric of his shirtsleeve. 'Were you acquainted with him fifteen years ago?'

Despite his sluggish mind and burning desire, Nicholas attempted to focus on the spoken words rather than the red lips speaking. 'I met Edwin eleven or twelve years ago.'

'Then you didn't know him when he was *my* Edwin,' Meggy said, stroking her finger along the ridges in Nicholas's upper arm, as if tracing the lines of his muscles over his shirt. 'I wish you had because he was wonderful. He was lively in a way our father couldn't be, for Papa was fifty years old when I was born. Edwin played with me. Hide-and-seek, ball games. He'd push me in the swing that hangs from the large oak near the pond. He taught me how to catch frogs and showed me they weren't frightening but instead quite lovely with their shiny eyes and smooth skin. I loved Edwin, and I *thought* he loved me. He said he loved me.'

Her words resonated profoundly with Nicholas.

A tear brimmed from the corner of Meggy's eye and ran down her cheek. She flicked it away with the back of a finger. 'One Christmas, Edwin came home, but he wasn't Edwin anymore. He slurred his words and stumbled and ignored me. And he and Papa argued so terribly it frightened me. Subsequent visits were even worse until he stopped coming altogether. It was addictions, of course – I didn't know it then, but I've learned since. Addictions to drink, to gambling, to . . . to whores, which is how he got . . . what's the disease one gets from whores?'

Nicholas nearly choked. His confused cock, which had resolutely clung to its state of readiness, gave up its fight and slumped against his loins. 'Er . . . there are several, but Edwin had the pox.'

Meggy's hand dropped from his arm as she studied Nicholas. 'Why don't *you* have . . . sexual intercourse diseases? Or *do* you, and I cannot tell?'

Nicholas's eyes widened. 'My God, what a question.'

'I'd like an answer.'

He turned slightly to pick up his brandy. He tossed back the drink, returned the glass to the table, and met her gaze. 'I do *not* have venereal diseases, as they are properly called, because there's a way to avoid them, which also prevents pregnancies.'

Meggy gazed at him for a moment through narrowed eyes, but then shrugged and looked down, her long lashes a dark smudge across the tops of her cheeks. 'When I saw Edwin years later for my mother's funeral, I barely recognised him, for the . . . pox had affected his appearance.' A fine line appeared between her brows. Her pretty lips frowned, and Nicholas's heart clenched as she lifted her hand to fiddle with his waistcoat buttons. 'That afternoon,' she continued, 'Edwin and Papa argued dreadfully. Sophy had never heard yelling before, and she was terrified. The poor darling was only two, and she was already heartbroken, wanting our mama and not understanding what had happened. So I . . .' Meggy dropped her hand, shook her head, and stared at Nicholas. 'But you can't possibly want to hear all this.'

He recalled the moment by the carriage when her maternal tenderness first struck him. 'Was that when you became a mama?'

She blinked. 'Why, how curious you should ask such a thing. I'm *not* Sophy's mama, of course, but when I took her upstairs that evening, she wouldn't go to her nurse. I sang her to sleep, and for many years after, she'd only fall asleep if I sang. So I suppose, in a way . . .'

'In more than "a way", my dear. Besides my sister Rose, I've not seen a better mother than you.'

Her eyes widened. 'Truly?'

Nicholas nodded. 'Yes.'

'I've wanted to be like a mama to them. Like a mama *and* a papa, in truth, for my father asked it of me.' Her fingers played with the ruffles at Nicholas's loosened shirt collar, pleating and releasing the fabric, and then pleating it again. 'It was lovely to have your help today, however.' She peeked at him from the corner of her eyes – shyly, not coquettishly.

An expansive warmth filled Nicholas's chest, and, to his astonishment, it pushed aside primal urges. He couldn't remember the last time he'd felt such a powerful urge to protect and comfort anyone other than his sister. Or perhaps he *could* remember, but he shoved those painful memories back into the hole where they resided.

He embraced Meggy closer, and she snuggled into his shoulder. 'Papa lived only six months after my mother's death. On the night he died, he told me I must carry the family's burdens alone until Harry became a man, and that I must ensure Harry never falls to Edwin's ways.' Meggy's eyes locked with Nicholas's. 'I've tried my best to live up to my father's expectations, and my best is *damned* good. But sometimes it's . . .' She trailed off.

'Lonely?'

She nodded, her chin quivering, and another tear escaped.

This time, Nicholas pressed his lips against its salty warmth on the curve of her cheek. 'I know,' he whispered against her soap-fresh skin.

Meggy placed her cool hand against his face. 'Lord Holbrook, I . . .'

She fell silent.

Nicholas tucked a golden-brown curl, glistening like a dark amber ribbon in the candlelight, behind her ear. 'What, my darling?'

'What' – she gathered a breath – 'what do you think of me, Lord Holbrook?'

Nicholas's answer escaped without a thought. 'You are utter sweetness.' He traced the line of her jaw with his fingertips. 'You're an angel.'

Meggy sighed, a faint smile on her lips. Lips that Nicholas needed to kiss.

Just once.

Nicholas leaned in, his cock rising to attention unbidden. He entwined his fingers in Meggy's tresses as his mouth sought hers, and this time, she met him with awkward eagerness. As her soft lips opened, he slipped the tip of his tongue into her sweet mouth. She tasted of the fresh anise flavour of toothpowder.

Oh, the heart-wrenching purity of her kiss.

Gently, so gently, Nicholas's tongue explored her lips, the tips of her teeth, as Meggy grew bolder, pressing back with increased need as she tightened her embrace.

Her breasts pushed against his chest.

She gasped, her mouth breaking its tight clasp. But Nicholas's lips still touched hers in an exquisitely sensual moment. His breath met Meggy's, and he gazed through half-closed lids into her beautiful eyes.

'Not lonely now, I hope?' Nicholas whispered the words against her mouth.

Meggy purred as she skimmed her fingertips along the back of Nicholas's neck, tantalising him. 'I want more kisses.'

She melted her mouth into his.

And kissed him *fervently*.

Desire blazed sudden and fierce within Nicholas, like a raging bonfire. The nascent tenderness in his heart gave way to something he recognised at once.

Fevered, focused lust.

To hell with his promises to Edwin and to Meggy. He needed more than one kiss from this lusty blue-eyed lady – pert and independent one moment, tender and gentle the next – although he wouldn't go *there*, he *couldn't* go there. She was a virgin, a debutante, an innocent.

Even still, even without *that*, there would be consequences for his actions. Tears, confusion, anguish.

Nicholas would deal with the consequences later.

After all, Meggy wanted him every bit as much as he wanted her.

He broke from her lips and trailed kisses along the curve of her neck. She arched against him as his hand ran down her spine. He half smiled into her lavender-scented skin. Every woman must be caressed differently and finding how each woman responded was part of the challenge.

Nicholas's lips hovered at the ribboned lace on the neckline of Meggy's gown. Her breath quickened; her nipples stood erect under the cotton.

'You glorious goddess,' he murmured as he brushed the underside of one luscious curve.

She whimpered; her eyes squeezed shut. Her expression was pained with desire; her lips were ripe and red from his kisses, her breath short and rapid.

Nicholas trailed his fingers along the pink ribbon and frothy lace of Meggy's nightdress. So feminine, so lovely. With a turn of his wrist, he untied the bow . . .

A rap sounded at the door from the hallway.

Nicholas's hand froze.

Meggy's eyes flew open. 'Who do you think it is?'

And sudden realisation flooded Nicholas: if they were caught like this, he'd be standing at an altar within the month. Moments earlier, in his bedchamber, he'd rejected the notion, but now, full of desire to possess Meggy's body, he also recalled her tenderness with her siblings and imagined her as his wife, passionate in bed but gentle and motherly with *his* child, *their* child . . .

A sudden wave of longing nearly deprived him of breath.

Another knock, slightly louder.

Nicholas must answer the door.

He brushed his lips against Meggy's mouth. 'I don't know, but I shall get rid of them.'

Meggy's eyelids grew heavy again, and she threaded her fingers into his hair. 'Don't answer it, and they'll go away. Kiss me more.'

She attacked him with new urgency, and Nicholas burned as he kissed her back, mindless of everything but Meggy's taste, her feel, her passion.

The cursed rap at the door repeated louder yet.

The others would awaken.

Nicholas broke the kiss.

Only then did he realise his fingers had released a button at his trouser waist.

His pulse pounded. What the *devil* had he almost done?

Fury at himself churned, rage rose at his lack of self-control. He pressed Meggy away with the palm of his hand, his throat too thick to explain that she must return to her room, to flee him, to think nothing but the worst of him, no matter what.

Because at his core, Nicholas was loathsome. Vile. Horrid.

'Door,' he managed, his voice raspy, his mouth dry.

Meggy nodded and stood, and Nicholas did as well, his throat constricting again, for even still, his cock thought on its own and bulged in his trousers, and Meggy must notice.

She did.

She flushed, glanced down, and then cast her gaze through her lashes – artless but maddeningly seductive.

Nicholas turned his back on her and opened the door.

The busty blonde maid from the courtyard stood in the corridor with her bodice loosened and her eyelashes fluttering.

Her presence cooled the remnants of Nicholas's ardour like cold water to the face. Thank God the door blocked Meggy's view.

But the maid's words, though whispered, were clear enough to be heard over his shoulder. 'Your lordship wanted my company tonight, and I'm desperate for yours.'

Meggy gasped behind him, and Nicholas froze. Meggy must think he'd arranged a tryst with a servant and then started with *her* instead. He gathered his breath to explain, but before he turned around, Meggy's bedroom door opened and closed.

'M'lord?' The maid still stood before him, but she was less confident.

Nicholas's rage swelled. 'Goddammit, no.'

She gasped. 'But I thought . . .'

How the devil had she got this impression? Did he ooze licentiousness as Edwin had oozed dissipation?

Of course, he did.

Look at how he'd just treated an innocent angel . . .

'No,' Nicholas said, more gently. He combed his fingers in his hair and cradled his head. 'Not at all.'

'But the last time you stayed here . . .'

Good God. He didn't remember, didn't even recognise her. 'Forgive me.' He shook his throbbing head and forced himself to meet her gaze. 'Forgive me.'

He spoke the words to the maid, but Meggy's face imposed on the serving girl's distraught features.

'N-Nothing to forgive, m'lord.' The maid's eyes darted from side to side as she tightened the laces at her bodice. 'But please don't tell the innkeeper. I could lose my place.'

Nicholas's shoulders slumped. 'Of course not, my dear. I shan't say a word.'

He closed and latched the door.

He leaned against it, one hand at his throat.

Meggy.

Nicholas must explain the misunderstanding about the maid to Meggy.

And he must apologise.

He crossed the parlour. His knuckles hovered over Meggy's door, but muffled sobs from within stilled his hand.

He closed his eyes. His conscience berated him. *You exploited Meggy's loneliness. You tempted her because you desire her, and she fell for it in her innocence. Without thinking, you might've taken her virginity – the right of the husband you promised to find – for your own goddamn fleeting pleasure and then been disgusted with yourself and with her. You would've destroyed everything she's worked towards since her father died. Walk away. Hurt her a little now rather than ruin her life, either by marrying her or not.*

Nicholas dropped his hand.

He must get out of Meggy's life, for her own good.

As Nicholas returned to his room, he planned for her protection. He'd keep his distance tomorrow – ride on horseback rather than in the carriage. He'd apologise when he had a private moment with Meggy. And he'd return to London as soon as she and the children were safely at Alton Park.

He'd rashly promised Harry a trip to Ipswich – an obligation that Nicholas would eventually fulfil – but first, he'd spend several weeks in London, in the arms of many different women, to clear his mind.

Meanwhile, Meggy must be married off as soon as possible.

Yet try as he might, Nicholas could no longer imagine pairing her with any of his friends.

5

'Lady Margaret?' Holbrook rested his hand atop the linen tablecloth near Meggy's elbow in his third attempt to address her that morning.

She bristled, ignored him, and applied herself to cleaning marmalade from Harry's sticky face by gasping her brother's chin in one hand and rubbing his cheeks with a corner of her napkin. She sat with the children, Miss Kimberley and Holbrook in their private parlour, in the same arrangement around the rectangular dining table as when they'd eaten dinner the evening before.

But Meggy had been in charity with Holbrook then.

She despised him now.

The humiliation by the pond had humbled Meggy, but the night before had mortified her. She'd told Holbrook things she'd never told another, allowed him to touch her body, and very nearly revealed the extent of her ridiculous feelings. Thank God she'd held her tongue and remembered at least one of Miss Kimberley's instructions regarding behaviour with gentleman: a lady should never declare her sentiments until after a gentleman declares his.

'Stop or you'll rub off my skin.' Harry, seated beside Meggy, squirmed out of her grasp and stuffed more toast in his mouth. 'And why do you ignore Nicky? He's trying to tell you I'm riding with him today.'

Meggy's brows shot up. *Nicky*? 'Harry, do not speak with food in your mouth, and address Lord Holbrook properly.'

Harry washed down the toast with a gulp of milk, leaving a creamy moustache on his upper lip. 'But he asked me to. Didn't you, Nicky?'

'I did, indeed.'

'May *I* call you Nicky?' Sophy asked. She'd nibbled the edges on two pieces of toast, saving the buttery and jammy centres for last.

Holbrook flashed a grin. 'You certainly may call me Nicky, Lady Sophia. Everyone at this table may call me Nicky.'

Miss Kimberley muttered 'such kindness, so generous, although I should never be so bold,' but Sophy giggled, spilling crumbs on the napkin tucked into the neck of her lilac-coloured gown. 'And you must call me *Sophy*, as you did yesterday, Nicky.'

Holbrook bowed his head. 'I'm honoured, Sophy.' His eyes darted to Meggy before returning to her sister. 'I did call you Sophy yesterday, but I realised this morning you never granted me permission to do so. A gentleman can never be too careful when it comes to protecting a lady. When he errs, perhaps encroaching on unwelcome familiarity, he must always correct his behaviour and make amends.'

78

Meggy gritted her teeth and glared, her pulse rising. Amends? Impossible.

Holbrook sought to fool her again with more honeyed words.

He'd tricked her twice, but he'd never succeed a third time.

The entrance of a maid with a plate of red apples and russet pears – the same blonde woman Meggy had glimpsed through her tears before she'd closed her bedroom door – deflated her spirit. A tight lump formed in her throat.

With effort, she swallowed. 'What do you mean you are riding with his lordship, Harry?'

The boy beamed. 'Nicky decided to ride today so there'll be more room in the carriage. He said I may sit before him on the saddle.'

'If that meets with your approval, of course, Lady Margaret.' Holbrook nodded at the maid as she refilled his coffee – did he wink, as well? Meggy's stomach lurched. What had transpired between the two of them after she fled? Had he transferred his passion to the maid, touching *her* breasts? Had he *coupled* with this blonde woman? Brought them both to whatever mysterious wonders arose from combining the passionate urges of two people? Did Holbrook and the maid experience together the sensations that were denied to a lady like Meggy unless a gold band encircled the ring finger of her left hand?

The sensations Meggy had throbbed for, yearned for, ached for in Holbrook's arms . . .

Meggy's innards coiled.

Never mind. She didn't want to know what had happened between them.

She fiddled with her coffee cup until the maid left. Then she snapped at Holbrook. 'I can hardly say no now without disappointing Harry, can I? But next time, I expect you to ask my permission *before* you promise treats to my siblings.'

'But Nicky is my guardian too, Meggy,' Harry said, sticking out his bottom lip and scowling.

'Only temporarily, Harry. Don't become accustomed to him. Furthermore, he's your guardian in name only.'

'I beg to differ, Lady Margaret.' Holbrook leaned back in his chair, his muscular frame encased in another magnificently tailored coat – this time an earthy green like oak leaves, paired with a linen waistcoat the shade of burnished acorns. The spurs on his tall brown boots with their pale leather tops scraped against the carpeted floor as he stretched out his long legs in a pair of trousers of the palest and softest buckskin, no darker than cream, and sipped his coffee. 'Until your marriage, you are, at best, equal with me in guardianship of Harry and Sophy. Of course, as a man, I hold the greater legal claim. But never fear, I promised Edwin I'd protect their interests.'

Meggy's nails dug into her palms. If the plate of fruit were closer, she'd hurl an apple at Holbrook's curled lips. Maybe she'd do it whilst he drank, so his coffee would splash into his mocking eyes and drip over the pristine whiteness of his shirt and cravat. '*Never fear*?' She spat each word out. 'Promised *Edwin*? The same person who landed me in this mess? Understand me now, Lord Holbrook. You have no claim to Harry and Sophy. You are a legal figurehead, nothing more.'

Holbrook lifted his eyebrows, and Miss Kimberley and the children gasped. But Meggy applied herself to her poached eggs and toast with renewed vigour. She wasn't going to let Holbrook push her around.

Harry crossed his little arms over his chest. 'You're horrid this morning. Horrid to Nicky and horrid to *me*.'

Meggy's fork stopped halfway to her mouth. She hadn't intended to hurt *Harry*. But before she could apologise, Holbrook patted her brother's shoulder. 'Harry, be patient with your sister. Remember how her head ached yesterday.'

Meggy tightened her grip on her fork, resisting the urge to stab it, eggs and all, into Holbrook's sanctimonious face. How dare he present her as weak? *He'd* caused her violent mood, and he knew it.

How she loathed him.

Never again would she fall into the marquess's sticky web. Never again would his false kindness deceive her. Meggy was innocent, but she knew what he'd intended when his hand reached for the button at his waist. And in her stupid, blind passion, Meggy might've spread her legs and welcomed her own ruin.

She'd been a fool.

But after several hours' travel in the swaying carriage, Meggy settled her thoughts more pleasantly. Holbrook was reprehensible scum, of course, and she'd never trust him again, but he'd provided her a service by physically answering a question she'd long had.

Sexual intercourse promised to be *extremely* pleasurable, just as the midwife Mrs Wright had suggested.

At the age of sixteen, Meggy learned about 'the marriage bed' from her governess. But Miss Kimberley, virginal herself, only relayed what *her* mother had told her. 'It's like what the stallion does to the mares, and it hurts terribly, but a wife must bear it for the sake of children. And, fortunately, it's over quickly.'

Meggy had furrowed her brow. 'But the *men* like it. Elsewise, Edwin would not be so much with . . .'

'Yes, yes. No need to name his vices, dearest. Men like it, although I cannot say why. Now I've told you all I know, and you are some years from marriage, so no need to think any more of it.'

But Meggy had thought of it a great deal indeed, and she'd observed the horses with new interest. The mating ritual appeared to consist of persistent stallions with terrifyingly large penises sniffing under the tails of jittery mares until the males suddenly mounted, thrust a few times, and jumped down. It didn't look appealing, and it didn't fit with Meggy's glimpses of courting villagers with their arms entwined and their lips brushing against flushed faces. These embraces, covertly watched, quickened Meggy's pulse.

Meggy had decided to consult a more knowledgeable source and settled on the village midwife. Mrs Wright was a tenant farmer's wife with eight round, jolly children. She and jovial Mr Wright hugged and kissed or slapped each other's bottoms constantly.

On a sunny autumn day when she was seventeen, Meggy had perched upon a weatherworn tree stump in the Wrights' kitchen garden as the midwife dug potatoes from the rich, moist soil. The youngest Wrights tumbled like puppies in the grass before their red-brick cottage's oak door.

'Mrs Wright, may I . . . ask you about men and women?'

Mrs Wright wiped perspiration from her forehead with the back of her hand, leaving a smudge of dirt above her twinkling eyes. 'Aye, m'lady. Anything you like.'

Meggy knitted her gloved fingers together. 'Is the marriage bed like . . . like what the stallion does to the mare?'

The midwife smiled tenderly. 'Oh, is that what you're wondering about, love? I suppose your dear mama – God rest her ladyship's sweet soul – didn't tell you much before she passed?'

Meggy shook her head, her heart longing, as it still did on occasion, for her mother's comforting embrace.

Mrs Wright sat back on her heels and cleaned her soil-dark hands with her apron. 'Well, the idea of the marriage bed is the same as the horses, but otherwise, 'tis not much like. Whilst I can't speak for the mares, they don't seem to have fun like I do with Mr Wright.'

Meggy leaned forward eagerly. 'So it's pleasurable?'

'M'lady, what happens between a man and a woman feels like heaven itself, done properly.'

Meggy's breath caught. She'd suspected as much when she peeked at the corded biceps of the young farmhands who stripped to the waist as they reaped hay in the golden autumn sunlight. Her own body had smouldered with heated urges, but the sensation was hazy, with no clear indication of what a farmhand would do to her, if she gave him leave, or what further feelings his touch would elicit.

'Mrs Wright, *how* does one do it properly?'

The midwife lifted her shoulders. 'Varies from person to person. Amongst our kind, we sometimes try it out a little before marriage. Have a tumble here and there. See what we like before we settle down. Once a baby's on the way, 'tis time to go to the parson.' Mrs Wright faltered and put a hand to her chin. 'But I oughtn't have told you that, Lady Margaret. You forget what I said, for 'tain't the same with your kind. One day you'll marry a fine gentleman, so you wait for him to show you these things. Be certain he's a kind man, and you'll have nothing to fear.'

Meggy knew a lady like herself mayn't go to bed with a man who wasn't her husband, because inheritance laws in England revolved around one thing: legitimate male primogeniture. No gentleman with land or a title to impart would marry a lady who wasn't either a virgin or a widow of spotless reputation. But knowing this didn't stop Meggy's attraction to young men, although she knew if she acted on her urges towards any of the strapping farmhands, she'd buy her family's ruin faster than Edwin had.

But last night, she'd got a little answer to her wonderings, and thinking of Holbrook's kisses and caresses as a *service* provided Meggy with delicious satisfaction. A satisfaction that *almost* distracted her from the throbbing longing aroused by watching his strong thighs rise and fall in the saddle.

Last night, she told herself, had simply made her more determined to do her duty and find an eligible husband, but she did hope the unknown gentleman wouldn't be ninety and toothless. He didn't need to be handsome exactly, but strapping would be good. And she'd not object if he could kiss her as Holbrook had done, but she couldn't dwell long on those thoughts without causing herself discomfort. No, regarding Holbrook it was important to remember the marquess was like a bull in a field moving from one cow to another, and that was the last kind of husband any woman would want.

With the roads dry and the weather clear, the carriage travelled fast. But as the day progressed, the air took on the stifling mugginess that precedes a storm, and rivulets of sweat dripped under Meggy's mourning gown as she wrote in her marbled pasteboard journal. By around half-past five, when the carriage turned off the main road leading south-east, the clouds formed threatening grey towers, and Meggy tucked her pencil into her reticule and fanned herself with the journal to relieve her discomfort. She leaned forward, eager for signs of Alton Park. As much as she despised Holbrook, a marquess's country seat would provide more creature comfort than two hot days on the road.

Meggy drummed her gloved fingers against the green silk armrest under the open window. How dreadful would Holbrook's sister be? Magnificence, hauteur and beauty didn't cow Meggy. But if Lady Rose proved to be as deceitful and callous as her brother, the upcoming weeks or months would be miserable.

The important thing, of course, was to protect Harry and Sophy from terrible influences.

Involuntarily, Meggy's eyes slid to the marquess riding on a bay stallion with one arm secure around her brother's middle and the other holding the horse's reins steadily. Harry reached his hand out, pointing, and turned his sun-flushed face to Holbrook.

Whatever the marquess replied, it made Harry laugh and bounce in the saddle.

Meggy fanned her journal faster.

She must marry. At once.

'It won't be long now,' Miss Kimberley said, holding her well-thumbed guidebook to the stately homes of England an inch from her bespectacled nose. 'It's a distance of two miles to the gate of Alton Park once one turns off the main road between Sudbury and Dedham, and the driver did that well-nigh fifteen minutes ago.'

It proved to be a prophetic speech, for at that moment, a towering, triple-arched stone gate came into view.

Meggy's journal fell to her lap.

Sophy gasped, clasping Dolly to her chest, and jumped to her feet to stick her head out of the window. 'Is this it, Nicky? Is this magnificent gate the entrance to Alton Park?'

'Come away, Sophy,' Meggy said testily. Why did her siblings adore the vile marquess? Everything would be easier if they could see through his façade, as Meggy now did. 'He can't hear you.'

But Holbrook pulled his reins, circled his horse back, and drew alongside the carriage. 'It is, Sophy,' he called through the window. 'Does Dolly approve?'

Sophy held her doll to her ear, as if the toy whispered a secret. 'Dolly says she must see the house before she decides.'

Holbrook nodded. 'Very sensible of Dolly. Harry and I shall ready it for her arrival in that case.' He spurred his horse and, leaning forward with Harry, they galloped ahead, passing through the entranceway the moment the middle of the three wrought-iron and gilded gates opened.

Miss Kimberley consulted her guidebook again. 'The gate is sixteenth century, as is the oldest part of the house.' She tapped her finger on the page. 'Three additional wings added in the subsequent three hundred years.'

The governess placed the book in her lap. 'In addition to Lord Holbrook's other perfections,' she said, peering out of the window as the carriage turned, 'he has a very fine seat, indeed. Doesn't he, Meggy?'

Meggy's cheeks burned, for she'd watched Holbrook's seat rise in the saddle until the marquess and Harry disappeared down the wide avenue, which stretched to infinity on the other side of the gate. Fortunately, a damp wind swelled to cool Meggy's face before anyone noticed her blush. She rested her head against the padded velvet carriage wall, gazing up at the arching branches of a double row of lime trees, which formed a leafy green canopy over the road.

Beyond stretched vast emerald lawns, as carefully mown as cricket fields. Steely clouds hung overhead like a heavy blanket.

A mile farther, the carriage rumbled over a stone bridge spanning a small river. Here the rows of trees ceased and either side of the avenue opened into parterre gardens with orderly geometric patterns formed by tightly pruned hedges.

Behind them, the house rose like a white palace.

Meggy's eyes widened.

Sophy squealed, and Miss Kimberley blessed her soul.

Alton Park's gleaming façade was symmetrical, with three storeys of leaded glass and snowy limestone under a turreted slate roof. The middle of the ground floor consisted of three wide, open arches. The carriage passed through the centre arch.

'Gosh!' Sophy blinked. 'I thought *that* was the front.'

On the other side of the arch, the carriage rounded a circular brick drive within an enormous courtyard. The house – four equally colossal wings of glistening windows and white stone – formed a quadrangle around the open square dotted with Grecian sculptures and paved with gravel. The team halted before sweeping steps and massive carved wooden doors on the far side of the courtyard.

At least eight Berksleigh Halls would fit inside the walls of this palace. Meggy couldn't even begin to imagine the window taxes, let alone the cost of staff to maintain everything. Why, gardeners alone must add to . . .

Her attempts at rapid calculation were interrupted when Holbrook opened the door to the carriage, looking tanned and more handsome than any man had a right to. He assisted Miss Kimberley and Sophy out, but when his gloved hand reached for Meggy's, she deposited Caesar into his arms instead.

'Take your beastly pig-dog,' she said, although guilt twinged. Caesar had curled beside Meggy on most of the journey, and when she wasn't scribbling in her journal, describing passing landmarks, she'd enjoyed scratching his round belly as Caesar kicked his back legs and snuffled in his dreams.

Whilst Holbrook released the pug to follow the others up the stairs, Meggy held up her black silk skirts and hopped down unaided. As the carriage drove off, the marquess placed his hand on Meggy's elbow.

Meggy snatched her arm away. 'Don't touch me.'

Holbrook bowed his head. 'I deserve that,' he said in a low voice. 'But, Lady Margaret, please allow me to apologise before you go inside.'

'No, I shan't.' Meggy held her chin aloft. 'I have no interest in your insincere words. If you were a *gentleman*, I'd consider hearing you, but as you are nothing better than a scoundrel who preys on women, I'd no more hear your apology than a rabbit would listen to the apology of a fox.'

The marquess drew back, and the glimmer of amusement that customarily hovered in his eyes and the corners of his lips vanished entirely. 'I . . . I see.' With his brow furrowed, he inhaled, held his breath, and then released it with a nod. 'In that case, I suppose I have only to welcome you to Alton Park.'

'Perhaps I shall remember my manners and thank you one day, but at the moment, it gives me nothing but dissatisfaction to accept your hospitality. I'd rather stay in a stable.' She tossed her curls and proceeded up two steps.

Only for his scoff to arrest her progress. 'Then you're going the wrong way.'

She turned. From her elevated position, she glared directly into his eyes. '*What?*'

'The stables are to the east.' Holbrook jerked his head to indicate the direction.

Meggy hesitated only a second before jutting her chin in the air. 'Very well, I shall sleep with the horses.' She marched back down the steps and past him, fully intending to follow through with her declaration.

But Holbrook ran to catch up. 'Please stop, my dear – you've made your point, and our discourse has descended into childishness.' His voice softened. 'Lady Margaret, if you'd allow me to apologise, we shall move beyond an . . . an impulsive accident—'

'An accident!' Meggy clenched her fists. 'You are so loathsome it pains me to speak to you. I shall marry the first eligible man who offers for me and be glad never to see you again.'

Holbrook held up his hands. 'By all means, apply yourself to finding the poor devil. No,' he added with

90

a half-smile, 'to finding the damned fortunate fellow.' His eyes gleamed, and he lowered his voice. 'But you may as well admit – because we both know it's true – that you *don't* find me loathsome. You wanted those kisses as much as I did.'

Meggy dug her nails into her palms in order to refrain from slapping the smug expression off Holbrook's face. She inhaled deeply and released slowly. 'In fact,' she said with perfect calmness, 'I wanted those kisses – my very first kisses – *more* than you did. They meant something to *me*.'

Holbrook drew back as if he'd seen a ghost. 'Oh, dear God,' he said, blinking. 'Lady Margaret, I warned you not to trust me—'

Meggy held up her hand. '*Stop*. Don't blame me for your faults. And don't speak another word. During our brief acquaintance, I've already endured lessons and lectures from you, and now it's your turn. Yesterday I thought I glimpsed something lovely: a dependable and kind *friend*, adored by my siblings. And that attracted me to you far more than your good looks. Telling you about Edwin and sharing those kisses were equally intimate moments for me. But regardless of what you did or did not do with the maid, her arrival reminded me of something. You were doing to me what you do to any woman who is foolish enough to fall in your trap. I shan't be your prey again. If you cared a snap of your fingers for me or for Harry, who idolises you already, you would never have touched me, never have tempted me, never have kissed me. Ruin me, and you ruin his chances and Sophy's chances. So, whilst I don't forgive you, I do thank you for proving that under your all-too-appealing exterior, you're a despicable man.'

He recoiled with a gasp — his face flushed, his eyes wide — and stared.

Excellent.

Meggy marched up the stairs, her back straight and her head held high. As she stepped into the marble entrance hall, thunder cracked, and the downpour began. She glanced over her shoulder. Holbrook stood at the bottom of the steps — lips parted, expression frozen — as the rain drenched him.

Perfect.

Now the marquess would know the extent of Lady Margaret Fairchild's resolve. And as for the ache in her heart — well, feelings that had come easily could flee just as rapidly.

Meggy swallowed as she loosened her bonnet ribbons. At least, she hoped they could.

6

The entrance hall of Alton Park was vast and *white*. White marble floors, white marble veneer on the walls, white marble statues. Meggy barely suppressed an eye-roll as she deposited her bonnet and gloves with the butler.

A dripping Holbrook straggled in, his fine green and cream clothes saturated, and his cravat plastered flat. Impossibly, the rivulets of water streaming over his chiselled cheeks and the raindrops on his thick black lashes only made him more handsome. With some difficulty, Meggy controlled an impulse to scowl. It wouldn't do to meet Holbrook's magnificent sister with an ugly grimace.

As Meggy composed herself, attempting to look as impassive and elegant as one of the marble statues, a valet materialised and expressed frenzied concerns for Holbrook's health.

The marquess dismissed his attentions.

Instead, he took Harry and Sophy's hands in his and smiled at Miss Kimberley. 'Please follow me, madam. With your permission, I'd like to introduce you to my sister, who will ensure your comfort after our long travels.'

Meggy fumed, for Miss Kimberley simpered.

One day, the others would see through Holbrook's treachery.

With the governess on her arm, Meggy followed Holbrook and the children across the entrance. The dogs' nails clicked on the marble until they passed through a set of gilded double doors manned by liveried footmen. The next room was a soaring wood-panelled great hall – Tudor, according to the description Miss Kimberley had read from her guidebook – with a flag-stone floor, a carved-stone hearth evidently designed to burn an entire forest at once, and a minstrel gallery looming from the upper level. Carved bears snarled from the stone and woodwork. The family's heraldic animal, presumably, as bears supported the crest on the carriage as well. No doubt a play on Holbrook's surname, Burton.

Fitting, as bears were predators.

Holbrook exited the great hall, turning into a vast corridor, where the wall of windows to Meggy's right looked over the courtyard, now dark grey with sheets of pouring rain. Lightning flashed, and a crack of thunder followed. Harry whooped, pointing, and Sophy tucked closer to Holbrook as she clutched Dolly to her side.

Miss Kimberley hung heavy on Meggy's arm.

'Tired, dearest?' Meggy asked.

The old woman shuffled on the thick gold carpet, but her pale eyes peered keenly behind her spectacles. 'Only a little. No doubt I shall be made comfortable very soon in this magnificent house. What a relief a bit of rest will be for you, Meggy, after all the years of hardship.'

Irritation rather than relief bubbled in Meggy's breast. Did Holbrook intend for an old woman to walk a mile around this pile of gilded bricks searching for the mysterious Lady Rose? And why didn't Miss Kimberley focus on Lady Rose's rudeness in not meeting them at the entrance, rather than allowing grand surroundings to enchant her? In the case of Holbrook – and likely his sister and estate – beauty disguised repulsiveness.

Vigilance was essential.

Holbrook stopped, turned with the children, and swept out the hand still holding Sophy's to usher Meggy and Miss Kimberley through an open door into a coffered-ceiling, crimson-coloured drawing room. A willowy woman sat straight-backed upon a rose-red sofa and wielded a needle into a snowy pile of linen. She gasped upon their entry; her eyes and mouth rounded.

'You've arrived,' she squealed, tossing aside her sewing. 'I didn't expect you until after dinner, and now with this dreadful, loud thunderstorm, I thought you mightn't come today at all, but here you are, safe and sound. Thank God.' She jumped to her feet and rushed to Holbrook's side, smothering his cheek with kisses. 'But darlingest Nicky, you're drenched. Change out of these wet things at once.'

Holbrook laughed, wriggling away from her attentions exactly as Harry wiggled away from Meggy's. 'I shall do so the moment I've introduced our guests. This, Harry and Sophy,' – he rested his hands on the children's backs

95

– 'is my sister, Lady Rose Edwards. And once, *ages* ago now, we were very much like the two of you.'

Meggy frowned slightly, surprised, for Holbrook and his sister bore no resemblance to each other besides height and grey eyes. Lady Rose was elegant, but her appearance was remarkable only for her pale thinness. Her skin was ivory, her eyebrows and eyelashes were light, and her hair was reddish gold under a lace cap. Her long, apple-green silk skirts fell in a wispy column from a modest bosom.

But more than anything, she looked kind and approachable; gentle eyes, a soft smile and graceful movements as she knelt and spoke to the children, holding both their hands and their attention.

For the first time that day, Meggy's tension eased. Perhaps Lady Rose wouldn't be as terrible as she'd imagined, although Meggy would reserve a final judgement until she knew the woman extremely well indeed. After all, Holbrook appeared kind sometimes, and he was a monster.

As Lady Rose knelt, Holbrook tousled Harry's curls. 'This young scamp is Henry Fairchild, eleventh Lord Berksleigh, and this little beauty' – Sophy giggled and hid her face behind Dolly – 'is his sister Lady Sophia. Although they prefer Harry and Sophy.'

A tremor passed over Holbrook's features when Rose stood and looked expectantly towards Meggy.

'Ah, yes,' he said, a catch in his voice. 'Their companion, Miss Kimberley, and their sister, Lady Margaret Fairchild.'

Rose shook Miss Kimberley's hand.

Then she stood before Meggy.

Her grey eyes – so precisely like her brother's except for her pale lashes – bore into Meggy's, but not unkindly. She lifted Meggy's hand and squeezed it between her own, which were slim, long-fingered and elegant. 'I've been exceedingly eager to meet you, Lady Margaret.' Her gaze swept across Meggy's face, and her smile widened. 'Allow me to offer you a very warm welcome indeed to Alton Park. I hope you will feel quite at home here.'

Unaccountably, Meggy's heart swelled.

Rose dropped her hand. 'And so must you all – Alton Park is your home for as long as you desire. Harry and Sophy, I have three *usually* delightful daughters upstairs yearning for new playmates. And Miss Kimberley, would you perhaps prefer a bedchamber on the ground floor? I'm afraid Alton Park contains far too many staircases, which do very well indeed when one enjoys sliding down railings but are a dreadful bore otherwise.' Her chatter ceased; her gaze fell upon her brother, and she drew her pale brows together. 'Nicky, why have you not gone to change? Leave,' she said, waving her hands. 'Do not return until you are warm and dry.'

Holbrook bid the children and Miss Kimberley goodbye but exited without a glance at Meggy.

Well, let him leave. The less Meggy saw of him, the better. In a house as massive as Alton Park, she likely would barely cross paths with the foul marquess.

If only that weren't an oddly unhappy thought . . .

★

Fifteen minutes later, whilst Miss Kimberley rested, Meggy and her siblings accompanied a chattering Rose to the top floor of the west wing. The warren of children's rooms consisted of a nursery, a schoolroom, the children's bedrooms, and the bedrooms of their attendants, but the playroom was nonpareil. Meggy smiled for Harry and Sophy's sakes as her eyes skimmed over rocking horses of every colour, blocks for castle building, armies of tin soldiers, shelves of picture books, and best of all, a three-storey, four-sided doll's house, every miniature room as elaborately decorated as a palace. Three red-headed girls stood beside this spectacular treasure.

A chubby-cheeked toddler with wispy copper curls ran forward with her arms outstretched. Rose scooped the baby up and smothered her in kisses before beginning the introductions. 'My eldest daughter, Maria,' she said, indicating a thin, quiet child with reddish-gold hair much like her mother's. 'And Elizabeth,' she continued, nodding towards a remarkably pretty girl with a mane of long auburn curls and something of her uncle's appearance in her fine dark brows and thick-lashed grey eyes. 'And my baby, Charlotte.' Rose kissed the toddler's little nose. 'Girls, make your curtsies to Lord Berksleigh and Lady Sophia.'

Maria curtsied. Sophy returned it, and Harry bowed.

But rather than obeying her mother's request, Elizabeth folded her arms across her thin chest. The child wore a white muslin gown and an expression of

98

supercilious hauteur worthy of a queen. 'Are you a marquess, Lord Berksleigh?'

Harry shook his head. 'I'm an earl.'

Elizabeth stuck her nose in the air. 'My grandfather was a marquess, and so is my uncle, so I'm not impressed by earls.'

Lady Rose gasped. 'Elizabeth, dearest. That wasn't kind. Apologise to Lord Berksleigh, please.'

Elizabeth smirked instead. 'No. I don't apologise for the truth.'

Meggy placed a protective hand on Harry's back.

'I'm so very sorry,' Rose said, addressing Meggy. 'She is sometimes a little naughty. Elizabeth, my love, you must go to your room if you cannot behave.'

Harry curled his lip and lifted his chin high over his bib-collared shirt. 'I don't mind what *little* children say to me, Lady Rose.'

This time, Meggy gasped. Her brother was never rude. Rambunctious, yes. Naughty, on occasion. But hurtful? Not once. Was this evidence of Holbrook's horrid influence?

Before Meggy could reprimand Harry, Elizabeth stamped her foot. 'I'm not a little child. I'm six and three-quarters, you beastly boy.' Elizabeth put up her small fists. 'And I can fight you.'

Rose dashed to Elizabeth's side. 'Elizabeth, stop this. You must apologise to Lord Berksleigh at once.'

'But Harry must apologise as well.' Meggy encouraged her brother forward. 'That's *not* how a gentleman speaks to a lady, Harry.'

The red-faced children glared at each other.

Meggy raised an eyebrow. '*Harry.* Behave like a gentleman.'

After a moment's pause, Harry's face softened. 'Forgive me, Elizabeth,' he said. 'I never thought you looked like a little child. In fact . . .' – he glanced at his feet before continuing – '. . . although I don't know you well, I can tell you have gumption in abundance.'

Meggy's heart burst with pride. She squeezed her brother and kissed his cheek before turning to a beaming Rose and sweetened Elizabeth.

'Do you really think I have gumption?' Elizabeth asked.

Harry stuffed his fists in his pockets and nodded.

'Maybe you do, too,' Elizabeth said. 'You scared of thunder?'

Harry lifted his chin. 'Of course not.'

Elizabeth held out her hand. 'Want to watch the storm with me?'

Harry clasped the offered palm, and they withdrew to the window.

After they departed, Rose put a hand to her forehead and sighed. 'I'm terribly sorry about Elizabeth's behaviour, Lady Margaret.'

But Meggy grinned as she watched her brother and Elizabeth exclaim over the lightning and thunder. Harry had proven himself every inch the wonderful, darling, noble boy Meggy knew him to be. 'Think nothing of it, Lady Rose. I've passed many sleepless nights worrying that inheriting a title at seven will turn Harry's head, but

I suspect Elizabeth will dispel any notions of grandeur he entertains whilst we're at Alton Park.'

Rose's laughter had a musical chime, like bells pealing. 'Yes, Eliza tolerates her own grandeur only.' Then Rose nodded her chin towards Maria and Sophy, who played together at the doll's house.

Meggy clasped a hand to her heart. At least her beloved siblings would be happy with these new friends and wonderful playthings.

A gentle rap on Meggy's bedchamber door just before dinnertime startled her, and for one heart-stopping moment, she wondered if Holbrook stood outside. She closed her book on Newtonianism and rose. 'Come in.' Her voice wavered.

Rose entered, wearing a light green evening gown as delicate as willow leaves, and Meggy's heart calmed. 'Are you pleased with your room, Lady Margaret?'

'Very much so.' The chamber was large and airy with primrose yellow floral wallpaper, a wide bay window, creamy damask drapes, and bed curtains embellished with pastel flowers. 'It's the prettiest room I've ever seen.'

Rose clapped her hands to her bosom. 'I call it the Spring Room, and I hoped you'd love it. I confess, it's my creation, as are most of the guest chambers.' She readjusted a white delphinium in a vase of flowers by the bed. 'I live at Alton Park whilst my husband is at sea, and Nicky often asks me to oversee refurbishments. I adore projects.'

Meggy suppressed a smile. Presumably, *she* was another such project. 'Is your husband often away?'

'Sadly, yes,' Rose said, perfecting a fold of the bed's drapery. 'The girls and I place pins in a map in the schoolroom of his journeys and his battles – I shall show you tomorrow, if you'd like. He's in the Americas now, on Lake Erie.'

In danger, then, since the United States had declared war in June. How dreadful that must be for Rose. 'Is there much fighting?' Meggy asked, uncertain of the best thing to say.

'As of yet, none on Lake Erie. I pray it remains so. Thomas is mostly occupied with ensuring the Canadian forts receive essential supplies. I know he finds it rather dull, but dull is so much better than the alternative.' Rose glanced towards the window as she knitted her hands together. 'I take on tasks so that I don't languish.'

Meggy recalled her parents' deep love for each other, and her heart warmed to Rose. Whatever faults the willowy lady might yet prove to have, she wasn't like her philandering brother. It was perfectly clear she loved her husband immensely. 'You must miss him.'

Rose smiled wistfully. 'I do. I sailed with Thomas for the first two years of our marriage. Comical, I know, to imagine me a sailor, but I *loved* the adventure. However, once Maria was on the way, I lost my sea legs, and after Maria was born, well, as much as I miss Thomas, motherhood comes first.' As if shaking off sorrow, Rose tossed her head and skimmed across the floor to clasp Meggy's hands. 'You cannot imagine how delighted I am you've come to stay. I adore my daughters, but to have another lady with whom to talk, and to have a London Season to plan for – I'm quite giddy, to tell the truth. And you're so breathtakingly lovely. I wanted to say so in the drawing room when we met, but I worried I might embarrass you.'

In order to show Holbrook what he'd *never* have, Meggy had made a special effort with her appearance after soaking in a refreshing bath. Although her low-cut, periwinkle blue evening gown was simple and several years old, it was pretty. She wore her mother's pearl jewellery set, and a maid had tidied her curls into a loose twist threaded with blue ribbons.

'My gown ought to be black,' Meggy said to Rose, 'but I'm afraid I didn't have time to order a black evening gown after Edwin's death. There were so many preparations for the new tenants.'

'Never mind, dearest. We aren't entertaining tonight. The only other guest is Nicky's friend Alexander – or Dr Mitchell, I suppose I should say – who's staying here for a few weeks to write his latest scientific treatise, and it's anyone's guess if he'll even leave his work for dinner.' Rose looked Meggy up and down, still clasping her hands. 'You possess *just* the type of beauty I most admire, and to tell the truth, I don't think you should wear black at all. What fun we shall have ordering your gowns for town. Blues to match your eyes, of course, but how lovely you'll look in white as well. And yellow – few can wear yellow, but I suspect you can. And peach, I think. I cannot *wait* to begin.' She danced on the tips of her toes.

Meggy laughed, genuinely delighted by Rose's enthusiasm. If Holbrook's sister possessed a nefarious nature, it was well hidden. 'I'm glad to hear you have an eye for such things, Lady Rose. I like pretty clothes and appreciate them once they're made, but I never know which style or colour to choose. Miss Kimberley has always done that for me.'

Rose threaded Meggy's hand through her arm and led her towards the door. 'Perhaps because you haven't had *time* to think of such things? You poor darling – Nicky told me a little of your circumstances, and I simply cannot imagine how you did it. You and I must have a tête-à-tête later but come now and we shall join the others in the drawing room before dinner. And call me Rose, dearest.'

'Then I must be Meggy, please.'

'Meggy.' Rose's eyes shone. 'How delightfully charming. It suits you perfectly.'

As Meggy walked down the corridor, arm-linked with a chattering Rose, a sharp prickle tingled behind her eyes. Only with effort did Meggy suppress a strong desire to hug the lady.

Meggy had never had a friend before.

Still, after Holbrook's cruelty, Meggy must be wary of Rose. An evening tête-à-tête was precisely what she needed to explore the lady's character more.

When Meggy re-entered the crimson drawing room, she noticed nothing but a freshly shaven, devastatingly handsome Lord Holbrook. His black evening wear clung to his muscular form, the points of his starched white shirt collar jutted up to his square jaw, and his shirt linen cascaded in snowy folds.

The confidence Meggy had whilst dressing fled like a horse at a gallop.

'Meggy,' Rose said, 'may I introduce Nicky's dear friend Dr Mitchell?'

Meggy tore her gaze from the marquess's dove-grey eyes.

You must forget Holbrook, Meggy reminded herself as she blinked to focus on Dr Mitchell. He was striking – tall and athletic, with auburn hair. His face brightened with a crooked grin, and a dimple appeared in one cheek. Meggy returned his smile as she attempted to ignore Holbrook's presence in her peripheral vision. Dr Mitchell possessed a charm of his own; perhaps he'd help push Holbrook from her heart.

Meggy offered her hand. 'A pleasure to meet you, Dr Mitchell.'

His eyes sparkled, gleamed with obvious admiration, in fact, which was an entirely pleasurable experience. Nothing of the predator lurked behind Dr Mitchell's frank regard.

'The pleasure is all mine, my lady.' He spoke with a soft Scottish accent.

His voice was as kind as his face.

'You're a scientist, I think Rose said?' Meggy turned her back so Holbrook's broad form wasn't visible at all. 'I find the sciences fascinating, although I'm an amateur student, of course.'

If possible, Dr Mitchell's eyes twinkled even more. 'I am a physician, ma'am,' he said, inclining his head.

Meggy hid her surprise. A physician as a guest in the home of nobility – and called a friend, no less – was an unusual blurring of class lines. At least Holbrook wasn't an elitist. He apparently had *one* admirable characteristic.

To Meggy's further astonishment, Rose had invited Miss Kimberley and Miss Johnson, the Misses Edwards's governess, to join them for dinner rather than eating with the children in their dining room. By the time the army of footmen had removed the cream soup and laid the first course out – oyster ragout, lobster fricassee, and an assortment of summer greens that stretched over the vast cloth-covered table – the two teachers were on congenial terms, having discovered not only that their opinions aligned on the education of young ladies, but that their hometowns in Nottinghamshire were only fifteen miles apart.

During the second course, the conversation turned to what must be done for Harry. Miss Kimberley confessed she didn't feel up to the task of a young earl's education beyond the age of seven.

'I can find Harry a tutor,' Holbrook said, sitting at the head of the table like a king. The light from the hanging chandelier, which must have held fifty beeswax tapers, played on his high cheekbones and the enticing line of his sideburns. His black coat contrasted strikingly with the gold-papered walls behind him, upon which hung full-length portraits of lords and ladies displaying three centuries of fine fashion. 'It would give me great pleasure to assist in this way.'

Meggy's brows snapped together. She'd told Holbrook she didn't want his intervention. He must be deliberately antagonising her yet again.

Holbrook answered her glare by bowing his head. 'With your permission, of course, Lady Margaret.'

Meggy forced a smile, pretending politeness for the sake of the others. 'Naturally, I cannot put you to so much trouble for my brother's sake, Lord Holbrook. *I* shall engage a tutor for Harry.'

He placed down his knife and fork and leaned forward. 'It's no trouble at all, truly, but even if it were, I'd do it gladly. You ought to be free to enjoy preparations for your time in London. Furthermore, Edwin desired I assist you—'

'Nonsense, sir. You have done *quite* enough already.' Meggy's patience was at an end. Holbrook needed to realise he was nothing to her, and there was no better way to effect this than to make use of the marquess's pleasant friend. 'But, Dr Mitchell, do *you* know any suitable tutors? Harry has a natural interest in the sciences, and I feel he'd do best with a tutor who could cultivate that. In this modern world, an education in the classics cannot compare with scientific knowledge.'

With a speared portion of asparagus halfway to his mouth, Dr Mitchell looked between Meggy and Holbrook, his crooked smile spreading as his eyes danced. 'I can certainly make enquiries for you, Lady Margaret. I would be immensely pleased to do so.'

'If you supply some names, Dr Mitchell,' she said, as sweet as honey, 'I'll send out the letters of enquiry. You have your own work, I know, but I shall have plenty of time, even with the crushing burdens of preparations for London.'

'I shall have a list for you tomorrow – sooner if you wish.'

She laughed. 'Tomorrow will be fine.'

Meggy reapplied herself to her roasted duck in chestnut sauce, awash in victorious warmth. From now on, every time Holbrook attempted to charm his deceitful self into Meggy's good graces, she'd fight back so he wouldn't mistake matters. Meggy would be civil enough whilst living under his roof, but they were enemies now.

He needed to know that.

It wasn't until the footmen served raspberry and lemon ices and a selection of nuts and fruit that Meggy ventured to peek at Holbrook. To her surprise, his expression wasn't hostile. His head was tilted, his brows drawn together, and a hint of a frown hovered on his lips.

He looked for all the world like he was trying to solve a puzzle.

Meggy shifted in her seat and lifted her spoon to her mouth, but the ice melted tasteless on her tongue.

In the crimson drawing room after dinner, Rose took up her sewing, arranging the same snowy pile of linen from earlier in her lap. Meggy, with no work of her own, offered to unravel a clump of silk flosses Elizabeth had jumbled. To do so, she withdrew to a delicate chair against the wall on the other side of the commodious chamber, directly under a lit wall sconce. She was untangling a particularly frustrating knot when the gentlemen joined the ladies.

Holbrook drew a matching chair beside her own, his bergamot-spiced fragrance mingling with the warm scent of port on his breath. 'May I help?'

She shrugged, for she'd made little headway alone. 'I suppose.'

Meggy's skin tingled as Holbrook lifted the silks from her hands. He began to untangle the threads, handing Meggy each floss as it slipped the knots. 'I am surprised you let me. You seem so defiant towards my offers of assistance.'

'When it comes to disentangling your sister's embroidery silks, I have no objection.' Annoyingly, Holbrook's nearness caused her hands to tremble. 'But in matters related to Harry, I don't need help.'

'I beg to differ.' Holbrook's voice was measured and calm, and he studied the silks carefully as he picked at the knots. 'You merely chose to rely on my friend Alexander's help instead of mine. That was, naturally, an excellent way to humiliate me.'

Meggy's cheeks warmed as she took another thread from him. 'You appear to have survived the embarrassment.'

'As it happens,' he said quietly, 'my pride has suffered far worse mortification.'

She peeked from the corner of her eyes. He did the same; their eyes met, and she dropped her gaze. He wouldn't breach the wall she'd constructed against him. 'I see no evidence your pride suffers in the least.'

Holbrook didn't reply at once. Meggy organised the untangled threads across her lap, sorted by colour, but her eyes were repeatedly drawn to the marquess's hands as he worked. They were strong, well formed, and masculine with close-clipped nails and beautifully raised veins. His skin was bronzed next to the white shirt cuff emerging from his black coat. His gold signet ring glinted as he deftly untwisted the flosses. 'I think you'll agree wounds are relatively easy to hide,' he said at last, handing her several newly untangled threads. 'You have some experience doing the same. The question, of course, is how much internal damage is inflicted when one shelters behind a hardened exterior.'

Meggy whipped her head up, but he focused on the knotted silks. 'I don't know your personal trials, Lord Holbrook, nor would I ever make light of them, but if you're attempting to suggest having internal wounds gives one allowance to behave poorly, I emphatically disagree. Having suffered ought to make one *more* compassionate, not compassionless.'

His grey eyes locked on hers. 'You think I have no compassion at all?'

Meggy recalled him playing with her siblings the day before, but she quickly replaced the image with the buxom maid's simpering. 'I think everything admirable about you is a façade. If it's not, I'm too inexperienced to know the difference between what's real and what's an illusion, so I shan't try.'

'I might—'

'No.' She sighed, exasperated. 'Don't you see? Whatever you *might*, I don't want you to. I shan't try to understand you because I don't want to understand you.' *Because otherwise I might begin to care*, Meggy thought, before she shoved aside her sentimentality for practicality. *Because I've been deserted once by a man such as you, and it won't happen again.* 'Furthermore,' she said, resorting to the protection of sarcasm, 'I don't have time to apply myself to the task. I shall be too busy readying myself for town; gown fittings and learning the steps to the waltz are such *consuming* endeavours.'

Holbrook continued to untangle the threads. For a long time, he didn't speak, but when he did, playfulness lightened his tone. 'The waltz when you are on the market for a ninety-year-old husband? A waste of energy, my dear. Apply yourself instead to the study of poultices to soothe gout and planning menus to ease the toothless invalid's digestion. Coddled egg, perhaps? Eel broth?'

He was teasing her, as he'd done with mortifying consequences before.

Very well. Meggy would serve him some of his own dish tonight and see how he liked the taste. 'Definitely not,' she said, deepening her voice. As Holbrook handed her another strand of silk, Meggy stroked his finger. His alert eyes jumped to hers – seemingly with a glimmer of hope – and Meggy triumphed. He wasn't the only one who could tease cruelly. 'A milk posset with stale bread, nutmeg and brandy is appropriate for the manly invalid.' She dropped the thread in her lap and traced the pearls lying across her décolletage as she pretended to think. 'I shall spoon-feed him as he rests upon my breast. Would he like that, I wonder?'

Holbrook's lips twitched, but his gaze didn't drop to Meggy's bosom, despite her suggestive efforts with the necklace. Instead, he frowned up at the ceiling, and then shook his head as he returned to working the last knot of the silks. 'Alas, I cannot say without having tried it myself. However, as I have pledged my aid in your quest for this old man, I could help you conduct an experiment.' He leaned forward, his breath tickling her ear. 'In fact, with an incentive like your breasts, I might *will* myself ill.'

She turned slightly towards him, his nose nearly brushing her cheek as she did so. Her eyes flickered involuntarily to his lips, and she froze.

How had he turned her tease around so effortlessly?

Holbrook half smiled as he placed the last threads on her skirt. 'Have I rendered you speechless, Lady Margaret? Pray tell me, was it because you enjoy hearing me speak of your breasts, or are you frightened when you imagine me ill? Either is perfectly acceptable to me.'

She recovered herself with a shake of the head. 'Neither, sir. I'm afraid I was overcome with exhaustion – or perhaps boredom. I'm not certain. Since you've finished with the silks, I shall try someone else's company and see if I revive.'

She gathered the rows of threads, draping each colour separately over her fingers.

'Before you go, Lady Margaret.' His hand brushed her bare forearm, his warmth infusing her skin for the brief moment they touched. 'You spoke outside about viewing me yesterday as a friend. I *would* like to be your friend.'

Her heart fluttered. What was wrong with her? Meggy steeled her mind again. 'I'm afraid that's impossible, Lord Holbrook. I cannot be friends with someone I cannot trust.'

He drew up his black brows, as if pleading. 'But if I earn your trust again?' His fingertips skimmed the back of her hand. 'Would you consider friendship?'

Meggy widened her eyes, astonished at his persistence. 'No matter how you hound me, you won't succeed with this seduction, sir.'

Holbrook blanched. 'Good God. I *truly*—' He stopped abruptly and ran his hands through his hair, tousling his curls and appearing even more handsome for it. 'But I mayn't apologise. Lady Margaret, perhaps it seems unlikely after how I've behaved, but, truly, I'd like to be your friend.'

Meggy pursed her lips. 'Why?'

Holbrook glanced towards an above-mantel portrait of a gentleman and a lady dressed in the styles of thirty years earlier, sitting with a fair-haired baby between them. 'I truthfully cannot give you a precise answer,' he replied slowly. 'Perhaps it's because I've never met a lady like you.' He paused, and when he spoke next, his voice caught. 'Or maybe it has less to do with you than I think. Perhaps it's because I enjoy Harry's company' – he paused, studying his hands before shaking his head and continuing – 'and Sophy's, of course. I'd genuinely like to be more than a figurehead guardian. Or . . . or maybe it's because I turn thirty soon. Or the heat addled my brains today.' He chuckled, then sobered. 'Whatever it is, I am sincere.'

Meggy looked at the rows of colourful threads on her fingers and considered her answer carefully. 'I confess, although it grieves me to do so because I'm extremely angry, that a significant part of me would love to believe your words, even if only because Harry and Sophy seem so fond of you already. But you told me two things within an hour of our meeting: firstly, that you aren't kind, and secondly, that I shouldn't trust you. Until I've seen tremendous evidence of your sincerity, I shall continue to do as *you* suggested and remind myself you are unkind and untrustworthy.' She lifted her eyes to his and grinned with false confidence. 'But it should give you some pleasure to know that in doing so, I take to your lessons remarkably well for a lady who dislikes being managed.'

Holbrook didn't smile back. 'That gives me no pleasure at all, but likely it's for the best.'

His words were clipped, terse.

He stood, bowed, and joined his friend across the room, leaving Meggy to stare at the coloured silks falling from her fingers over her skirt like a serpentine rainbow river.

7

The crimson drawing room's gilded mantel clock struck the hour, setting off a chorus in other rooms so precise that the nine strikes reverberated together. Meggy placed the last of the embroidery silks, now tied into skeins, into Rose's work basket.

Rose snipped off her thread. 'You were a darling to do that tedious work, Meggy.'

'I cannot take all the credit,' Meggy said, folding her hands in her lap. 'Your brother unknotted most of it.'

Rose glanced at Holbrook, who chatted with Dr Mitchell. 'Yes, I noticed he helped you.' She lifted the white linen she worked on – a fine-sewn man's shirt, such as the one Meggy had run her palms over the night before when she'd stroked Holbrook's hard, sculpted muscles. As Rose folded it neatly, Meggy dropped her gaze and stared resolutely at her tight-pressed hands.

Rose placed the shirt on top of her work basket and smiled. 'I usually see the children to bed at this time. Do you wish to come?'

Meggy lifted her head. 'Oh, very much so, yes,' she said, eager to return to the familiar, uncomplicated presence of her siblings. 'I love to read to Harry and Sophy before they fall asleep.'

The announcement of their intended departure precipitated more of the same. Miss Kimberley and Miss Johnson declared themselves unable to keep their eyes open, and the gentlemen left to play billiards.

After the children were kissed and cuddled under cotton-fresh feather counterpanes – with Meggy holding a glowing Sophy and Harry a little tighter than usual as they waxed lyrical about their new playmates – Rose took Meggy's hand. 'Will you drink a glass of wine in my room and tell me about yourself, Meggy?'

The promised tête-à-tête! Holbrook had irritatingly absorbed Meggy's thoughts so much she'd forgotten, but her before-dinner enthusiasm for a companionable chat with Rose rushed back.

Meggy grinned, not even attempting to hide her eagerness for friendship. Any qualms Meggy had had about Rose vanished when the elegant lady, attired in her fine evening gown, had crawled under the bedsheets of Maria's bed, pulled down her bodice to put a sleepy-eyed Charlotte to the breast, and read aloud with her elder daughters' cheeks resting against her upper arms.

'I'd enjoy that very much, Rose.'

Rose squeaked happily; her ivory skin tinged with the faintest hint of colour as she pulled Meggy down the corridor. 'I shall show you a painting of Thomas.'

Meggy gasped when she entered Rose's bedroom on the first floor, for the grand chamber was awash in every shade of pink imaginable. Deep raspberry papered the walls, and pink-bottomed cherubs frolicked in rose-tinted clouds on the frescoed ceiling. A thick mauve carpet covered the floor, the shimmering silk bedclothes were rich ruby, and the upholstered chaise lounges were the whispery colour of inside a shell.

Rose clapped her hands together and laughed delightedly. 'Shocking, isn't it? I *adore* pink, but I never wear it, for it clashes terribly with my hair. But in *here*,' she said, sweeping her arms wide, 'I may have as much pink as I like, and, although they tease me, Nicky and Thomas indulge my fancy. Look.' She motioned Meggy to a row of gilded cabinets with mirrored shelves lined with pink ornaments. From as small as a penny to as large as a pineapple, they comprised everything from pinkish rocks to dried roses to elaborate bejewelled figurines. 'I began this collection in childhood. My papa – my wonderful, wonderful papa – gave me the first pieces. Every time he had to leave for a few days, he'd find me *something* pink. Pink for his pink Rose, he'd say. When he arrived home, it was my task to discover which pocket it was hidden in.' She pointed at a porcelain figure of a young lady holding an armful of roses. 'This one was for my sixteenth birthday. He died soon after, but when Nicky came home from Eton for the funeral, he told me to look in his pocket and inside was that tiny pink bunny you see there. Nicky was only fourteen, but that was the moment he began to take care of me. Or so I let him *think*, the darling.'

Meggy frowned, not wanting to hear heart-tugging stories about Holbrook.

Rose pulled Meggy to the last cabinet. 'Most of the curios in here come from Thomas or Nicky. Look – this is the one Nicky brought me today.' She tapped the glass, indicating a carved coral flower the size of a peach stone. 'Oh, I've forgotten our wine.'

Rose danced across the room, opened a brilliant rose-gold cabinet, and extracted a small crystal decanter.

'Only a little for me, please, or I shall fall asleep here, I'm afraid,' Meggy said, grateful Rose had concluded the tour of presents from Holbrook.

Rose handed Meggy a tiny wine glass. 'My collection is a bit of silliness, really. All the same, I know the story behind every single item.' She curled into a corner of a sofa and settled her green silk skirts about her. 'Now, dearest, have a seat and tell me about yourself.'

Meggy reclined on a chaise lounge and answered a steady stream of questions about life at Berksleigh Hall for half an hour, whilst Rose occasionally refilled their miniscule glasses. Talking so much about herself was an unfamiliar sensation, but Rose nodded and murmured encouragingly.

After a companionable lull in the conversation, whilst they both sipped their wine, Rose cleared her throat softly. 'Your mother died when Harry was an infant, I gather. If you don't mind my asking, did she die in childbirth?'

Meggy shook her head. 'In a dreadful accident.' She swirled the burgundy liquid in her wine glass. The unaccustomed drink had loosened her tongue earlier; now, thinking of her mama, it incited strong emotions, and Meggy's eyes prickled. 'My mother loved to take her little phaeton on long trips across the countryside. She was an excellent driver, and she taught me quite early to handle a team. But the first time she drove out after Harry's birth, she was thrown. Killed instantly, the physician said. When our steward and coachman investigated the accident, they determined she'd hit a rut at a blind curve. The road had washed out in heavy rains a month earlier, but she couldn't have known because of her confinement.' Meggy traced the rim of her glass with her finger. 'Her death destroyed my poor father. Twenty-five years separated them in age, but theirs was truly a love match. I don't think he ever imagined she'd die first.'

When Meggy raised her gaze to meet Rose's, the sweet lady's eyes glistened.

'I'm terribly sorry, Meggy.'

Meggy smiled wistfully. 'That's kind of you to say. I miss my parents dreadfully, but the saddest thing is that neither Harry nor Sophy remembers them at all.'

'Ah, yes. Grief is hardest when one grieves alone.' Rose studied her wine glass. 'It's the same for Nicky. He has no one with whom to remember Arabella.'

Meggy tilted her head. 'Remember who?'

'His wife, Arabella.'

The room seemed to swirl, pink on pink churning together. Meggy, caught up in her silly and confusing thoughts about Holbrook, had entirely forgotten he was a widower. 'I see,' she said with some difficulty, for the words caught in her throat.

Rose looked over the rim of her wine glass. 'Did you know Nicky was married?'

Meggy licked her dry lips. 'Y-yes. I'd heard that, I-I think . . .' Meggy hesitated, aware her stumbling might appear odd. 'In truth, I'd forgotten.'

'Oh, and no wonder,' Rose said. 'Everyone forgets, for Nicky never speaks of her. Never utters her name. Not even to Alexander, who is Nicky's dearest — although not his oldest — friend. There's not a single painting of her, even in Nicky's room — at least, not that I've seen. Can you imagine? I don't know what she looked like.'

Meggy's legs trembled under her skirts, but Rose's words drew her in. 'You never met . . .' — for some reason, Meggy couldn't form Arabella's name — '. . . her?'

'No, I was at sea with Thomas when they met, and Arabella died before I returned to England.' Rose sipped her wine. 'Nicky doesn't speak of their son either. The poor babe was stillborn, but that's no less devastating, of course. He'd be nearly nine now, slightly older than Harry.'

Meggy's stomach sank like a rock in the water. *Harry.* Holbrook had spoken of enjoying Harry's company and genuinely wanting to be a guardian, and now the words took on heartbreaking new meaning. Harry reminded Holbrook of his dead son, the boy who'd never thrown his arms around the marquess's neck or held his hand, as Harry had done. A child for whom Holbrook would never choose a tutor. Meggy pressed her fingers to her throat.

Rose was talking, *had* been talking whilst Meggy's thoughts wandered. '. . . not far along in my first pregnancy when we received word about Arabella's death. I wasn't well, and when Thomas read Nicky's letter, he brought me back to England at once. Nicky was in such a terrible state – mad with grief – that at first Thomas hesitated to leave me with him. But knowing I was with child gave Nicky purpose. He focused all his energy on my care. In fact, that's how he met Dr Mitchell. Alexander is an obstetrician.'

'A what?' Meggy forced the question out.

'A physician who devotes his practice solely to women's concerns. He mostly delivers babies, and he studies and writes about safer methods of childbirth. Alexander was quite young when Nicky sought him out, but now he's one of the most respected obstetricians in Britain. He's accepted everywhere. Nicky sponsored him at first – and I don't mean only in society. With Nicky's patronage, Alexander built the Mayfair Maternity Hospital. Every woman who stays receives the best of care, even if she hasn't a penny. Now Alexander's hospital has dozens of sponsors – he's terribly popular – but Nicky was his first.'

This was an altogether surprising side to Holbrook.

Meggy adjusted herself on the chaise lounge. The upholstery was suddenly quite stiff and uncomfortable.

Meanwhile, Rose gazed at her cherub ceiling, as if in thought. 'It's a little amusing,' she said with a giggle, 'that Alexander is so intimately acquainted with many of the society hostesses who welcome him into their homes, including myself.'

Meggy gasped as she caught Rose's meaning.

Rose's twinkling grey eyes met Meggy's; the elegant lady's laughter pealed. 'That was a shocking thing for me to say, wasn't it? Forgive me. Truly, there is never any awkwardness with Alexander. He's a wonderful physician. He delivered my daughters, and I never had a moment's difficulty.' Her expression sobered, and she tapped her fingernail against her wine glass. The crystal chimed. 'I suspect one reason Nicky's so unhappy much of the time is because he wonders what might've happened if he'd found Alexander before Arabella died.' Rose finished her wine and placed down her glass. 'But that's enough dreariness. Tell me, dearest, have you ever been to London? What would you most like to see? Oh, and I haven't shown you my Thomas.' She flittered away like a butterfly and returned with a miniature of a sea captain with dark red hair.

Later that night, Meggy lay between crisp cotton sheets as rain pummelled the glass panes of her bay window. Sleep was impossible, for thoughts of Holbrook, his dead wife and child, and his care of Rose, churned in her mind.

Holbrook's words – *you think I have no compassion at all* – haunted Meggy, and the lost baby tugged at her conscience until she reached a decision that gave her some peace. As an act of kindness, she'd allow Holbrook to locate a tutor for Harry.

Then Meggy *must* find herself a husband before Harry and Holbrook became too attached.

★

Nicholas released a cloud of smoke from his cigar as the billiard balls rolled to a rest on the green felt. 'Dammit, Alexander. You've made it impossible for me to score.' They'd been playing for two hours in the oak-panelled room, and Nicholas had yet to win a game.

Alexander grinned roguishly, the candlelight from the low-hanging chandelier reflecting in his dark blue eyes as he stepped back from the table and took up his glass of whisky. 'Don't play billiards or golf with a Scot unless you wish to lose.'

Nicholas aimed the leather tip of his stick at his cue ball, assessed his options, and shot, but he failed to cannon or pot his own ball off his friend's, just as Alexander had intended.

Nicholas downed the dregs of his glass of brandy. Then, with his cigar clamped between his teeth, he sprawled on one of the oxblood-coloured leather sofas lining the wall. 'Finish me,' he said morosely.

Alexander aimed his cue stick and scored, achieving the agreed-upon two hundred points. 'You're not usually so terrible a player, Nick. What's troubling you?'

'I'm tired after days on the road.' Although it wasn't the complete truth, it wasn't a lie either.

Alexander grinned. 'Not all bad, though, eh? It can't have been misery to travel with a companion like Lady Margaret. I was never more shocked in my life than when I saw her. That beauty the sister of Edwin Fairchild? Seems impossible.'

Nicholas controlled a flicker of jealousy. '*Half*-sister.'

Alexander ran his ink-smudged fingers through his thick auburn mane. 'I say, Nick – what are your thoughts on her?'

Again, that spark of annoyance. Nicholas puffed his cigar as he stared at the vaulted wood-carved ceiling. 'What do you mean?' he asked, feigning ignorance.

'I wouldn't mind knowing her better, but I also wouldn't tread on your toes, my friend. You could hardly take your eyes off her all evening.'

It was true. Drawing his eyes from Meggy had taken effort every time. Nicholas had burned feverishly when she entered the drawing room in that periwinkle silk, a colour that intensified her blue eyes and highlighted her rosy cheeks. He craved her, desired her. Wanted her lips on his, her breasts against his bare chest. Wanted her to pant his name, to moan with longing, to writhe in pleasure at his touch.

And also, he didn't.

Because she stirred deeper sensations in him – sensations ignited the night before and fanned into substance by the harsh but well-deserved reprimand Meggy had delivered at the base of Alton Park's front steps. Sensations Nicholas thought he couldn't feel anymore – and wasn't at all certain he could feel with lasting significance.

But those thoughts were new, tender, precious, *terrifying* – and for all he knew, an illusion of frustrated lust – and he wasn't about to share them with Alexander. 'What the devil else was I supposed to look at? Your ugly mug? *You* can't have been so taken with her if you were watching *me* all evening.'

Alexander laughed as he crossed the room to the sideboard, where decanters of amber and red-gold liquids stood in a crystal cluster. 'Ah, but that was only to see if you had a prior interest.'

'I met her two days ago.' Two potentially life-altering days ago . . .

'I spent two hours with her, and yet *I* see her worth.' Alexander refilled his glass with a splash of whisky. 'I find it impossible to believe *you* don't, especially as you whispered in her ear in the drawing room for a quarter of an hour.'

'I was helping her untangle my sister's embroidery silks.' *And* breathing her lavender scent *and* observing the lustre of pearls on golden skin, the bounce of honeyed curls, and the fullness of soft red lips.

'Whilst whispering in her ear.' Alexander grinned over the rim of his glass.

Nicholas inhaled on his cigar and blew out a slow stream of white smoke. 'You seem committed to your opinion, so I shan't argue more. Since when are you in the market for a wife?'

'I'm two-and-thirty,' Alexander said, resting his bottom against the edge of the billiards table. 'I'm well established and able to provide a comfortable home. What man in those circumstances *doesn't* think of a wife and children?'

Nicholas raised his brows pointedly. 'I recall feeling the same way nine years ago.'

Alexander started, coloured, and sipped his whisky. 'Forgive me, Nick – I spoke without thought.'

'Never mind.' Nicholas held his cigar away from his mouth and watched the black-rimmed tobacco leaf recede from the silver-grey ash. 'You're correct – any sensible man in your circumstances would, just as many widowers would consider remarriage after nearly a decade. But not me, so let's change the subject, please. Set up another game, and I shall win this one.'

Alexander complied, but as he arranged the balls he continued. 'So, you *haven't* any interest in Lady Margaret?'

Their gazes met; Alexander's eyes shone with scrutiny as intense as if the physician were examining one of the dissected specimens in his laboratory. Nicholas twisted on the sofa, uncomfortable under his friend's inspection. 'I cannot say I have no interest at all,' he admitted with a sigh. There was no point in disguising the truth from Alexander. 'She mesmerised me from the moment I met her, and two days' travel didn't diminish her charm. Quite the opposite, in fact.' Nicholas dug the fingers of his free hand into his hair and cradled his head. 'The truth is that I have so great a respect for her I wish her happily settled with a husband who deserves her *and* doesn't mind living under the cat's foot. Neither of which describes *me,* Alexander. If you're such a man, I wish you the best of luck. You'll have a diamond of a wife in terms of beauty and intelligence. But trust me, she'll rule you.'

'I shan't mind if my wife rules me if she keeps me warm at night.' Alexander sipped his drink. 'And Lady Margaret would keep a fellow *very* warm at night.'

Nicholas clenched his jaw but refrained from punching his friend.

'Ah, I see you didn't care for that comment,' Alexander said. 'Never fear, Nick, you've convinced me not to pursue Lady Margaret. Not *yet*, anyway.'

'Why should I care if you marry the chit?' Nicholas bit down on his cigar and spoke through his teeth. 'Please, do me a favour and take her off my hands. If you wish to be henpecked, she's perfect for you.'

'No, she's too perfect for *you* for me not to give you a chance.'

Nicholas extracted his cigar and blinked. 'Were you not listening when I listed two excellent reasons why she and I don't suit? If you wish, I can enumerate a hundred more arguments against pairing a wide-eyed innocent with a man who'll only break her heart.' Even worse than Edwin did . . .

Alexander's gaze fell to his whisky; he tilted his glass and appeared to study the amber liquid as it swirled. 'Lady Margaret would bring out the best in you.'

Nicholas's mouth went dry. An overwhelming wave of yearning washed over him, as it had when he imagined Meggy as the mother of his child.

Was Alexander correct?

Did Nicholas have a chance for redemption after years of mistakes?

Alexander chuckled. 'How wonderful – you're thinking about what I said.'

Was he?

He was.

Nicholas sat up.

But he oughtn't.

He jammed the lit end of his cigar into his discarded brandy glass. The ash sizzled as it hit the remnants of liquid. 'Marriage isn't for me. Not again.'

He couldn't, because even after his marriage to Meggy, when another woman's body enticed Nicholas, the same thing that had happened the night before would occur again. Nicholas's lustful urges would unbutton his trousers without thinking.

Then, in time, he'd destroy Meggy's loving heart – so inclined to trust, despite the injuries it had sustained from Edwin's desertion – until eventually Meggy's eyes would lose their lustre. Turn to deep wells of despair, such as Nicholas had seen before.

'What I need,' Nicholas said, standing and brushing an ash flake off the black sleeve of his coat, 'is to go to town. I shall leave in the morning.'

Alexander jolted upright. 'You've only just arrived. Why do you need to go to London?'

Nicholas picked up his cue stick and inspected its tip. 'Because I'm in urgent need of women, my friend. Many, *different* women, although I believe I'll start with one or two, unless I happen upon very good luck indeed.'

Alexander's hand tightened around his whisky glass. 'I warn you now, Nick, if you ruin this opportunity, I shall happily swoop in if Lady Margaret will let me.'

Nicholas placed his cue ball on the table and leaned forward, readying his cue stick, gauging its feel and the way it slid over his fingers. He narrowed his eyes to aim. 'What's stopping you?'

He thrust his stick; his cue ball smacked against the red ball. Both spheres spun across the green felt and landed in a perfect double baulk.

The rain continued throughout the night and into the next morning. The children bounced around the breakfast table, and Meggy smiled at their joy as she stirred hot milk into her coffee.

The sky-blue, octagonal breakfast room, with its towering vases of sunny dahlias, white delphiniums, and azure hydrangeas, contained only the ladies and children. Determined not to enquire about Holbrook's absence, Meggy heartily applied herself to grilled ham, boiled eggs, watercress salad, and a macedoine of fresh berries as the children planned a morning of hide-and-seek.

'After all,' Rose said, as excited as the little ones, 'hide-and-seek will be an excellent way to familiarise yourselves with Alton Park.'

'But I wonder how we shall ever find each other,' Sophy said, pretend-feeding Dolly a raspberry. 'The house is enormous.'

Maria whispered a suggestion. 'Perhaps we should hide in only one wing at a time.'

Elizabeth crossed her arms and stuck out her bottom lip. 'Bah – what poor sport, Maria.'

'I think your sister's plan is excellent, Elizabeth,' Rose said. 'Remember, Harry and Sophy don't know the house so well as you do. Now, my loves, as soon as everyone has eaten an excellent breakfast, we shall begin.'

As the children shovelled food into their mouths, Rose sipped tea from a floral cup and stared towards the windows. Rain streamed down the panes. 'I *do* wish Nicky had delayed going to London until after this storm. I simply cannot think what was so urgent . . .'

She stopped speaking as a faint flush covered her pale cheeks.

Meggy's food turned to ash in her mouth. In the brief span of Rose's words, she'd firstly been disappointed to hear Holbrook was gone, secondly terrified as she imagined his carriage overturned in a muddy ditch, and thirdly disgusted. Had Rose flushed because she realised, as Meggy did, that Holbrook was likely either eager to flee *from* Meggy or return *to* someone in London?

'Business, Rose,' Dr Mitchell said from the door. The physician wore a well-tailored, rust-coloured tailcoat that emphasised the burnished gleam of his auburn hair. A folded newspaper was tucked under his arm, and ink smudged two fingers and the thumb of his right hand. 'Urgent business, as I understand it.' He lifted a plate and served himself from the steaming silver dishes heaped on the sideboard.

Meggy pursed her lips. Urgent business, indeed.

'Coffee, please,' Dr Mitchell said to a footman as he sat in a vacant seat across from Meggy.

'Did you see him today, Alexander?' Rose asked. 'He was gone before I came down.'

The physician pinched salt from a silver cellar and sprinkled it over his eggs and meat. 'He left around seven perhaps – shortly after dawn.' He peered towards the rain-drenched windows. 'As much as there *was* a dawn this morning.'

Rose tapped her nails on her cup. 'Did he mention how long he'll be away?'

'I'm sorry, no.'

Harry swallowed his mouthful of food and licked a sticky finger. 'Nicky said he'll be back in a fortnight. Or three weeks at the latest. And then he is to take me and the girls to Ipswich.' Harry's eyes jumped to Meggy. 'But, Meggy, he said only if you and Lady Rose approve and only if we're good whilst he's away and . . .' – Harry tapped his chin – '. . . oh, and I was to remind you he didn't need to ask you first because he'd already told you about it. So there's no need to have at him like you did yesterday morning. He didn't say that – but *I* do.'

Meggy's cheeks burned. She applied herself again to her breakfast. 'Yes, he mentioned something about Ipswich,' she said to her plate.

'Lady Rose, my sister was *beastly* to Nicky at the inn—'

'Harry!'

'Well, you were.' But Harry dropped the subject and stuffed half a roll in his mouth.

Meggy clasped her coffee cup in both hands and stared at the steaming liquid. Embarrassment over Harry's revelation raged next to personal triumph. She'd been correct, after all. Holbrook *wasn't* dependable. He'd fled the moment he'd dumped them at Alton Park. Meggy needn't feel pity for him anymore, and she wouldn't ask for his help.

There was silence at the table until Dr Mitchell cleared his throat. 'Did I overhear whispering about a game of hide-and-seek? Might *I* join in the fun?'

'Of course,' Meggy said at once. She put down her coffee and smiled brightly at the physician, full of fresh resolve. Dr Mitchell was exactly the type of role model her brother needed. Steady, hard-working, scientifically minded. 'If you can spare the time from your work?'

Alexander's dark blue eyes sparkled. 'I can for an hour or so.'

Meggy peeked at the physician through her lashes, giving him the look Holbrook had appeared to enjoy. 'Perhaps you'd tell me about your treatise sometime?'

Dr Mitchell's fork stilled halfway to his mouth. A decided flush pinked his cheekbones. 'Would you truly like to hear about my treatise, Lady Margaret?'

'I'd enjoy it immensely.' Meggy twisted her finger in a curl that lay upon her shoulder. Could she be a physician's wife? The notion intrigued her. Rather than the fervid passion and joy-laced, child-centred playfulness she'd briefly imagined in a (false) future with Holbrook, her mind evoked a lifetime of quiet evenings by a cosy fire, discussing scientific journals. She threaded her index finger through the handle of her coffee cup and sipped the hot drink. 'Are you like other gentlemen, Dr Mitchell, who are quite certain young ladies read only novels and poetry?'

The dimple appeared in the physician's cheek. 'Lady Margaret, if my profession has taught me anything, it's never to presume to know a lady's heart or mind. But I, myself, enjoy novels on occasion, especially when I'm at Alton Park. Nick's collection of fiction and poetry is unparalleled. Other than newspapers and his correspondence, he reads nothing else.'

Meggy nearly choked on her coffee. She almost uttered an exclamation of surprise – Holbrook had teased *her* about reading novels – before reminding herself she didn't care about the marquess's interests.

Instead, she smiled at Alexander, who bestowed his crooked grin in return.

He really was a handsome man.

But, for some reason, dark blue eyes weren't as attractive as clear grey ones.

8

On the evening of the day he had departed Alton Park, Nicholas left his townhouse on Piccadilly and strolled towards the brick terrace houses of Half Moon Street. Carriages splashed through the puddles in the cobblestones, but Nicholas deftly dodged their spray. His evening wear – black breeches, white stockings, polished-leather evening shoes, and one of Weston's finest tailcoats, which moulded against his broad shoulders – remained unblemished. He banged the brass ring knocker of number twenty-nine, seeking companionship for tonight's adventure.

Wenching was more fun with his friends.

Kindly old Mr Smith, the manservant, opened the door. 'Good evening, your lordship. You'll find the gentlemen at their dinner.'

'Everyone is at home?' Nicholas asked as he surrendered his tall-crowned hat and his gloves to the grey-haired servant. It was a rare evening when the three bachelors who resided at number twenty-nine Half Moon Street dined together.

'Aye, m'lord.'

Nicholas spanned the depth of the panelled entrance vestibule in four strides. The townhouse was a modest,

Spartan residence. Typically, discarded coats, muddied boots and tossed-aside hats littered the otherwise bare floorboards near the front door, but the harried house-keeper Mrs Smith and her niece Ellen had obviously achieved some recent success with tidying.

Nicholas threw open a wooden door and grinned at the occupants of the dining room. The three men feasted in their shirtsleeves around a circular, polished-oak table. They were Nicholas's oldest friends – his closest companions from his days at Eton.

John Tyrold, the owner of the townhouse, sat to Nicholas's left, with his dishevelled black hair bowed over a newspaper laid flat beside his bowl of stewed beef and vegetables. Before the age of eighteen, the gentry-born Tyrold had increased a respectable fortune to the wealth of a king through canny investments.

Yet the cuffs of Tyrold's shirt were threadbare, and a button hung loose on his linen waistcoat, because the eccentric businessman was a renowned miser. Likely, he'd refuse to accompany Nicholas tonight, as Nicholas's intended destination generally left a sizable hole in a gentleman's pocket.

Dear, sweet Sidney Wakefield sat to Nicholas's right, his handsome face shining under his thick blonde hair. The younger brother of the debt-ridden Earl of Eden, Sidney earned the paltriest of sums as a curate at St George's, Hanover Square. He probably wouldn't join Nicholas either.

Nicholas focused on the gentleman directly ahead of him, for Lord Edward Matlock was Nicholas's most likely companion for tonight's quest. Tall, elegant, chestnut-haired Lord Edward, who dipped cheese-toasted bread into his stew, was the youngest son of the Marquess of Lockington. An excellent artist, Edward followed his fickle but passionate heart in all his endeavours – and into the arms of most of his models.

Nicholas flung himself into the fourth chair at the table. Within seconds, mob-capped Mrs Smith plopped a plate of stewed beef before him. Ruddy-cheeked Ellen handed him a glass of wine, with her face pinker than usual.

Tyrold's green eyes glared through his too-long black hair. 'I thought you were in Suffolk, dragging Edwin Fairchild's siblings about the country.'

Nicholas stabbed his fork into a tender chunk of beef and swirled it in the thick dark gravy. 'I've completed that task, Johnny. The current Lord Berksleigh – as excellent a scamp as ever there was – is no doubt pretending the dining table at Alton Park is his pirate ship, whilst his sisters and governess add to the already rather overwhelming number of females at my estate.' Nicholas brought the beef to his mouth; it melted on his tongue and warmed his throat as he swallowed. Mrs Smith cooked simpler food than Nicholas's French chef, but it was remarkably tasty. 'I left them all – including my sister and multitude of nieces – to Alexander's excellent care.'

Lord Edward propped his chair back on two legs and swished a mouthful of wine. 'How hideous is the old maid sister?'

Nicholas bristled at his friend's words. Meggy's laughing blue eyes and crinkled nose popped into his mind's eye, accompanied by a powerful tug on his heart. Had she missed him today? Or was his absence a relief? 'Not hideous in the least, surprisingly,' he said, spearing another chunk of beef. 'And not an old maid. She's as fresh and lovely as any debutante. Rather, she's more so.'

Sidney leaned forward, his light brown eyes twinkling. 'Do I detect a tendre, Nicky?'

The other two gentlemen perked up, alert.

A wide grin splashed Lord Edward's face. 'Are we to wish you joy?'

Nicholas put a hand to his heart, as if in mock horror; in truth, that organ pounded within his chest. 'Good God. Since when do my friends think I'm halfway to the altar simply because I said a woman wasn't hideous? I routinely praise the attributes of the fair sex.'

Tyrold steepled his fingers over his plate and rested his elbows on the table. '*Certain* members of the fair sex. Widows, matrons of questionable repute, actresses, opera dancers—'

'Covent Garden nuns,' Lord Edward chimed in. 'Women of the town, canary birds—'

Tyrold chuckled. 'The occasional obliging chambermaid, other men's mistresses—'

Nicholas held up his hand. 'Are you quite done?' He looked round at his friends, whose faces shone with amusement. Even Sidney's shoulders shook as he covered his mouth with his fist. 'You've only proven my point. I enjoy women.'

'*Women*,' Tyrold said, 'being the operative word. Not ladies, and certainly not the debutante daughters of earls.'

Nicholas scoffed. 'I may not speak of my admiration of beautiful young ladies, but that doesn't mean I fail to notice their loveliness.'

'Oh, beautiful, is she?' Edward laughed. 'That's rather a step up from "not hideous in the least". Do please tell us more about the future Lady Holbrook.'

Edward went too far when he evoked *that* title.

Nicholas smacked his palm flat upon the table, rattling the glasses and silverware. 'Keep your mouths shut when you don't know what you're speaking about,' he snapped. 'Yes, I found the chit attractive, but I'm far from nurturing noble sentiments.' Far from *nurturing* them, but not far from possessing them – but that was the very reason Nicholas was on his mission. He must rid himself of this nascent but overwhelming tenderness for Meggy at once, for her own good. 'In fact, I called to see if any of you wish to accompany me to the Preece sisters' weekly entertainment tonight, for I find myself in desperate need of a shag.'

The Preeces were London's most renowned courtesans. The five dark-haired sisters, ranging in age from their early twenties to their mid-thirties lived like jewel-encrusted queens in an opulent mansion on Mount Street. The sisters themselves were only attainable through contracted arrangements at an immensely high price, but every Thursday evening, they hosted 'entertainments for gentlemen' as grand and luxurious as any society hostess's ball. London's finest ladies of the night attended.

'Maybe two or three shags,' Nicholas added for emphasis.

There was silence around the table.

Good.

Nicholas picked up his fork again.

Tyrold cleared his throat. 'I never go to the Preece sisters' house, so I shan't accompany you.'

Nicholas looked at Edward. 'Well?'

'I'll accompany you,' Sidney said. 'I shall take my poetry.'

'Thank you,' Nicholas said politely, although Sid's companionship wasn't useful when philandering. Sidney never indulged in the lustier side of the entertainment on the rare occasions he went to the Preeces' Thursday nights. Instead, he wrote poetry and stories in a corner of the drawing room. The middle sister, Kitty, was his 'muse and inspiration'.

Edward snorted. 'Good God, Sid.' He quaffed his wine. 'I'll go, Nick. But rather than poetry, I shall bring my rammer, fully cocked. Ten guineas says I capture more rabbits than you.' He held out his paint-stained hand.

The stew churned in Nicholas's gut.

Meggy's words flooded his memory: *If you were a gentleman, I'd consider hearing you, but as you are nothing better than a scoundrel who preys on women, I'd no more hear your apology than a rabbit would listen to the apology of a fox.*

Nicholas brought his hand to his throat. His starched cravat lay in stiff unmovable folds, but something seemed to tighten and constrict his breath.

Blue eyes, so soft, so brave, so lonely. A clear tear-drop on the curve of a freckled cheek.

Kissed away.

'What do you think of me, Lord Holbrook?'

'You are utter sweetness. You're an angel.'

A sigh. A faint smile.

Trust.

The purest of kisses.

A clock ticked too loudly, reverberating in the otherwise silent room.

Nicholas's friends stared, their expressions growing quizzical.

And although his stomach curdled at his own vileness, Nicholas reached across the table, grasped Edward's palm, and shook it firmly.

Two hours later, Nicholas – thoroughly exhausted and longing for his own, *unoccupied* bed – leaned forward on the azure silk sofa where he sat with Sidney in the shadows of the Preece sisters' steaming-hot, raucous drawing room and cradled his aching head. The vast dark-blue chamber, as magnificent as a ballroom, undulated with close-pressed bodies. A three-tiered crystal chandelier, which hung from the centre of the frescoed ceiling, provided the only light, so that the edges of the chamber were as dark as dusk.

The room was a pulsing din of noise and movement,

throbbing from dozens and dozens of dancing feet. Jewel-toned silks swirled. Over-loud gentlemen stumbled and swayed. Perspiration-damp skin brushed against Nicholas's bent knees, his hands, his hair, his cheeks. Brandy and wine splashed as gesticulating arms waved glasses too wide. Nicholas's black kid-leather slippers stuck to the parquet floor, glued by spilled champagne. Violinists sawed at their instruments, doggedly determined to be heard over it all.

Edward had long since vanished with a carmine-lipped redhead.

Sidney's golden head bent over a scrap of paper resting on his lap. His pencil ran across the page and back again, repeatedly, as row upon row of tiny words filled the blank space.

In Nicholas's peripheral vision, the gaunt young baron Lord Murden stretched on a chaise lounge. A woman straddled him, with her long red skirts draped over Murden's supine body. They pressed their heads together under the curtain of her curls, but the woman's rhythmic movements left no doubt as to what happened beneath her gown's shield.

Nicholas's stomach hadn't settled, and Murden's occasional grunts, audible despite the pandemonium, brought bile to the back of his mouth.

How had these evenings *ever* appealed?

Heavy cosmetics, loosened bodices and cloying fragrance disgusted Nicholas when compared to memories of a riverside stroll, a purple wildflower held to a pretty nose, and the scent of lavender soap on freshly washed skin.

Why hadn't Nicholas saved the flower and pressed it between the pages of Byron's passionate verse, rather than throwing it out of the window? He'd tossed away his chance . . .

A hand fell on his shoulder and interrupted his thoughts.

'Lord Holbrook?' A feminine voice, raised over the noise, her words slurred.

Nicholas lifted his head, hopeful that whoever she was, she'd strike a spark of lust. He'd take her into a corner and prove he wasn't worthy of Meggy. Confirm that he must cast Meggy's smiles and laughter from his heart . . .

But when his gaze met the kohl-rimmed eyes of a vaguely familiar prostitute, Nicholas felt nothing but sorrow.

At least he remembered a past lover's face, this time.

'Are you lonely?' she asked through blood-red lips.

So lonely. He had been for years.

'My friend is here.' Nicholas nodded his head towards Sidney.

Her brow furrowed, but she shrugged and moved on, vanishing into the crowd.

Nicholas collapsed against the back of the sofa.

Sidney's pencil stilled. 'That's the twelfth one you have rejected tonight.' He leaned close to speak over the din. 'Will you make it a baker's dozen?'

Nicholas rubbed his temples. 'I mistook my feelings tonight.' The clamour of the room almost absorbed Nicholas's voice. 'I thought I wanted company in bed, but sleep is what I truly need.'

Sidney indicated the door. 'Shall we leave?'

Nicholas nodded.

The night air struck with a refreshing blast when they at last stepped through the cherry-red front door into the streetlamps' glow, after shouldering past countless moist bodies.

Nicholas's ears hummed.

He jammed his hat on his head and trudged down the front stoop.

'Edward's coming,' Sidney said from behind Nicholas. 'I saw him across the room and signalled our departure.'

Although his bed called to him, Nicholas stuck his hands in his pockets and leaned against the iron railings. 'We'll wait, then.'

Sidney stood in a halo of light from a flickering gas lamp. He extracted his paper and read to himself.

'Are you happy with what you wrote?' Nicholas asked.

Sidney folded the paper and tucked it into his waist-coat pocket. 'It's a start. This story's infested my brain for some time, and seeing Kitty tonight . . .' He paused. 'Well, you know how it is for me, Nicky. She inspires me. Something fell into place. I'm quite excited to get on with it because I think it'll be another novel.'

'I'd enjoy reading it sometime,' Nicholas said.

A little smile tugged at the corner of Sidney's mouth as he stared at his feet. 'You know I only let Kitty read my work.'

'Do you love her, Sid?' The question burst out before Nicholas could stop it. Although Sidney and Kitty had been unlikely close friends for over five years, Nicholas had never asked. Sidney was delicate, in need of protection, and Nicholas disliked making him uncomfortable.

Sidney spoke to the pavement. 'I admire her. I see what she has overcome; I know what she suffers—'

'Suffers?' Nicholas waved a hand at the house behind him. 'Within that splendour?'

'It comes at a cost, Nicky. She shields her essence, of course. They all do.' He jutted his head, indicating the Preece sisters' house. 'Even the men, I think, have a nobler side than these animal instincts. There is always an undercurrent of unhappiness amidst all the gaiety.'

Sidney's words resonated profoundly. Unhappiness had *flooded* Nicholas's life for nearly a decade.

But not on that one perfect day with Meggy and the children.

Nicholas jolted upright, realisation dawning.

That day was what Nicholas yearned for, not debauchery and meaningless sex.

The Preece sisters' door opened, spilling light and muffled noise onto the pavement.

Edward's voice boomed. 'Well, Nicky? How many rabbits did you bag?'

Not even one. Tonight, with temptation surrounding him, Nicholas had longed only for home, hearth, quiet . . . and Meggy.

Nicholas's heart swelled in his chest.

He'd changed. That's why he couldn't take a prostitute into his arms tonight.

Nicholas faced Edward, beaming. 'I owe you ten guineas, my friend. But if you come with me to

Warwickshire for a week, I'll pay you fifty times that.'
With Edward's artistic help, Nicholas would procure a
peace offering for Meggy designed to show his heartfelt
sincerity.

A gift that illustrated his sensitivity and caring.

His compassion.

Then Nicholas would court her honourably.

9

Russets and golds tinged the leaves three weeks later when Nicholas journeyed back to Alton Park from London. The day was brisk, but the sun shone in a blue sky amongst fluffy clouds. He rode ahead of his carriage, his head high, and applauded his clever scheme.

Soon – *very* soon – Meggy would forgive him.

After he passed through Alton Park's gate, he spurred his horse to a gallop. He daydreamed of Meggy's reaction to the book of Lord Edward's paintings as his horse's hooves thrummed along the long avenue. Maybe she'd want to kiss Nicholas, but this time, he'd insist they save the kisses for a time when he might claim them by right. Perhaps he'd add, *'should I ever be so fortunate'* or something to that effect.

As he crossed the bridge, he reminded himself to proceed with caution. There was no rush. He must be certain he was willing to relinquish the freedom of bachelorhood before he declared his intentions. He should consider the pros and cons. For example, Meggy might be a managing wife, forever demanding explanations for Nicholas's actions, but there were things worse than a nag – and besides, once she fell in love with him, she'd likely be as darling as she was in his arms that one night.

Nicholas closed his eyes as he rose and fell in the saddle and tried to clear his mind, because when he thought of that interrupted evening – her kisses, her moans, her breasts – he wanted Meggy so much it hurt. Dull throbs of aching longing and frustrated desire.

He needed her. He needed her to want him, and then he needed to thrust into her hot pulsing body every night for the rest of his life.

If he could stay faithful.

But he'd not think of that right now.

Meggy's singing filled the entrance of Alton Park when Nicholas arrived. She was an alto, her skin-tingling voice rich and warm. Perfection. What a welcome.

He tossed aside his hat, crop and gloves, crossed the entrance and great hall, and propped himself against the door to the light-filled music room. Rose played at the grand pianoforte, and Meggy leaned over her shoulder, singing a ballad. Her back was towards Nicholas, but he glimpsed some of her profile – a soft cheek and long lashes, the exquisite line of her jaw and curve of her neck. Sunbeams streamed in from the tall windows, silhouetting her body under her sheer muslin gown and thin petticoats. Curls tied into a twist with a wide yellow ribbon tumbled on her head. She was as lovely as a daisy, and *so* ripe for plucking.

'Bad news, bad news, to old England came,
Bad news to fair London Town,

There's been a rich vessel and she's cast away,
Cast away, cast away,
And all of the merry men drown'd.'

'What a dreary tale for a beautiful day, my dears,' Nicholas said, shedding his lustful thoughts. 'May I request something cheerier?'

Rose jumped up from her seat, blocking Nicholas's view of Meggy. 'Nicky,' she squealed, dashing across the room, throwing her arms about his neck, and smothering his face in kisses. 'You've been gone an *age*, and we've missed you dreadfully. Haven't we, Meggy?'

Rose released him, and Nicholas met Meggy's steady gaze.

Unless he was very much mistaken, a deeper pink tinged her cheeks.

But her voice was curt. 'Welcome back, Lord Holbrook.'

Nicholas bowed. Of course, it would take time for her to trust him. But once she saw his gift – which he'd show her in their first moment alone together – her animosity would vanish.

'Come, Nicky.' Rose pulled him by the hand towards the pianoforte. 'Your request next, but you must sing with Meggy.'

Meggy held up her hand. 'No, I—'

'*Please*, Meggy.' Rose clasped Meggy's upraised hand as well, forming a bridge uniting Nicholas and Meggy. 'Nicky sings beautifully, I assure you.'

But Meggy glowered, clearly annoyed.

Nicholas placed his free hand over his heart. 'Rosy, I hope Lady Margaret will honour me with a duet one day' – he smiled munificently at Meggy – 'but not today. I'm far too thirsty from the road.'

'Then you must have tea.' Rose dropped their hands and danced across the room to pull the brass wall lever to ring for a servant.

Nicholas laughed. 'Not tea. Brandy.'

The butler materialised in the doorway. 'Does your lordship wish for brandy?'

'No, Hammond.' Rose spoke firmly, like the little mother she'd always been to Nicholas – like Meggy was to Harry and Sophy. 'His lordship wishes for *tea*.'

'Rosy, one day you must learn I'm a grown man now.' Nicholas smiled at his butler. 'Hammond, tea to appease Lady Rose, and brandy to appease me.'

When the butler left, Rose returned to Nicholas's side and patted his coat and waistcoat pockets. 'Where is it?' she asked.

'Where's the fun if I tell you?' But Nicholas spread his arms out so she could search more easily, as was his custom.

Rose checked for lumps under his coat sleeves. 'Where do you think he's put it, Meggy?'

Meggy's eyes cut to Nicholas. He tapped his ankle with the heel of his other boot and winked, glad of the opportunity to demonstrate his brotherly devotion to Rose.

'His boot, he says.' She lifted her chin and looked towards the window.

Rose stepped back. 'Is it in your boot, Nicky?'

'Perhaps you'll have to take it off to find out, and I cannot guarantee the smell will be pleasant. I've been in the saddle for hours.' Nicholas glanced at Meggy to see if she laughed, but she stared stone-faced out the window.

'Bah! I'm not taking off your filthy boot.' Rose stuck her finger into the rim and extracted a slim circle wrapped in pink silk. She skipped to the sofa, pulling Meggy with her. 'See what Nicky has brought for my collection.'

The two ladies collapsed together on the rose-coloured silk like a frothy confection of white and green muslin. Huddled next to Rose, Meggy's frostiness melted. Her eyes sparkled; she smiled and laughed. Her freckled nose crinkled. Tawny curls pressed against Rose's thin shoulder.

Nicholas's heart sang.

He accepted a brandy from Hammond and relaxed in an armchair, his legs resting on the footstool before him. Rose gushed as the silk slipped away to reveal a pink jade disc carved with a stylised scene of a Chinese village.

'Oh, Nicky. Where did you find such a treasure?'

Nicholas described the dark, incense-heavy store near Shadwell Market in East London, which he'd visited during the fortnight he'd spent in town after Warwickshire. Rose's eyes shone as she and Meggy sat with their arms clasped about each other's waists, and Nicholas settled deeper into his seat. The warmth of the brandy, the warmth of the feminine friendship before him; for years, he'd undervalued domesticity, but not anymore.

When he'd answered Rose's subsequent questions, he quaffed the rest of his drink. 'How have the scamps been? Well enough behaved for me to take them to Ipswich?'

Rose fluttered her hands. 'They've been darlings, as always.'

But Meggy tilted her head, her ribbon-threaded curls bouncing. 'Now, Rose, that's not quite true . . .'

The ladies burst into laughter, foreheads pressed together, noses touching.

Precious.

Since Rose and Meggy adored each other, Meggy would fall in love with Nicholas quickly indeed. The difficulty, of course, was that the moment Nicholas attempted gallantry, the ladies would order the wedding clothes in anticipation.

And Nicholas must be *certain*.

Nicholas refilled his brandy from the decanter at his side. 'What trouble did they cause?'

Meggy giggled; clearly, she'd already overcome her earlier reservations, for she was amiable and content now. 'I'm afraid my brother isn't the best influence on Elizabeth, Lord Holbrook.'

'And vice versa,' Rose said. 'There have been several *incidents*.'

They'd only begun to relate a tale about Harry and Elizabeth's night-time kitchen pilfering when thundering pandemonium down the corridor announced the arrival of the two menaces accompanied by Copper, Caesar and Alexander. The physician's coat was off, his hair stood on end, and he grinned from ear to ear.

'Nicky *is* here, Eliza.' Harry pointed his finger. 'You were lying when you said the carriage arrived with Caesar but no Nicky.'

'I wasn't lying!' Elizabeth pounced on Harry.

A flurry of white muslin frock and dark-blue one-piece suit twisted like a tempest on the Turkish rug. Auburn curls mingled with brown ones as little arms flailed. Copper barked and pounced on the children, wanting to join the fun, and Caesar yipped as he bounced on his stubby legs.

Meggy, Alexander and Rose swooped on Harry and Eliza like hawks on mice. Rose scooped a kicking and screaming Elizabeth into her arms, and Alexander grabbed Harry by his bib collar and dragged the boy to his feet. Together, Alexander and Meggy knelt, one on either side of the young earl.

'Harry, you mustn't call names,' Meggy said. 'And to call someone a *liar*, of all things, is simply abysmal.'

Harry drew his brows together and crossed his arms over his chest.

Meggy continued. 'Furthermore, it's not true. Lord Holbrook said he rode, presumably ahead of the carriage.'

Harry's shoulders slumped. 'Oh.'

'Not too late to apologise to her, eh?' Alexander patted Harry's back. He and Meggy exchanged smiles over the boy's hanging head.

Nicholas sat as straight as a rod, suddenly alert.

What was this doe-eyed simper in Meggy's eyes as her gaze met Alexander's? Why did the physician break into a ludicrously over-large grin?

And their *hands* – were their fingertips touching on Harry's shoulder?

Harry cleared his throat. 'I'm sorry, Eliza. But sometimes you *do* lie, like yesterday when you told me the alum used for pickling was a sugar lump so I'd put it in my mouth.'

Elizabeth shrieked from her mother's arms. 'You blabbed, you horrid boy.'

Before another fight erupted, Nicholas spoke. Clearly, it was time for him to manage the children. 'I was just enquiring as to your behaviour whilst I was away, Harry and Eliza.'

Instantly, both children's faces shone angelic, as Nicholas had expected. Hopefully, Meggy would appreciate that Nicholas dealt with the scamps much better than Alexander had.

Elizabeth approached with her small palms extended. 'Our behaviour has been *extremely* good, Uncle Nicky.'

Harry tugged at his collar. 'We are the best of friends, sir.'

'Only teasing each other on occasion.' Elizabeth bestowed a pretty smile on Harry. 'Isn't that correct, Harry, my dear friend?'

The earl nodded solemnly. 'All in good fun.'

They climbed into Nicholas's lap to continue more of the same, but Nicholas only half listened to their chatter. His stomach writhed, for Meggy whispered to Alexander as she prepared the physician a cup of tea. Alexander looked damned pleased with himself – and why wouldn't he be, with Meggy's pretty hand resting on his sleeve . . .

'Uncle Nicky? Were you attending? I asked when you'll take us to Ipswich?'

With effort, Nicholas drew his attention to Elizabeth. 'I . . . er . . . tomorrow? If the weather holds and your mother and Lady Margaret approve.'

The children squealed. 'May we, may we?'

Rose and Meggy granted permission.

'And Dr Mitchell, will you come as well?'

'I wouldn't miss it.'

Meggy and Alexander smiled at each other whilst Nicholas glared.

'May we tell Maria and Sophy, Mama?' Elizabeth asked.

'Yes, away with you,' Rose said, fluttering her hands to shoo the children out the door. 'And I must away as well. I want to write in my journal about my new treasure before I forget the details. Thank you, Nicky, dearest brother. How lovely that you are home again.'

She blew Nicholas a kiss and followed Harry and Sophy.

'I should be back to my work.' Alexander stepped backwards towards the door, his eyes on Meggy.

Meggy placed a hand on his arm again. 'Shall I come and help, Alexander?'

Nicholas's grip tightened on his glass of brandy. *Alexander*?

The physician glanced at Nicholas and cleared his throat – damned nervously, the devious dog. 'Thank you, Meggy, but I'm not yet finished with the case files you organised yesterday. Perhaps the day after we return from Ipswich?'

Nicholas fumed. *Meggy*, as well as Alexander? The bastard had absolutely stolen a march in his absence.

'I'd enjoy that,' Meggy said, and – Nicholas shifted in his seat, trying to achieve a better view – appeared to bat her lashes. 'I find your work fascinating.'

'You're a scientist through and through, ma'am.' Alexander bowed and departed, tossing a 'Glad you're back, Nick' over his damned shoulder.

Meggy followed.

Nicholas jumped to his feet. 'Lady Margaret,' he said, before she reached the door. 'May I please have a moment of your time?' And to remind her she'd liked *him* before Alexander, Nicholas smiled sweetly.

Which appeared to have no effect on Meggy. She glanced between him and the door. 'I suppose,' she said at last. 'But only a moment.'

Nicholas rang the bell; his butler appeared framed in the doorway. 'Hammond, ask Bloomfield to send down the package from town. Lady Margaret, please have a seat again.'

She perched on the edge of a sofa with her eyes narrowed as if he were a rat. Nicholas sat on the other end. His mouth was suddenly dry, but the brandy remained by his previous seat.

'Well?' She crossed her arms.

Even scowling, she was lovely. The honeyed tones of her brown curls glistened in the sunbeams; her blue eyes shone like sparkling water. 'I . . . I, er.' Nicholas swallowed and shook his head. 'Forgive me, I find myself rather tongue-tied.'

'In that case, our conversation appears to be over. I should help Rose with preparations for tomorrow.'

She stood, but Nicholas caught her hand. 'No, please stay. Rosy will write in her journal for a while. I . . . as it happens, Lady Margaret, I have a gift for you as well.'

She yanked her hand back. 'I shan't accept any gift from you, Lord Holbrook.'

'Then not a gift. A peace offering. An olive branch, I suppose you might say. Ah, here it is.' Nicholas gestured to the footman who'd arrived holding a large, flat package wrapped in brown paper and tied with twine. 'Thank you, William, that'll be all.' Nicholas took the package and offered it to Meggy. 'For you, my dear.'

She looked from the package to Nicholas's face several times before receiving it with a glare. She plopped onto the sofa, huffed, and fiddled with the twine. Nicholas withdrew his penknife from his coat pocket, but she pushed it away.

After spending five minutes unknotting the twine, Meggy began to unwrap the paper by lifting each corner delicately.

Nicholas suppressed his annoyance with difficulty. 'You can tear the paper.'

Her eyes cut to his. 'I don't *want* to tear perfectly good paper. I shall use it to make paper dolls with the girls.'

'No need – I can buy paper dolls for the girls.'

'I thought you said this . . . *peace offering* is for me. If I value the paper it's wrapped in, that's my choice.' She laid aside the collection of paintings – bound between leather covers – to roll the brown paper into a cylinder that she fastened with twine. 'To smooth the creases,' she explained with a smirk.

She was trying to antagonise Nicholas. He wanted to find it adorable, like flirting or teasing, but it was as irritating as she intended. He'd put an immense amount of effort into this present.

Meggy lifted the book and slowly drew her eyes down to the first page.

Her smirk vanished.

Now she'd regret her behaviour. Nicholas smiled. 'Do you like it?'

Meggy flipped through the pages, observing Lord Edward's watercolour paintings: Berksleigh Hall, no windows blackened; the water-lily pond; the brambles by the River Avon; the estate village. At the depiction of the mediaeval castle in Warwick, she paused. 'Harry loves Lord Warwick's castle.'

'I confess much of my intelligence came from your brother. I asked him about your favourite things and your favourite places, but I suspected some might be *his* favourites.'

'Ah, that explains the painting of the kitchen cat.'

'Yes. And I can have the cat brought here, Meg – Lady Margaret.'

'No – Harry knows it would break Cook's heart if we took Miss Mouser away. But these paintings *will* bring back wonderful memories. Did you paint them?'

'No, I commissioned a friend to do so.'

She nodded, still flipping through the book. 'She did a lovely job.'

'*He*,' Nicholas said, too sharply. She was still deliberately provoking him.

'Hmm.'

Nicholas swallowed and tried again. 'I can commission him to do your favourites in oils.'

'This is better. I haven't anywhere to hang oil paintings.'

'In your bedchamber here if you like.'

'No,' Meggy said, shaking her curls, 'it wouldn't do. Paintings of Berksleigh Hall in the autumn won't match Rose's decoration scheme for the Spring Room.'

'Perhaps you'd like a different bedchamber.' A brilliant idea arose in Nicholas's head. 'Perhaps you'd like to decorate one in *your* favourite scheme?'

She held up her hand. 'No, no. Quite unnecessary, as I shan't be here long.'

Nicholas faltered. Why was she so certain?

Meggy leaned forward, and her blue eyes locked with his. 'Thank you, Lord Holbrook.'

Ah, a glimmer of hope after all. 'You're most welcome, my dear.'

She nodded, stacked the paper cylinder on top of the book, and stood.

Nicholas stood as well. 'Perhaps we might be friends now?'

Meggy blinked, outwardly incredulous. 'Oh no. *Definitely* not.'

She didn't appear to be in jest, and Nicholas's stomach dropped. But he forced a smile; surely she simply didn't understand. 'The book is my peace offering.'

'Very well,' she said. 'We're at peace, Lord Holbrook.'

His smile deepened into a grin. She was a playful thing. 'Ah, so we're *allies*. Very near to friendship.'

Meggy raised an eyebrow. 'We aren't actively at war, but we aren't allies or friends. I was quite clear I cannot be friends with someone I don't trust. Giving me a collection of watercolours was lovely, but it doesn't make me trust you.'

Nicholas's smile vanished, and his shoulders tensed. 'I was demonstrating my kindness to prove I'm willing to exert considerable effort to help you.'

'Ah, I see. But unfortunately, providing me with paintings of Berksleigh in no way *helps* my current situation. If that was your goal, it was a wasted effort, and you would've done better to stay at Alton Park. In fact – rather ironically, I now realise – I went to bed the evening of our arrival feeling somewhat guilty about refusing your help to find Harry a tutor, and I came down to breakfast ready for your aid. But then I discovered you'd fled.'

Nicholas curbed his anger. 'I went to London to commission these paintings for you.'

She laughed. 'But is that all you did? No cavorting about town?'

'I . . . I . . . well, not in the way I think you mean.'

'Please don't mistake me. You're perfectly free to cavort as much as you wish. I'm merely pointing out that it didn't *help* me. Not to worry, though: Alexander's been *invaluable*, and I've engaged a tutor for Harry who'll arrive next month. But I digress. I only mean to suggest, sir, if you wish to help me, perhaps ask me *how*.'

Nicholas took a deep breath and spoke with forced calm. 'How may I assist you, Lady Margaret?'

Meggy tilted her head. 'Why, at this moment, I cannot think of any way at all.' She smirked and skipped from the room, her golden-brown curls and yellow ribbons bouncing.

Nicholas turned on his heel and stormed to the library, a large room lined with leather tomes on cream-coloured shelves under a coffered gilded ceiling. Alexander sat at a beech wood desk covered in papers. 'On your feet, Alexander.'

His friend's head flew up. 'You look as if you wish to challenge me.'

'Dammit, perhaps I should.'

Alexander rubbed his chin, as if contemplating. 'In that case, it'll have to be swords. You're too good a shot, and I'm not wasting my life to appease your fury.'

Nicholas seethed at his friend's mockery. 'On your feet, I said.'

'Really, Nick. I have work to do.' But Alexander tossed down his quill and squared his shoulders. 'What do you have to say?'

Nicholas leaned over the desk and spat his words in his friend's face. 'You said you'd give me a chance.'

'What are you talking about?'

'A chance with Lady Margaret. But whilst I was gone, you ingratiated yourself to her. Made yourself *invaluable*, she says.'

Alexander's crooked grin and dimple appeared. 'Did she say that? What a darling she is.'

Nicholas clenched his fists. 'Damn you!'

Alexander held out his palms. 'Be fair, Nick. I said you must use the opportunity. You fled the next morning, by your own admission planning to seek out other women for casual dalliance. What was I supposed to do? Ignore an engaging young lady who wanted to help me with my work? I'm only a man, my friend. And Meggy's damnably pretty, and devilishly clever. Why, she—'

Nicholas grabbed his friend's waistcoat. 'Have you kissed her, you dog?'

'*What*? No! I wouldn't take such a liberty. Good lord, what do you take me for?'

Nicholas recoiled, releasing Alexander.

Alexander's jaw dropped. 'Dammit, Nicholas, did *you* kiss her? Oh, I can tell you did. You villain – she's in your care!'

Nicholas tugged on his cravat. 'She's not in my care. Her siblings are in my care.'

'You are grasping at straws to defend your conduct. Good lord! She's a fatherless young lady whose seven-year-old brother is her only male relative. How do you live with yourself, Nick?'

Nicholas glared, his face warming. 'I find it damned difficult, as I thought you knew.'

'Perhaps you should address *that* before you attempt to address Lady Margaret.'

'I did address it. I went to one of the Preece sisters'

Thursday night affairs whilst I was in town, and I wasn't the least bit interested in anyone.'

Alexander's brows shot up. 'Do I understand correctly, Nick? After taking liberties with a virtuous young lady, you attended a debauched party, and because you kept it inside your breeches for one evening, you consider yourself worthy of Meggy's regard? The regard of a lady whose honour you played fast and loose with? You imagine yourself a reformed rake, now, do you?'

The room suddenly felt stifling. 'Well . . . when you put it *that* way.'

'There is no other way to put it. I merely restated facts. Nick, that's not improving yourself in the least.' Alexander poked him in the chest. 'You haven't even begun. And if you want my advice, consider why it is you find it so damned difficult to live with yourself. You'll never win Meggy's heart if you're ashamed of your own, my boy.'

Nicholas shook with fury. 'You have a lot of nerve.'

'Bah! What nerve? I'm older *and* wiser than you, and I'm not impressed by a title, as you damn well know. Now, leave. I have work to do if I'm to come to Ipswich.'

'You are welcome to stay here, you bastard. Better yet, go back to London.'

'And miss an outing with Rose, Meggy, and the children?' Alexander grinned. 'I wouldn't dream of it.'

10

The moment Meggy awoke the next morning, she knew there'd be no trip to Ipswich.

Rain lashed at her bay window. Grey mist swirled beyond the streaming panes. The Suffolk sky had unleashed another torrent of rainfall such as had plagued the entire summer.

Whilst a chambermaid built up the fire in the hearth, Meggy crawled out from under her covers and pulled her woollen dressing gown over her nightdress. She slid her feet into her pink slippers and hastened from her bedroom with her hair tumbling loose over her shoulders.

Her mind schemed as she hurried down the corridor. She must offer the children some other entertainment, or there would be disappointment and tears, which would lead to arguing and headaches.

But even before she reached the closed door of the playroom, peals of laughter and gleeful shrieks pierced Meggy's ears.

She opened the door and leaned against the jamb.

None of the boisterous occupants noticed her presence.

Accompanied by the two dogs, the four older children ran about in their long white nightdresses, screeching, screaming, climbing upon furniture and hiding behind rocking horses as Holbrook chased them in his shirt-sleeves, roaring, with his dark curls standing on end.

Meggy's heart twisted.

Why did Holbrook still wield power over her?

She'd known the day before, when his deep voice reverberated behind her in the music room, that despite her best efforts to fall in love with Alexander, she'd missed the marquess terribly when he was in town.

The scene before her illustrated perfectly *why*: she'd never seen her siblings happier than when they played with Holbrook, and Meggy understood Harry and Sophy's sentiments. At play, Holbrook exhibited the same wild, unbridled, joyful energy Edwin had possessed, so many years ago, when he played with little Meggy.

Edwin had been the light of Meggy's world in those days.

Sophy, blonde curls bobbing, dashed in front of shy Maria, who protected a squealing baby Charlotte as Holbrook advanced, growling.

'I shall save you from the bear, Charlotte.' Sophy flung herself, full force, onto Holbrook's back.

The marquess buckled and collapsed to his knees, laughing, as Sophy flung her fists, battering his head, chest and arms. 'Beastly bear! Bad bear! To frighten a baby, of all things!'

Not that Charlotte was frightened. She bounced on Maria's lap, clapping her fat, dimpled hands and chortling.

'Now *you've* incited the bear's wrath, Sophy,' Holbrook roared, rising as he bundled Sophy into his strong arms, his muscles bulging under his fine white linen shirtsleeves.

Sophy kicked her legs, twisted and pounded the marquess's back, full of vigour. 'I'm not scared of you, you horrid bear.'

Harry and Elizabeth joined in the attack, yanking at Holbrook's limbs to save Sophy, until the marquess knelt – no doubt at his own will – and the children pulled him recumbent to the floor. Elizabeth pinned Holbrook's ankles, Harry clasped the marquess's wrists, and a triumphant Sophy plopped directly on his chest.

From her perch, Sophy's eyes met Meggy's. 'Meggy's here,' she said to the other children, as she bounced her bottom on the marquess's abdomen. Holbrook gasped for breath through his laughter. 'Look, Meggy, we captured the bear! Help us skin him for a rug.'

Meggy could most definitely *not* help the children pretend to skin Holbrook.

The smattering of dark curls at his loosened shirt collar was distracting enough.

She entered the room and sat demurely on a sofa, folding her hands in her lap. 'I came expecting to find tears because of the rain. I've discovered five exceedingly wild bear hunters instead.'

'Nicky said bear hunting was our first order of business,' Sophy replied, as solemn as a Methodist preacher. 'We must accomplish a great deal today.'

'Oh?' Meggy said, hiding a smile with difficulty.

Harry counted off on his fingers. 'Blind man's buff in the ballroom followed by a picnic in the attic!'

'Don't forget the fancy dress,' Maria added, tucking a silken strand of red-gold hair behind her ear. 'Uncle Nicky said we must eat our luncheon wearing fancy dress . . .'

'There are trunks of old clothes in the attics,' Elizabeth explained to Meggy, her clear grey eyes sparkling.

'And last of all,' Harry continued, 'we shall hunt tigers in the conservatory.'

'Tigers,' Meggy gasped, fully entering the fun, for it sounded like a delightful way to spend a rainy day. Holbrook or no, there was nothing more enjoyable – or exhausting – than play-acting with the children. 'Are there tigers in the conservatory? If I'd known, I would've asked one of you to protect me yesterday as I watched the parakeets.'

Sophy, still perched on Holbrook's stomach, shook her head. 'Not *real* tigers, Meggy.'

'Uncle Nicky is to be the tiger,' Elizabeth said.

Holbrook nodded from the floor. 'I am to be the tiger,' he agreed. 'I assure you, under normal circumstances, Lady Margaret, the conservatory is quite safe.'

Meggy raised an eyebrow pointedly. 'When *you're* not in it, you mean?'

Holbrook burst into laughter. As always when faced with the marquess's infectious, unrestrained mirth, merriment bubbled spontaneously to Meggy's own lips.

Sophy looked between Holbrook and Meggy. 'What Meggy said wasn't *that* amusing.'

166

With difficulty, Meggy stopped giggling, although her shoulders still shook. 'You're correct, Sophy, it wasn't in the least.' She rose. 'And, as we have such a very busy day ahead, I should return to my room to dress.'

Only as the words slipped from her mouth did Meggy remember she stood before Holbrook in her night-clothes – as she had on one other, disastrous occasion. Her ears burned at the memory; thank God she'd worn her thickest dressing gown.

Maria leapt to her feet. 'Oh, but Meggy, Uncle Nicky also promised to help us make paper dolls if you show him how.' Meggy met Holbrook's eyes, which gleamed like a naughty boy. 'Can you draw out the dolls before you leave?' Maria asked, pulling Meggy towards a small table, upon which rested the brown paper from Holbrook's gift, scissors, paints and pastel crayons.

As Meggy and the girls sat, Harry groaned. 'I hoped you'd forgotten that one. Eliza, *you* don't want to paint paper dolls, do you?'

But Elizabeth leaned forward on her elbows, watching as Meggy folded the brown paper into strips, like pleats on a skirt. 'Sometimes I like to paint paper dolls,' Elizabeth said.

Harry stuck his fists in his pockets. 'It's a girlish thing to do.'

Elizabeth smoothed her long, auburn curls. 'Well, I *am* a girl, and exceedingly glad to be one. Girls are better than boys.'

Harry scowled. 'Are not. Are they, sir?' he asked, looking at Holbrook.

The marquess sat in a too-small chair beside Meggy, his long legs folded with his knees comically high. 'Girls are infinitely better than boys, Harry.' He reached across the table for a pair of scissors; the movement stirred a whiff of bergamot. 'It's a sad fact for us, but there you have it, and the sooner you learn to recognise it, the happier your life will be.'

Meggy took up a pencil. 'Not that *you* recognise it,' she said before she could stop herself. She busied herself sketching the outline of a woman's shape from one folded crease of the pleated paper to the other.

'I assure you I recognise ladies' superiority, Lady Margaret.'

Meggy drew a parasol on the doll's shoulder. 'And yet I recall a lecture about *managing* women. It was accompanied by a scold on young ladies filling their heads with nonsense.' She tilted her head and blinked with feigned innocence. 'From reading too much Byron, I believe.'

Holbrook's grey eyes livened. 'Ah, but when I acknowledged ladies' superiority, I didn't say they had *no* vices.' He grinned cheekily. 'Now, tell me what I must do with these scissors? Cut upon your lines?'

'Yes,' Meggy said. 'But you mustn't cut on the creases at the corner of the lady's skirt or at her parasol. If you do it correctly, we shall have four ladies joined together, walking in a row.'

'How clever.' Holbrook plied the scissors into the paper, cutting perfect lines along Meggy's drawing with the long, thin steel blades. Five small heads leaned over his labour, a circle of red, blonde and brown ringlets watching strong masculine hands manage delicate work.

Again, Meggy's heart twisted. When Holbrook was like this, it was impossible not to imagine the marquess as the most magnificent of papas. Handsome, stalwart, playful . . .

She put her hand to her forehead, for the room spun.

His eyes met hers at once, as if he were attuned to her discomfort. 'Are you well, Lady Margaret?'

Meggy gave a light-hearted chuckle, although her mouth had gone quite dry. Best to jest, so he didn't know how his presence affected her. 'Oh, I'm terribly unwell. You've just explained that women have vices; I dread to think what mine are.'

His lips twitched. 'No doubt I should declare that you have none. But I never lie, Lady Margaret.'

Meggy's eyebrows shot up. 'Indeed?' Her dry mouth no longer bothered her. 'Dare I ask what my vices are?'

Holbrook bent his head over his work. 'You are yourself so exceedingly strong that you cannot endure weakness in others.'

Meggy stiffened. 'How is it a *vice* not to celebrate weakness?'

Holbrook didn't respond to her question. 'Shall I tell a fairy tale, children?'

'Lord, yes,' Elizabeth said, 'for your conversation is dreadfully dull.'

'There was once a beautiful princess who lived at the top of a magnificent tower,' Holbrook said as he snipped the brown paper carefully. 'The tower's sides were as smooth as glass and there were no stairs to the top. All the princes in the land wished to be her friend, but the princess declared that only those who succeeded in climbing to the top of her tower could speak to her. Therefore, all around her tower, princes climbed upon ladders that slipped and slid on the glassy sides, trying to reach the top. One prince – a terribly handsome one, as a matter of fact – climbed with more determination than he'd ever applied to anything else, because he *especially* wanted to be friends with the princess. He admired how she'd climbed to the top of the tower on her own, although dragons had snapped at her hands and feet.'

He paused briefly to unfurl the paper dolls. The chain of ladies spread perfectly over the table. 'Just as the prince approached the princess – near enough to say one or two words – he stumbled and lost his grip . . .'

'Oh, no.' Maria put her hand to her mouth.

'Never fear, Maria, for although he slipped very far indeed, he managed to find himself before he hit the bottom. The prince grabbed onto the sides of the ladder. He pulled himself up again, one foot at a time . . .'

Holbrook stopped speaking. He leaned back in his seat.

Silence filled the room.

Meggy, suddenly aware she'd held her breath, exhaled.

The girls stared wide-eyed.

'Well?' Sophy asked. 'What happened? Did he make it to the top?'

Holbrook held up his hands, palms out. 'I'm afraid I told you the best part, for, with this particular princess, it doesn't matter if he made it to the top. Once the prince stumbled, she never liked him again. It was her vice, you see. She herself was perfect; thus, she couldn't admire anyone who wasn't perfect as well.'

Meggy drew in a sharp breath, for the marquess's ending nettled. She was not so narrow-minded. Twice Holbrook had betrayed her trust in a most abhorrent manner. 'I believe you have the story wrong,' she snapped. 'The particular prince you refer to never made it to a ladder at all. He is many miles from the tower, so bogged down in mud and muck as to *never*—'

Harry's heavy sigh interrupted Meggy. 'This is the *worst* story. Can you tell one about pirates instead, Nicky?'

Holbrook smiled. 'Of course.'

Meggy picked up the brown paper, and, with a scowl on her face, drew the lines of another row of paper dolls. She barely listened to Holbrook's silly pirate tale, although he was so engrossed in telling it, he fell behind with cutting, and Sophy took up a second pair of scissors to assist.

After he'd completed the story, Holbrook leaned near Meggy's shoulder and whispered, his breath warm against her cheek. 'Do you suppose if that poor sod ever makes it to the top of the tower, the princess will look favourably upon him for how difficult his journey was?'

Meggy nudged Holbrook with her elbow, pushing him away. 'How can she?' she asked through clenched teeth. 'She won't even see him through the muck.'

Holbrook sighed, audibly. 'Forgive me if my story angered you.'

Meggy whipped her head around, glaring into his long-lashed eyes. 'Angered me? Lord Holbrook, it's more serious than that. You play predator with the children, but to me, your threat is real.'

He put his hand, splay-fingered, over his heart. His bronzed skin contrasted beautifully with the white silk of his waistcoat. 'You have nothing to fear from me, Lady Margaret. Not anymore.'

Meggy fumed. Oh, he was a *terribly* talented actor. It would be so easy to slip into his deceitful web again. 'I required two cruel lessons, Lord Holbrook, but I've learned now. You are not kind, and I do not trust you.' She placed her pencil on the table. 'I think it's best if I help Alexander with his treatise today rather than play with you and the children.'

Holbrook stared at her for a moment. Then he closed his eyes and rubbed the bridge of his nose. 'Perhaps I should leave Alton Park again.'

Harry's head, bowed over his painting, popped up. 'No, don't leave, Nicky.'

Sophy stopped cutting. 'Is Nicky leaving again? Please stay . . .'

Then Sophy gasped. Her face crumpled, and she released a long, high-pitched whine, which caused both dogs to sit up, heads cocked and ears perked.

Meggy frowned. A bit excessive, really . . .

Holbrook vaulted from his seat.

His chair crashed to the floor.

By the time Meggy realised what was truly amiss, scarlet blood covered Sophy's fingertip, and the marquess had enfolded her sister in his arms. Even before Meggy rose – intending to assume responsibility for Sophy's care – Holbrook had extracted a pristine handkerchief from his waistcoat pocket and secured it around the child's finger. He kissed the bandage and rocked Sophy, singing a lullaby into her blonde curls as she sobbed against his shoulder. He possessed an exquisite, rich baritone voice.

'There, there, sweet darling,' Holbrook murmured once Sophy's sobs quietened. 'I shall take you to Dr Mitchell now.'

Something compressed Meggy's chest so painfully she couldn't breathe as Holbrook carried Sophy from the room, with the other children and the dogs trailing in his wake.

Meggy *must* find a husband.

If she waited much longer, her siblings would love Holbrook too much to leave him.

I I

The Ipswich trip occurred on a warm, cloudless day a fortnight later. When Meggy emerged from the house into the morning sunlight to join the rest of the party upon the front steps, her gaze flickered to Holbrook instantly. The excited children clung to him adoringly – as they'd done every day during the two-week deluge – swinging on his arms and pulling at his dark blue tailcoat and buff trousers. Even toddling Charlotte embraced him around his black boots.

Meggy turned her head so the brim of her poke bonnet shielded her face. She reminded herself for the thousandth time that Edwin had been appealing like that until other temptations pushed all thoughts of the little sister who loved him from his head, and he'd left Meggy, still a frightened and grieving child herself, to raise babies and manage an estate on dwindling resources.

Meggy ignored the ache in her throat, lifted her chin, and smiled at Rose, who organised everyone into the carriages.

They set out in three equipages. A closed carriage conveyed the two governesses, as well as Charlotte and her nurse. The four older children travelled with Rose and Meggy in an open-top landau, and the gentlemen led the procession in Holbrook's two-seater curricle drawn by a matched pair of greys. The journey took over an hour, but the day was glorious, and the children's excitement infectious as Rose entertained them with stories of her sea adventures.

The Ipswich shipyards, loud with hammering and sawing and the singing and cursing of workers, were located at the bend of the River Orwell, and the fishy odour of the tidal river mingled with the smell of fresh-cut wood. The vessels under construction rose mighty and tall along the banks, supported by scaffolding, and Meggy delighted in Harry's beaming face. Her brother held Holbrook's hand and bombarded the leather-skinned master shipwright, Mr Palmer, with questions.

After a tour of the factory rooms, Harry pointed at a towering vessel. 'May we see *inside* a ship under construction?'

'Aye, m'lord,' Mr Palmer said. 'I hoped you'd want to.' He spoke to Holbrook. 'My builders will hoist the ladies and children in nets so they needn't climb the ladders.'

The two governesses declined this service, preferring to remain upon solid ground, but baby Charlotte and her nurse went up, as did Rose with her elder daughters.

Meggy assisted Sophy into a net that hung from the side of the ship like a teardrop-shaped web. 'Harry, come up with Sophy and me. It'll be like flying, for the ships reach to the sky.'

Harry, still holding Holbrook's hand, shook his head. 'I shall climb the ladder like Nicky and Alexander.'

The rope ladder dangled down like a wavering vine. One slip and Harry would fall to his death, either upon the hard ground or against the wooden scaffold beams supporting the soaring ship. 'No, Harry,' Meggy said, 'it's not safe.'

Harry looked to Holbrook with pleading eyes, and Meggy prepared herself for a fight.

But the marquess knelt and took both of Harry's hands in his. 'Harry, why does your sister ask you to go in the net?'

Harry jutted out his bottom lip. 'Because she thinks I'm not man enough to climb the ladder.'

Holbrook shook his head. 'No, my boy. Because she loves you, and she cannot bear the thought of losing you. Furthermore, she and Sophy *need* you, don't they?'

A lump sprang to Meggy's throat. She hadn't expected Holbrook's support.

But Harry still frowned. 'So am I never to have fun, Nicky?'

'I didn't say that. But you mustn't take *unnecessary* risks.'

Harry nodded, but his chin trembled.

Meggy swallowed the lump – and a considerable amount of dignity. 'What . . . what is your opinion, Lord Holbrook?'

The marquess, still kneeling, looked up at her and blinked. '*My* opinion?'

'As Harry's joint guardian, yes.'

Holbrook stood and wiped the dirt from his knee before responding. 'My opinion, ma'am, is that Harry will be an excellent climber, and I shall ensure his safety.'

Harry's eyes shone, and he bounced on the balls of his feet. 'May I, Meggy, *please?*'

Meggy wrung her hands. She couldn't protect Harry for the rest of his life. One day, he'd be a man, with all the temptations and dangers of the world laid out before him, and he must navigate those risks without falling to Edwin's way.

'Very well,' Meggy said at last.

She arranged herself on the net seat with Sophy as Harry began the arduous climb on the rope ladder. Holbrook, true to his promise, stayed immediately behind the boy. If Harry fell, the marquess's body would catch him.

Holbrook shielded Harry from harm, as a father protected his child. As an elder, grown brother *should* protect a young, orphaned sibling . . .

The sight played on Meggy's sentimental heart. She closed her eyes, reminding herself of the urgency of finding a trustworthy husband before she cared too much for Holbrook.

As they toured the fresh-cut, yellow wood hull of the ship, which opened like an upturned shell to the sky, Holbrook offered Meggy his arm. At first she determined to ignore him, realising he thought he'd won because she accepted his help with Harry. But a clever plan to put him in his place formulated, and, with a smile, she slipped her hand onto his elbow.

He pressed against her a little, and his whisper rumbled at her bonnet brim. 'You took my arm. I thought you might leave me looking the fool.'

Meggy fully intended to leave him looking the fool . . .

She brushed her breast against the firm muscles of his upper arm, and his beautiful grey eyes danced. He was already smug – and heart-achingly handsome, so tanned and magnificent in the sunlight. Meggy forced herself to ignore the titillation in her nipples as she continued her tease. 'I owe you a *little* kindness after your help with Harry, so I decided not to emasculate you before these carpenters. You already appear to a distinct disadvantage near them.'

Holbrook raised his perfect eyebrows. '*I* appear to disadvantage?'

Pleased with herself, Meggy continued. 'Yes – by wearing your finery when all a man needs are muscular, tanned arms and rolled-up shirtsleeves.'

'If that's what you'd prefer, I can oblige.'

She knew he could. She'd run her palms over his thick, hard biceps once, and she revisited the memory nightly. But *he* mustn't know that. 'Nonsense.' She flittered her free hand in the direction of an especially brawny builder. 'Why should you when there are plenty of handsome arms before me?'

He tensed, stiffening at her side. 'Ah. You hope to incite my jealousy in an especially shallow way. I advise you against such a tactic.'

Meggy's temper flared. How dare *he* belittle *her*? 'I

don't care tuppence for your *advice*. Nor do I care if you're jealous or not.'

'I believe you don't care for my advice,' he said tersely, 'but of course you wish to make me jealous. Otherwise, you would've kept your thoughts on the carpenters' arms to yourself.'

Meggy's blood boiled. 'Yet *again* you know my feelings better than I do. You imagine all I think about is you.'

'I imagine no such thing,' he snapped, 'and, as I've said before, you should minimise your use of sarcasm. It's your least attractive quality.'

Meggy controlled her urge to hit him only with the greatest effort. Instead, she sweetened her tone to deliver a large dose of the sarcasm he despised. 'Thank you for showing me the error of my ways. Making myself attractive to you *is* my primary aim in life.'

His jaw clenched. 'How quickly you've made me regret my gallantry, ma'am.' His breath came short and quick. 'I would've preferred you not take my arm rather than to engage in such a manner.'

She glared into his flashing eyes. 'I only took your arm out of pity, so I'm happy to release you.'

His words sliced the air between them. 'Please do.'

Meggy retracted her hand. Holbrook inclined his head without eye contact and joined Harry and Elizabeth. With false composure, Meggy walked between Sophy and Maria. The girls embraced her, but their hugs didn't calm her roiling stomach.

Perhaps she'd achieved her purpose, but the victory was inexplicably sour.

179

After luncheon, to appease Alexander, Nicholas arranged a tour of the century-old Ipswich medicinal gardens made famous by Dr Coyte. That eminent physician had died two years earlier, but his daughter maintained the gardens.

Nicholas trailed behind Meggy as they strolled along the garden paths. She peppered Miss Coyte with questions and exclaimed over the rare and exotic plants with Sophy, Maria and Elizabeth. The girls adored Meggy; they gazed at her as if she were an angel and patted the frothy muslin of her soft skirts.

Meggy was stunning, and her new gowns did justice to her beauty. Rose had spared no expense with the clothes, as Nicholas had instructed the day he'd arrived at Alton Park with Meggy and the children.

'Papa said that to you when we were children,' Nicholas reminded his sister when she'd visited his rooms shortly before dinner that evening. 'Do you recall? "Spare no expense, Rosy, when you dress your dolls."'

Rose smiled, her eyes glistening. 'I remember, Nicky.'

She put her arms around him. Nicholas almost sobbed against her lace cap as he thought of his papa, but instead, he breathed deeply. 'Well, I've brought you a doll to play with. Lady Margaret hasn't had an easy time of it. Take care of her, will you?'

Rose tilted her head back and placed a hand on his cheek. 'Of course. And may I also take care of *you*, Nicky?'

He laughed to hide his pain. 'I don't need taking care of, Rosy.'

She opened her mouth to say words he didn't want to hear, so he gently waved her away. 'Enough nonsense, sister. Put your energy into your new project. In fact, go now and see if she's comfortable.'

Powerful sentiments now swelled Nicholas's chest as the tip of Meggy's gloved finger alit upon the edge of an orchid bloom, and he silently forgave her for her hurtful behaviour in the ship's hull. She was young and innocent, and she couldn't possibly know the insecurity she'd evoked. Certainly, Meggy possessed healthy physical urges – she'd displayed as much – but she did *not* indulge that appetite unless nobler sentiments accompanied it.

She hadn't kissed Alexander.

She wouldn't have kissed the carpenters.

She'd kissed *Nicholas*, on that one perfect day when he'd earned her admiration.

After an hour at the gardens, little Charlotte – according to Rose – felt feverish. Miss Coyte suggested a variety of herbal remedies, but Rose, level-headed except when it came to her daughters' illnesses, wanted to return home.

Her anxiety over the child necessitated a change of seating for the journey. Rose insisted on travelling with Alexander and Charlotte's nurse in the closed carriage.

'I shall take Harry with me, in that case,' Nicholas said.

'No,' Rose said. 'Three adults and three children are too much for the landau. Meggy must ride with you in the curricle.'

Nicholas, surprised, observed his youngest niece more closely. She lay with her chubby cheek pressed against Rose's shoulder, one dimpled fist clutching at her mother's jacket, the other fist resting under her round chin. Charlotte looked sleepy, but there was no hint of fever – no glassy eyes, no flushed cheeks.

How thoughtful of Rose, Nicholas concluded. And, perhaps, of Alexander, who seemed most willing to perjure himself.

Meggy had avoided private conversation with Nicholas during the last fortnight, but an hour's tête-à-tête would allow him an opportunity to smooth the disastrous misunderstanding in the ship's hull, and perhaps he could at last convince her of his trustworthiness.

Meggy didn't talk as they began the journey. Nicholas, unwilling to push her into conversation but desperate to make the most of the opportunity, trotted the horses at a leisurely pace though the countryside, allowing the others to outstrip them. Shadows cast by the late afternoon light lengthened over the newly reaped fields as several miles passed without a word from her. Cattle lowed as they grazed; the sheep, their fleeces thickening again, were woolly clouds in the green and gold meadows; and the only traffic was an occasional farm waggon laden with produce.

After a half an hour of silence, Meggy spoke abruptly. 'Who receives your bills, Lord Holbrook?'

Nicholas replied with some difficulty. His heart had leapt to his throat at the sound of her voice. 'My what?'

'Your tradesmen's bills. I need to know, and neither Rose nor your housekeeper could tell me.'

'I receive them myself,' he said, puzzled. 'Why do you ask such a question?'

'I wish to see the bills I've incurred for myself and the children so I may pay them.'

Nicholas smiled. 'I shall pay your expenses whilst the children are in my care.'

'Most certainly you will not.' She snapped the words, like a whip lashing. 'I've spent a fortune on new gowns for London.'

Nicholas tried again. 'But I *want* to pay for you. As I told you, I want to be helpful.'

Meggy stomped a foot against the floor of the curricle. 'And yet the moment I ask for specific help – namely, for you to give me my bills so I may pay them – you refuse to give me what I ask for.'

She was clearly furious, and Nicholas recognised his defeat. 'When you put it in such a way, I really have no choice,' he said. 'I shall hand them over to you.'

Some of them.

She relaxed. 'Thank you.'

Her sincere tone bolstered Nicholas's hope. 'But as you wish to speak of financial matters, Lady Margaret,' – he turned the horses off the highway and onto a country lane – 'whilst I was in London, I met with my friend John Tyrold regarding the remnants of the Fairchild fortune. Tyrold's shockingly brilliant with

183

repairing and growing wealth – he's increased his own manyfold – and we diversified your investments—'

Meggy whipped her head around, her blue eyes burning like fire. 'You did *what*?'

Nicholas swallowed. 'Diversified your investments. Rather, diversified Harry's invest—'

'I don't want you making such decisions without me.'

'B-but you don't understand. I *must* make the decisions about Harry's fortune. It was precisely for this reason Edwin wanted a male guardian for the boy. As a woman, you haven't the legal—'

Her hands clenched into fists. 'I don't want you making any decisions regarding Harry without me. You must stop assuming you know how to help and *ask* instead. Why do you not understand this?'

Nicholas's spirits deflated.

Then, quite suddenly, Meggy pounded his left arm and shoulder with both her fists. 'You *infuriate* me, you horrid, pompous, beastly man! I think you must *plan* how you can most annoy me.'

She continued to batter him, rising in her seat to pummel him with considerable force, and Nicholas struggled with the reins. 'If you must beat me,' he said between blows, 'at least allow me to stop the team. I cannot drive under these conditions.'

Meggy plopped down on the seat and crossed her arms. 'I shan't beat you anymore. But you're as horrid a driver as you are a man.'

Nicholas laughed. 'I may be a horrid man, but I'm an extremely good driver.'

She huffed in an almost playful manner.

Nicholas pulled up the team. 'Can *you* drive better?'

Her eyes brightened. 'Indeed, I can. Move over.'

They switched places. Meggy took the reins in her small hands, and calling to the team, got them up to a trot.

'Gallop them,' Nicholas said, delighted with her skill.

She did. Nicholas, half smiling, settled back against the armrest. Although her bonnet brim shielded her face, there was plenty to admire. Her peach-coloured spencer hugged her full bosom, and her soft skirts flapped in the breeze.

She glanced at him.

He winked. 'Keep your eyes on the road, my dear.'

'You're distracting me.'

'How?'

'I can feel your eyes on me.'

He chuckled. 'If I don't have to drive, I shall enjoy the view.'

For two miles, Meggy raced the team along the narrow country lane. She managed difficult twists with skill, but at a blind curve in a forested strip between two fields, she suddenly called out, shrill and terrified. 'Pull them up for me!'

She strained with the reins, her shoulders tense and her arms shaking. She was in tremendous distress.

Nicholas threw his hands over hers and stopped the team.

Meggy trembled like a leaf, and Nicholas attempted to reassure her. 'You needn't make yourself miserable merely to prove a point. You're a wonderful driver. They're a spirited team – difficult for *me* to handle, and I have many years' experience over you.'

Her hands shook under his. 'I don't like blind curves . . . m-my m-mama d-died in an accident . . .' She released her hold on the reins and covered her ashen face.

Although Rose had mentioned it, Nicholas had forgotten. 'Oh, my sweet darling.' He embraced Meggy as he held the reins with one hand. She clung to his coat and burrowed her face into his chest, and Nicholas's heart swelled. 'There now, my lovely, brave girl.'

A farm waggon rounded the turn and ambled past as Nicholas held an unmoving Meggy. When the sounds of the waggon wheels had vanished down the lane, Meggy exhaled slowly and lifted her face.

Their gazes met for a moment.

And then her lips clasped his fervently. She drew her body up, brought her hands to Nicholas's head, and knocked off his hat as her fingers clawed into his hair. She was forceful, almost violent in her passion, and if not for the necessity of maintaining an awareness of the team, Nicholas would've joined her desperation in a moment.

As it was, he did the best he could one-handed. He drew his arm around her waist and pulled her to him, pressing his body against her push until they were like two opposing forces fighting for control. His erection was instant, painful, urgent, and when lack of air forced them to separate, his mouth still needed her, and he kissed her cheek, her brow, her chin, all sloppier than he intended, as she did the same to him. Her tongue flicked into the curves of his ear, and he groaned. 'Good God, Meggy—'

'*Lady Margaret!*' Her voice was husky, breathy as she sucked and nipped.

'You torture me.' He nuzzled his face into her neck, breathing in lavender combined with the natural, musky scent of her skin after a day in the sun. He kissed under the blue satin ribbons of her bonnet, and he kissed her soft curls as they spilled onto her shoulder. 'Lady Margaret, please acknowledge we have feelings for each other which we can no longer ignore.'

'I can ignore them,' she said. She drew herself up so she knelt on the seat, with one leg across Nicholas's lap, her soft thigh and skirts pressing against his erection. They kissed again, his tongue thrusting with the urgency his cock felt, her sweet tongue answering back.

And then she drew away, her face flushed, her lips swollen and red, her breasts heaving. 'I can ignore my feelings *most* of the time.' She crawled over his lap, returning to the passenger side of the curricle seat. 'I couldn't ignore them *then*, but I can now. You should drive on, or the others will wonder what's become of us.'

Nicholas's breath was ragged, and his eyes struggled to focus. He wanted to take her into a field and release the team – to hell with his curricle, if the horses wouldn't stay around – and have her, thus settling the matter. He would make her his wife, and he would do his damned best to be a good husband.

He *wanted* to, but he couldn't. Not yet.

He must be certain he was ready before he made another terrible mistake.

'Lady Margaret, *I* cannot ignore my feelings for you. I want this animosity between us to end so I may gauge the extent of my sentiments.'

'The extent of your sentiments?'

'Whether I should ask you . . .' He stopped. Saying more was tantamount to a proposal.

'*Yes?*'

'I feel I've said as much as I should at this time.'

Her cheeks reddened, and her nostrils flared. 'You cannot say more lest you raise hopes in my tender maiden breast? Hopes of being the wife of a notorious rake? There is absolutely no chance of that *ever* happening. When I marry, it won't be to a man I must share with every woman willing to spread her legs. He'll be mine alone.'

The team tossed and pulled at the reins, restless to move, but Nicholas held firm. 'I've not been with another woman since I met you.'

Meggy rolled her eyes. 'Slightly more than a month. My heart is aflutter.'

'You and your damned sarcasm again.' His body tensed as the tightness returned to his chest. She was devilishly irritating at times.

'How recently before me did you have a woman, I wonder?'

'If it was before you, what does it matter? I cannot be judged on anything I did before I met you.'

'I disagree. You've known me a few weeks – you lived nearly thirty years before that. If I were ever to consider a life with you, I'd want to know all about those thirty years because *that* is the man you truly are.' Her words chilled Nicholas. 'So how many days was it?' she asked.

'Good lord.'

'How many?'

He sighed, defeated. 'Three days, I think.'

'And what was her name?'

Nicholas's throat thickened. What *was* her name? Had he even known? He had only the vaguest recollection of a boring coupling, his thoughts more on his frustration with Edwin than on the woman gasping as he thrust.

'You don't know, do you, sir?'

'You took all thoughts of other women from my mind.'

Meggy recoiled. 'Is that supposed to flatter me? Lord Holbrook, you disgust me. Whatever you imagine you feel for me, you feel because you can't have me. You told me yourself that once you have what you want, you don't want it anymore.'

Nicholas swallowed.

'Ah, yes,' Meggy said. 'You agree with me. Now, let's have no more hints about your honourable intentions. I don't trust you any farther than I could throw you, and I shan't marry a man I can't trust.'

The horses pulled on the reins again. 'You're not indifferent to me, Lady Margaret.'

She met his gaze coolly. 'Everything you raise in me is entirely primal.'

'I don't believe that. When we play with the children together—'

She held up her hand to silence him. 'Then let me be perfectly clear about my feelings. I despise being indebted to you. I *sometimes* enjoy your company for brief moments, especially when we are with the children. I'm attracted to you physically, which I find *annoying*. However, you're the last man I'd ever marry. When I go to London, I shall meet a man whom I trust, whom I enjoy, who is *manageable*, and who attracts me. And you and I, sir, need never speak again. Now, can we please return to Alton Park?'

She crossed her arms under her breasts and turned her shoulder.

Nicholas stared at the leather straps of the reins falling across his hands. 'Search your heart, Lady Margaret. Are you so certain it feels nothing for me?'

'My *heart*?' she hissed, looking at Nicholas over her shoulder. Venom laced her eyes. 'Why would I search my heart? My mind informs my decisions, Lord Holbrook. A mind that looks for patterns; a mind that analyses information and forms predictions based on logic. A mind that is wholly and completely against you and all your ilk, sir. Now drive on or I shall get out and walk.'

She might as well have ripped out Nicholas's heart.

After only a moment's pause, he started the team at a breakneck pace. He held back impending tears by concentrating on driving whilst Meggy remained silent for the duration of the drive, with her body resolutely turned away from him.

But in the fleeting glimpse Nicholas caught of Meggy's face before she dashed up the front stairs at Alton Park, he thought he perceived slightly reddened blue eyes.

Perhaps there was hope.

As long as Nicholas made no more mistakes . . .

12

As the trees lost their leaves, and winter's chill cast silver-white frost over the fallow fields, Meggy's new life at Alton Park fell into a rhythm. Alexander returned to London, and Harry's tutor, a bewigged old scholar with twinkling eyes and a youthful fascination with life, arrived. Schoolroom adventures with Mr Davis included battle re-enactments, paper boat regattas on the river, and night-time excursions with the telescope.

Meanwhile, Meggy applied herself to her singing and dancing lessons, paid social calls with Rose, and began a correspondence with Holbrook's friend John Tyrold about finances.

And she *tried* to apply herself to receiving her new admirers.

Her most eligible suitor was a gentleman named Robinson, the owner of a prosperous estate twenty miles to the south. Though nearing forty, with sandy hair and a ruddy complexion, he wasn't unattractive, and he promised to be extremely manageable. His favourite phrase, besides the repetition of the word 'capital', was 'ladies know best'.

It grated on the nerves after a time.

One day in late January, Meggy sat alone with Mr Robinson in the music room, and after ten minutes of stuttering and stumbling over his words – and gulping three cups of coffee – he said, 'Lady Margaret, I hold you in the highest esteem. You're a capital lady.'

Meggy forced a smile. 'How kind.'

Mr Robinson's eyes lingered on her mouth and fell to her breasts. Neither were unfamiliar experiences for Meggy – even Holbrook still glanced, although when *his* gaze trailed along her body, it was like butter sliding across a hot pan – but she didn't currently have the patience for ogling. 'My eyes are on my face, Mr Robinson.'

He flushed scarlet. 'Oh, I say. Forgive me.'

'Of course.' She rose; he did as well, leaning towards her until his coffee breath warmed her face. Meggy drew back, but the sofa restricted her, so she bent awkwardly backwards. 'Mr Robinson, I've enjoyed our chat, but I ought—'

He grabbed her hand in his clammy one. 'My lady, I have something of importance to say to you. Ever since I met you, I've thought you awfully pretty. Then last week after we dined here, my mother told me I'd do well to marry an earl's daughter, even though your dowry is depleted. Now I've always said that ladies know best, and there's much sense in what Mother says.' He eagerly leaned closer, and a trickle of sweat dripped down his temple. 'Mine isn't an old family, and our fortune was made in trade. By birth you are above me, but as Mother said, there are advantages to the match for you. I've four thousand a year—'

Meggy oughtn't flaunt eligible proposals, and yet she was far from ready to give serious consideration to a man who proposed because his mother suggested it. She was struggling to compose words that would neither encourage nor discourage Mr Robinson when Rose and Holbrook entered.

'Mr Robinson, I hoped you'd not left yet.' Rose spoke as if there was nothing odd about that gentleman grasping Meggy's hand as Meggy leaned backwards over a sofa. 'I want your opinion on my new riding mare. Holbrook says she's a daisy cutter, and doesn't pick up her legs at a canter, but I think she's a rum prancer and *quite* the prettiest thing I ever saw. Do come and settle the debate, please. No one is as good a judge of horseflesh as you are.'

Meggy maintained a serious demeanour with the greatest difficulty whilst Holbrook stood as impassive as a statue beside Rose.

Robinson, mouth ajar and scarlet forehead covered in a damp sheen, looked between the occupants of the room. 'At this moment, Lady Rose?'

Rose smiled. 'Unless it's quite inconvenient.'

Holbrook's lips twitched, and his grey eyes twinkled at Meggy. She bit her bottom lip to refrain from giggling.

Robinson gaped. 'I . . . I . . .'

Meggy suppressed her merriment. 'Do go with Lady Rose, Mr Robinson. We can continue our conversation another day.'

'Er . . . yes . . . that is to say . . . yes, yes. Ladies know best, of course. Capital! Capital! We shall continue another day, as you say, Lady Margaret.'

Meggy collapsed onto the sofa when Rose and Robinson departed. A grin spread across Holbrook's face, and Meggy laughed. 'Stop it. You said yourself I cannot afford to be choosy, and at least he has all his teeth. So, be gone with you, Lord Holbrook.'

The marquess raised his eyebrows. 'What have *I* done to deserve banishment? I said nothing until this moment.'

'You didn't have to. I understood your thoughts perfectly.'

He laughed. 'Did you? Have you reached such an elevated level of understanding you can read my mind? I wish the same were true for me.'

'Oh, nonsense.' But Meggy, heart aflutter, wished she could think of a wittier reply.

Holbrook approached her. He tugged gently at the flounced short sleeve of her pink and white striped silk gown, and Meggy's skin tingled although he hadn't touched her arm. 'This is lovely,' he said.

She was so breathless that it was difficult to speak, but she managed a few words. 'Your sister chose it.'

'I'm not surprised.' His hand still hovered near Meggy; his perfect fingers frozen as if waiting for deployment. 'Are you all right? Did Robinson trouble you?'

Meggy wanted to clasp Holbrook's hand and pull him down on top of her. She wanted him to kiss her breasts as she wrapped her arms and legs around his hard body, because, despite the impossibility of ever accepting a man so certain to be unfaithful, Meggy hungered for his touch. They'd not given in to their passion since the trip home from Ipswich – although it smouldered almost tangibly between them on occasion – nor had Holbrook made any overtures about courting Meggy again.

He'd behaved, she had to admit, like a proper gentleman. Like a *friend*. Meggy frequently wanted to respond in kind, but it had become a habit to pretend she despised him. She wasn't certain how to change the habit, and she wasn't certain she wanted to. If she stopped pretending she loathed Holbrook, her last defence would drop – and how soon then until she fell completely under his spell?

'He troubled me less than *you* trouble me,' she said.

Holbrook dropped his hand. 'If he'd troubled you more than I do, I'd take a horsewhip to him.'

Meggy laughed despite herself. 'I don't let anyone else trouble me like you do.'

'I should hope not, my dear.' His hand reached. Again, it halted and waited.

A deafening silence filled the room. The ticking of a pendulum clock in the next chamber echoed.

Meggy spoke contrary to her will. 'I did ask you to leave.'

'You did.'

'And yet you're still here.'

His hand hovered one moment more, and then he dropped it. 'Very well, I shall make myself scarce. After all, ladies know best.' He grinned.

As his broad back turned into the great hall, Meggy closed her eyes.

If only Holbrook were all he seemed at some times. If only Meggy could trust him.

Three days later, Robinson's voice floated from the entrance hall to the crimson drawing room where Meggy and Rose sat.

Rose's grey eyes widened over her embroidery. 'Do you know your answer?'

Meggy placed her book aside, grimacing. 'Lord, no. I've tried not to think about it.'

'Then *go*. Quickly, before he's announced. I shall say you're indisposed. Go through Nicky's office into the library, and you can flee upstairs whilst Robinson is with me.'

Holbrook's office, as Rose termed it, was an ante-chamber between the drawing room and the library. A masculine room with oak wainscotting and paintings of hunting scenes, it was where Holbrook retreated to answer correspondence or speak with his steward. Meggy intended to walk through it as Rose suggested; instead, she hesitated once she'd closed the door behind her.

The room *felt* like the marquess. Handsome, orderly, manly; the faintest hint of rich tobacco from the cigars Holbrook smoked on rare occasions. An entirely pleasurable shiver ran down Meggy's spine as her eyes swept the chamber.

A stack of unanswered correspondence lay to one side of Holbrook's large oak desk, a tidy pile of answered correspondence lay on the other. Between them were writing instruments: a row of trim quills and a penknife; an H-embossed silver writing service which included an inkwell and a container of blotting sand; a stick of red sealing wax; and a tray of crisp ivory paper.

Meggy stepped closer to the desk, overwhelmed with an urge to discover with whom Holbrook corresponded. Heart pounding, she sat in the leather-upholstered seat. The smell of paper, ink, wood, and the faint scent of Holbrook's bergamot fragrance enticed her as she looked through his letters. All were addressed in his sloping hand; they bore his frank across the front and the seal of his signet ring in red wax on the back.

And all were written to gentlemen.

Meggy sighed, inexplicably relieved.

She restacked the letters and slid her hands over the smooth desktop. She hesitated a moment, and then she slowly opened the middle drawer of the desk. Its contents were unexciting but beautifully tidy: stacked blotting paper; more red rectangular prisms of wax; and a perfect row of unused quills.

The side drawers revealed boxes labelled with the names of Holbrook's estates in Kent, Rutland and Norfolk. Another was labelled Holbrook House – the townhouse in Mayfair – and a final box contained investment papers. Parliamentary correspondence filled one drawer, and, in the first somewhat disorderly part of the desk, a stack of newspaper clippings related to the war in the Americas and various other political concerns.

Meggy closed the last drawer. Holbrook's diligence was powerfully attractive. She breathed the marquess's faint scent again as she smoothed her fingers over the satin wood. A thrill ran up her arm and settled in her breasts. Meggy squirmed on the leather chair. She throbbed between her legs; and a little spark of pleasure – just a hint – shot up when she clenched the muscles in her private place.

Again, she slid her hand across the wood. This time, she imagined Holbrook laying her upon it, his trousers tented as they'd been that evening at The George in Huntingdon. She envisioned him undoing his buttons, pulling up her skirts, bringing her bottom to the edge of the desk, right by *this* corner . . .

Meggy's hand paused, and the daydream slipped away. The outside of the top-right drawer was taller than the interior had suggested. Brow furrowed, she investigated further. There was a drawer within a drawer, not visible unless one looked for it.

Breathless, Meggy pulled it out.

The drawer contained a collection of miniature portraits laid upon red velvet. Maria, Elizabeth and Charlotte; Rose as a very young lady, and a man with Holbrook's curling lips, recognisable at once as Rose and Nicholas's father. Portraits of him hung throughout the house.

And an exquisitely beautiful young woman. Unfamiliar, and yet Meggy knew instinctively who it must be. With her heart pounding, she picked the portrait up. Its gold frame rested heavy in the palm of her hand.

Holbrook's wife possessed a delicate, heart-shaped face with lips like a pink rosebud, large dark eyes, and rich blonde hair without a trace of brown or brass. No freckles marred a porcelain complexion, and her nose was straight perfection, rather than small and somewhat upturned.

Meggy, mesmerised, couldn't put the painting down.

The frame was a locket, and the inside contained golden hair woven into a true love's knot, and a dark, feathery wisp tied with a strand of embroidery silk. A lock of infant hair from a dark-haired baby, too fine to weave or braid, and added later – undoubtedly by a grieving father.

A lump formed in Meggy's throat. She closed the frame and turned it over. Inscribed on the back were the words: *'To my dearest Cole from his Bella'.*

Meggy's eyes blurred as she lay the miniature on its velvet bed. Here was Holbrook's true love: the beautiful wife whose untimely death – in the very act of trying to give Holbrook a son – drove him to a wild, reckless grief.

Meggy could never replace that kind of love.

She closed the drawers, fled Holbrook's office, dashed across the library and the entrance hall, and ran up the stairs two at a time, until she arrived at her room. She stood by the bay window, tears flowing down her cheeks, and hugged herself as she looked out on the bleak landscape towards the Dedham Vale.

For the first time, Meggy acknowledged the full extent of Holbrook's presence in her heart.

13

The next day dawned bright with a fresh blanket of snow. Meggy bundled up in her blue velvet pelisse and went for an early morning walk to clear her mind. She'd passed the night in restless confusion, wondering about her feelings for the marquess.

Copper accompanied her. He snuffled in the snow and dashed in circles, his long ears flapping. When the novelty wore off, he trotted beside her past the stable blocks and the fallow kitchen gardens and onto the east lawn. Meggy's leather boots crunched through the snow, leaving the first marks on the pristine pillow, but the glare of the sun on the expansive white lawn stung her eyes. She changed her course.

On the south side of the lawn, a footpath led from Alton Park to the village of Longford. Ancient, red-barked yews, their evergreen boughs cradling snowy clumps, shaded the walkway. Despite the early hour, Meggy and Copper's were not the first footfalls on the heavily traversed path.

When Meggy approached the low stone wall of the parish churchyard, she discovered one source of the footprints. Holbrook stood amongst the Burton graves, his back to Meggy, and his tall-crowned black hat tilted towards a stone monument with two carved angels. A dark blue greatcoat fell to his mid-calves, and his gloved hands, holding his walking stick, were clasped behind his back.

Meggy's heart hammered. She'd intruded on a private moment. After months of solitary rambles, she knew the tombs in the churchyard, and Holbrook was at his wife's grave. Meggy would've fled back to Alton Park, but Copper barked a greeting to Caesar.

Holbrook turned.

His eyes were red-rimmed, his cheeks damp, his lips turned down. But with a shake of his head, he tipped his hat and bowed. 'Good morning, Lady Margaret.' His breath clouded in the winter air.

'Good morning, Lord Holbrook.' Meggy's voice wavered. In her months at Alton Park, he'd never appeared to pay any notice to his wife's grave. Of course, he came alone to mourn.

Holbrook cleared his throat. 'On a walk?'

'Yes.'

'Are you going into the village?'

'I was . . . wandering, I suppose. No purpose in mind.' *Other than to think about you*, Meggy added to herself.

He extracted a handkerchief from his pocket and wiped his cheeks. 'In that case, may I join you?'

'Oh!' Breathless. 'Yes, yes, I suppose so.'

They met at the churchyard gate. Caesar and Copper exchanged sniffs and leaps, and Holbrook offered his arm to Meggy. She slipped a gloved hand out of her fur muff and rested it in the crook of his elbow. The fresh scent of winter morning clung to him, and his body radiated heat through his greatcoat. Meggy shivered.

'Are you cold, Lady Margaret?'

'A little, perhaps.' But the shiver wasn't from the weather.

'You don't wish to turn back?'

'No, the snow is lovely.'

'It is. I agree.'

They walked to the village green. The fragrant smoke of coal and wood fires wafted from the brick chimneys of the trim, shingled cottages. Several boys threw snowballs at each other, but the play paused in their presence.

'We should have a snowball fight with the children this afternoon, perhaps,' Holbrook said. His earlier tears had thickened his voice.

'They would like that.' They passed the last straggling houses of the village and crossed the wooden bridge over the Stour tributary. Beyond was the expanse of the communal pastures. Cows and sheep huddled together, chewing the hay thrown out by the farmers. 'Lord Holbrook, I'm sorry I intruded on your privacy.'

Holbrook released a long breath. 'There's no need to apologise. I'm not often in such a miserable condition, but it's rather a difficult anniversary for me, I'm afraid.'

Meggy recalled an early February death date on Lady Holbrook's monument. 'Is today the day your wife died?'

A pause elapsed before Holbrook replied. 'Yes.'

Their footsteps crunched in unison through the snow as they crossed the pasture and came upon the road that led to the main branch of the Stour. 'D-do you wish to talk about it?'

His next inhalation was ragged, and Meggy peeked from under the short brim of her velvet capote bonnet. He was crying.

'Oh, Lord Holbrook.' She pressed into his arm.

He grasped her hand on his elbow and squeezed. Again, he released a slow breath. 'I'm afraid I'm rather pathetic at times.'

'That's perfectly understandable.'

At the river, they turned towards Alton Park and walked without speech until they reached the ha-ha which separated the parklands from the pastures and fields. The ha-ha was much too high to climb, but a path ran along the wall to the wilderness gardens at the back of the house. In this relatively private space, hidden from view of the house and gardens, Meggy stopped. 'I feel badly I haven't been kinder to you, Lord Holbrook.'

The fresh air had cleared the traces of his crying, but his eyes didn't have their customary liveliness. 'Please, don't pity me.'

'But why?'

'Because I neither deserve it nor appreciate it. Your brother Edwin was inclined to pity me, and I never forgave him for it. He'd adopt an expression like *this*' – Holbrook drew his brows into a peak and turned down his bottom lip – 'whenever he saw me. Used to make me want to beat him. Upon no account *ever* show me such an expression, Lady Margaret.'

She smiled. 'But you wouldn't beat me.'

'No, I certainly would not. It's *you* who beats *me*. You've done so on two occasions already.'

Meggy dropped her gaze. A solitary pearl pin nestled within the folds of Holbrook's cravat. She took a step closer and met Holbrook's eyes again. 'I've been beastly to you. Forgive me.'

Holbrook lifted his brows. 'You're making Edwin's pitying expression right now.'

'I'm not – and anyway, it's not pity.' It was so much more than that.

His head cocked. 'Hmm.'

Meggy laughed. 'Truthfully, I'm in earnest.'

'Oh, very well, then,' he laughed. 'I forgive you for your general beastliness, but not for beating me. Truth be told, I enjoyed that.'

Meggy's cheeks warmed, despite the chill air.

'Come, my dear,' he said, gently leaning towards the house. 'You'll be cold if we stand still too long. Your velvet pelisse is fetching, but it cannot be warm.'

Meggy tightened her grip on his elbow and stood her ground. 'I'm not cold. Not much, anyway.' Holbrook stood still, watching her quizzically. 'May I ask you a question, Lord Holbrook?'

He narrowed his eyes. 'You may *ask*. I don't promise to answer.'

Meggy studied her gloved fingers on his arm. She

stroked the fine blue wool as she gathered her nerve. 'How did Edwin save your life?'

'Oh!' His eyes softened; his mouth relaxed.

'I've long wondered, and I should like to know some good of Edwin.'

'It's rather a horrid story, I'm afraid.' Holbrook studied the toe of his boot as he packed the snow with his foot. 'But your brother appears in a good light.'

'Please tell me?'

He sighed. 'Very well, but don't tell Rosy.' Holbrook frowned and continued to examine the ground as he began. 'I have . . . rather a tendency towards melancholia, I suppose you might say. I keep it well hidden – at least, I *think* I do – but it's there, and it's been there my whole life. Perhaps it started because I found my mother difficult, or perhaps it's simply woven into my character. I don't know. But I do know I loved my father dearly, and whilst he lived, he always knew what to say to help me feel better. I was fourteen when he died, and Rose and my guardianship fell to our paternal uncle. *That* man, I'm afraid, was not the guardian he ought to have been, and . . . well, I found myself in rather a terrible state after a few years.'

Holbrook paused, now gazing towards the river, his mouth set, and Meggy waited breathlessly for him to continue. 'On the evening of . . . an important day, I became quite miserably unhappy, and it seemed as though I'd never recover from the depths of despair. I left my house – I was in London at the time – and went to . . . various places, and I drank, and with each drink, my misery increased. By the middle of the night, I was very drunk, and I was very alone. I stumbled along the Strand, past the Temple Bar, and onto Fleet Street, hardly aware of where I was, placing one foot in front of the other, swigging a bottle of brandy as I staggered.'

Holbrook's grey eyes locked with Meggy's. A flicker of mocking amusement gleamed. 'Do you know where my pathetic tale is leading?'

'It's not pathetic. It's heart-wrenching.'

Holbrook placed his free hand on top of Meggy's at his elbow. He rubbed her fingers between his own, and powerful emotions swelled Meggy's heart. 'A fog had settled in by the time I got to New Bridge Street, and my eyes were drawn to . . . well, you haven't been to London so you wouldn't know, but there's an obelisk at that junction, and at night it's lit with hanging street-lights. Those lamps seemed like heavenly halos in the dark haze. And then I thought of Blackfriars Bridge at the end of the street, and I thought of the Thames. I've always enjoyed water – swimming, sailing, sea-bathing, rowing – and the idea of a watery grave appealed to me. I stumbled towards the river, congratulating myself on the simplicity of the solution. I decided I'd make my death look like a robbery, so Rosy wouldn't be ashamed. There was a boy, perhaps twelve years old, poverty-stricken, with two little siblings clinging to him – the only people out, as far as I could tell. I tried to give him everything of value I had, but he'd only take my money and the brandy, saying he'd hang for anything else. He was frightened, the poor child, and he grasped the coins and the bottle and fled into the mists. After he left, I staggered to the middle of the bridge, crying some, but mostly filled with determination. One by one, I threw my valuable possessions into the Thames. My father's pocket watch, a diamond cravat pin, the original signet ring of the first marquess, nearly three hundred years old – the one I wear now is a replica, but Rosy doesn't know. I kept only one thing to identify my body. Something I once thought was my most prized possession, but that very day its value had become nothing at all to me, and I wanted that despised object – the cause of my misery, as I saw it – to identify my swollen corpse.'

Meggy blinked, and a tear fell from the corner of one eye. Holbrook observed it with a frown. 'No pity, my dear.'

'You aren't fair,' she said ardently. 'How can I feel nothing as you tell me such a story?'

He wiped away the tear with his thumb. 'I don't believe I deserve it, Lady Margaret. You were fourteen when you were left with an undesirable guardian and great responsibilities, and yet *you* never gave in to drink and despair.'

'Yes, but I had the children. I was too busy, too *needed*, to give a thought to myself.'

'And now that you aren't so busy? Do you languish or engage in self-destruction?'

'No, but you aren't fair to yourself, Lord Holbrook. You don't account for other differences.' *Your wife, your child* – but Meggy didn't voice those thoughts. 'Please continue.'

Holbrook sighed. 'I looked over the bridge to the fog swirling below. I imagined that falling into it would be like falling into a cloud, and I longed for that. But I had to make my death look like a murder, so I climbed upon the stone side and stood backwards with the heels of my boots over the edge and a knife to my neck. My idea, you see, was to slit my throat and fall over so my corpse would later be mistaken for that of a victim tossed into the river. But as I made to plunge the knife, both of my legs were seized, and I was pulled down onto the bridge. I struggled with my saviour in the fog, and escaped, but my knife had slipped from my hand when he grabbed me, and it was lost. As I scrambled to find it, my saviour grasped my coat and said, "Dammit, it's never as bad as that."

'Of course, you know it was your brother. He'd not recognised me when he first saved me, but he recognised me then, and I him, and he was surprised – for, as I mentioned, it had been an important day which no one would've expected to end in my suicide. We looked at each other for a time, until at last he said, "At least, if it is as bad as that, don't kill yourself whilst you're drunk. Come home with me and sleep off the drink, and if you want to die in the morning, after a good breakfast and plenty of coffee, I shan't stop you."'

Holbrook played with Meggy's fingers again, his brow creased. 'Things didn't look much better in the morning, but my mind was clearer, and I realised killing myself would've played into my enemy's hand.

I determined not to do that, at least. I stayed with your brother for many days – he still had the townhouse on Berkeley Square at the time – and when I at last went home, although I was no happier, I remembered Edwin's advice: I decided if I were going to kill myself, I'd do it sober. That's saved my life a few times.' He chuckled joylessly. 'So, there you have it, Lady Margaret – my debt to your brother explained. But I ask you once more not to pity me. I don't want pity from anyone, but certainly not from you.' He squeezed her hand.

Meggy stepped closer and searched his face. His grey eyes were unreadable. 'What about my friendship, Lord Holbrook? Do you still want that?'

He rubbed the tips of her fingers with his thumb. 'I've made myself ridiculous begging for your friendship, but I don't want it if it merely stems from pity.'

'But it doesn't,' Meggy said, desperate for him to understand. 'I *do* want to be your friend, but I haven't known how to break myself of the habit of pretending I despise you.'

'Pretending?' Holbrook's eyes shone, alert and focused. 'Has it indeed been pretence? For how long?'

Meggy scrunched her nose. 'It's far too embarrassing to admit.'

His face softened, and his lips widened into the same sweet smile he gave to Rose and the children. 'Well, I shan't push you to tell me then.'

Holbrook whispered the words tenderly, and they hung between them like the mingling clouds of their breath. So intimate was the moment that Meggy would've closed her eyes and offered a kiss, but the spectre of heart-faced Arabella hovered in the cold air.

'Come,' Holbrook said, 'shall we see if the scamps want a snowball fight after breakfast?'

Meggy shivered. 'Yes – hopefully, breakfast will warm me.'

'Poor darling, I knew you were cold.' Holbrook slipped off his greatcoat and hung it like a cloak around her shoulders, tucking the lapels into one another under her chin. It reminded Meggy of being snuggled into bed years ago by her mother – a secure, warm, comforting, *loved* feeling. 'Is that better?'

Meggy couldn't speak, but she nodded. With her hands under the coat, she couldn't hold his arm, but they walked side-by-side back to the house. She pressed her nose against the fine wool, and the smell of bergamot and spice, fresh air and winter chill infused her with a warmth so intense her heart ached.

14

A magical month followed at Alton Park.

Or very nearly so.

There were just enough hints of Holbrook's past promiscuity to remind Meggy of the risks of following her heart. The most generous supplier of these intimations was Lady Harradine, a widowed, son-less baronet's wife who lived nearby in her brother-in-law's care. The black-haired and catlike widow was over forty, but she was alluring. She didn't merely flirt with Holbrook, like other ladies; she oozed invitation. She whispered to him behind her fan. She caressed him – a hand under Holbrook's coat, breasts pressed against his arm – as she flickered smug smiles at Meggy.

Whilst playing whist at one of Rose's evening card parties, Lady Harradine's elbow brushed against Meggy's hand. When Meggy bent down to retrieve a dropped card, the widow's stockinged foot ran *all* the way up the inside of Holbrook's thigh under the table and came to a rest fully against his crotch. Meggy's stomach heaved, and she couldn't look at the marquess.

The day after the card party, Meggy was snappish for the first time in weeks.

That evening they neither entertained nor went out. Rose vanished soon after dinner to reply to a letter from her husband, and the governesses and Mr Davis retired early. Meggy and Holbrook remained in the crimson drawing room.

Meggy, curled on a sofa with her legs tucked under her white silk skirts, read an engrossing treatise on aerial navigation whilst Holbrook, also reading, lounged in an armchair closer to the crackling fire.

Sometime after ten, Meggy sensed his eyes on her, and she peered over her book. The marquess's legs stretched out upon a footstool, and his head rested against the upholstered back of his chair. He still held his book, but he smiled tenderly at Meggy.

Meggy's breath caught. 'What?'

He shook his head. 'Nothing at all.'

'Why do you stare at me, then?'

'Because I love to look at you.'

'Oh!' Meggy's heart leapt. 'Well, go back to your book. I cannot read when you look at me.'

Holbrook nodded obediently. 'As you wish.'

But after reading the same paragraph three times with no greater understanding of the second obstacle in the way of aerial navigation, Meggy again glanced over her book at Holbrook. He looked up, held her gaze with a small smile, and then winked. 'Ready to build a flying machine? Or are you reading that merely to impress Harry's tutor?'

She narrowed her eyes. 'Bah! Why should I care to impress Mr Davis?'

Holbrook placed a hand beside his mouth, as if telling a secret. 'Given your penchant for old men, I thought perhaps . . . you know.' He waggled his eyebrows.

'You're *not* amusing.' But she giggled. 'What are *you* reading?'

'Marlowe's poetry.'

Meggy crinkled her nose. 'I find poetry remarkably dull.'

Holbrook placed a hand over his heart and blinked. '*Dull*? May I attempt to change your mind?'

Meggy pursed her lips. 'You may *attempt* it, I suppose.'

Holbrook opened his book. When he spoke, his words were honey. '*Come live with me and be my <u>love</u> . . .*'

On the word 'love' he lifted his eyes to Meggy's. She gasped involuntarily, and her heart thudded a pounding rhythm in her chest.

Holbrook smiled and continued.

> '*. . . And we will <u>all</u> the pleasures prove,*
> *That Valleys, groves, hills, and fields,*
> *Woods, or steepy mountain yields.*
>
> *And we will sit upon the Rocks,*
> *Seeing the Shepherds feed their flocks,*
> *By shallow Rivers to whose falls*
> *Melodious birds sing Madrigals.*'

Again, he raised his eyes.

> '*And I will make thee beds of Roses . . .*'

Meggy couldn't breathe until his glance returned to the page.

> '. . . And a thousand fragrant posies,
> A cap of flowers, and a kirtle
> Embroidered all with leaves of Myrtle;
>
> A gown made of the finest wool
> Which from our pretty Lambs we pull;
> Fair lined slippers for the cold,
> With buckles of the purest gold;
>
> A belt of straw and Ivy buds,
> With Coral clasps and Amber studs:
> And if these pleasures may thee move,
> Come live with me, and be my love.'

Holbrook recited the last verse from memory, his eyes locked with Meggy's.

> 'The Shepherds' Swains shall dance and sing
> For thy delight each May-morning:
> If these delights thy mind may move,
> Then _live_ with _me_ . . . and be my _love_.'

Meggy, incapable of movement, could only stare.

Other than the whisper of the fire, silence reigned until Holbrook spoke again. 'Was that _dull_?'

'I . . . I . . .' Meggy blinked, broke their eye contact, and licked her dry lips. 'Yes, terribly dull.'

An utter lie – and Holbrook knew it, for he grinned slowly. 'Then please read me some of yours.'

'You won't understand it.'

'Allow me to try?'

Meggy opened her book. '*The act of flying is continually exhibited to our view; and the principles upon which it is effected are the same as those before stated. If an attentive observer examines the waft of a wing—*'

'The what of a wing, my darling?'

'The *waft.*'

'Ah yes, how the wing flows through the air, I presume.'

'Yes. Well done.' She continued. '. . . *he will perceive, that about one third part, toward the extreme point, is turned obliquely backward; this being the only portion, that has velocity enough to overtake the current, passing so rapidly beneath it, when in this unfavourable position. Hence this is the only portion that gives any propelling force.*' Meggy looked up. 'Do you wish for me to continue?'

Holbrook lifted his brows. 'My darling, I'm riveted. You may read to me about propelling force all night.'

Meggy's face burned. 'You're making it improper.' She didn't dislike it.

He grinned. 'Please continue.'

She placed the book on a nearby table. 'I don't want to.' But she looked at him through her lashes and smiled.

He tilted his head. 'Did I offend you earlier today?'

Only then did Meggy recall she'd been irritated about the widow. 'No.'

'Yesterday then?'

Meggy twisted her hands. 'Never mind. Forget about it.'

He removed his legs from the footrest, leaned forward, and rested his elbows on his knees. 'Please tell me what I did. I thought you'd bite my head off this morning.'

She chewed her bottom lip. 'I didn't like . . .'

'Yes?'

'Lady Harradine . . . stroking your leg.'

'*Ah*. I wondered if you perhaps saw that.'

Meggy scowled. 'You are so dispassionate?'

He held up his palms. 'I didn't invite her touch, and it was entirely unwelcome. Nor did I return her advances in any way.'

Meggy softened. 'Truthfully? But have you ever returned her advances?'

'My sweet darling, can it not be enough for you to know I could never think about a Lady Harradine now that I've met Lady Margaret? Do you truly have no idea of the strength of my feelings for you?'

Her heart pummelled her chest. 'I . . . I'm uncertain what to think about anything, Lord Holbrook.'

'Then let me assure you I have eyes and feelings for one lady, and one lady only, and *you* are that lady.'

'Oh!' She was breathless again.

Holbrook crossed the room, sat beside her on the sofa, and offered his arm. Meggy hesitated only a moment before snuggling into his embrace, her legs still curled under her, her cheek against his shoulder, his chin on her head. He held her, not passionately, but securely – his arms solid and sure shelter.

She sighed.

He matched her deep breath, and after they both exhaled, Meggy slipped her free arm under his coat and around the silk waistcoat covering his hard chest. She closed her eyes. Her arm rose and fell with his breath.

The moment lasted forever.

Holbrook kissed the top of Meggy's head. 'May I *please* stop calling you Lady Margaret?'

She smiled into his shoulder. 'What will you call me instead?'

'My dearest love. My darling, beloved Meggy.'

His words stole her breath. 'Am I that?'

'You are indeed. Do you mind that I feel that way?'

There were a million butterflies fluttering inside her. 'No, but . . .'

'But what, Meggy?'

She answered honestly. 'But it feels like a dream, Lord Holbrook.'

'Ah, I agree. A long-awaited dream, on my part.' His lips brushed the curls on her forehead. 'Please stop calling me Lord Holbrook, my love.'

'What shall I call you instead?' *To my dearest Cole . . .*

'Nicky?'

Meggy didn't understand why her heart fell. She hadn't wanted him to say Cole, of course, but for some reason, she wanted a name of hers alone to call him, just as his wife had.

She shook her head.

'No? Nick, then? Or Nicholas?'

'No.'

'I'm afraid I'm out of options.'

Meggy forced a laugh. 'Holbrook it shall be then. I shall drop the "Lord" to celebrate our new terms of familiarity.'

'If you insist, I shan't object. But call me it with feeling.'

'How do I do that?'

'Try this: my darling Holbrook.'

She nestled deeper into his shoulder. 'My *darling* Holbrook.' Her voice was muffled.

'That was a good start. But can you look at me when you say it, Meggy?'

Her breath came shallow and rapid. Never had he been so handsome: his grey eyes full of tender feeling and his lips soft and curling, with no hint of mockery.

'My darling Holbrook.' Meggy smothered a rising panic – was she committing herself without thinking? – and allowed herself to relish the moment.

His smile vanished. 'Yes.' His voice was husky. 'That's lovely.'

Meggy's gaze fell to his mouth, and her eyes were too heavy to keep open. She parted her lips and tilted her chin up, hoping, trusting he would take the lead.

He did. She gasped when his lips clasped hers, for it was not like before. It was a soothing balm over a wound – comfort for an ache, a longing, a burning want. His tongue slipped hot and firm into her mouth, and she opened for him, wanting all of him in her, wanting to take him deep into her body, wanting to feel as one with him. All reason floated away with her body's urges.

His fingers were in her hair, threading in her curls, cradling her head, and she reclined, trusting he would hold her, trusting he would come with her. He lay her onto the silk of the sofa and leaned over, the length of his body above her but his weight not pressed into her. She was liquid, flowing into the upholstery, flowing under him until they aligned; her legs parted and his slipped between, her hips sought connection. The impossibly hard length of his erection pressed in that place that ached most desperately. Although her skirts and his trousers were between them, there was torturous pleasure as he rubbed her. She moved her hips in rhythm with his, but with each rock, she sought him with more desperation. Her hands slipped down the linen back of his waistcoat until they came to a rest over the muscular curve of his bottom. And then she gripped. She lifted her hips higher, pushing against him.

'Oh, God, Meggy.' His words were harsh, guttural, pained. His lips kissed down her neck, into the cleavage of her breasts above her low-cut bodice.

She fumbled at the waist of his trousers, trying to release him, as she'd done in her vague but passionate dreams. Her desire flamed so intensely she was almost angry. 'You started a burning ache in me, and you need to soothe it.' The buttons were too complicated; she gripped his thick cock through his trousers.

He groaned. 'Yes, I shall, but not here. Come, my love.'

Holbrook stood and offered his hand.

And Meggy, suddenly terrified, widened her eyes. 'B-but not . . . not . . .' She didn't have the words.

Although she hadn't said anything coherent, he replied. 'I know, Meggy. Trust me.'

After only a second's pause, Meggy clasped his hand, and he led her from the room.

15

Nicholas led Meggy to the State Bedroom. It was the nearest bedchamber, rarely used, and no one would think to look for either of them there.

When he entered the dark room, he put down the candle in his hand. Then he closed the door and pressed Meggy against it, desperate to feel her body against his again. Her kisses were nectar, her taste as sweet as syrup; they were life-giving water in the desert; they were fire and passion. He was consumed with ardent need to have her, to satiate his lust and hers. But he also wanted to make adoring, reverent love to her – to *Meggy*, who'd become the greatest hope of his heart.

He pulled away. Though wild with desire, his tender sentiments reigned. He wouldn't hurt her, and he couldn't *have* her. Not really, not completely, not *yet*.

But she must be satisfied – *now* – and that he would do.

Afterwards, if she seemed receptive, Nicholas would ask Meggy the question he'd been yearning to ask.

Meggy clung to his arm. Nicholas knew her passion was feverish. Driven by instinct, fed by need, and – he hoped – fuelled by love. He moved the candle to the bedside and drew back the bed curtains. A feather duvet with a white cotton sheet covered the mattress. It would do. Nicholas kissed Meggy again, but tenderly, concentrating on her taste, the feel of her lips, the silkiness of her tongue. He allowed her to explore his mouth as much as he explored hers. She moaned, threaded her fingers in his hair, and pushed herself against him.

Nicholas broke from her sweet mouth to turn her so he could unlace her gown. He kissed her curls and the back of her neck, for he didn't need to see his hands to untie a lady's gown. He twisted gently, and the silk fell with a rustle to her feet.

He repeated the action with the stays. Laces loose, straps pulled off her shoulders, and the silly thing slipped down and joined the dress. Her petticoat followed. Nicholas rubbed his hands down Meggy's back, kneading and stroking over her cotton chemise. She leaned over the mattress, her bottom pressing into his erection, her moans soft. He cupped her luscious breasts. Her nipples were erect, poking against the delicate fabric, and he rubbed the nubs until she panted with rapid breaths. 'Holbrook, I need you.'

Nicholas's skin burned; his cock ached.

But this moment was entirely about Meggy.

Nicholas had imagined her body, dreamt about it, pleasured himself to the thought of it, and tonight, he would worship it. He turned her around, kissed her slowly, gently, achingly on the lips whilst cupping her breasts. He slid his hands to her waist, over the curves of her hips, and onto her round, lush bottom. And then he inched her chemise up until he could grip her bare skin, smooth and taut, as Meggy breathed hot against his cheek. He worked his way up her curves, and then, pulling away from her just enough, he slipped her chemise over her head.

Nicholas drank in the sight of her nude body in the flickering candlelight: full, shapely breasts, a belly rounded as a woman's should be, a dark feathery triangle between her legs. He lay her on the bed. Her fingers gripped him as she tried to pull him with her. He couldn't leave her aching for long. She must be satisfied, but a little more torture first would bring her pleasure to a more intense release. He trailed his fingertips over her body, from her lips, over her breasts, along her stomach, and down one thigh. 'Exquisite, my love.' His voice was thick and heavy. As thick and heavy as his need, as thick and heavy as his cock.

Meggy's eyes were hazy, and her breath panting as Nicholas took off his coat. She stroked her breast. '*Yes*, my love,' he said. 'Pleasure yourself whilst you wait for me.'

Her hand stilled. 'What?'

Nicholas smiled tenderly. 'You needn't be ashamed. I shall enjoy watching you.'

'Watching me what?' Her brow furrowed, her voice wavered.

Nicholas released the first button of his waistcoat. Did she truly not know?

'Have you ever climaxed, Meggy?' he asked, pushing the second button through its hole.

She bit her bottom lip.

Good lord.

What a sweet angel; Meggy was the most enticing juxtaposition of womanly passion and pure innocence.

Nicholas brushed a curl from her forehead. 'Climax is sexual release, my love. A sexual release which our bodies need.' Very gently, Nicholas placed Meggy's free hand between the warm, wet folds within her feathery curls. 'I shall help you tonight, but you can achieve it on your own if you stroke here.' He guided her to her silky clitoris and demonstrated with his finger on top of hers.

Meggy's eyes widened. Then her head fell back, her eyes closed, and her mouth opened with a breathy gasp. Nicholas let her continue alone for a time as he finished removing his waistcoat, but he anticipated an unexpected pleasure: *he* would bring her to her first orgasm, her first exquisite experience.

Nicholas untied his cravat, unwrapping the long strand of linen and tossing it to the floor. His shoes were next, followed by his shirt. But not his trousers.

He crawled into the bed at Meggy's feet. He removed her delicate slippers, stroking his thumb along the arch of her foot over her silk stockings and rubbing her heels. He untied the ribbons at her knees and slipped the first stocking down the curve of her calf and past her ankle. He flung the flimsy fabric over his shoulder.

Nicholas kissed Meggy's toes as her moans increased. He slipped off the other stocking and massaged that foot. Her hips rocked and her fingers stroked with increased speed. She was bringing herself close.

Time to intervene.

He kissed up one leg. His cock strained in frustration when Nicholas breathed in the sweet scent of her vulva, but he maintained control. He placed his own hand over Meggy's, and as he kissed up her stomach, he slipped a finger between her folds.

She whimpered, her breasts heaving before him.

She was engorged with desire and slippery with lubrication. His fingers located the centre of her pleasure, whilst his tongue licked around one areola. Nicholas intensified his pressure on her clitoris as he took the whole nipple in his mouth and suckled.

A moan ripped from her throat – a low, guttural sound, an ache, a cry of pain and pleasure. Her hips rolled as he teased the nub, teased her nipple. But she wanted more. His fingers were good, but she deserved better for her first time.

Nicholas spread her legs and knelt between them.

Again that scent. The natural aphrodisiac scent of a woman.

But not merely any woman. Of Meggy. The scent of the woman he loved.

He spread her. Pink, glistening, soft, hot. One lick through the silky folds and up to the centre of pleasure. Then around that, the taste of her slightly sweet, slightly salty, all Meggy. Her breath caught, held, then released low and gasping as he sucked and licked. She didn't question his offering, and that was powerfully attractive. Instead, she gave in to pleasure. She entwined her fingers in his curls as his tongue matched the rhythm of her hips. As she intensified her grip on his head, he slipped a finger into her tight opening, his heart yearning, his need urgent, but he focused on her with his strokes and his suckles, and her muscles tensed, her breath caught, her hips reached, and then she pulsed, slow and deep, ongoing, both on his finger and at his mouth. She cried out her pleasure – deep, low and unrestrained.

'There, my love.' His fingers stroked her as the pulses grew slower, and she fell back into the feathers, gasping but satiated. 'That's *once*.'

Three times Holbrook brought her to climax, and each time Meggy's urgency built in layers of intensity before all-encompassing, shuddering waves of exquisite release.

But always with his fingers and tongue.

After the third time, he turned her on her stomach and rubbed her back until she was a puddle, her muscles relaxed into liquid on the soft feather duvet. He ran his hand over the curve of her bottom.

But when Holbrook's fingers again slipped between her thighs, Meggy rolled to face him. He rested his hand on her stomach as he lay beside her, propped up on one elbow, a gentle smile on his face. He was handsome clothed, but he was beautiful half nude. His neck and shoulders were broad and solid, his arms defined with muscles. But his *chest* – hard bulges and ridges, his stomach as firm as wood, and a deep vee cutting down on either side of his hips and vanishing into his trousers – tantalised Meggy.

She ran her fingertips over these ridges, his skin tight, his muscles rigid. His breath caught and his smile vanished as her fingers trailed that enticing vee. The enormous swell in his trousers moved.

'What about *you*, Holbrook?' She glanced at him through her lashes.

His voice caught. 'What about me, my love?'

'How do I make you feel . . . that way?' She slipped her fingers under his trousers and touched the rounded tip of the bulge. Smooth, slippery, hot. 'How do I make you climax?'

His eyes hazed with her touch, but he stroked her hair and smiled. 'You don't, Meggy. Not tonight. Tonight is about you.'

Meggy released one button of his trousers. Holbrook's smile vanished. She released another button. He fell back upon the mattress, one arm folded behind his head, and his breath heavy. She opened his trousers.

She inhaled sharply.

His penis was erect – thick, veined and long, with a satin-smooth head. It stood powerful and ready for Meggy, and her body knew what to do. *Straddle him*, it told her. *Take it between your legs, and he will slip into you and stroke you into deeper peaks of pleasure.*

But when she put her leg over him, Holbrook cried out the moment her silky wetness touched his cock. 'No, Meggy – don't, my love. I shan't be able to stop if you do.' His voice was thick, pained, agonised. 'And I can't, my darling. You know I can't.'

Meggy nodded, clearing her mind.

Of course.

She lay down beside him, nestled into one muscular arm, and rested her cheek on his chest. His heartbeat sounded in her ears, but her eyes were still drawn to his erection. Perhaps she could touch it . . . perhaps she could take it in her mouth and use her tongue as he'd done to her . . . would such an action please or horrify him?

Meggy skimmed her fingers over his hard abdomen. 'Is there anything I can do?' She didn't want to leave him aching.

'Not tonight, my love.' His palm slid up and down her arm. He pressed his lips into her curls, inhaled, released a warm breath, and then kissed the top of her head. 'Unless . . .'

'Unless what?' Meggy asked, hopefully.

Her head rose and fell with his chest as he inhaled and exhaled again, slowly. 'Meggy.' His voice was firm.

She lifted her head and looked into his eyes. 'Yes?'

He studied her, a fine line between his drawn brows. 'My darling, will you marry me?'

16

At first, Meggy was aware only of exhilaration. Yes, yes, she would marry him. Why would she not? He was amusing, playful, handsome. Rose would be her sister, Holbrook's nieces would be her nieces, and Alton Park would be her home. Harry would be delighted.

Holbrook had even proven himself manageable enough lately when he'd been desperate to please her.

But that was the thorn.

He'd been desperate to please her because he wanted her. He wanted her now, but he'd proposed before doing *that* thing which ought to be saved for marriage. All that was exactly as it should be.

But some things weren't as they should be. *I am not kind, do not trust me.* Lady Harradine's foot along his thigh. The unanswered question about his past with the widow. And most haunting of all: *Once I have what I want, I don't want it anymore.*

A husband was forever. No matter how appealing Holbrook had been lately, his past was concerning, and the wounds of Edwin's abandonment festered too deeply for Meggy to dismiss them without certainty of Holbrook's faithfulness.

Meggy sat up, tucking her legs under herself.

Holbrook sat as well and buttoned his trousers. 'Surely you expected this declaration, my love? I've not made a secret of my feelings for you.'

Meggy studied her hands. 'I wasn't certain if you were sincere. I thought you might be teasing or playing with me.'

'No, Meggy. I'd not do that to you.'

'You *did* – the first time you kissed me.'

He took her hands in his, holding them securely in his warm grasp, and leaned his head down until she looked up at him again. 'You never allowed me to explain myself, Meggy. Yes, I behaved reprehensibly that evening. I oughtn't have kissed you. You were vulnerable and innocent and under my protection. And for that, I'm sorry. But I didn't arrange a tryst with the maid, and I didn't kiss you to seduce you – not initially, anyway. When I first kissed you, before passion clouded my judgement, my feelings were nobler. I was already falling in love with you.'

In love. Warmth filled Meggy's heart, and she glanced down again.

But Holbrook lifted her chin with his fingers. 'And now, Meggy – *now* I'm deeply, passionately in love with you, and my feelings are all that is noble, all that is honourable. Be my wife, darling. I shall make love to you for the rest of the night, and we shall wed as soon as Rosy recovers from her exultations enough to order your gown and plan the breakfast.'

Meggy laughed softly. That was exactly what Rose would do.

Holbrook grinned. 'Come, what do you say, sweetness?'

Acceptance was on the tip of Meggy's tongue, but a heart-shaped face and blonde curls stilled her response. Arabella, whose graveside Holbrook sobbed at, whose miniature he kept, whose pet name he cherished too much to share with anyone else.

Holbrook's first wife would always have her well-deserved place, and Meggy couldn't – and shouldn't – compete. But there was one thing she must know. One thing which would tell Meggy if she could risk her future – and the future of her siblings – on this man who *seemed* to be perfection, but whose reputation was the opposite.

Her heart hammered. 'One question, Holbrook.'

'Anything, my darling.'

'Were you faithful to your wife whilst she lived?'

The candlelight was dim, but it was enough. Holbrook flinched, blanched, and held up his hand. 'Meggy . . .'

And the illusion fell away.

Bile burned at the back of Meggy's throat. Dearest Cole hadn't been faithful to his Bella. How would Holbrook be faithful to Meggy? He wouldn't be. It was that simple. It wasn't possible.

Meggy felt the full exposure of her nudity. How had the coldness of the room escaped her notice before? She wrenched her hands away from Holbrook and stumbled off the bed. 'It doesn't matter. I know your answer, and my answer is the same. No, Lord Holbrook, I won't marry you.' She fumbled on the floor for her chemise.

He climbed down from the bed. 'Meggy, you must allow me to explain myself.'

'There is no explanation you can give that will change my mind. Please don't try.' She pulled her chemise over her head and searched on her hands and knees for the rest of her clothing.

'I was extremely young when I married Arabella . . .' He touched her shoulder, but Meggy jerked away.

'You were essentially my age now.' Meggy slipped her gown over her chemise. She gathered her stays and petticoat.

'. . . and I mistook my sentiments—'

Meggy tasted bitterness in her mouth. She choked it back. He *mistook* his sentiments? Holbrook tried to take her in his arms, but Meggy wriggled out of his grasp and struggled into her slippers.

'—the feelings I have for you are different, such as I never truly had for Arabella.'

Meggy dashed for the door, desperate to be out of the room. Is this how he would have spoken about her to another young lady if *she* lay dead in the churchyard?

His arm grabbed her, and he pulled her close. 'Meggy, the situations are not the same, and—'

Meggy's ears pounded, and her emotions rose like a tidal wave. 'The situations are *precisely* the same.' She tried to pull away from him, but he held firm. 'She was your wife. You made vows to her you ask to make to me. If you didn't keep them with her, you won't keep them with me.'

'I shall, Meggy. It's true I was a terrible husband before, but with you I shall try—' He caught himself, and Meggy escaped his grasp. 'With you, I *shall* be different.' His voice pled. 'Please, Meggy.'

With her hand on the knob, she gathered her breath. 'I shall give you this, Lord Holbrook: undoubtedly in your unbelievable conceit, you believe what you say. But I know that you won't change simply because you're married to me. Do you imagine I'm flattered when you tell me you didn't love the poor lady who died having your child as much as you love me? Or that in your youth, you mistook your sentiments for her? Sir, in your frustrated passion, I suspect you mistake your sentiments for *me*. I don't know what madness convinced me during these last few weeks that you're kind and trustworthy, but it's over now.'

'Meggy, when I told you I wasn't kind and trustworthy, I believed that to be true. And yet haven't I been *both* for months?'

Meggy didn't answer. Her hand was on the knob, and Holbrook put his own over it. 'Answer me, please. Haven't I been both kind and trustworthy? Haven't I?'

She drew in a ragged breath. 'Yes.'

'Because I changed for *you*. Because I love you. Give me a chance to change as a husband. Marry me.'

'No, never.'

'Don't say that, my darling.' His voice cracked. 'Please don't. For years, I thought I'd never marry again. Now, for months, I've dreamt of a life with you. Please don't take that dream away. I love you so much.'

He tried to take her in his arms again, but Meggy pushed him off. 'Don't touch me and don't speak to me of love.'

'But I believe you love me too.'

'You are mistaken.' The words lashed, as she intended. Never would he know the extent of her feelings. Never would he have that satisfaction, at least.

He inhaled a ragged breath. 'Not at all?'

'No. I love my siblings, and for their sakes I shan't take any chances with a husband. Who are *you* to set an example for Harry? Who are *you* to show Sophy what to expect from a husband one day?' He flinched, and Meggy continued. 'I learned years ago that selfish people don't change, and you are a selfish person. The way you speak of your wife—'

He held out his hand. 'Please allow me to explain—'

She snapped. '*Nothing* will justify what you said about your mistaken sentiments!' And to cut him as deeply as she could, she added, 'What *dearest Cole* said about his *Bella*.'

Holbrook recoiled, his mouth ajar, his eyes wide. But as he stared, his expression changed: first he frowned, and then he curled his lips into a sneer. 'Did you go through my possessions?'

Meggy licked her dry lips. Her words had been the impulse of the moment, and she regretted them. 'I happened to find it.'

'You *happened* upon the back drawer of my desk? And then you happened to pick up a portrait of Arabella and read its inscription?' He ran his hands through his

234

hair. 'What else did you do? Read my correspondence? Go through my bedroom?'

Meggy hugged her clothes tighter to her chest. 'N-no.'

Holbrook narrowed his eyes. 'Perhaps you're correct, after all.'

Her heart thumped. 'What do you mean?'

'About us.'

'Of course, I'm correct.' She spoke with more conviction than she felt, for something now burned in her chest.

He nodded. 'I shall go to London tomorrow. Leave you in peace.'

'Go back to other women, you mean.'

Holbrook shrugged. 'Doesn't matter anymore, does it?' His voice was as cold as ice. 'Could you leave, Lady Margaret? I'd like to be alone.' He turned his back.

Meggy fled through the door and down the deserted corridors. Tears burned her cheeks as she ran upstairs, and she flung herself across the bed, gasping for air because of the violence of her emotion.

And she wished with all her heart that she'd never, ever met Nicholas Burton.

17

Three days later, Meggy sat at a table in the crimson drawing room surrounded by ribbon and silk flowers, attempting to trim a new bonnet, but the results looked nothing like the illustration in the fashion journal.

She threw down the hat and buried her face in her arms. 'Why is the bow *still* lopsided?'

Rose's silk skirts rustled. Her slippers whispered across the carpet, and her hand cooled Meggy's neck. 'Shall I help?'

Meggy lifted her head. 'What does it matter? I've ruined it. The ribbon is creased, the flowers crushed, and now I've bent the brim. I oughtn't have attempted to trim it myself. It was false economy.' She cradled her chin and scowled as her thoughts drifted to Holbrook, three days gone – his lust slaked by another woman by now, no doubt.

Meggy squeezed her eyes shut before the tears arrived. She *didn't* care.

'Let me try, dearest.' Rose settled in an adjoining chair and dismantled an hour of effort in a moment. She re-pinned the yellow silk lining so it no longer crumpled on the left side and discarded the blue flowers

Meggy had lumped together, selecting a combination of soft oranges and greens instead.

'I thought *blue* was meant to be nice with yellow,' Meggy said.

Rose smiled. 'Sometimes it is. Especially if there's a hint of red. If we had some artificial cherries, I might arrange them with the blue flowers. But given what you have here, I believe these three colours are best. What do you think?'

The oranges and the greens were light and yellowish; paired with the sunny ribbon and silk lining, the colours harmonised. Meggy's shoulders slumped. 'It's lovely.'

'You don't seem happy. You can tell me if you don't like it.'

'I *do* like it. But it's depressing that other ladies know exactly how to make bonnets pretty, or which trim complements which gown, and I've never understood it in the least.'

'You shouldn't be so down on yourself. You can speak intelligently about crop rotation and market price and – what's the breeding one?'

Meggy blinked. 'The *breeding* one?'

'What you spoke of last night with Mr Davis. About the Lincoln sheep.'

Meggy chuckled, grateful for a little amusement. 'You mean Mr Bakewell and the Lincoln Longwool. *Selective* breeding.'

Rose tied the yellow ribbon into a perfect bow under the flowers. 'That's it. Selective breeding.'

'Well, I doubt my agricultural knowledge will make me any more likely to catch a husband, and once I *do* catch one, what are the chances of his giving a damn about my opinions on estate management?' Meggy flicked the silk flowers scattered on the table and sighed. 'Everything would be so much simpler if I were a man.'

Rose threaded a needle and began to sew fine white lace from her own workbasket around the bonnet brim as Meggy fiddled with the flowers. 'Rose, aren't you frustrated that men have power, influence and control over their lives and possessions, and we must learn to trim bonnets?'

'I like trimming bonnets.'

'Yes, but you are like me, Rose – the elder sister of a peer. If we'd been born male, *we'd* have the title, the position, the management of the estates. It's not that I begrudge Harry, but at the same time, it's not fair. Do you never feel that way?'

Rose's fair eyebrows drew together. 'It was a blessing from God that I'm female.' Her voice was unsteady, and her lips turned down, quivering.

'Why, Rose,' Meggy said, straightening her back in surprise, 'you're upset.'

Rose was never melancholy.

Rose tossed aside the bonnet with the strung needle and unsewn lace hanging and covered her face.

'What did I say, Rose? What did I do?' Meggy, distressed, rubbed her friend's shoulder. She hadn't meant to make Rose sad. 'I'm terribly sorry, whatever it was.'

Rose uncovered her face, but she kept her fingertips pressed to her lips. 'No need to apologise, dearest. You don't know.'

'Don't know what?' Meggy asked, still rubbing Rose's thin back.

Rose studied her hands.

Meggy's heart thudded. 'Will you tell me, Rose?'

'Yes,' Rose said at last. 'You need to know before London.' She lifted her eyes and nodded her chin towards the portrait above the mantel that Meggy had noticed during her first night at Alton Park: the former marquess and marchioness dressed in the styles of thirty years earlier, sitting with a fair-haired baby between them. 'You know, of course, that's a portrait of me with my parents before Nicky was born.' Rose paused and chewed her bottom lip as she studied the painting. 'What do you think of Mother's appearance?'

'She was a *tremendously* handsome woman,' Meggy said truthfully. The former Lady Holbrook possessed a slender figure, ivory skin and a beautiful face. Her grey eyes shone under sweeping brows, and her thick ringlets trailed over one shoulder, powdered in the fashion of the time. 'I thought so when I first saw her portrait.'

Rose nodded. 'Yes, she was an "*Incomparable*". A Paragon. Hailed as the great beauty of her generation, and the darling of the Royal Academicians in the late 1770s, before she married.' Rose's voice grew stronger, but it was oddly flat. 'She modelled for many of them, and they painted her as Aphrodite, Diana, Cecilia,

Cleopatra – there are countless portraits of her – and every painting produced a small war as the nobility and the royal dukes bid and outbid each other for them.' Rose faced Meggy, her grey eyes distressed. 'But for the exhibit in 1779, an artist named Isaac Henderson painted her entirely in the nude as Helen of Troy, and that's when her reputation took a turn. She became known as *The Face* – as in, the Face that Launched a Thousand Ships. And I should say, the intent was quite improper.'

Meggy's eyes widened. 'Your poor mother.'

Rose held up her hand. 'Save your compassion, Meggy. My mother was beautiful, but her beauty ran no deeper than her skin.' She sighed as she examined the portrait. 'Nicky looks a great deal like her, doesn't he? But his colouring is more like Papa's. Mother's hair was red. Not pale like mine, but a rich, deep auburn like Elizabeth's.'

Meggy looked at the former Lord Holbrook, his skin bronzed, his eyes dusky. Even powdered, his hair was as dark as steel. He wasn't especially handsome, but he looked approachable. Kindly, gentle – with a soft, curling smile – like Nicholas had appeared when he'd first stepped from his carriage at Berksleigh Hall. 'Your brother has your father's smile,' Meggy said quietly.

'Yes! So I've always said to Nicky, but he doesn't see it. Do tell him you think so; perhaps he'll believe you.' Rose paused. 'Nicky despises his resemblance to Mother. They were not close at all.'

'He mentioned that.'

Rose tilted her head. 'Did he, indeed? Did he say anything else about Mother?'

'No. But he said he loved your father dearly.'

'Papa was an angel.' A tear dripped over Rose's pale lashes. 'Which of my parents do I look like?'

Meggy considered. 'You have your mother's *eyes* – and her ivory complexion.'

'Yes.' Rose clasped Meggy's hand. 'And Meggy, you might look all day, but you'll find no feature Papa and I have in common. Because whilst he was my papa and my father in all else that that word can mean, he was not the man who sired me.'

Meggy gasped. 'Oh!'

'Papa *always* claimed me, of course. The church register declares him my father; I bore his name before I married. But no one *believed* it. I was born three months after my parents' wedding and the vicious gossipmongers tittered that Papa was the only gentleman in London who *hadn't* been with my mother before their wedding night. You see, the man who sired me might be any of several men; Mother had affairs with many of the artists who painted her, as well as with a royal duke who bought several of her portraits.'

Ah, like *mother*, like *son*. The bile burned in the back of Meggy's throat again.

'You wonder, perhaps, why Papa married her, especially since she carried another man's child?'

'Yes,' Meggy said emphatically. 'I do wonder that.'

Rose nodded. '*Everyone* wondered. But whilst many men loved Mother's face and body, Papa loved *her*. She was younger than he, but he'd known her all her life – the Burton lands in Kent neighboured my maternal grandfather's small estate – and when my ashamed grandfather ordered Mother to an aunt in Yorkshire for her confinement, she fled to Papa for help. Not because she loved Papa, but because she didn't want to be secreted away in Yorkshire. She wanted to be admired, celebrated, a society leader. She wanted wealth and position. Papa proposed, as she likely knew he would, although any other nobleman would've offered only an *arrangement*, and then he married her, knowing there was no chance the child she carried was his, not knowing if I'd be a boy or a girl. He was prepared to love my mother's child as his own, even as his son and heir, if such were the case. I praise God I was a girl, but it wouldn't have mattered to him, Meggy. *That* was the type of man Papa was.' Rose wiped her eyes with a lacy handkerchief and gazed again at the portrait.

Rose released a shuddering breath. 'She was never faithful to him, Meggy. She broke his heart over and over again. No one can be perfectly certain Nicky is Papa's son, but Mother insisted he is. When Nicky would yell at her – even as a child, he was furious at how she flaunted her lovers in Papa's face – she'd snap back, "I gave your father *you*, his own son, which even *he* never asked of me, so who are you to ask more?" And I, at least, always believed her. I think after her pregnancy with me, she learned how to . . . well, I needn't go into details. The point is, I think she did, indeed, do that one thing for Papa. She gave him his own son, and then, despite countless lovers, never fell pregnant again. But Nicky struggles to believe any good of her.'

Meggy pressed her hands to her churning stomach. So, *this* was the background, and these were the parents, which had produced Holbrook's mercurial personality. It made sense, but it didn't excuse the marquess's vices. Rose had grown up in the same environment, the child of the same heartless mother, and yet she was steady and faithful in all her relationships.

Rose bit her bottom lip. 'Papa bore the shame of cuckoldom with no complaint. He never scolded Mother, never reprimanded her. But my uncle was a different matter.'

Meggy recalled portraits from the gallery: Holbrook's father and uncle as young men, both swarthy and strapping, but the younger more handsome than the elder. 'Uncle Walter loathed my mother,' Rose continued. 'And he loathed Papa for marrying her, for marrying a woman who carried another man's child. You can see his perspective. To lose your chance at a title because of the law of legitimate male primogeniture is one thing, but to be usurped by an unknown man's bastard is quite another. He never forgave Papa; I don't think he ever truly believed Nicky was Papa's son either. He's the one who made Nicky doubt it. But Meggy, Papa *raised* us – *that* made him our father. I was his daughter – his little pink Rose, and Nicky was his son – his little lump of coal, he called him.'

His lump of coal.

243

Cole.

It was like a blow to the stomach. 'His *what?*'

Rose chuckled, twisting her handkerchief. 'I know it sounds dreadful, but it was a pet name. You'd never know, as fastidious as Nicky is about his appearance now, but he was a rough and tumble boy, always a little grubby, always dishevelled – much like Harry. And he had long, dark curls past his shoulders. He didn't want them cut, and he didn't like them brushed. Mother said his hair was like tangled lumps of coal. She said it scornfully, but Papa made it a pet name. Cole, you know – for Nicholas. Pink Rose and Cole-lump. Silly, I know, but coming from Papa, they were the loveliest names in the world.'

Meggy's outside composure had returned, but her stomach remained unsettled, and a sharp ache radiated behind her forehead. Why had Arabella used the father's pet name when Rose didn't? It must be that Holbrook had asked it of his first wife, although he'd not requested Meggy do the same . . .

Meggy rubbed her temples. Trying to understand Holbrook and his convoluted, twisted life was like chasing a shadow, and she had no patience for fruitless ventures.

Rose sighed again. 'Meggy, there was no one like Papa, although both Thomas and Nicky are extremely close indeed.'

Meggy couldn't suppress a raised eyebrow and pursed lips.

Rose cocked her head. 'Don't you agree?'

'I am certain your husband is all you say. And I have no doubt Lord Holbrook is an excellent *brother*.'

Rose's eyes searched Meggy's. 'You don't see Nicky's excellence in other ways? His gentle heart? His sensitive nature?'

'I don't wish to distress you, Rose, so let's not speak of him.'

Rose's face creased with concern. 'I think you must've quarrelled with Nicky. Quite truthfully, I thought perhaps you and he were about to announce some wonderful news. But then he vanished to London in a foul temper, and you've been in a mope.'

Meggy drew her brows together. 'I've not been in a mope.'

'Please forgive my choice of words. But you've not been yourself since he left.'

Meggy jumped to her feet and walked to a window.

'Don't go.' Rose followed her. 'I'm sorry if I've made you angry, but you must understand I'm concerned.'

Meggy gazed outside. The March day had dawned overcast, but the sun broke through the clouds and shone light on the bright green of the early spring grass. '*You* haven't made me angry, Rose. I'm furious at the situation I find myself in. I don't want to be indebted to your brother.'

'But Nicky doesn't mind, Meggy. I've never seen him happier than he's been in the past months. He's never stayed so long at Alton Park, and he's never been so engaged with the girls. To tell the truth, dearest, I believe Nicky is *very* much in love with you.'

Meggy's heart fluttered – an instantaneous reaction that irritated her. 'Your brother doesn't know what love is, Rose,' she snapped. 'He's no more capable of faithfulness than your mother was.'

'But I don't think that's true at all. I know Nicky has a certain reputation, but that's not who he really is. It's just how he's foolishly chosen to behave out of grief and lack of purpose. But with *you*, with a *wife* and a family – Meggy, Nicky is like Papa. I know he is. That's what he was like as a child. That's what he was like until mourning for Arabella brought him to a dark place.'

Meggy spat out her words. 'Mourning didn't change him.'

'What do you mean?'

'Your brother was unfaithful to Arabella whilst she lived, Rose.'

Rose recoiled. 'That cannot be true.'

'And yet it is, by his own admission. Even during their brief marriage, he couldn't stay away from other women.'

Rose's eyes widened. 'He told you?'

'Yes, because I asked him to. I needed to know, for he . . . proposed to me, and I wasn't certain if I could take a risk on him. Rose, your father was perhaps capable of an utterly self-sacrificing love, but I'm not. I cannot live with constant suspicion, and I cannot ignore infidelity or selfish behaviour. It would fester in me. I'd be jealous and angry. Therefore, I shan't put myself at the mercy of a man destined only to hurt me. I suffered too much at my brother's hand.'

Rose wrung her much-abused handkerchief again. 'I understand.' Her lips turned down. 'I'm so sorry, Meggy – I am. I wouldn't have thought that of Nicky – Mother's behaviour infuriated him.'

'But Rose, such is the way of people with addictive personalities. I believe that somewhere, deep inside, Edwin wanted to be a good man, but his addictions were more powerful than his intentions. Your brother is the same. Like your mother, he's unable to control his impulses – at least in *that* matter – and I shan't live like your father did.'

Rose dabbed her eyes. 'I couldn't either, Meggy. B-but I did so want you for a sister.'

Meggy held out her hand, her heart aching. 'We shan't be sisters, Rose, but I hope we shall always be friends. I cherish our friendship.'

Rose threaded an arm around Meggy's waist and kissed her cheek. 'Always friends, dearest.'

As she embraced Rose, Meggy fancied that the late marquess watched them from the mantel, and his gentle smile didn't conceal the sorrow in his dark eyes.

18

Nicholas clutched a glass of brandy and frowned at his father's painted eyes over the mantel. With his other hand, he rubbed Caesar's velvety ears. The pug was curled in a warm ball in his lap; the dog's loud snores were the only sound in the cavernous bedchamber in Holbrook House, Nicholas's palatial London residence.

Nicholas hadn't permitted his staff to clean his room in days. Twisted sheets lay in the middle of the curtained bed, the green and gold carpet was strewn with books and clothes, and the drawn damask drapes allowed in little light. But Nicholas's eyes were accustomed to the gloom.

Nicholas treasured the portrait above the fireplace. The background was Holbrook House's rose garden at the height of its June glory, and, like most paintings, the composition formed a triangle. Tall, dark Papa stood in the middle. An eight-year-old Rose, in a flowy white frock with a blue satin sash, leaned her cheek against Papa's arm, a bouquet of pink roses in one hand, the other entwined with their father's. Six-year-old Nicholas, dressed in a blue-velvet, buttoned-up, lace-collared one-piece suit, grasped Papa's other hand. A subtle smile brightened his boyish face, and his long, dark curls – tidied for once – tumbled down his shoulders.

It was painted after an especially horrid spring. Engrossed in a torrid affair with Lord Wingrove, Mother had been wild, unpredictable and merciless. Wingrove was not her only lover, and he was viciously jealous. Every few days, the viscount arrived in a red-faced rage, stormed to Mother's dressing room, and slammed the door. He and Mother then exchanged screaming accusations until gasping moans and loud grunts began, which, dispersed with more arguments, lasted for hours. The next morning, Lord Wingrove would breakfast with the family wearing a silk banyan and a smug smile, and Papa, at the head of the table with eyes like two dark pools, would chatter with Nicholas and Rose as if everything were normal.

Meanwhile, Mother watched, her lips curled into a sneer, her taunts directed at everyone: children, servants, husband, lover.

Even now, Nicholas's rage rose like lava when he remembered her cruelty.

Early that June, Wingrove's jealousy had reached a fevered peak, and he fought a duel in Hyde Park with another one of Mother's lovers. Both gentlemen were wounded, and Mother deserted everyone to travel to Brighton with a third man.

Peace had descended on Holbrook House the moment her carriage rolled out of the gilded iron gates and onto Piccadilly Street. It wasn't the fleeting peace afforded by Mother's afternoon or evening absences;

this was an all-encompassing relief. Nicholas and Rose ran about in unbridled joy with no fear of viciousness. And although sadness lingered in Papa's eyes, he stood taller and laughed more.

Papa had commissioned the painting the next week. After each afternoon sitting, their father strolled through the gardens with Nicholas swinging on one arm and Rose on the other – exactly as Harry and Sophy clung to Nicholas during the journey to Alton Park in September. Instinctively, the two Fairchild siblings – very like a little Pink Rose and a little Cole-lump – had trusted that Nicholas was safe and strong.

He didn't realise it then, but that was the moment he began to believe again he could be a kind and honourable man. Kind and honourable – but without his father's weakness.

Nicholas thought he'd found the balance.

Instead, he was a disaster.

Papa's painted eyes gazed at Nicholas.

'Dammit, Papa, it's not that I didn't *try*.' His words slurred.

But, of course, Papa didn't answer. Nicholas didn't know what his father would've said, but it would've been exactly what he needed to hear.

Nicholas tipped a decanter to refill his brandy glass, but the decanter was empty. 'Bloody hell.'

He placed Caesar on a cushion and stumbled in stock-inged feet across the room, running his fingers through his unwashed hair and across his scratchy cheeks. He recoiled from the brightness when he opened his door and leaned against the wall to counteract the swirling world. A footman stood in the adjoining antechamber.

'Stephen, isn't it?' Nicholas's words were sluggish. He tugged at his loose shirt collar, as if it would help his enunciation.

'Yes, my lord.'

Nicholas licked his lips. 'Brandy.'

Stephen's brow furrowed.

'Did you hear me? Brandy, dammit, man!'

'Y-yes, my lord.'

Nicholas stumbled as he turned back to his room. He shook off Stephen's offered hand. 'Get me my blasted brandy!'

But before the footman could leave, the door to the antechamber opened, and Alexander entered. 'No more brandy for you, Nick. Doctor's orders.'

Nicholas scowled. 'What the devil are you doing here? Weren't you told I'm not at home? Do none of my servants follow my orders?'

Alexander ignored him to converse in a low voice with Stephen, and the footman disappeared.

'He'd better bring me my bloody brandy, or he can find a new situation.'

'Nonsense, Nick. You'll have tea and a solid meal.'

'But I'm ill, dammit. The brandy's medicinal.'

'Ill, are you? Very well, let's have a look at you.' Alexander grabbed Nicholas by the arm and returned him to the bedchamber. 'Good God, man – this room *stinks*. It's a beautiful day out. Why are your windows closed and your curtains drawn?'

'Bah! I see no beauty in the world anymore. And the sun hurts my eyes.'

Alexander threw open the drapes and pulled up the sashes. Fresh, cool air gusted as dust motes flickered in the glaring sunbeams, and Nicholas shielded his face.

'Nick, the sun hurts your eyes because you are as drunk as a . . . as drunk as a lord. Ha, what truth in some idioms. Now sit down. What are your symptoms?'

Nicholas collapsed into an armchair, and Alexander clasped his fingers to his wrist. 'I cannot sleep,' Nicholas said. 'I twist and turn for hours but cannot relax. My heart flutters as if I've run a race. I cannot breathe – the agony in my chest feels like a boulder. There's a pain down my arm, my throat burns, my head aches.'

'Your head aches from drink.' Alexander tilted Nicholas's chin and examined his eyes.

'Brandy is the only thing that allows me to rest.'

'Open your mouth.'

Nicholas did as bid, and Alexander peered into his throat. He massaged behind Nicholas's ears and along his neck. 'Why are you examining me, Alexander? I don't have the body parts you specialise in.'

The physician chuckled. 'Your body parts are less complicated. Take your shirt off so I can listen to your heart and lungs.'

Nicholas tossed aside his unbuttoned waistcoat and pulled his shirt over his head. Alexander placed an ear to his chest.

'How did you know I was here, Alexander?'

'I'd say a little bird told me, but that would be a lie. It was a flower. A Rose, to be exact.' Alexander stood up. 'Put your shirt back on.'

Nicholas picked up the limp cotton. But after sniffing the shirt, he tossed it aside. The crisp air *was* restorative, but its freshness heightened stale odours. 'Why did my sister write to you?'

'She was concerned. She thought you might be in a terrible condition. But I'm happy to report there's nothing wrong with you that wholesome food, exercise, and the love of a wonderful woman cannot help.'

Nicholas buried his head in his hands and cried.

Hours later, Nicholas had bawled some of his sorrows to Alexander. He'd also eaten, shaved, bathed, and rested between clean sheets in his tidied room.

But he hadn't slept. Not well at least.

He needed brandy, and there was a decanter in the library.

Nicholas threw on a dressing gown and slippers, and padded down the carpeted corridor into the marble entrance hall. It was dusk, but not yet night; evening light still filtered through the soaring stained-glass roof as footmen lit the wall sconces and gilded candelabras.

The butler glided to Nicholas's side. 'Does your lordship wish the chandelier lit tonight?'

The two-tiered, cut-crystal chandelier held over fifty candles. 'Good lord, no, Stinchcombe. Not for me. I shall be in the library.'

'As you wish, my lord. Dr Mitchell is in there reading.'

The library was an oval room with a domed glass cupola roof. Alexander – coat off, feet up, and whisky in hand – read in one of the gold silk armchairs.

'What are you still doing here?' Nicholas asked. 'Don't you have babies to deliver?'

'My servants know where to find me. I shall enjoy your lavish hospitality until Rose comes to town next month.'

'The devil you will.' Nicholas picked up his decanter.

Alexander grinned. 'Come now. You're ill, don't you remember? Best to have a physician in the house.'

'*You* said I shan't be better without Meggy's love.' Nicholas raised his glass to his lips.

'Put down that brandy at once, Nick. You may have some tea, and you should eat some more food. But lay off drink entirely.' Alexander rang the bell. 'Tea and dinner for Lord Holbrook, please, Stinchcombe. And no wine.'

Nicholas crumpled onto the sofa with a sigh. 'Overruled in my own house, am I?'

'It's for your own good. Do you remember what I said months ago, Nick?'

'That you would woo Meggy if I failed? Yes, I remember perfectly well, damn you.'

Alexander sipped his whisky. 'I was referring to my suggestion that you consider *why* you find it difficult to live with yourself. Did you ever do so?'

Nicholas dug his fingers into his hair and gripped his head. 'I know why I find it difficult, yes.'

'And have you resolved that?'

'I cannot change the past.'

'No, but you can make peace with it.'

'Not always.'

Alexander shook his head. 'You must not want Meggy very much at all.'

Nicholas shot up. 'How the devil can you say such a thing?' His voice caught. 'I *told* you how much I love her.'

'Then why waste your time drinking yourself into a stupor? Win her heart.'

'I have no chance of winning her heart. She's disgusted by me, and I don't blame her.'

Alexander sighed. 'Nicholas, what do you want in life?'

'Meggy.'

'And if you can't have her? What then? Will you waste away like Edwin? Leave this world no better – and possibly worse – than if you'd never been born? Dammit, Nick! I shall ask you what you want in life one more time, and I want a better response.'

'Because you want Meggy for yourself?'

'I'm trying to help you, and you are severely trying my patience. I shan't ignore a comment like that again – the next time you accuse me of attempting to steal Meggy, I *shall* thrash you. Now, Nicholas Burton, what do you want in life?'

Nicholas fell against the back of the sofa. He closed his eyes and imagined Papa's strong and safe arms, with two giggling children swinging upon them. 'I want to be a good man. I want to be a loving husband and father.'

'There. And what prevents you from doing so?'

'Meggy won't marry me.'

'Try again, Nick. What prevents you from being a loving husband and father?'

Nicholas opened his eyes. Glimmering candles reflected like starlight in the glass cupola above his head. 'I'm not sure I can do it, because I didn't do it the first time.'

'How do you feel about your marriage, Nicholas?'

'I'm utterly ashamed of myself.'

'Don't you see? It is as I said to you months ago: you'll never win Meggy's heart if you are ashamed of your own. You scoffed then. Will you scoff now?'

The butler slipped in. 'My lord, your dinner awaits in the dining room. And Dr Mitchell, your manservant arrived. Mrs Chalkley, I understand.'

'Ah, about time. I've expected this baby for a fortnight.' Alexander put on his coat. 'Well, Nick, Mrs Chalkley is a first-time mother, so I likely shan't be back tonight, but, with a bit of luck, I may breakfast with you. Don't drink, or I *shall* hear of it.' He patted his coat pocket and extracted a folded paper. 'Before I go, here's a letter from the young earl. It was encased within Rose's.'

Nicholas smiled wistfully as he took the missive. Harry had scrawled *The Most Honourable* – that was always a laugh – *The Marquess of Holbrook* across the front.

The dining room adjoined the library. Nicholas sat at the head of the endless table and unfolded the paper. Ink splotches splattered a page full of misspelled and crossed-out words. He dipped his spoon into the steaming bowl of creamed cauliflower soup and read.

Dear Nicky,

Please forgive my penmanship. I miss you terribly, and even though Rose says I shall see you after Easter and you will take me to the Menagerie at the Tower and to the circus at Astley's Amphitheatre, I cannot be happy. Coming to London means Meggy will marry, and I might not like the man she chooses. I'd hoped you *would marry her and be my guardian* and *my brother — a brother who'd be like a father, for that is how I feel about you, Nicky. But when I asked Meggy, she said she wouldn't have you if you were the last man on earth. Meggy is usually kind, but she wasn't at all nice when she said that, and now I feel even sadder.*

Please write back. I'm certain you will know how to make me feel better.

Your very obedient, sir,
Harry

Nicholas placed down his spoon and blinked at the last line.

I'm certain you will know how to make me feel better.

Tears sprang to his eyes.

Nicholas's dreams were far from fulfilment. But, right now, there was a boy he loved who needed a father's guidance. He could do that.

★

Dearest Harry,

*Please remember this, my dear boy: every decision
your sister makes, she thinks first of you and Sophy.
She loves you tremendously. Treasure that love. It is
a selfless gift — and in return, respect her wisdom.*

*I know you admire me, but I haven't always been
a good man, and your sister — quite justifiably —
holds me accountable for my past actions.*

*We never know what the future holds. Nor can we
change the past. But we can better ourselves in the
present. I have determined to do so; you must
continue to be the capital fellow you already are,
Harry. Mind Mr Davis and learn your lessons. Play
outside every day. Be a loving brother to your sisters.
Be a friend to Elizabeth, Maria, and Charlotte. Take
care of Copper.*

*And whatever happens, I shall be there when you
need me, whatever mistakes you make, whatever
accidents befall you, whatever joys and successes you
experience. Our friendship, Harry, is like a sturdy
ship such as we saw in Ipswich. Whatever tempests
the seas churn, we shall work together to stay afloat.*

With much love, Nicky

Nicholas folded, directed and sealed the letter. He leaned
back in the leather chair at his library desk and steepled
his fingers as he gazed across the room.

He'd never known how to make peace with his past. Perhaps, in part, because no one else knew the details of his disastrous marriage.

He suddenly wanted to tell the person he admired and loved most in the world.

If she would listen.

He drew out another sheet of paper.

Dear Lady Margaret,

I have done little to deserve your attention, so I appeal to your <u>compassion</u> when I ask you to read this letter. I promise I shan't renew the proposal that was so distasteful to you, nor shall I attempt to justify my past actions. I behaved deplorably during my marriage to Arabella. For nine years, shame has festered in me, and I've been too disgusted to speak of it.

Please allow me to lay out the facts of my marriage. If you don't want to know, cast this letter in the fire. But if you can bear it, please read my words – and <u>then</u> burn this letter and think of me what you will. If you despise me, it's exactly how I feel about myself much of the time.

I met Arabella at my uncle's estate in Sussex the summer before I turned one-and-twenty. I'd just completed my studies at Cambridge, and I was full of the vigour and determination of youth. I meant to serve King and Country selflessly in the Upper House. I intended to steward my estates wisely. I determined to sponsor charities with a philanthropic spirit. And I wanted, above all else, to marry and have a family.

That dream I'd shared with my uncle the Christmas before when he visited me at Alton Park, because I needed his permission to marry before my majority. And in July, he invited me to his estate. He wished to introduce me to a most perfect young lady . . .

19

August 1803 – February 1804

Arabella smiled, and Nicholas's heart expanded a thousand times. 'Of *course* I shall marry you, Cole.'

He stroked her tiny hand, marvelling at its daintiness. She was a living version of one of Rose's porcelain figurines. 'May I kiss you, Bella?'

She pressed her cheek against her shoulder and twisted a golden curl. 'Yes, Cole.'

The kiss was chaste, her lips like butterfly wings upon Nicholas's.

Arabella was a distant cousin of his aunt's, a poor relation educated on his uncle's generosity. Her voice was hushed, her touch cool and soothing, and her interests aligned with Nicholas's like a hand in a glove. They loved the same books. They shared identical opinions on art. She knew his favourite poems by heart. She adored the colour pink, just like his beloved sister Rose, whom Nicholas had missed terribly since her marriage two years earlier.

Arabella was shy, deferential, modest. And she whispered the exquisite words that Nicholas had never heard from any woman but his sister, for his mother had never uttered them: 'I love you. I love you, dearest Cole.'

She'd invented the pet name three days after they met. Coincidentally, it was the name Papa had called him. The one no one else ever used.

Nicholas's heart had nearly stopped when she'd suggested it, for it had been a sign.

A sign Papa smiled down on them from heaven.

'You've made a fine choice, Nicholas.' Lord Walter Burton leaned back in the leather seat behind his heavy oak desk, a smile on his handsome, swarthy face. 'I confess it surprised me when you mentioned in the winter you wanted to find a wife. But over the spring I wondered if you might consider Arabella. I realised how very alike you are – you seem to share a mind. Simply astounding.'

'She's perfection.' Nicholas had grown to love his uncle in the last few days, and he regretted all the years he'd thought the man despicable.

'Don't take this amiss, Nicholas, but after your mother, after the *last* Lady Holbrook . . . well, perhaps I should say no more.'

'But I perfectly understand you. My mother did nothing but make my life miserable – and what she did to Papa . . .' Nicholas clenched his jaw.

His uncle shuddered. 'It doesn't bear thinking of, does it, my boy? How your poor father suffered. But you won't. You've chosen well. And you do right to take a wife so young, under the circumstances.' Lord

Walter examined his folded hands with drawn brows. 'Nicholas, as you know, your aunt and I never had children. The nearest heir to the title, besides myself, is a fourth cousin I haven't even met. I hope you and Arabella are blessed with a son *soon*.'

Nicholas leaned forward. 'I have the same wish, Uncle, although son or daughter doesn't matter to me.' Nicholas wanted a child so much his heart ached. He yearned to be a father, to bestow love like Papa's on a tiny new soul. Sweet, pure Arabella would be an angelic mother, so entirely different from the monster who'd given birth to Nicholas. 'With your permission, I'd like to marry within the month. In town, although I know London is sparse of company in August. But still, I want a society wedding. The ceremony at St George's, Hanover Square, and a wedding breakfast for hundreds at Holbrook House. Everyone must know how much I adore Bella.'

'My dear nephew,' Lord Walter said, beaming, 'how like your sainted father you are.' He held out his hand. 'I bestow permission without reservation. In fact, your aunt and I shall arrange *such* a wedding breakfast that we shall draw half the *ton* to town for the event.'

Nicholas grinned and grasped Lord Walter's hand.

Their wedding wasn't quite the grand affair Nicholas desired, but everyone knew of it, and six hundred guests from the most elevated ranks attended despite the unfashionableness of London in August. Society-watchers lined George Street as Arabella arrived at the church in her silver and white crepe de chine gown, and all the newspapers reported the details.

It was afternoon before the last breakfast guests departed. Nicholas had consumed too much champagne, for his glass was always full. The moment they were alone, he wanted his wife, and she wanted him in return. Arabella dragged him into her bedroom, unbuttoned his breeches, and bent over fully clothed. 'Take me from behind, Cole.'

He struggled to understand. 'What?'

Arabella reached and grabbed his cock. It was the first time a woman had touched him, and he nearly ejaculated as she slid her hand up and down and positioned him between her legs. Instinctive understanding took over; Nicholas placed his hands on her slender hips.

And his fingers brushed her abdomen.

She tried to push his hands away, but it was too late. He'd already felt what she wanted to hide. Her stomach was hard and tight – and *swollen*.

Horror gripped him as he backed away. Arabella's eyes flitted to his. Then she knelt, as if to take him in her mouth, but Nicholas buttoned up his breeches.

'Don't you want me, Cole?' she asked, reaching again for his crotch.

Nicholas dodged her hand. A drum beat against his temple. 'Arabella, show me your stomach.'

Arabella bit her lip. 'Cole . . .'

'Show me your stomach *now*, dammit!'

She paled, but she lifted her long, loose skirts to display thin legs, slim hips, and an abdomen as round and hard as if a ball sat under her skin. Perhaps she wasn't many months pregnant, but on her tiny frame, the bulge was unmistakable.

The betrayal released a savage beast in Nicholas. 'Whose child do you carry, you *whore*?' His words lashed like a whip.

Arabella dropped her skirts, her eyes cast down and her chin quivering. 'Your uncle said you would be as kind as your father was to your mother.'

Nicholas clenched his hands into fists. 'My vicious slut of a mother ruined my father's life. My uncle's a damned fool if he thought I'd roll over and accept such a fate.'

Arabella drew her brows together. 'Your uncle's no fool. He's brilliant and . . . and gentlemanly and a *true* noble.'

Nicholas's breath caught, his chest tightened, and his body burned as if aflame. The drumming in his head became the galloping hooves of a thousand horses.

'Whose goddamned child do you carry, woman?' He ripped each word from a constricting throat.

Arabella cradled her swell, her hands rubbing the roundness under the gossamer silk of her wedding gown. 'This baby is a true Burton.'

Nicholas's stomach heaved; his mouth filled with an acrid tang. The world swirled; he staggered to Arabella's bed and collapsed against the pink brocade.

Arabella's voice echoed as if he were in a tunnel. 'You cannot object, Cole. *You* could be anyone's son. What other choice did your poor uncle have, deprived of his title by a whore's bastard and locked into marriage with a barren woman?'

Everything made sense at once.

'Did my uncle tell you to call me Cole, Arabella?'

A pause. 'Yes.'

Nicholas nodded as he stared at the draped folds of the canopy above him. 'And what else did he tell you? My favourite books and poems? My sister's favourite colour, perhaps?'

'I think you know the answer.'

The rage receded, but it left a desert in its wake. A dead wasteland where his hopes and dreams had flourished until moments before. 'Ah, I see. You are a stranger – a puppet my uncle created for his own purposes.' Nicholas sat. 'How did he convince you to do it?'

She shrugged. 'I must make my way in the world, the same as anyone else. If not for your uncle's generosity all my life, I'd be impoverished – a working man's wife at best.' She smiled. Not cruelly, but contentedly. 'Instead, I'm the Marchioness of Holbrook, Cole.'

Nicholas stood. 'You mayn't call me that anymore. And sadly for you, your plans will come to naught. I shall annul this marriage, and my uncle can make his own arrangements for his mistress and his bastard.'

'You cannot seek an annulment without your uncle's permission.'

'I can after my birthday.'

'Nicholas, be reasonable. You won't annul this union.'

'Of course I shall, Arabella.'

266

'No, you *won't*. Because if you do, *everyone* will know the story. You would be more mocked than your father.' She held out her hand. 'Dearest, you're overreacting.'

'Overreacting! Ha! Are you *mad*?'

She dropped her unreceived hand. 'You *are* over-reacting. After all, I carry your cousin – your father's nephew.' Then Arabella rubbed salt in his wound. 'This baby is your beloved papa's *true* relation, unlike you.'

'That's my uncle's lie.' Nicholas's voice cracked.

'It isn't a lie. Your uncle says half a dozen men might've sired you.'

'But my mother swore I was my father's son.'

'And did your mother always tell the truth, Nicholas?' Arabella tried again to take his hand; he yanked it away. 'I shan't be like her. Once I have borne your uncle a son as your heir – whether this child or another – I shall be loyal to you. No one else will ever know.' She leaned forward and whispered in his ear. 'And whilst I am with child, I shall be your wife and *only* your wife. I know you want my body. I'm *very* skilled in bed – I shall give you the most exquisite pleasure.'

She stroked him through his trousers. Although his penis betrayed him by rising at once, her touch was a violation. He pushed away her hand.

'I shall never, *ever* lie with you, Arabella.'

Nicholas stormed from her room, slammed and locked his own door, and collapsed onto his bed.

He'd known depression, darkness, fear and grief, but nothing like this. The depth of this despair suffocated him. For hours, Nicholas lay in the darkening room as nausea from the betrayal and self-loathing for his stupidity washed over him like waves on a beach. But he was most furious at an evil whisper within him, which demanded he make Arabella love him, force her to be the woman he thought he'd married. In his mind, a poisonous voice hissed he should go to her bed and show her he was in control. His cock hardened at the thought.

Betraying him again.

He sat up. Arabella was not the only woman in London. He could find one who'd pretend with him. He'd pay her to tell him she loved him and to whisper his name. After all, there was no point in virtue anymore. He'd prove himself a man. He needed to *fuck*.

An hour later, Nicholas stepped out to a dampening London evening. A diamond pin flashed within the folds of his pristine white cravat. His three-hundred-year-old signet ring glinted as he flipped open his father's pocket watch – nearly nine o'clock – and then returned it to his fob pocket. Only then did he realise he'd absent-mindedly tucked the miniature Arabella had given him as an engagement present into his waistcoat pocket. It had already become a habit to carry it with him. Until that evening, he had thought it his most treasured possession.

The slender blonde whore tried to please him, but Nicholas wept through his first sexual experience. Pretending didn't help at all. He took off the condom, buttoned his trousers, paid her generously, and visited another prostitute.

She was plump and black-haired, past thirty and lusty. She crooned he was handsome and lovely, and *such* a man; she told him to lie back and nurse his bottle of brandy whilst she enjoyed him. The hours with her were eye-opening – increasingly sweaty, vigorous and *loud* as she taught him skill after skill and praised his progress with feverish screams of pleasure – but they didn't erase the pain.

By the middle of the night, Nicholas stumbled along the Strand, past the Temple Bar, and onto Fleet Street, hardly aware of where he was going, placing one foot in front of the other, swigging from a bottle as he staggered. A fog set in by the time he arrived at New Bridge Street, and his eyes were drawn to the obelisk at the junction, its streetlights like heavenly haloes in the dark haze. Then Nicholas thought of Blackfriars Bridge at the end of the street, and of the River Thames.

And if Edwin Fairchild hadn't been walking north after an evening spent at an unsavoury gambling hell south of the river, Nicholas's life would have ended then.

A month after the wedding, Arabella's pregnancy was no longer concealable, and Nicholas took her to Alton Park. In front of the servants, he pretended kindness. Alone, he was as cruel as his mother. He rebuffed Arabella's attempts at intimacy. He denied her access to the carriage and refused to let her socialise. 'How otherwise can we pretend, *wife*, that your bastard is legitimate? Six weeks married, and you're already as big as a cow. You chose to play this hideous game, but now I determine the rules.'

Nicholas neither knew nor cared how Arabella spent her days locked away at Alton Park, but he spent his in whatever pleasures took his fancy.

And lots of pleasures – in all shapes and sizes – took his fancy. At least, they took his fancy *once*, and then he'd leave, no matter how much they wanted him back.

He'd *never* be so foolish as to give his heart to someone again.

Love made one vulnerable. And vulnerability was weakness.

In early February, Arabella began her labour. She laboured for thirty hours, and when her screams ceased, the silence was deafening. Nicholas froze with his glass of brandy halfway to his lips, unable to identify why the silence distressed him.

And then he realised: no baby cried.

The doctor entered the library minutes later, two days' stubble on his pallid cheeks. He shook his head.

Nicholas placed down his brandy. 'The baby?'

'I'm sorry, my lord. Your son never lived.'

There wasn't time to register his reaction before the doctor continued. 'My lord, Lady Holbrook . . . she's dying.'

'*What*?' A thrum, thrum, thrum began in Nicholas's head.

'She cannot survive. She's losing blood as we speak.'

'Then why the *hell* are you with me, man? Go back to her at once and stop her bleeding!'

The doctor shook his head. 'There is nothing to be done. I cannot prevent her death. She will die and very soon.'

Terror gripped Nicholas with icy hands upon his throat and heart. Why had he not been a decent person, a humane man? Perhaps he'd willed this terrible fate on Arabella and the baby. 'Good God, then send for the vicar.'

'My lord, there's no time. She needn't know she's dying – it'll be like slipping into sleep – but you should go to her. Your presence will make her comfortable. She's grieving for the baby. Give her what peace you can.'

How could *he* give her peace?

But, as if in a dream, Nicholas rushed to the bedside where an ashen-faced Arabella lay beside the baby – a swarthy, dark-haired Burton.

She lifted hazy eyes. 'He's dead.' Her words rasped from lips as white as marble.

Nicholas choked out his words. 'I'm so sorry.'

Her head tilted almost imperceptibly. 'You are?'

'Bella, I would've loved him as my own.' Nicholas cradled his wife's head against his shoulder. 'I didn't know that before, but I do now. I've been a monster. I shan't be, anymore.'

'You called me Bella.' Her voice whispered like rustling leaves.

'Yes, I did. My Bella, m-my wife.' He fought back tears, regretting too late that he'd never been kind to the woman he'd vowed to love for better and for worse.

A sigh. 'I've been so lonely these months. Terrified about childbirth as the baby grew larger and larger. And through it all, I thought you despised me. Do you still love me, Cole? *Can* you still love me?'

Although his wife was a stranger to him and Nicholas never lied, he gave the only answer he could give under the circumstances. 'Yes, Bella. I love you. Can you forgive me for how I've behaved?'

But she'd slipped away.

Waves of despair and self-loathing threatened again to overwhelm Nicholas in the months after he buried Arabella and her son in the churchyard.

He wondered, on occasion, what his uncle felt – if he mourned or was at all remorseful. In the end, it didn't matter because Nicholas hated himself more than he hated Lord Walter. Given the opportunity to be as honourable a man as his father, he'd failed.

He'd proven himself to be his mother's son instead.

But after he stirred himself to care for Rose during her first pregnancy, Nicholas buried his shame deep within himself and reconsidered his life. He was a callous bastard, incapable of honour and unwilling to be kind. Horrid, vicious, selfish.

His hopes and dreams were dead; his heart hardened against love.

He might as well make the most of it.

20

After seven weary hours on crowded roads – *everyone* seemed headed for London – the carriages from Alton Park passed through the gilded gates on the north side of Piccadilly Street. Harry and Elizabeth squirmed, ready to be released from confinement, and Mr Davis concluded his lecture on the history of London at last.

Meggy's stomach fluttered, her palms prickled, and the toes of her kid boots tapped against the carriage rug. She brushed aside the green velvet curtains as the carriage passed the gates.

Comprised of three storeys of white stone and sweeping colonnades, Holbrook House and its surrounding gardens occupied an entire block. Within the brick walls enclosing the property, trees unfurled tiny new leaves in gentle breezes, rows of tulips and daffodils bloomed, and birds chirped.

It was a haven inside a loud, crowded, malodorous city.

Meggy stepped from the carriage. Harry, Sophy and Copper tumbled behind her, followed by Mr Davis. A peacock dragged iridescent feathers across the wide front steps, and when Copper barked his disapproval, the bird fanned his impressive plumage. The spaniel retreated with his tail between his legs. Harry and Elizabeth, hands clasped, burst into laughter, and ran towards the oak doors.

Into the outstretched arms of a grinning Holbrook.

Meggy smoothed her muslin skirts. Holbrook certainly hadn't suffered during the separation. He looked in fine fettle: handsome, tanned, healthy.

Rose paused on the bottom step. 'Coming inside, dearest?' she asked Meggy.

'Not yet. I'd like to walk first. Enjoy a little peace after seven hours with Harry and Elizabeth.'

'You were *such* a dear to take them with you.' The sun passed behind a cloud, and Rose glanced up. 'Don't stay long, Meggy; the sky's darkening.'

'I shan't.'

The earthy scent of rain permeated the damp air as Meggy walked the brick-paved pathway around one sweeping colonnade to the vast back garden. A central lawn lined with lime trees stretched over the middle of the grounds behind the house, but Meggy headed towards the hedged walkways enclosing smaller gardens along the periphery.

Since it was early April, many of the mysteries of the enclosures were concealed, but each smaller garden possessed its own character and purpose, like different rooms in a house. A greening rose garden led to the shell-lined tunnels of an artificial grotto. The man–made cave was drier and brighter than a real-life counterpart, but Meggy smiled as she traversed the passageways. The children would delight in games

274

of pretence here. Mermaids or pirates or giants – the possibilities were endless.

Rainbow mists and the sound of splashing water at the end of the grotto foretold the next garden before Meggy exited the cave. A fountain featuring Poseidon rising from marble waves stood within trim parterre hedges. Beyond was the entrance to a maze constructed of tall, square-trimmed boxwoods.

A *large* maze. It appeared to stretch the width of the grounds, for the entire north edge of the lawn was an eight-foot wall of hedge. Presumably, the maze exited on the far side of the property and led to the smaller gardens along the eastern wall.

As Meggy considered whether she should walk across the lawn or attempt the maze – and possibly find herself lost inside when the rain began – the click of boots on bricks arrested her attention. She stepped into the hedge, her heart racing.

But she hadn't reached the first turn before Holbrook caught up. 'Lady Margaret.'

Meggy paused. Might as well get the first meeting behind her.

She turned and met his gaze.

He stopped mid-stride. 'Ah, I see you don't want me here. I shall return to the house.'

She sighed. 'No, wait.'

'*Yes?*' He looked like Harry hoping for a sweetmeat. Or Copper begging for a game of fetch.

Meggy closed her eyes to focus her mind. It was difficult to see Holbrook and maintain her resolve, but after reading his heart-wrenching letter dozens of times, she'd finally decided. Whilst she believed he strove to be a good man – and even believed that, like Edwin, at his core Holbrook *was* good – he fell far too easily into vice when confronted with challenges or with temptations.

Just as Edwin had.

Just as Harry must *never* do.

Meggy's deathbed promise to her father was a sacred thing. It had eased his passing, and the future of the Fairchild family depended upon it.

Therefore, Meggy must put aside her own feelings because Holbrook's impulsivity posed a volatile risk, both for her and for Harry. She *must* find another mentor for Harry. One without vices – or, at least, whose vices were mild and easily influenced away by the firm guiding hand of a wife.

Meggy needed a husband she could control. Dull, predictable, safe.

This first meeting with Holbrook was critical; Meggy couldn't fail. A deep breath calmed her nerves.

She faced the marquess again and began her prepared speech. 'I want to say thank you for trusting me with your confidence. It was undoubtedly difficult to communicate such distressing memories, and I'm aware of the honour of your sharing them with me. I hope confiding gave you some peace—'

His shoulders drooped. 'But you loathe me even yet.'

The words were on the tip of her tongue: *I don't loathe you – quite the opposite.* But she left them unspoken.

'My opinion is irrelevant, sir.'

'Your opinion is all that matters.'

'It oughtn't be. Nor is it fair of you to burden me so. *Your* opinion should matter most.'

Even sheltered amongst the boxwoods, a damp wind swelled. The evergreen leaves rustled, the smell of rain grew stronger, and the clouds took on the colour of iron.

Holbrook studied the toe of his boot. 'You sound like Alexander.'

'Alexander is wise.'

Holbrook's jaw tightened. '*Wise*, is he?'

Meggy sighed. 'I didn't say that to make you jealous. I can agree with a man without being in love with him.' She stepped closer. His scowl softened, and he held out a hand. Meggy shook her head; his arm fell to his side. 'Lord Holbrook, I'm terribly sorry for what happened. If it gives you any comfort, anyone who heard your story would agree you were the more aggrieved party. You were betrayed by those who ought to have had your best interests at heart.'

Holbrook leaned towards her. 'So, you think my behaviour justifiable?'

'I didn't say that.'

He released a heavy breath. 'I see.'

'As I told you before, being wounded doesn't give one allowance to wound others.'

'But what ought I have done when I discovered Arabella carried my uncle's child?'

'Let's start at the beginning. I don't mean to be cruel, but you oughtn't have been so impulsive in your choice of a wife in the first place, especially after how your father suffered. And considering your previous distrust of your uncle – why, it baffles me that you fell for the trap.'

Holbrook didn't answer at once. Instead, he pulled a leaf from the hedge and studied it. 'You don't account for how unloved I've felt much of my life.' The leaf fluttered to the ground. 'It's no small thing never to hear your mother say she loves you.'

'As every orphan can attest to. Holbrook, you made your choice willingly – albeit impulsively – and therefore were accountable to abide by it. You made vows to your wife – vows which aren't to be dismissed. Vows which are sacred.'

He threw his palms up. 'And yet she made vows to me which she never intended to keep.'

Meggy stepped closer and almost placed a gloved hand on his arm. 'But we're speaking of *you*, not Arabella. By your own admission, you knew nothing about her. We don't know her true motivations, and we don't know how your uncle manipulated her.'

'You say having wounds doesn't give one allowance to behave poorly.'

'Yes, and it's certainly fair for you to be upset with her, just as I am upset with Edwin. But to repay pain with pain . . . no, Holbrook. Not justifiable.'

He bowed his head, shielding his eyes with a hand. 'Arabella died before she could forgive me.' When he dropped his arm, his eyes glistened. 'And everything you say reinforces my self-loathing.'

'Self-loathing is not something anyone else can take away.'

A tear trickled from the corner of his eye, tracing a path over one cheekbone and down his cheek before it disappeared into the starched points of his high collar. 'I could love myself again if you would love me, Meggy. Then I could believe I have worth.'

Meggy swallowed the three words she mustn't utter. 'I shall say again, it's not fair to burden me so.' It was the truth, after all – he *shouldn't* ask such a thing of her.

He stepped closer, and although they didn't touch, she felt the warmth of his body and smelled bergamot mixed with the pre-storm air. The dark clouds above his head churned with their unshed burden. 'Is there no hope at all, Meggy? No hope for my love to be returned?'

She closed her eyes and gathered her resolve. 'I shan't marry you, Holbrook. You aren't what I want in a husband.' *What I* need, she corrected herself silently. *You aren't what I need in a husband. Want is another matter entirely.*

His eyes glistened with unshed tears, but he nodded. 'I understand. Why would you, after all?'

A stab of pain originated in Meggy's heart and reverberated through every nerve. It was tempting to give him some respite from his self-loathing by telling him what he wanted to hear. If she had any guarantee that his love would last, she might do it. But she'd made her decision, and she would adhere to her resolution.

'Holbrook, I do care. I'm grateful to you for your generosity to me and to my siblings. I want to be your friend. Truly. You may share your feelings with me

– let me be your confidante as you discover how to forgive yourself. I shall listen.'

He ground the toe of his boot upon the brick path, the fine lines again between his brow as he studied the gleaming tip of his shoe. But when he at last lifted his gaze, his eyes had brightened. 'I shall accept what you offer with gratitude. Thank you for your friendship, Meggy.'

'You're welcome. And . . . and have you forgiven *me*, Holbrook?'

'Forgiven you? What do I have to forgive you for?'

'For prying into your desk drawers.'

He half smiled. 'I'd forgotten. But you're welcome to pry amongst my possessions. I have no secrets from you anymore. I reacted foolishly at the time in an attempt to protect my heart. It didn't work – it shattered into a million pieces the moment the door closed behind you.'

His words stole Meggy's breath and pulled at her own heart like a magnet. She stood on tiptoe and leaned towards Holbrook before she recalled herself and stepped away. She'd nearly failed already.

But Holbrook had noticed. 'Oh, Meggy.' His voice was thick, guttural. 'My dearest love.'

She focused on the rustling leaves of the boxwood and breathed until her writhing heart calmed. But he was by her shoulder, his words whispered in her ear. 'Meggy, perhaps you *do* love me?' His hand slid up her arm, his touch against her cotton spencer radiated throughout her body. Her eyes fluttered with the exquisite pleasure of his closeness, and she savoured it a moment longer than she ought.

'Holbrook, you mustn't touch me.' She turned as his arm dropped. 'I cannot marry you, but I also cannot resist your touch.'

He parted his lips, his eyes yearning. 'My love – my sweet love, my only love – *please* don't do this to us.'

'*No!* Don't speak like that. Don't attempt to change my mind. And you must promise not to touch me.' *Because if you do,* she thought to herself, *I shall give myself to you.*

His brow furrowed as he studied her, but he didn't press her for more explanation. He released a heavy sigh instead. 'As you wish, Meggy.'

The first raindrops fell.

Meggy looked at the dark sky. Cool droplets landed on her hot cheeks.

Holbrook offered his arm. 'Shall we go inside?'

She reached out her hand instinctively. Then she drew back.

'Forgive me,' he said, a new lightness to his voice. 'Force of habit, I assure you. I shall remember the next time.'

They fell into step as they retraced Meggy's earlier path through the gardens. Despite the weather, they didn't rush. The raindrops were plump but gradual, splashing upon the budding spring leaves and lush grass.

'I must ask, Meggy – what if you stumble or trip? May I catch you?' He jested, teased – and his eyes twinkled.

Meggy chuckled, a warmth infusing her as she settled back into playfulness with her friend. 'No, you must let me fall.'

Holbrook placed his hand to his heart. 'Dear God! But if you are about to drown? Surely then I may save you?'

She lifted her chin and tossed her curls. 'It won't be necessary. I'm an excellent swimmer.'

'So, truly under no circumstances may I touch you?'

Her smile fell away. 'Yes, Holbrook. I think it's for the best.'

A flicker in his eyes. Then he resumed the dramatics. 'Very well, I shall do as you bid. I expect I shall look a scaly cove, however, escorting you and Rose this season and never offering my arm.'

Meggy laughed. She brushed against him accidentally due to the narrowness of a turn in the grotto. Although he must've noticed, he said nothing. As they continued in silence, she peeked from under her bonnet.

He looked remarkably well for someone who claimed to have a broken heart.

A dark thought, one that she'd often wondered during their weeks apart, returned to her.

Had Holbrook released his desire into some woman's willing arms? It was his right, it was his nature, and Meggy had no cause for jealousy, but nevertheless, the thought sickened her.

'You look well, Holbrook.'

The fall of their footsteps and the splatter of rain-drops were the only sounds for a moment. 'Thank you. I've made some effort on that account. I have little to recommend myself to the lady I love besides my devilishly handsome face – do please excuse my vanity – so I thought I'd make the best of it.' He grinned and winked. Then his smile fell away, but his voice retained a playful lightness. 'Not at once after I left Alton Park, you understand. In the first week of my coming to town, I was rather a mess. Spent my days and nights drinking alone in the dark. It was pathetic, and you would've been disgusted. But then I chose a different course of action. I cleaned myself up, didn't touch drink, rode and boxed every day, and ordered new clothes. What do you think of this coat?'

Meggy considered. 'It looks very much like most of your other blue coats, although lighter in shade.'

'Does it? And yet Weston declared this one of his best. Never mind; I shan't tell him your verdict lest he end in tears. But what is your opinion of the shade? Does it make my eyes look less severe? Less like cold steel?'

'Your eyes don't look like cold steel.'

'No? Dare I ask what they do look like?'

They were the soft feathers of a dove's wing; the pillowy piles of spring rain clouds; the shimmer of grey silk. But Meggy couldn't say those things. 'I shan't tell you.'

'Shall I tell you what yours look like?'

'They're blue.'

'They're the blue of a cool lake in summertime. Of forget-me-nots blanketing a meadow. The blue of an endless sky on a cloudless day.'

When Meggy at last regained the ability to speak, she said, 'Yes, well. Blue.'

She wasn't capable of more.

21

Meggy knelt upon the yellow upholstered window seat and leaned her forehead against the sash, watching Holbrook, Mr Davis, and the four older children play a ridiculous game upon the lawn in the late May sunshine. It employed cricket bats and wickets but appeared to follow an improvised set of rules.

The children and Mr Davis comprised one team. They batted the ball to keep it from the opposing team, which consisted of an exuberant Copper, a panting Caesar, and a hatless Holbrook.

A hatless *and* coatless Holbrook, wearing tight buff-coloured trousers. A grinning and laughing Holbrook – as he'd been increasingly often over the last weeks – with dark curls falling over his forehead and loose shirtsleeves pushed up his tanned forearms.

Meggy shivered, despite the warmth of the day. She remembered those arms embracing her, cradling her, holding her almost three months earlier. Her hands recalled cupping his muscular bottom as his hard cock rubbed against the throbbing between her legs. She could almost feel his lips trailing her body, suckling her aching breasts, and . . .

Rose's voice chimed from across the room. 'Have you decided whose suit you will accept, dearest?'

Meggy's smile vanished. She sighed, as she did whenever she thought of her suitors. She needed to decide *soon* which she'd accept. It wasn't fair to leave them dangling. She couldn't accept all three, and the other two might wish to look elsewhere before families dispersed to the country in July.

Meggy tore her eyes from Holbrook and stood.

'No, I haven't.'

They were in the magnificent ground-floor drawing room of Holbrook House. The painted faces of Burton ancestors hung in gilded frames upon red walls. Gold damask draped the tall windows overlooking the lawn and back gardens, and gilded furniture with yellow silk upholstery provided seating for dozens.

Rose embroidered, her slender, pale hands plying a needle as rows of lilies of the valley blossomed along a white muslin hem. She often embellished Meggy's gowns, and she completed the work with astonishing speed and precision. 'It's almost June, dearest. Mr Harrison especially seems to grow impatient.'

Meggy plopped upon a sofa and took up her own embroidery. Although she despised sewing, one needed an occupation when afternoon callers arrived. She sighed as she threaded her needle with green floss. 'Does he? I hadn't noticed, but if I do, I shall reject him at once. An impatient husband won't do.' She knotted her floss, breaking one of the many embroidery rules she cared nothing about. 'Besides, I have a strategy for choosing.'

Rose's pale eyebrows lifted. 'Oh?'

Meggy began the second half of a leaf she'd worked on for three days. 'On the first of June, I shall line up Mr Carow, Mr Webb and Mr Harrison – unless I've already rejected Harrison for impatience – and count them off. *What will my husband be? Tinker, tailor, soldier, sailor, rich-man, poor-man, beggar-man, thief.* Except I should add barrister, sugar baker, and Parliamentarian to the list.'

Rose's laughter pealed. 'You wouldn't.'

'I'm considering it.' Meggy wasn't really. Her marriage was a critical decision, both for her and for her siblings; she'd never be impulsive. But the idea amused her. They were all exactly the sort of staid man Meggy's father would've wanted her to marry. 'One is very much like the next: perfectly eligible, reasonably handsome, pleasingly pliable, and none proposes because his mother wishes it, which was Mr Robinson's unforgivable sin. Mr Carow is the cleverest, Mr Harrison possesses the finest eyes, and Mr Webb is the most obliging. I suppose as a tradesman, he has the most to gain from a union with an earl's daughter, even if she is the sister of Edwin Fairchild.'

Holbrook's early prediction had been accurate. Meggy's association with Edwin was a millstone that made her more determined than ever to set the Fairchild family to rights. The unsavoury recollections *must* be a dim memory by the time Sophy and Harry grew up.

'Every family has some skeletons,' Rose had said early in the season. 'You see not everyone is perfectly kind to me. The older ladies despised my mother.'

286

'Your brother doesn't suffer from the connection,' Meggy had replied. It was true; despite Holbrook's terrible reputation, on the few occasions when he'd accompanied them into society, he was sought after by debutantes and their mothers alike. Which just proved people would do anything for a title, Meggy had thought, and then remembered she oughtn't judge what she couldn't understand. She'd carried the privilege of an honorific all her life.

'Nicky is more easily forgiven for being Mother's child,' Rose had said. 'Matchmaking mamas agree on only one thing: there's a deplorable shortage of titled single men in Britain.'

Like Rose, Meggy learned to compensate for another's sins by being especially pleasant. Not ingratiating, and certainly not toad-eating – such behaviours were unforgivable – but mild-mannered, well spoken, and, above all else, willing to encourage the chatter of others for hours.

But she was hardly a raging success on the marriage market. Her dowry was uninspiring. She was old for a debutante – she felt positively ancient next to the flittering seventeen- and eighteen-year-olds. And she was too freckled and short – or 'rather common-looking', as some said – to be an Incomparable.

Rose drew Meggy's thoughts back to the present. 'But, dearest, which of the gentlemen do you *love*?'

Meggy tugged at her needle. The second half of the leaf was not symmetrical, but it was too tiresome to pull it all out and start again, so she continued sewing. 'I've decided love is something that must come *after* marriage. I know it wasn't so with you and your Thomas, but generally, I think it best to choose an acceptable partner and then will oneself into loving him.'

Rose's eyes widened. '*Will* oneself?'

'Yes — settle upon what features and characteristics are most pleasing and then ignore the rest until one falls in love. I'm certain it can be done.'

'You might wait, Meggy, until you find a gentleman you love.'

'No, Rose. I need to marry. I mustn't keep imposing upon your brother.' Meggy couldn't live much longer with Holbrook. Her carnal impulses were nearly impossible to resist. She needed to commit to another man and let *him* satisfy her. 'Besides,' she continued, 'I turn two-and-twenty in a few weeks — I shall be an old maid next season, fit only to sit against the wall with the dowagers.'

Rose chuckled. 'Hardly.'

Meggy didn't argue, but she knew that a lady who refused eligible proposals was deemed a flirt, a tease or a jilt — and respectable men didn't pursue elusive quarry for marriage. If Meggy developed such a reputation by rejecting all three of her perfectly eligible suitors, it would tarnish Sophy as well.

Meggy *had* to marry either Carow, Harrison or Webb. She and Rose sewed in silence.

'*Dearest* . . .'

Meggy recognised the pleading tone. 'Rose.'

'But, Meggy, please hear me out. You and Nicky enjoy each other's company. Your daily walk—'

'We're friends, as you know.'

'He loves you so much, I'm convinced of it.'

'Rose, you know my feelings on this matter. I'm going to be happy with one of my utterly predictable, utterly dull suitors—'

The butler cleared his throat from the door. 'Dr Mitchell, my ladies.'

Alexander entered, grinning his crooked grin. 'Do tell me about your dull suitors, Meggy.'

Meggy laughed. 'Thank goodness it's only you. How dreadful if one of them had overheard.'

The physician stretched out in an armchair near Rose. 'Prepare yourself, Meggy. I saw Carow walking across Green Park.'

Not three minutes later, Mr Carow was announced. He sat beside Meggy and launched into a not entirely unamusing story about his latest court case. Mr Harrison arrived ten minutes later, and the two gentlemen vied for Meggy's attention until Mr Webb joined last of all.

Meggy listened half-heartedly to their conversation as she struggled with her embroidery.

Then Holbrook, coat on and curls tidied, entered. Meggy's hands, still holding her needle and square of silk, fell to her lap.

The marquess glowed from exercise as he chatted and laughed with Rose and Alexander. His coat was Meggy's favourite, although she'd never admit it to him, as impossibly conceited as he was. It was dark green, and when combined with Holbrook's tanned complexion and grey eyes, Meggy was reminded of a cool, shady forest.

A hand brushed her forearm. 'Don't you think, Lady Margaret?'

'I'm sorry, I didn't catch your question.' She answered without knowing who'd spoken, and whilst still watching Holbrook. His gestures indicated he was describing the ball game. Rose and Alexander laughed.

'I say, Lady Margaret, do you attend?' Meggy turned and blinked at a scowling Harrison, whose narrowed eyes flitted between her and Holbrook.

'Forgive me, Mr Harrison,' Meggy said. 'I'm afraid my thoughts were elsewhere. What were you saying?'

Harrison's lips compressed. 'Never mind, ma'am. I don't wish to intrude upon your thoughts. I ought to be leaving anyway.'

Alexander took his leave as well, but Carow and Webb lingered.

'Harrison was asking your ladyship's opinion about *The Grecian Daughter*,' Carow said. 'The play we saw at Drury Lane last week when he and I had the privilege of sitting in your box. Specifically, he wished to hear your thoughts on Sarah Bartley's performance.'

Meggy took up her embroidery again. 'Oh, she was very good.'

She barely recalled the actress. It had been on one of the rare evenings that Holbrook accompanied them, and he'd amused Meggy with whispered commentary about the other theatregoers for the duration of the performance.

Carow chuckled. 'I'm glad you enjoyed it. Harrison wasn't certain if you could *hear* the performance. The audience was especially chatty that evening.'

Fury rose hot within Meggy. *Damn* Carow for laughing at her. She wouldn't have a husband who bristled about her enjoying her friendships. 'I heard what I wanted to hear.'

The barrister's lips curved into an amused half-grin. 'Touché, my lady.'

Webb cleared his throat. 'Lady Margaret, would you . . . that is, would your ladyship be so good as to accompany me on a ride in Hyde Park this afternoon?'

Meggy softened her demeanour. 'I'm sorry, Mr Webb, but I cannot today. Lady Rose and I are engaged to attend Lady Frampton's ball.'

'I shall be there as well,' Carow said. 'May I take this opportunity to request the first dance?' The barrister smirked at Webb. The wealthy confectioner wasn't invited to the parties of the *haut ton*, although no assembly was complete without his shop's exquisite treats arranged in pastel pyramids upon the refreshment tables.

Meggy accepted, but she pursed her lips. If she chose Carow, she'd have to rid him of his elitist views.

At last, both gentlemen finally left, and Meggy tossed aside her embroidery.

'Thank God they're gone,' Holbrook said. He threw his feet onto the sofa and lay down, placing his head atop the cascading muslin in Rose's lap with his hands folded over his waistcoat. 'I can at last rest in my own house.'

'You won't rest if my needle pricks you, Nicky,' Rose said. 'You're lying upon it.' She patted his curls, much in the manner of one petting a puppy, and Holbrook grinned at her.

Meggy laughed. 'Did the children exhaust you, Holbrook?'

'Ha! I exhausted the children.'

'Yet you look tired.'

'Tired, no. Sunburnt, maybe.'

'You didn't wear your hat. I saw you.'

Holbrook propped himself on one elbow. 'And did you also see your *sweet* little sister maul me viciously not five minutes into the game? How can a man wear a hat under such circumstances?'

'You should've been better on your guard. You know how violent Sophy is during tiger and bear hunts – or last week, when we played pirates in the grotto.'

Holbrook grinned. 'I confess I encourage it. She must learn to fight off blighters now. It's preparation for *her* first Season.'

Meggy smiled. 'I suppose you're too tired for a walk?' she asked, teasing. Nothing prevented their daily walks. Even in rain, they bundled under *separate* umbrellas and trudged forth.

'I told you I'm not tired.'

'I don't believe you, of course. I've played ball with the children. They exhaust *me*, and I'm nine years younger than you.'

'I shall prove I'm full of energy by racing you across the lawn.'

Meggy laughed. 'I accept your challenge. Rose, will you join us?'

'No, but thank you.' She replied thus every day.

'Give me a moment, Meggy,' Holbrook said. 'I shall meet you upon the lawn.'

22

Meggy waited for Holbrook in the shade of a lime tree. She savoured the warm breeze, which fluttered the skirts of her muslin frock and cooled her bare arms. The day was a glorious testament to late spring: the gardens abloom, the sky cloudless, the lawn like green velvet. Muffled city sounds of carriage wheels and hooves upon cobblestone, and the cries and calls of people, faded into the background. The tweets and warbles of birdsong chorused louder within the enclosed grounds.

Meggy squeezed her arms around her chest. She closed her eyes and inhaled warmth and sunshine.

It was almost like the country.

'You look happy.'

Meggy hadn't heard Holbrook's approach. She opened her eyes and smiled.

'Because I *am* happy. What's in the bag?' The strap of a leather satchel crossed his chest.

'You shall see, in due course. Now, a fair race across the lawn to the entry of the maze?'

'The maze!' Meggy placed a hand to her breast in mock surprise. 'Are you *finally* allowing me to enter the maze?'

'Yes, after weeks of your tiresome begging, I've decided to indulge you.'

'And why today of all days?'

'Ah, because the maze is ready for you now. It's at its best in June, and it's very nearly that month.'

Meggy tilted her head. 'At its best? It's an evergreen hedge; it looks the same all year long.'

'Not the centre of the maze.'

'What's in the centre?'

'I shan't spoil the surprise.'

Meggy lifted her chin. 'Something grand and ostentatious, I imagine. A Grecian temple folly with a statue of Apollo – for which you posed, no doubt.'

His eyes sparkled. 'Very likely. At any rate, if there's not one yet, I ought to rectify that. But will you model as Daphne to my Apollo, my darling? It seems so fitting, especially as we begin our race.'

Meggy's cheeks warmed. She blushed less frequently in Holbrook's company now, but his reference was a bold reminder, and she'd walked right into it. According to myth, the god Apollo was passionately in love with Daphne, a water nymph who loathed him. One day they ran a race, and the moment Apollo caught Daphne, the nymph pleaded to the river god for help. She transformed into a laurel tree in Apollo's arms.

Meggy stood tree-like herself, her improper thoughts unspoken: *I wish you would catch me. I'd not plea to be turned into a tree; I'd beg you to carry me away with you.*

'Meggy? Shall we begin our race?'

294

Meggy snapped out of her daze. Her daydream was titillating, but she'd think of it alone in her bed later. Holbrook as Apollo and herself as Daphne promised to be an especially delightful imagining of the sort she indulged in every night before drifting to sleep.

'Count us off,' Holbrook said.

Meggy did as she was bid.

The wind whipped in her face as she sprinted across the lawn with her skirts pulled up to her knees. Holbrook was behind her – his boots pounded the grass, but he never passed her. She glanced over her shoulder, laughing, and he winked, not even winded.

'You're letting me win.'

'Perhaps you're too nimble for me, Daphne.'

By the time Meggy reached the maze entry, her heart hammered. She laughed as she doubled over to catch her breath. 'That was wonderful. How I miss running across fields. There's far too much sitting in drawing rooms in London.'

'Yes, you always seem more at home outside.'

Meggy hugged her arms tightly across her chest, aglow with the warmth of exercise. She turned her face to the sky. 'If I could, I would live in a . . . oh, perhaps in a house amongst the tree branches, or a cave beside a bubbling brook.'

She smiled at Holbrook.

He wore *that* look, the one that made Meggy's heart ache. Tilted head, darling smile, soft eyes. 'Do you mean, Meggy, that you would *all the pleasures prove, that valleys, groves, hills, and fields, woods, or steepy mountain yields*?'

Meggy laughed to disguise her yearning. 'You and your improper Marlowe.'

Holbrook shrugged. 'It's a fitting poem for you. But go on then.' He nodded towards the entrance. 'Let's see how quickly you can find the centre.'

'You won't show me the way?'

He grinned. 'Where's the fun in that?'

Meggy tossed her head. 'What a taskmaster you are today.' She put her right hand to the boxwood hedge. In this way, one might traverse a maze and always end in the centre. It was a slow method but ensured success.

'Why not try to find the centre without using that tiresome trick, Meggy? We shall be at it until evening otherwise.'

'I don't take risks, Holbrook. Certainly, I *might* find the centre more quickly otherwise, but I'm just as likely to end up thoroughly lost.' She peeped over her shoulder. 'However, if you would simply *show* me the way, we might be there in moments.'

'You'd memorise the key, and then you'll never have the fun of the puzzle.' He put a finger to his chin. 'Unless . . .' He shook his head. 'But no, that won't work.'

'Unless *what*?'

'Never mind, I wasn't thinking.' His eyes twinkled.

Meggy lifted her chin. 'You are playing with me, of course. You obviously have a nefarious scheme in mind, and you may as well confess.'

'I was only thinking *if* you would allow me to touch you, I'd tie my handkerchief around your eyes and lead you.'

Meggy glared. 'This is a ruse.'

'Not in the least. However . . .' Holbrook glanced at the toe of his boot.

'Yes?'

He met her gaze. 'If you *did* allow me to touch you, and I behaved myself, I wonder if you might then grant me the dance of my choosing at Lady Frampton's ball tonight?'

Meggy's heart pounded – and not from exercise. 'I thought you weren't attending Lady Frampton's ball.' Her voice was more breathless than she intended.

'I shall attend if you'll dance with me,' Holbrook said. 'And please don't say no yet. Allow me first to lead you through the maze. I promise you can trust me.'

She pretended to be reluctant. 'Oh, very well.'

The moment his fingers brushed her skin, her body tingled to every extremity. But he never lingered in one spot; his movements were brisk as he took off her bonnet and tied his crisp handkerchief around her eyes. He plopped the bonnet on her head again.

'There,' he said. 'Place your hand upon my arm, and I shall keep you perfectly safe.'

They walked down a path and turned back on themselves. The next turn was a right, followed by a left. Continuing to focus on the order of the turns kept Meggy's mind off Holbrook's muscular arm.

'Are you memorising the turns, Meggy?'

'Of course.'

'I anticipated that. Therefore, I intentionally led you down some wrong paths.'

She smiled. 'Yes, you certainly have.'

He burst into laughter. 'What a cutting reply, Meggy. But admit it, my darling – I've been a gentleman this spring.'

She squeezed his arm. 'You're a lovely *friend*, Holbrook.'

He stopped. 'Thank you for trusting me. You took a risk. Now tell me – do you appreciate the reward?' He removed her blindfold.

And Meggy gasped.

Clematis vines laden with snowy blossoms trailed green and white tendrils over a gazebo. Three majestic draping willows surrounded the structure, and tall delphiniums bloomed blue, pink and purple. Butterflies fluttered, furry bees buzzed, and the air was heavy with the scent of flowers. Meggy clasped her hands before her heart. 'It's a magical fairyland.'

'There's no pond, of course, but I wondered if it might remind you of your favourite spot at Berksleigh Hall. To me, there's a commonality between them.'

Meggy nodded. 'I sense it as well. There's a similar peaceful seclusion. And an intimate connection with nature.'

'Recently you told me you enjoyed going to the pond to read. I wondered if the gazebo might serve such a purpose for you whilst you're in town? I shan't take your hand, but come, look inside with me.'

He swept aside the clematis, for the vines fell like a curtain around the open sides, and Meggy stepped inside. Sunlight filtered through the greenery and cast fluttering dappled shadows against the marble interior. The gazebo was circular, the sides comprised of Doric columns and curved benches.

Holbrook chuckled. 'You weren't far off with your guess before our race. It's a bit like a Grecian temple. And when you stand in the centre, you are Daphne. But *your* Apollo shall behave. Would you like to read a book?'

'I haven't a book.'

He opened his bag. 'I have a selection. Geology? Chemical philosophy? Newton? Or perhaps – although I think it unlikely – a novel?'

'But I'm in a garden. Didn't you bring something on horticulture?'

Holbrook lifted his brows. 'Shall I return to the house and see what I can find?'

She laughed. 'No, I'm only teasing you. Geology will do.'

'I'm glad you didn't choose the novel – otherwise, I might be very bored indeed.' Holbrook removed his coat, rolled it, and placed it upon a bench as a pillow for Meggy's head.

'I'll read upon *that* one.' He indicated the adjacent bench. 'And I shan't look at you even once. In fact, I may fall asleep.'

'I knew the scamps exhausted you.'

'I admit nothing.'

Meggy reclined with her head upon his coat. She clasped her book to her chest.

'Comfortable, my darling?'

'Very,' she said. Sunlight and shadows flickered over Holbrook's face as he smiled down.

'And have I behaved well enough to earn my dance tonight?'

'Yes.'

His eyes lit. 'Truly?'

'Don't make me regret it, Holbrook.'

'Not I.' He winked and disappeared from her view, but Meggy listened as he settled himself on his bench and opened his book.

Meggy didn't open hers. Instead, she continued to hug it to her chest as the clematis fluttered in the breeze.

She indulged herself in the daydream she'd begun on the lawn. She was Daphne racing across a meadow of delphiniums – but a Daphne only *pretending* she didn't want to be caught – with Holbrook as Apollo in pursuit. She wore the sheerest muslin without a chemise, and the breeze blew against her skin. Holbrook wore linen draped to expose his muscular body. When they reached the Grecian temple, Daphne let herself be caught. When Apollo took her in his arms, his cock was hard as it pressed against the soft skin of her thigh. And his lips were hot on Daphne's, and she succumbed willingly.

Gratefully.

Desperately.

Meggy throbbed.

It was a fantasy she could create at this very moment. Surely Holbrook would enact it with her. They'd be best friends taking their play to another level – a place safe for them to pretend whatever they wanted because they were secure in their trust.

If only she could trust him.

If only she could take that risk.

Meggy indulged her imagination until her desire reached a fevered pitch. She needed to go inside, or she would kiss Holbrook. And if she kissed him, she wouldn't stop.

Meggy stood.

Holbrook lay reading. One hand propped up his head, and his elbow rested on the bench.

He lifted his eyes. 'Yes?'

'Take me back inside, please . . .' – and although she couldn't say the words he longed to hear from her, she offered him a small gift – '. . . Nicky.'

He blinked. 'What did you call me?'

'Nicky.'

He sat up. 'Why, Meggy? What does it mean?'

She couldn't tell him what it *truly* meant. 'Merely that I wish to call you by the name you like best.'

Silence stretched between them for some time.

'At one time,' Nicholas said quietly, 'Cole was my favourite. But not anymore.'

She nodded. 'I know, my dear friend. I know.'

Lady Frampton's ball was a proper squeeze, so crowded with damp bodies the air steamed. Heavy perfumes masked the smell of heated humans, and wine-dense breath warmed Meggy's cheeks as old men pressed unnecessarily close against her, as they did to most young ladies.

According to the *haut ton's* reasoning, the ball was a raging success.

According to Meggy, it would've been another tiresome, sweaty evening if not for the promise of a dance with Nicholas.

She fully admitted – but *only* to herself – she couldn't *wait* for that dance.

She'd dressed in the evening gown Rose said became her the best: a pale blue satin underdress overlaid with sheer, white silk net with a square-cut neckline and short, puffed sleeves. Like all dancing frocks, the hem fell just above the ankle, and Meggy's blue satin slippers peeked out from below, their long ribbon laces crossed over her silk stockings and tied under the knee with her garters.

Mr Carow claimed her for the first dance, a country reel.

'Lady Margaret, you look spectacular this evening. Beauty beyond compare. Please tell me you have an affirmative answer at last so that I may be the happiest of men.'

'Not yet, Mr Carow.'

The barrister frowned. The dance separated them for a short time, and when they rejoined, he said, 'If you are holding out for an offer from Holbrook, you might wish to rethink your strategy.'

Meggy's heart stopped. When it resumed beating, it pumped boiling blood through her veins. Carow needed a tongue-lashing for his impertinence but making a scene at a ball wasn't a behaviour she could risk.

She compressed her lips instead.

But Carow was evidently just beginning. 'I'm certain Holbrook makes himself appealing enough from time to time, but everyone knows he's a heartless debauchee. No one would speak to him if not for the title, and if he weren't so damned rich and handsome. Never trust him, Lady Margaret. He'd think nothing of hurting you.'

Meggy clenched her jaw to keep her words inside. Carow knew nothing at all about Nicky.

But then she realised Carow echoed her own fears.

'The more you are seen with him,' Carow continued, 'the more your reputation will suffer. If not for the fact that Lady Rose's behaviour is without fault despite . . . well, never mind. I only mean to say, if not for Lady Rose, you and your siblings would already suffer for the association. Only your brother would be so foolish as to appoint Holbrook guardian to anyone. Not that I blame *you*, my lady. Quite the opposite . . .'

Carow droned on in a similar vein. Meggy ignored him as her eyes trailed Holbrook. A gaggle of matrons surrounded him everywhere he went. As always when women flirted with Nicholas, Meggy wondered how many of them he'd bedded. How many of their breasts had he kissed, how many of their bodies had he taken pleasure in?

She knew that wondering such things about the past would be daily life if she became Lady Holbrook. And at some point, Nicholas's resolve would falter. Not at first, certainly. In the beginning, everything would be lovely. But at some point, he would tire of her. Perhaps when she was with child, or once her body changed as a woman's invariably did after childbirth. Or maybe it would happen even sooner. After their first argument. Or the first time another woman touched him invitingly.

And once it happened, it would happen again and again whilst Meggy bore the shame as Nicholas's father had.

She shuddered at the thought.

She *couldn't* risk marriage with Nicholas.

But she wanted him.

Every fibre of her body yearned for him.

And she knew with sudden clarity what held her back from accepting one of her other suitors: before she committed herself to another man, she needed Nicholas.

Once she had that one treasured memory to cling to for the rest of her life, she could face being another man's loyal and dutiful wife.

After her dance with Carow, Meggy accepted the hands of other partners one after the other, hoping at the end of each dance that Nicholas would claim her next.

At last, he approached.

Meggy's heart lurched, her body blazed.

The orchestra struck the opening bars of a waltz. Nicholas placed a hand around Meggy's waist and drew her close. His embrace stole her breath.

She tilted her head back, her eyelids as heavy as lead, her feet as light as feathers. 'Did you choose the waltz on purpose, Nicky?'

He smiled – not mocking, not teasing, not grinning. He smiled a tender smile, a smile full of love. 'If I may have only one dance with you, I'd be a fool not to take the waltz.'

And they swirled.

Meggy's feet glided across the polished wooden floor. She was weightless in Nicholas's arms, her silk net overskirt swishing against his tight trousers, his gleaming black kid-leather dance slippers sliding near her blue satin ones. The music was a universe away, the flickering candles like starlight. She couldn't draw her gaze from his grey eyes.

'Meggy, you are so beautiful you take my breath away.'

Her reply came without thinking, straight from the heart. 'I feel the same about you.'

His hand tightened around her waist. 'I love you,' he said. 'With every thought I have, every moment of every day, I love you, Margaret Fairchild.'

It was as if gravity vanished. Meggy's heart was falling into a deep, deep well, with no bottom in sight, and the fall was luxurious. There were no people in the world but the two of them, swirling together amidst the crowds.

Near the end of the dance, she whispered his name into the linen folds at his neck. 'I . . . I'd prefer to go home early tonight. In fact, I want to leave now.'

A moment stretched between them like an eternity.

Then he nodded. 'Let's find Rose.'

23

Nicholas ran his fingers through his hair and gripped his head. He paced his bedchamber's green and gold carpet, his wine-red brocade dressing gown flapping at his trousered legs.

He stopped, and his arms fell by his side. He stared at the single candle casting a flickering circle of light into the vast darkness of the room. Caesar snored on his velvet dog bed and cricket song floated in from windows open to the warm night, but Holbrook House itself was as silent as a tomb.

Nicholas extracted his pocket watch. Nearly one-thirty. Two hours since a flush-cheeked Meggy whispered good-night, her blue eyes peeping through dusky lashes, offering an unspoken invitation. Two hours since her trembling fingers had trailed across his palm and lingered before she dashed upstairs, the shimmering satin and gauzy silk of her skirts swishing around her lovely ankles.

Nicholas knew Meggy wanted something. He thought he knew what that something was, and he thought she wanted it tonight.

But he couldn't afford an error. Not when hope had just begun to blossom.

At that moment, the door cracked open. Nicholas's heart stopped.

Meggy was a phantom in the dim light as she pushed the door closed with her back. She leaned upon it, her hand still on the knob, her wide eyes locked with his. Honeyed curls tumbled loose upon her shoulders, a soft silk dressing gown tied under her breasts, and her lips parted.

'You didn't come to me, Nicky.'

'Oh, my darling – I didn't come because I didn't dare. I thought wishful thinking might've misled me, that my love might've driven me to madness.'

'You weren't misled,' she said, her voice breathless.

Nicholas's heart soared. Meggy wanted *him*. Despite his flaws, in spite of his faults. She had come to him; she had chosen him.

He spread his arms. Meggy released the doorknob, ran forward, and buried her face in his shirt linen. He rested his cheek upon her head, her lavender-scented curls soft against his skin.

They inhaled and exhaled together.

United.

'My dearest love.' Nicholas rubbed her silk-clad back, his hand gliding over the smooth fabric. The heat of her body radiated through the dressing gown, and her breath warmed his chest.

She raised on tiptoes. 'Kiss me, Nicky. Kiss me and don't stop.'

Euphoria. Everything Nicholas had longed for his adult life: a partner, a lover, a wife – and in Meggy, a lady more marvellous than his dreams had ever foretold. Her practicality would unite with his romanticism; her steadfastness would counterbalance his impulsivity. Nicholas would have the honour of providing for her, of protecting her.

Nicholas brushed the curls away from her cheek and cradled her face with both hands. He trailed his thumb over her bottom lip, and her eyelids fluttered.

His lips grazed hers.

'Not like *that*.' Meggy's nails dug into his cheeks, and she pressed her mouth to his. She kissed him with bruising passion as he supported her head, for he couldn't be gentle either. Months of pent-up desire gushed like water from a collapsing dam. Nicholas's erection was a thick rod between their close-pressed bodies.

He walked her towards the bed. He'd give her the satisfaction she urgently craved whilst preserving her virtue, as he had before.

Meggy broke their kiss, but her wet lips brushed his as she whispered into his mouth, her hands still on his face, her thumbs stroking his cheeks. 'I want you, Nicky, but not here.'

'Where then?' His throat was swollen and tight.

Her eyes twinkled in the candlelight, and she laughed.

She was playful, teasing. Delightful. He'd do anything she asked.

Nicholas grinned. 'Where, you angelic rogue?'

Meggy's dimples deepened as she slid her arms around his waist. Her breasts pressed against him, and his hands cupped her round bottom. The luscious curves he'd desired for months were like heady drink; his thoughts slowed as his senses heightened.

'Will you think me silly, Nicky?'

'Not a chance, my love.'

'Then take me to the gazebo. I can't stop thinking about it. Take me there and make love to me *completely*. That's where I want my first time.'

Her first time.

Nicholas would do anything Meggy asked – except *that*.

Nine months earlier, he wouldn't have hesitated to make love to Meggy at her request. Even now, his brain struggled to focus on any thought but *yes, yes, yes.*

His brain struggled, but Nicholas *could* resist for the sake of Meggy's honour.

Because he'd changed.

'Meggy, I shall satisfy you, but we must wait . . .'

'Please, Nicky. No more waiting.' She whispered the words hot against his tingling cheek. 'Do you know how much I've longed for you to touch me this spring? How much I've longed to touch you?'

'Oh, Meggy.' Nicholas closed his eyes, breathing her, embracing her. Her face was sweet and warm against his as he held her beautiful body secure in his arms.

'May I touch you, Nicky?' she asked, sliding her hand between their close-pressed chests and trailing the opening of his dressing gown.

Oh, God, *yes.*

He kissed the shell-like curve of her ear. 'Anywhere you want.'

Her hand slid under his dressing gown.

And Nicholas's breath drew ragged as her fingers slipped under the waistband of his trousers. A guttural groan wrenched from his throat as she grabbed his cock, enflaming him. He buried his face in her tumbling curls.

'I cannot wait anymore,' Meggy said. 'Nicky, I must choose one of my suitors to marry . . .'

What?

'. . . and, once I marry, there can never be physical intimacy between you and me . . .'

Nicholas's hopes plummeted.

Meggy continued. 'But I cannot choose one of them because I think only of you. This is my last chance to satisfy the passion for you which has raged inside me for nine months.'

Nicholas calmed.

All was not lost, by any means.

'Darling Meggy,' he said, tenderly, gently, as he threaded his fingers in her hair and traced the curves of her cheek with his lips. 'You needn't marry one of them. Marry *me*.'

Meggy shook her head. 'I cannot marry you.'

Stay calm, Nicholas told himself.

'Then I cannot do what you ask of me,' he said softly. 'I won't dishonour you.'

She tilted her head. Her hand, agonisingly still on his erection, stroked him. 'If I ask for it, how is it dishonouring me?'

Nicholas swallowed. Focus, concentrate. She was young and innocent; it was his responsibility to help her understand the consequences of her request.

He brushed his thumb over her bottom lip. 'Because you don't know what you are asking.'

'I know perfectly well what I'm asking.' Her voice was husky, sexual, carnal – and perhaps a little irritated. 'I'm asking for my dearest friend to be my first lover.'

Nicholas held her closer. 'But, Meggy, if you and I make love, our bond is irrevocable.'

'Our bond is already irrevocable. Don't you understand that? Although I cannot marry you, you are my friend, and I want you to remain so, always.' Nicholas's heart swelled with hope as Meggy continued. 'No one else makes me laugh as you do; no one plays with me as you do. If I do not have you once, what might have been will torment me forevermore.'

Meggy kissed Nicholas, and when she drew away, she sucked his bottom lip.

Her face was part shadow and part aglow in the flickering candlelight, as Nicholas traced the line of her jaw, her neck. She had expressed her reasoning clearly, as always. She was a logical thinker, not an impulsive one.

And she'd indirectly said she loved him.

Perhaps her practical mind needed this experience to understand what was in her heart.

Once they made love, she'd know.

Nicholas could help her realise how closely bonded they already were.

'Very well, my love,' he said, with a heart full of devotion. 'I am yours to command.'

Meggy smiled, dimples deepening on both cheeks, eyes dancing in the candlelight. 'Truly?'

Nicholas kissed the tip of her adorable crinkling nose. 'Truly.'

She pulled back from his embrace slightly with a coy giggle and peeked from under her lashes. 'Nicky,' she purred as her fingers played with the buttons on his trousers. 'Nicky, do you remember the night you . . . kissed me? Down *there*, I mean?'

'I'm hardly likely to forget.'

Her eyes darted up. 'Well, sometimes you have difficulty remembering details about past lovers.'

Nicholas recoiled. Why would she say such a thing? 'Meggy, it's not like that with you.'

She shrugged. 'I wondered that night, when I asked what I could do to make you . . . climax, if you'd like me to do the same to you? If you'd like me to' – she gripped the girth of his cock – 'kiss you . . . down there?'

Nicholas's breath hitched. Oh, good God.

'Would you like that?' She bit her bottom lip, her teeth pearls against a ruby cushion. 'May I try?'

Nicholas nodded. His throat was too dry to speak.

Meggy knelt, her soft lips poised at his shaft.

She opened her mouth; her tongue brushed him. Nicholas threaded his fingers in her hair and clasped her head to refrain from yelling out. Meggy hesitantly took him in her hot, wet mouth; she circled her tongue around the head of his cock.

She paused, and her blue eyes gazed up. 'I don't know how, Nicky.'

'A little deeper,' he said, guiding her open mouth down, although not too deep, for of all things, Nicholas didn't want to cause her any discomfort. 'Now suck, my love.'

She did.

Nicholas groaned. Torturous pleasure ripped through his body. He held Meggy's head and looked into her eyes, past the point of no return. He'd need to focus all his effort on being gentle because he was mad with desire.

But then again, she was none too gentle herself. She grew more adventurous and took him deeper into her mouth.

Nicholas was dangerously close to release.

'That's enough, my love,' he said, pulling her up.

Her eyes widened. 'Did I not do it well?'

'You were spectacular.' Nicholas kissed her face – her eyelids, her nose, her forehead, her cheeks. 'There's only one climax for me, however, and you come first.'

Literally.

Meggy giggled. 'Then ravish me, Nicky, for *pretend* – because I know what that word means now. I looked it up in Dr Johnson's dictionary.' She pressed herself against him, and her head fell back as if she were powerless in his arms.

Ah, so she wanted a *little* playful roughness.

Nicholas kissed her offered throat, loosened her dressing gown, and yanked her ruffled and beribboned neckline, ripping the thin cotton to expose the tops of her breasts.

Meggy's eyes gleamed. 'You tore my nightdress.'

He grinned as he cupped her breasts. 'It's a damned nuisance, although a very pretty, very frilly, very

feminine damned nuisance. I shall buy you another.'
He nuzzled his face into her bosom; his mouth found a nipple, his tongue encircled it, and flicked the hard nub.

She gasped.

And he suckled her.

She whimpered, grabbing his bottom, pulling him towards her. 'Take me to the gazebo.' Her voice was assertive, certain. No longer playful. 'Now.'

He broke from her nipple. 'As you wish, my love.'

'I can't wait much longer, Nicky. I *ache*. I hurt.'

He empathised.

Nicholas adjusted his clothing. He grabbed the green damask bedspread, balling it in his arms, and extracted a sheath from a drawer.

'What's that?' Meggy asked, alert and curious as always.

He showed her the tube of softened animal intestine. 'A condom, my love. I'll wear it to protect you.'

She studied it, touching it as it rested in his palm. 'Is this what you spoke of at the inn – how you prevent diseases and pregnancy?'

Nicholas nodded.

'You always wear one?' she asked. 'Every time you've been with a woman?'

'Always.'

Meggy bit her bottom lip and seemed to consider. 'But I don't have any . . . venereal diseases, I think you called them. Is there another way to prevent pregnancy? Because I don't want that thing inside me – I want only *you* inside me.'

Nicholas's heart leapt to his throat, and his cock rejoiced. 'Yes,' he said. 'I can pull out of you before I climax. But it's not without some risk.'

She didn't respond at once. Her brow furrowed; then she nodded. 'Leave the condom.'

Nicholas threw it back in the drawer, desperate to be at the gazebo. He blew out the candle, casting the room into darkness.

Meggy was a warm shadow at his side as she grabbed his arm.

Nicholas buried his nose in her curls. 'Shall we go out the window, my love?'

'Yes.' Her voice laughed. 'Although it seems *so* improper.'

'And yet it's the least improper of our actions tonight, my dear Lady Margaret.' And whilst holding the bedspread, Nicholas scooped Meggy into his arms and carried her over the window ledge. Once his slippers touched the ground, he put her down. The waxing moonlight shone silver on the lawn as he wrapped them both in the blanket.

'I'm not cold, Nicky.'

He kissed her forehead. 'This is for concealment. Best if the night watchmen don't see us.'

Her eyes widened. 'You have watchmen upon your grounds?'

Nicholas wrapped his arm around her. 'I imagine so. Seems plausible.'

She laughed. 'You know perfectly well if you do or don't.'

'It might be an excuse to keep you close so I may fondle your breasts as we walk. But either way, do snuggle beside me and keep to the shadows. Do you feel like a thief?'

She chuckled. 'A little, yes.'

He kissed her under the blanket.

The city noises were reduced because of the lateness of the hour, but the odd carriage rattled over cobblestones on the other side of the brick wall as they traversed the gardens. When they reached the entrance of the maze, they no longer huddled under the bedspread. Nicholas clasped Meggy's hand, and they ran together through the turns.

And then they were in the centre.

Meggy tilted her chin up, her curls falling back from her smiling face, and twirled. She was an angel amongst the delphiniums and beside the clematis, her dressing gown silver in the moonlight.

She stole his breath.

He smiled at the wonder of her. 'Oh, my love.' His heart burst as she tiptoed to him and kissed him.

'Take me to the gazebo, Nicky.'

'But are you *certain*?'

'Oh, *yes*. I've dreamt of you for so long.'

They entered the gazebo in a half-embrace.

And they were in a magical universe.

Nicholas lay the bedspread over the marble floor. Meggy trailed her fingers in the clematis and watched him undress.

'Come here, love.'

316

And then Meggy was with him, soft, willing, beautiful. He untied her dressing gown, and the silk rippled to the ground. She pulled up her nightdress.

Waving vines curtained them as they stood nude in their own temple. When their bodies brushed together – skin against skin in the moonlight – Nicholas gasped into a kiss, but his lips and fingers only grazed because every sensation was heightened. Her touch was electricity, and the hot smell of arousal permeated the air.

But then long-repressed hunger consumed him, and Meggy answered back.

Meggy threaded her arms around his neck, and her mouth cupped his. Nicholas grabbed her bottom and lifted her; she jumped into his arms and wrapped her legs around his body. Her slick wetness rubbed down his hard length, they gasped in unison.

'Go in me, Nicky—*please.*'

He wanted to push Meggy up against a column at once, but, mindful of her virginity, Nicholas lay her down and cocooned them both in the damask blanket.

'Are you cold, darling?' The chill of the marble radiated through the silk and wool blend.

'A little.' Meggy snuggled next to Nicholas, and he cradled her. 'And it's harder than I imagined.'

'Why, thank you, my love.'

She blinked, her wide-eyed expression just visible in the moonlight. He grinned.

And then she laughed. 'I meant the *floor*. But that too, perhaps.'

317

Nicholas pushed the curls back from her face, his palm against her cheek, and found her lips.

Their kiss was long and deep. Meggy pressed into him until his back rested against the floor, and her curls tickled his face. He stroked her breasts as they brushed against his chest. He teased the hard nipples, and then cupped their full, heavy weight in his hands as she broke from his kiss, inviting him to suckle her.

Not one to deny her, his mouth gave her what she desired as his hands trailed to her waist and then to her rounded hips. He slipped his fingers between her legs.

His touch ripped a cry – loud, urgent – from her lips. She was hot, slippery and engorged, bursting with need. Fully ready for him. He rubbed her clitoris with his thumb and inserted a finger into her, stroking her on the inside and outside as she panted.

She was so aroused it took only moments to bring her to climax as he suckled her breasts. But as she pulsed hard on his hand, her whimpered moans softening, she said, 'I didn't want to, *yet.*' She knelt beside him. A curtain of hair hid her face.

'Never mind, love – that was only the first course.' And he lifted himself up and moved his kisses down her body.

Her sensitivity was heightened – almost too intense, he suspected – as he flicked the tip of his tongue over her clitoris. But she soon relaxed, resting her bottom on her heels and spreading her knees to accommodate him. Nicholas thrust his tongue into her passage and then licked up through her folds again to the centre of her pleasure, the scent and taste of Meggy his only sensory awareness. He was powerfully aroused; his cock strained as if he would burst.

Meggy was getting close to another climax, but rather than accept it from his tongue, she pushed his head away and straddled him, and she started to slip over his aching tip.

His eyes flew open at the feel of her on his unsheathed cock. He groaned in sweet, exquisite pain, the sound pulled from his gut. Meggy was hot and wet, her entry tight. Her body offered heat to stoke his passion; slick balm to soothe his need.

But she was struggling with the position, so Nicholas rolled her onto the blanket and arranged himself with his weight on one elbow. 'I need to be inside you all the way, my love.'

Meggy's hands cupped his bottom. 'Why do you hesitate?'

'I don't want to hurt you.'

'Not having you in me hurts. *Please*, Nicky.'

Nicholas caressed her cheek, his heart full of love, his body full of need.

And then he thrust, stretching her over him as he plunged into the woman he loved.

He swallowed back a cry that would've woken London, and Meggy bit into his shoulder.

It was paradise. Blissful, *aching* paradise.

Their hips soon rocked in unison. Waves of pleasure, each swelling to a new peak, surged. But beyond the carnal sensation was something so much more: Nicholas was coupling with the woman he loved.

His dearest friend.

And on top of everything else he adored about Meggy – her playfulness, her intelligence, her devotion to her siblings, her dimples and freckles and crinkled nose when she laughed – was yet another perfection: she was passionate.

Very passionate.

For there was soon nothing gentle about their love-making: their rhythm frenzied, their unconstrained cries called into the dark night, and their bodies slick with sweat and noisy with wet coupling.

After many minutes of intense union, Meggy arched her back and lifted her hips to push him deeper. Her tight passage squeezed his cock, and she dug her nails into his back. And then she pulsed on him, over and over, crying out with each hot, wet throb, until she fell back at last, and Nicholas, who couldn't restrain his climax any longer, withdrew, and spilled himself over her stomach. Her name ripped from his throat as his orgasm shattered him.

24

Nicholas melted beside Meggy. Their spent bodies entwined as the residual waves of pleasure ebbed, their breath heavy as they kissed, their hands caressing. Meggy's stomach was wet, and Nicholas cleaned her using a corner of the bedspread.

'What is that?' Her voice was soft, sweet. The purr of a satiated woman.

And her words were another stark reminder of her innocence.

'Semen.' Nicholas kissed her forehead. He enveloped her in his arms and wrapped the blanket around them. She'd begun to shiver.

'Is semen what makes babies?' Her teeth chattered.

'Yes.' He held her closer. Whether her body was reacting to the night air on her damp skin or the after-effects of lovemaking, she needed warmth and comfort. She snuggled her face into Nicholas's chest. Her head rested on his arm, and her curls nestled under his chin.

'This was a first time for you as well, Nicky.' Her fingers played with the hair on his upper chest. 'Since you've never been with a woman without a condom, I mean. I wanted to be your first in that way.'

Nicholas's heart swelled with love for her. 'Meggy, there are so many firsts for me in this moment. This is the first time I've been with a woman I love.'

She traced the muscles on his abdomen, and Nicholas held her tighter although her shivering had stopped. 'What else, Nicky?'

Nicholas took a deep breath. Now was his chance to make Meggy understand they belonged together, as husband and wife, and that what she felt for him was the type of love which would last a lifetime. 'My darling,' he began, whispering into her curls, 'this was the first time I made love to the woman with whom I wish to spend the rest of my life. The woman with whom I hope to make a family.' Her hand stilled; her palm rested flat against his skin. 'If you will marry me, Meggy, then this is the first time I've been at the beginning of forever.'

Meggy stiffened. Her arms and shoulders tensed; her breath paused.

She wasn't responding as he'd hoped, even after making love.

Suddenly the crickets' chorus was deafening.

'Meggy?' Nicholas tried to keep his voice light. 'Can you not feel how strong our love is? This is not mere friendship, my darling.'

She wriggled out of his grasp and searched for her nightdress. 'I don't know about that.'

A drummer beat a slow rhythm inside Nicholas's head as he sat up. 'Meggy, my darling, we should marry.'

She pulled her nightdress over her head. 'Why?'

Nicholas's chest tightened, but he kept his voice as calm as possible. 'Because I love you, and you love me.'

She put her feet into her slippers. 'We're friends, Nicky.'

Nicholas's mouth went dry. Why did she persist in calling their love friendship? 'But you cannot seriously mean to accept the proposal of another man after what has passed between us?' His voice was sharper than he'd intended.

'I don't know what I intend to do.' Meggy tied on her dressing gown. 'But I know I don't like your angry tone.'

'I'm not angry,' he replied, levelling his voice with effort. His emotions writhed; he couldn't fail. He must help her to understand the strength of their love. 'I'm distressed. Frankly, I thought you'd change your mind after we made love. I thought you'd comprehend the depth of our connection.'

'I do comprehend the depth of our connection. You will always be the first man I made love to, and I'm *very* happy I did. It surpassed all my expectations. But, Nicky, I'm not yet ready for more. I'm sorry.'

Nicholas's body tensed, and his blood began to boil despite his efforts. 'You're *sorry*? You know how desperately I love you, Meggy, and yet you dash my hopes again with an *"I'm sorry"*? That's remarkably heartless of you.'

Meggy sighed. 'I'm not heartless, Nicky. I simply need more time.'

Perhaps her answer oughtn't irritate him, but it did. It was the same one she gave to all her suitors. 'So, even after we share an experience like *that*, you dismiss me as you do Carow, Harrison and Webb – with a request for more time.'

'Yes, because I need to think about what I feel for you.'

'Dammit,' Nicholas cursed, his temper snapping. The thought of falling into failure from such elevated hopes shredded his heart – no, it destroyed his soul. How could he face a lifetime without Meggy *now*? He'd pulled himself from despair and weakness to win her regard – a regard he thought he'd earned at last, after months of single-minded focus on self-improvement. 'Why did you not think about what you feel *before* you came to me tonight?'

Even in the moonlight, Nicholas saw the flash of her eyes. 'You, sir, may *never* question why I succumbed to physical need without forethought!'

Nicholas's stomach turned. His anger fell into anguish. 'Yes, I deserved that,' he said penitently. 'Please forgive me.' The pounding was no longer a drummer; it was a hammer upon his temple. He cradled his head, still kneeling nude upon the twisted bedspread. 'Meggy, you cannot fathom the depth of my disappointment.' Even after all his caution since Meggy had arrived in London, Nicholas had ruined everything. He'd known he shouldn't make love to her without a betrothal, but he'd let desire win. 'I've tried so hard to be a better man.'

Meggy sat on a bench and folded her hands in her lap. 'I know you have,' she said quietly.

He looked up. 'And does that mean nothing to you, darling?'

'I'm very proud of you, Nicky.'

A glimmer of hope, perhaps. 'Then please tell me why you hesitate to be my wife?' he asked, gently. Cautiously.

She studied her hands. 'Several reasons. Partially because Harry idolises you to the point where you can do no wrong. If you were ever to slip back into your old habits, he'd follow you on that path when he becomes a man, if he has any of Edwin's tendencies, and I'd have failed my promise to my father.'

Nicholas put his hand over his heart. 'Meggy, I take my responsibilities to Harry seriously. I'd never lead him astray.'

She shrugged. 'Perhaps, but it's a risk. One of many risks with you. Then there's what you said to me at the beginning: once you have what you want, you don't want it anymore.'

Ah. That old concern still troubled her.

'That's not true of *you*, my love.' Nicholas leaned forward, trying to make eye contact, but Meggy stared resolutely at her folded hands. 'That's not true of *me* anymore. I'm no longer the foolish and bitter man who uttered such a ridiculous statement. My God, Meggy, my desire for you consumes me. No, it's more profound than that – it *inspires* me. Become my wife, my sweet darling, and I shall prove I want you every day for the rest of my life.'

'You feel that way now.'

'Yes – and I might point out that I very much just had you,' he said with a smile, hoping to lighten her mood.

But Meggy's expression remained solemn. A frown tugged at the corners of her lips and two faint lines creased her brow. 'Oh, I believe you care for me enough to want me more than once. Maybe for weeks, months, or even a year. But forever, Nicky? When I've borne you children? Once I've grown older?'

'Unquestionably,' he said, his chest aching with longing as fleeting images crossed his mind. Meggy pregnant. Nursing their baby. Tucking shadowy future children into bed with kisses. And, finally, the two of them, aged and grey but arms entwined as they sat together, here in this gazebo, reflecting on a lifetime of love. 'You grow more beautiful to me every day, Meggy.'

Meggy knitted her hands. 'I don't share your conviction.'

Nicholas shook his head in disbelief. 'What more can I possibly do to convince you?' he asked, his throat tightening.

'You can't, Nicky. You've done everything possible, and yet I cannot trust you, which is why I cannot accept your proposal – not yet, anyway. I must have more time to think.' She chewed her lip as she looked beyond the clematis into the flower-strewn maze centre. 'Logic informs my decisions, and logic rules against you, my friend. Logic tells me you are a risk, and you know I don't take risks. Not normally, at any rate, although I admit I took one tonight. And whilst I shan't regret doing what *I* wanted to do for once, I also shan't let passion determine the course of my life.'

'But this isn't passion.' The unpleasant edge had returned to his voice somehow, and Nicholas steadied his breath before continuing. 'This is love. Lasting, all-consuming love.'

'Perhaps. Or perhaps it's merely especially intense lust.'

Good God! How could she still deny their love?

'I'm telling you it's not,' Nicholas said through clenched teeth.

Meggy narrowed her eyes and frowned. Her slippered foot tapped the marble. 'And you know because you have so much more experience than I? Because you've made love to countless women?'

'I've only made love to one woman.'

'There you go, then. Don't pretend to be any more of an expert on lasting love than I am, Nicky.'

Nicholas gripped an edge of the bedspread at his knee and fisted it. His jaw ached; his muscles twitched. 'I know what I feel, Meggy, and I shan't allow you to continue to diminish my love by telling me it's lust or frustrated desire. Naturally, you may refuse me for whatever reason you wish, and I must abide by your decision, but I shan't accept nonsense from you without calling it out.'

'I'm not speaking nonsense.'

'You are when you belittle our love,' Nicholas said, his voice rising significantly despite his efforts to stay

327

calm. Meggy spoke of applying logic and reason, and yet she failed to acknowledge the strength of the love that blatantly existed between them. 'And, yes, I said *our* love – for you love me as well, although you certainly fight it. You've been that way since the beginning of our acquaintance: hot one moment and cold the next. You tell me you don't want me, but you kiss me passionately. You push me away, but you go through my possessions. You're my friend, then you're not, then you are, then you aren't. And worst of all, you come to my bed, but you refuse my hand.'

Meggy stood, fists clenched at her sides. 'Are *you* lecturing *me* on virtue, Nicholas Burton? This is a sermon I won't hear. I'm going inside.'

She turned on her heel and marched out of the gazebo, the clematis wavering in her wake.

Nicholas followed her. 'Stop. You don't know how to get out of the maze.'

She tossed her head. 'I'll figure it out. Right hand against the wall.'

'I'm escorting you back,' Nicholas snapped.

'Come then. I'm not waiting.'

Nicholas indicated his nude body. 'May I clothe myself, *please*, madam?'

Meggy crossed her arms. 'If you hurry.'

He returned to the gazebo and breathed deeply as he dressed. He'd let his insecurities get the better of him; the underlying fear of his inherent unlovability had reared itself in anger. But the fact of the matter was that Meggy, who professed to such rationality and sensibleness, wasn't being reasonable when it came to this matter of the heart.

And that was as infuriating as the very devil.

'You know,' he said to Meggy as he covered her in the bedspread again, 'for someone who dislikes riskful behaviour, you certainly seem to want to throw your-self into it now. For your information, I was serious about my watchmen, and in your pale dressing gown, you'd be spotted in a moment. If you won't accept my proposal, we'd better be damned certain no one knows we were together tonight.'

Meggy huddled under the draped damask next to Nicholas's warm body as they returned to the house. He smelled of heat and spice and musk and love.

His closeness was intoxicating. *And* infuriating.

Meggy wished Nicholas a million miles away. And also, she wanted him to envelop her in the blanket and cradle her as if she were a child. To press his lips to her forehead and rub her back. To reassure her that he understood her bewilderment. That her confusion was reasonable and perfectly comprehensible.

Because whilst Meggy's feelings and thoughts coiled around each other like clinging vines, they almost never aligned. Her heart hungered for Nicholas. But her mind warned that he'd betray her one day, as Edwin had done. Yes, Nicholas was lovely *now*, but so too was Edwin, *once*. He'd been the big brother with strong arms and a bright smile who greeted Meggy by swinging her into the air as she giggled. He'd been someone who'd loved her and whom she'd adored in return.

And then Edwin had deserted her. He'd forced a fourteen-year-old orphan to bury her heartbreak and loneliness in order to shoulder the burdens of a mother, a father, and a manor lord.

Learning that she couldn't depend on others – even on those who claimed to love her – had been a bitter lesson to learn. It now seemed an impossible lesson to *unlearn*. Meggy's mind preached that she needed a stable and predictable husband. Someone mild-mannered and dull. Someone she'd never be tempted to depend upon. Someone who didn't cloud her judgement with over-whelming, all-encompassing, powerful emotions.

But her heart yearned for scarred, troubled Nicholas.

And for several exquisite minutes during and after their lovemaking, Meggy's heart had silenced her mind's protests. All she'd wanted was to lie in Nicholas's warm arms and savour that peace. To nourish her emotions within a loving embrace until her brain was forced to accept a fresh way of thinking – that *maybe* her heart wasn't weak and foolish. That maybe, with time, her heart could lead her mind back to trust.

But Nicholas hadn't understood at all. He wanted a decision now.

And Meggy was furious with him for that.

She planned to run to her room and bury herself in her duvet the moment she climbed over the window ledge. She needed to let her boiling blood cool. She needed to organise her tangled mind and her desperate heart. To make the two of them work together, one way or the other. With her other suitors pressing her for a decision as well, Meggy didn't have much time; therefore, she must make use of every moment she had.

She needed to think. On her own, alone.

When they reached the window ledge – undetected by any watchmen – it was higher than Meggy expected. Nicholas had carried her down it when she'd been weightless and alive with tingling anticipation. Climbing up would be a different matter entirely.

'I'll lift you, Meggy.' Nicholas's powerful arms encircled her, but she pushed him away.

'I didn't ask for your help.' Her words were childish and her tone petty. Meggy was ashamed the moment she uttered them.

Nicholas threw up his palms, scoffed, and turned his shoulder.

Meggy shoved aside her sorrow and stretched her arms over the wide ledge. Her fingers struggled to grasp the inside of the window, but at last she established a precarious hold. The outer ridge dug into her breasts.

Positioned as she was, she couldn't use her arm strength to pull up. She'd have to hoist herself with her feet.

But her satin slippers slid off the smooth stone façade, and Meggy soon half dangled from the window, unable to progress. '*Dammit!*'

'Do you need some assistance after all?'

She spoke through gritted teeth. 'What do you think?'

Again, childish. But before she could add a 'yes, please', Nicholas grabbed her bottom and tossed her over the ledge. Meggy tumbled onto the plush carpet of his room, with her dressing gown wound around her legs and her curls covering her face. The bedspread landed on top of her.

The nerve of him, treating her like a bag of wool!

Meggy swept back her hair and leapt up, intending to pummel Nicholas the moment he popped over the ledge. But a snuffled growl, like the grunt of a pig, began behind her. A second warning, higher and more urgent, joined.

And a small but mighty voice rang out. 'Halt, you dirty gallows-bird, or I shall swinge you soundly with this candlestick!'

Meggy froze as Harry emerged from the shadows.

Nicholas hoisted himself into the room. 'Don't, Harry! It's me.'

Caesar and Copper dashed to the window to offer whimpered apologies and frantic tail wags.

'Nicky! But then who's *that*, sir? Why – it's you, Meggy.'

Meggy's heart thudded. How could she explain to her brother why she was in Nicholas's bedroom in the middle of the night? 'Yes, Harry. It's me.'

A flare of light and the rotten egg smell of sulphur permeated the room as Nicholas lit a candle. Harry, clad in his cotton nightdress and nightcap, with rumpled woollen socks upon his feet, grasped an empty candlestick. He looked from Nicholas to Meggy and back again, his mouth drawn into a circle.

Nicholas knelt beside the boy. 'Did you have a nightmare, Harry?'

Harry's lips turned down as he nodded.

Nicholas embraced him. 'And I wasn't here when you sought me, was I? Forgive me, Harry. I'm here now.' Harry leaned his cheek on the marquess's shoulder and threw his arms around his neck, still clutching the candlestick.

Meggy tilted her head. Harry had experienced night terrors all his life, but he'd not had them often in the last few months. 'What happened, dearest?' she asked, relieved Harry hadn't asked any awkward questions but concerned by the return of his bad dreams. 'Did you read a frightening story before bed? You haven't had a nightmare since we left Alton Park.'

Harry rubbed his eyes and stifled a yawn. 'Yes, I have,' he said sleepily, nestling closer to Nicholas. 'But I come and sleep with Nicky when I do. He carries me upstairs again before morning so the girls don't know I was scared in the night. Nicky, now that you're here, will you please sing to me until I fall asleep?'

'Yes, of course.' Nicholas scooped the boy up and plopped him on the curtained bed. Harry was a round-eyed speck amongst the white sheets and the thick feather duvet, like an owlet in a nest.

Meggy tucked the covers under his chin. 'Snug, dearest?'

Harry nodded, his head nestled within pillowy piles. He was adorable, and Meggy smiled despite her argument with Nicholas. She leaned over and kissed her brother's nose. 'Now, upon my orders, you may dream only the sweetest dreams tonight. Sunny days running in

333

a meadow, white sailboats on blue waters, Copper and Caesar digging holes with their tails wagging, and . . .'

'Pirates!'

'Pirates? Would that be a sweet dream?'

'No, but it'd be a jolly fun one.'

Meggy laughed. 'Very well, pirates too. But friendly pirates, with bright parrots upon their shoulders.'

'And their enemies' skeletons hanging from gibbets upon the masts,' Harry added.

'Good lord!' But Meggy laughed again and kissed Harry's forehead, her mood lifting. 'I love you, you darling squirrel.'

'Well, Harry,' – Nicholas's voice was thick – 'if *that* doesn't chase away the nightmares, nothing will.' He half smiled at Harry. 'Hand over your club, sir. An excellent choice of weapon, and I'm glad you didn't clout either me or your sister over the head with it.'

Harry surrendered the candlestick with a giggle. 'Why were you and Meggy crawling through the window?'

The dreaded question hit like a blow to Meggy's stomach.

Ashamed, she cast her eyes to the foot of the bed where the dogs pawed and snuffled as they dug at the bedcovers, circled, and plopped into self-made nests. How could she possibly answer?

Nicholas sat on the edge of the bed and took Harry's hand. 'Meggy and I were walking outside together, Harry.'

'In the middle of the night?'

'Yes. And I oughtn't have done so. It wasn't the behaviour of a gentleman, and you have every right to be extremely angry with me.'

'But I couldn't be angry at you, Nicky.'

Meggy's eyebrows shot up, for Harry's reply perfectly illustrated the worry she'd expressed in the gazebo. Her brother idolised Nicholas unquestioningly, even when the marquess was in the wrong. '*See*?' she asked Nicholas, pointedly. 'Do you not comprehend my concern when Harry says something like that? Surely you must understand now.'

Nicholas's forehead furrowed.

'What do you mean, Meggy?' Harry asked. 'What should Nicky understand?'

'Never mind, Harry,' Meggy said. 'It is something Nicky and I discussed during our . . . our walk.' Meggy cringed, her stomach knotting. How had the beautiful experience of lovemaking turned foul so rapidly? Why had she taken such a foolish risk? Rather than clearing Meggy's mind to allow her to consider her options, it had complicated everything. And if Harry told *anyone* else, matters would worsen. 'Darling squirrel,' she urged her brother, 'do please listen. You mustn't tell anyone Nicky and I were walking outside.'

Rumours spread in a moment amongst the *haut ton*. A word overheard by a servant could be Meggy's undoing . . .

Nicholas interrupted her thoughts *and* dispelled her authority. 'Meggy, you mayn't ask that of Harry. You mustn't burden a child with keeping an adult's secrets.'

Meggy clenched her fists. 'But if he says anything—'

'*Stop!*' Nicholas held out his hand. 'Harry, please allow me to speak with your sister for a moment.' He strode to Meggy's side of the bed and gripped her upper arm. 'Tell Caesar and Copper a bedtime story until I return.'

Meggy attempted to twist away as Nicholas propelled her into the antechamber adjoining his bedroom. But his hand was firm, and his palm warm through the soft silk of her dressing gown. Once the bedroom door closed, they were shrouded in darkness. Nicholas's hot breath whispered in her ear. 'I knew I shouldn't have agreed to take you outside tonight without having an under-standing. There *will* be consequences for our behaviour.'

Meggy stopped resisting his grip and crumpled against the wall. After years of rational thinking, would she be forced into a decision because she surrendered to impulse *once*? 'I suppose you'll be happy if I'm compelled to marry you to save my siblings from scandal.' Her voice choked with repressed sobs.

Nicholas stepped back. '*Happy?*' The word slashed like a knife. 'How can you say something so childish and unreasonable, Meggy?'

Meggy blazed with fury. Childish and unreasonable when all she'd asked for was time? 'And I might ask how you can claim to love me when you clearly don't understand me in the least, Nicky!' Meggy's throat thickened, for the truth of what she'd said hit full force. If Nicholas didn't understand her, then he *didn't* truly love her – not a lasting love which would withstand

336

time, anyway. 'Soon you'll see what you feel for me is not love at all. Then you'll recognise – and be grateful for – my reticence. My wisdom.'

There was a long pause.

At last Nicholas spoke, his voice soft but devastating. 'This night was an utter debacle. I regret every moment. I should never have made love to you.'

The words sliced Meggy's heart, but it was what she'd expected. He'd leave her now, and it would hurt, but it would be so much easier than if she were bound to him for her entire life.

He opened the door, and a sliver of light shone over half his face.

His cheeks were damp with tears.

And Meggy's heart screamed that she'd made a terrible mistake.

But Nicholas was gone. The door clicked closed behind him, and Meggy stood alone in the dark, forcing her mind to repeat its reassurances, hoping to soothe her tortured heart. She'd been correct all along, she told herself. Nicholas didn't *love* her – he'd *wanted* her. Now he'd realised. He even regretted their lovemaking. This nonsense about his undying love would cease.

It was better this way.

Better for her, better for Harry.

Meggy hugged herself to force her breaking heart back into one piece.

'What song do you want, Harry?' The thick oak door muffled Nicholas's voice.

'Anything, Nicky.'

A pause. Then the now-familiar rich baritone, muted for a bedside song, began:

> *'Fond love, why dost thou dally,*
> *And mock my passions with thy disdain?*
> *Seek not thy pleasure in my pain—'*

'Stop! What sort of song is *that*, Nicky?'

'The first thing that came to my mind.'

'Could you *please* bring another to mind? Something not about *love*? Bah! What a scaly thing to sing of.'

'I agree.' Nicholas's voice sounded choked, strangled. 'Especially unrequited love.'

'Unre-what? I don't know what that is.'

'I hope you never do, my boy.'

'Are you crying, Nicky?'

Nicky's reply was muffled, but Meggy couldn't endure hearing more, anyway. She inhaled with a shuddering breath and dashed from the antechamber to the sounds of a popular ditty, sung without joy.

> *'I go through the north country,*
> *The fashions of the world to see,*
> *I sought for merry company,*
> *And go to the City of London.'*

Unrequited love, Meggy thought as she ran up the stairs. No, not unrequited at all.

Not in the least.

She needed to *think*. She needed to decide, and time was running out.

And if rumours spread, there was no time left at all.

25

An overwhelming weight lay in Meggy's stomach as she listlessly stabbed a fat strawberry with her fork at breakfast the next morning. A thin thread of pink tinged the heavy cream as she trailed the fruit across the painted roses on her plate.

The fork slipped from her fingers and clinked against the silver rim of the porcelain. Meggy tore a portion from her buttered scone but didn't lift it to her mouth. Instead, she absent-mindedly crumbled it like snow over the cream.

A shout of laughter startled her. Elizabeth had snorted elderflower cordial through her nose, dampening the front of her frock, and the other children giggled as Rose murmured about table manners. Meggy's eyes fluttered to Nicholas's unoccupied chair. She dropped the rest of her scone on her plate and wiped her fingers upon her napkin.

A sultry breeze carried the heady scent of wisteria from the garden into the breakfast room. Meggy stifled a yawn. She'd lain awake for much of the remainder of the night, unable to resolve her conflict. Only the hope of seeing Nicholas at breakfast had dragged her from her bed.

But Caesar snuffled with his nose to the carpet, licking up the children's crumbs. And if Caesar was in a room without Nicholas, then Nicholas wasn't at home.

Meggy wanted to return to her bedroom and *think*, but Sophy placed a warm hand on her bare forearm. 'Play outside with us?'

She sighed. 'Certainly, love, if you wish it.'

Sophy's blue eyes shone as she tilted her head. 'Come then, for you seem melancholy and sunshine will make you happy.'

Oh, darling Sophy.

Meggy kissed her sister's blonde curls. 'Allow me five minutes to drink a cup of coffee,' she said as steadily as she could muster, 'and I shall join you.'

The children tumbled out of the dining room with Copper and Caesar jumping at their heels.

Rose handed Meggy a steaming cup of coffee with boiled milk. 'You didn't *eat*, Meggy.'

'I'm not hungry. The heat, I imagine.' The bitter drink burned her tongue.

'I've never known heat to bother you before.'

Footsteps at the door made Meggy whip her head around, but it was only Harry returning. He dashed to the table and put a sticky palm on her shoulder. 'Now that the girls are gone, I wanted you to know I shan't tell anyone you were walking outside with Nicky in the middle of the night.'

The room was suddenly suffocating. 'Never mind,' Meggy said, her chest tight. 'No need to speak of it again.'

Rose appeared fascinated with the tablecloth, but her pale brows drew together.

Harry patted Meggy's cheek. 'And you needn't feel as if you're burdening me with an adult's secrets, as Nicky said. After all, I don't want the girls to know I had a nightmare.'

'Th-thank you, Harry.' Meggy's mouth was so dry her voice croaked.

Harry grinned. 'Hurry and drink your coffee. We plan to solve the maze today, but we'll wait for you.' He planted a rather wet, strawberry-scented kiss on her cheek and dashed away.

Meggy sighed. Why the *maze*?

She swirled her coffee. Tendrils of steam warmed her chin.

'Dearest?' Rose's voice was little more than a whisper.

No – Meggy hadn't the strength to withstand Rose's questioning. She'd confess all, and Rose would echo Nicholas's arguments. Neither of them understood the power Meggy's logic wielded over her. Everything but promises pointed to Nicholas's future unfaithfulness, and promises were too easily broken.

Meggy gulped her drink, the too-hot liquid burning as it travelled down her throat into her empty, unsettled stomach. 'I should join the children.'

'But, Meggy—'

'They're waiting, Rose.' She placed her cup on the white tablecloth and managed a half-smile.

'Very well, dearest,' Rose said softly.

★

When Meggy trudged back from the maze two hours later, five scampering bundles of energy surrounded her, and a nascent headache budded at her temples. Only Caesar plodded slower than she, his wide mouth drawn into the comical grin of his breed, and his tongue curled up to his nose.

'Come then.' Meggy picked him up. He perched on her arm and panted hot breath on her cheek. She nestled her nose into his velvet fur and whispered into one floppy ear. 'You and I shall go upstairs where no one will bother us and *rest*. And you can help me think about Nicky. Tell me what I should do.' Caesar's round eyes shone, and Meggy chuckled. 'Never mind, I know what you would say. But, still, we shall have a delicious rest until luncheon, and perhaps Nicky will be back then.'

But the moment the pug's paws landed upon the marble floor of the back vestibule, he dashed into the adjacent drawing room. Meggy pulled off her gloves, untied her bonnet, and placed them in the butler's waiting hands. 'Mr Carow desires an audience with you, my lady. He awaits you in the drawing room.'

Meggy whispered. 'I have a headache, Stinchcombe. Tell him I'm indisposed, please.'

The butler lowered his voice. 'He's rather persistent. He *says* he had an appointment to call upon your ladyship at half-past eleven.' Meggy blinked, and Stinchcombe continued. 'Lord Holbrook is with him now.'

Meggy's heart skipped a beat. 'Oh! Thank you, Stinchcombe. I shall see Mr Carow.'

She smelled tobacco before she stepped into the red and gold room. Carow bowed when she entered, but Meggy's eyes travelled to Nicholas. He puffed a cigar – an infrequent habit he *never* indulged in in the drawing room – and stood to bow. His buckskin breeches buttoned at the knee above dusty top boots.

Riding – he'd been riding that morning. He hadn't even removed his spurs.

Thank God, for riding was an innocent occupation which helped Nicholas think clearly. Perhaps Meggy could have a calm, rational discussion with him as soon as she got rid of Carow.

Meggy curtsied, but Nicholas's face remained an unreadable mask behind a white haze of smoke. 'Good day, Mr Carow. Morning, Ni—Lord Holbrook.' She perched upon the edge of a yellow silk armchair.

As the two men stared at each other, Nicholas stretched his long legs and spurred boots on an uphol-stered footrest and continued to puff his cigar. His free hand stroked Caesar, curled up at his side.

Carow drew his gaze from Nicholas. 'Would your ladyship walk with me in the gardens?'

'No, thank you, Mr Carow. I've been outside for the last two hours.'

'Nothing amiss, I hope?'

'Amiss? Not at all.'

'Excellent news. I was concerned some injury might've befallen you. Last night you granted me permission for a *private* audience' – his eyes darted to Nicholas – 'with your ladyship at half-past eleven this morning, and it's now five minutes past twelve.'

Meggy's cheeks warmed. Nicholas watched her now as he smoked, but the hand petting Caesar had stilled.

'Forgive my tardiness, Mr Carow. I was playing with the children.' Meggy put a hand to her throat, wondering how to extract herself from this interview. 'I'm sorry to say—'

Mr Carow interrupted her. 'A moment, Lady Margaret.' He turned to Nicholas. 'Your lordship must have many demands on your valuable time.'

Nicholas's eyes narrowed. 'I'm not in the habit of having other men instruct me in how to manage my time, Mr Carow. I shall leave only if Lady Margaret asks it of me.'

Carow's eyes cut to Meggy, expectantly.

'I see no reason for Lord Holbrook to leave, Mr Carow,' Meggy said, as pleasantly as possible. 'Furthermore, it would be better if you spoke with me another time. Unfortunately, today I don't quite—'

The barrister interrupted. 'You promised me this interview, ma'am, and you cannot expect me to conduct it in front of *him*.'

'Don't tell Lady Margaret what she may or may not expect, Carow,' Nicholas said, his voice edged with hostility.

Meggy sighed. If the two men continued in this vein, there would be trouble, and an argument wouldn't further Meggy's objective of putting Mr Carow off until she spoke again with Nicholas. 'Lord Holbrook, thank you for your concern, but please allow me a few minutes to hear Mr Carow.'

Nicholas drew back. Pain flickered in his grey eyes before a hard glint replaced it. He removed his boots from the footrest. 'I see that my presence is superfluous, after all.' He rose. 'Come, Caesar, we aren't wanted here.'

The pug hopped down and padded after his master, and the clink of Nicholas's spurs and the fall of his boots faded.

Meggy's heart ached for the pain she'd caused, but it would be of short duration. She'd ask Carow to call another day, and then she'd speak with Nicholas at once.

'Did your ladyship forget our appointment?'

Meggy's headache flared. 'Quite honestly, I don't recall your asking, Mr Carow. And I don't feel at all well this morning—'

'Afternoon.'

'This afternoon. Under the circumstances, I'd appreciate if we delayed this conversation for another time.'

Carow shook his head. 'No more delay. I realise you've lived always in the country, so I've been patient with your provincial ways. But to continue to dangle three gentlemen's proposals – rather, I should say, *two* gentlemen and a tradesman's proposals – as you yourself set your cap after Holbrook is the inside of enough.'

Meggy bristled. 'Perhaps you are correct that I dangle only two gentlemen's proposals. But I'd say rather that I dangle two gentlemen and a barrister's proposals. To force yourself in my presence when I've already told you I don't feel well, and then to *insult* me, is the inside of enough, as you say. I shall bid you good day.'

'A moment, Lady Margaret. Don't be so quick to send me off, for if you do, I shan't return. Forgive my frank speech, but it's kindly meant. Holbrook leads a merry chase, and you follow like a hopeful child. He must delight in seeing you so smitten. I grant you he glowered at me from upon that sofa for all the world like a jealous lover, but he's toying with your affections. Not an hour ago, I saw him riding in Hyde Park with Kitty Preece. Although I hesitate to mention that woman's name in the presence of a lady, you ought to be aware what sort of man Holbrook is . . .'

Meggy's heart shattered as Carow's voice receded into the distance.

Kitty Preece, as *everyone* knew, was the middle – and most renowned – of the five courtesan Preece sisters. Although the Misses Preece didn't attend the balls and assemblies of the *haut ton*, they flittered around Mayfair like bejewelled butterflies. Plumed and dazzling, they rode in an elegant pastel landau driven by smart coachmen wearing the livery of some nobleman or another and held court at the theatres. Draped in diamonds against the red velvets of their opera box, they glittered more than Queen Charlotte herself, and wealthy men, young and old, fawned upon them.

Meggy's hands trembled. If Carow spoke the truth, Nicholas's resolve had crumbled even sooner than she thought. Only hours after their coupling, she could still feel Nicky in the soreness between her legs. Had Nicholas truly gone already to another woman?

Carow took Meggy's hand in both of his, clasping it so she couldn't pull away. He'd been droning on the entire time, but now he stopped. 'And even yet you hesitate. I mean what I say: I must have a definitive answer one way or the other today. I shan't play this game any longer.'

Meggy's head pounded. She no longer wanted to speak to Nicholas, but she needed to flee Carow. The cool sheets of her bed called.

Rest, she needed rest.

She spoke her next words without thinking. 'My answer is no.'

And a weight lifted from her shoulders.

That, at least, had been easy.

Carow's face reddened darker than the crimson walls.

Meggy sighed. 'Naturally, what I meant to say is whilst I'm sensible of the honour of your proposal, I'm unable to—'

'Save *those* sorts of words for Harrison and Webb.' Carow dropped her hand. 'Or Webb, rather, as I doubt Harrison will be back after your rudeness yesterday. But if you think for one moment you'll ever catch Holbrook or that he'll make you happy if you *do* . . .'

Meggy didn't attend to the rest of his tirade as she strode from the room. When she reached the foot of the carpeted marble staircase, she ran up the steps two at a time.

She threw open the door to her own bedroom, ready to fling herself into the feathery softness of her canopied bed, but Sophy and Maria sat at her dressing table, playing with her ribbons and jewellery.

Maria beamed. 'You're back, Meggy. We've been waiting for you.'

Sophy patted the cushioned chair before the dressing table. She burnished Meggy's silver brush. 'Please sit. We want to style your hair.'

Meggy collapsed onto the seat. Her dream of rest fell away like the hairpins the girls yanked from her curls.

By luncheon, Meggy still hadn't had a moment to herself..

Because Rose's eyes bore into her, Meggy ate for the first time that day, swallowing mouthfuls of herbed sorrel soup followed by cold salmon and buttery new potatoes. But the food tasted of chalk.

And Nicholas wasn't there. He might be *anywhere* . . .

Perhaps with another woman in his arms.

Afternoon callers arrived soon after the meal, and Meggy submitted to social duty. But tedious small talk exacerbated her headache; thus, she agreed at once when mild-mannered Mr Webb offered to drive her in his high-perch, open phaeton. It wasn't time alone, but it would provide a change of scenery.

The sky was a clear blue with a white blazing sun. Horses and people wilted like dying plants in the heat, but, as always, Piccadilly Street jostled with pedestrians and equipages. Once they passed into Hyde Park, Mr Webb urged his team forward. Fashionable Rotten Row – the sandy bridle path running through the park on the south side of the Serpentine – was less crowded than the streets. Meggy shielded her face with her blue silk parasol and closed her eyes. The wind blew the curls that peeked out from under her silk-covered straw bonnet.

'You're lovely, Lady Margaret.'

Meggy opened her eyes. Webb attended to his pair of spirited bays, but he smiled.

'You're kind, Mr Webb.'

Peals of laughter chimed to their right. A team of white horses pulling a light blue landau cantered by. Within it sat four of the Misses Preece dressed in gauzy pastel silks as lovely as marzipan confectioneries. They twirled parasols and fluttered dainty gloved fingers at passers-by.

Even next to her magnificent sisters, Kitty shone like a diamond. Her appearance was pure perfection, as if painted on canvas by a master artist. Long, dark ringlets cascaded down one broad lily-white shoulder. Her almond-shaped eyes dazzled; her wide lips were as lush as cherries. She possessed a resplendent bosom, as fully displayed as if it were evening. Her bare arms looked as if they'd been sculpted from marble.

Meggy's chest compressed. Nicholas had ridden with a goddess on the morning after he'd made love to Meggy. Of course, lust would've spiked his thoughts with such temptation before him; even Meggy could've gazed at Kitty for hours . . .

Meggy couldn't compete with beauty and sensuality like that if she tried for a thousand years.

Mr Webb cleared his throat. 'May I mention my proposal again, my lady?'

Meggy pulled her eyes from Kitty with the greatest of difficulty. 'I'd rather you not, Mr Webb, for I cannot give you a favourable answer today.'

Webb frowned. 'Lady Margaret, please forgive my impertinence, but I worry about your happiness. You are, of course, very much in love with Lord Holbrook—'

Meggy's heart lurched. She'd not told anyone that secret. '*What?*'

'—and he's a fool not to propose, for you seem to be quite perfect friends. I suppose he doesn't because . . . well, no, I oughtn't hazard a guess when I don't know the man. But I . . . I . . . what I mean to say, is if you decide you *could* marry me, I shan't mind that you are in love with Lord Holbrook.'

Meggy regained the ability to speak. 'But why do you think I'm in love with him?'

Webb shrugged. 'Your face glows the moment he enters a room. Your eyes sparkle and cannot be drawn away from him.' Webb half smiled. 'I'd give anything for you to look at me in such a way. Lady Margaret, although I haven't Lord Holbrook's looks and his position, I have a bit of wealth, as you know, and you and your siblings would never lack for anything. And I'd never, ever hurt you.'

Meggy's throat and eyes burned with unshed tears. 'You're a darling, Mr Webb, truly you are, but don't marry me. You must wait for the lady who *does* look at you in such a way.'

'I'm not sure that will ever happen.'

Meggy squeezed his arm. 'I'm certain it will. If I'd met you before Holbrook, I might've been able to do so. But you're correct about me. Perhaps I cannot marry Holbrook, but I cannot marry anyone else either.'

Not whilst she was so madly in love with Nicky.

26

When Webb had driven away, Meggy hastened up the wide front steps of Holbrook House. She intended to dash to her bedchamber and indulge her long-restrained tears. Then she'd soak in a refreshing bath, eat dinner alone in her room, and *rest*.

She must restore her energy and calm her emotions so she could speak with Nicholas about Kitty. Would he confess the truth on his own? Was there an innocent explanation for his actions?

But Nicholas blocked her plans – literally. He leaned hatless against the open front door, still in his riding clothes, and smoking again. His cheeks and chin were dark with unshaven shadow.

Meggy must pass him by. She wasn't stable enough to discuss Kitty yet.

'Good afternoon, Nicky,' she said when she reached the top of the stairs.

He inhaled on his cigar and exhaled a slow stream of white smoke. 'Afternoon.'

'You're smoking a great deal.'

He shrugged. 'It's that or drink. I decided smoking was wiser.' His lips compressed, and he blinked rapidly as he turned his cheek to her.

Impulsively, Meggy longed to ask about Kitty Preece, for at that moment her writhing heart yelled that Carow was mistaken. But before the words escaped, Nicholas met her gaze and coldness glinted in his eyes.

He puffed his cigar. 'Your suitors have been active today.'

Meggy wrung her hands, trying to rub out the tingling of her palms under her kid gloves. 'Yes.'

'Am I to wish you a lifetime of joy with some spineless fool? Or did you request *more time* of them as well?'

Meggy recoiled. 'Why would you be so cruel?'

'Me, cruel? Ha!' He flicked his cigar down the stone steps. It arched and then lay smouldering on the cobblestone drive. '*You're* the cruel one.'

Meggy's tears, long in abeyance, surged like a tidal wave. She threw her gloved hands over her face, turned her back, and fled back down the steps.

'Meggy, wait! Please come back.'

She didn't return. She sobbed into her hands as she ran unseeing. Her foot slipped, her ankle gave way, and she tumbled into strong, wool-clad arms. She pressed against a broad, sturdy chest and buried her face in folds of shirt linen.

But the scent was wrong. Soap and books rather than bergamot and tobacco.

Meggy withdrew. Through blurry eyes, she saw furrowed auburn brows and a frown upon lips customarily curled into a crooked grin.

'Are you hurt, Meggy?' Alexander asked.

'I tw-twisted m-my ankle.'

353

'Allow me to look, please.'

Alexander supported Meggy's back with a strong arm – how lovely to lean on a safe friend – as she sat upon the sun-warmed stone step. Ever so gently, Alexander removed her leather slipper and palpated her ankle through her silk stocking.

Nicholas's footsteps approached, then stopped. 'Meggy,' he said, tender-voiced, 'I shall carry you inside so you may rest comfortably whilst Alexander examines you.'

Fresh tears burned Meggy's eyes. Until she knew what had happened between Nicholas and Kitty, Meggy didn't want him to touch her. 'No, thank you. If I wanted that, I'd ask.'

'You can't stay on the front steps.'

'Pl-please go away, Nicky.' Now more than ever on this turbulent day, Meggy needed peace. The warm steps, the outside air, and Alexander's tender-kneading, knowledgeable fingers on her throbbing ankle provided more relief than anything else had.

'Meggy, please forgive me for what I said . . .'

'Not right now. My ankle hurts.' She buried her face in her hands. Why couldn't he leave her alone? All she'd wanted, all day, was time to reflect. Instead, she'd played with children despite an aching head, been subjected to two more marriage proposals in addition to Nicky's last night, and now she'd twisted her ankle.

'Nick,' Alexander said, 'I think you should give Meggy time before you ask for forgiveness for whatever you've done.'

Nicholas huffed, but his footsteps receded up the stairs.

Meggy winced as Alexander lay her foot on the steps, although the ache had lessened. The physician handed Meggy a handkerchief and sat beside her. She cradled her head and breathed through the thin cotton.

'Does your ankle still hurt?'

Meggy wiped her eyes. 'Not much anymore. Truthfully, it only hurt badly at the very beginning.'

'There's no swelling, so I think you merely turned it.' Alexander replaced her shoe. 'Do you want to go inside?'

'No, not yet.' Surely Nicholas hovered in the entrance hall, and she couldn't face him.

'Are you able to walk with me? Movement should help stabilise the joint.'

Meggy nodded, and Alexander helped her up.

'Put your arm through mine,' he said. 'Only a little weight on the ankle until you're quite certain it's strong again.'

Meggy's ankle soon recovered, but when she entered the rose garden with the perfume of the myriad blooms heavy in the air, she burst into a fresh bout of tears.

'Forgive me, Alexander,' she said through her sobs. 'I've been restraining these tears all day, and I simply cannot anymore.'

'No apology necessary. Cry as much as you need.'

She sat upon a marble bench and bawled into the damp handkerchief. But violent tears don't last forever, and when Meggy's at last subsided, tension released in her chest. Her eyes and nose felt swollen, but her mind had cleared, as she knew it would.

'Did you and Nick quarrel?' Alexander asked.

She dabbed her face with the tortured handkerchief. 'We quarrelled *terribly*. He wants me to marry him. Did you know that?'

Alexander coughed. 'Er, yes. I'm aware. I take it you'd rather not?'

'It's not as simple as that.' Meggy twisted the handkerchief. 'I've not told anyone else, but I . . . I love Nicky with my whole heart. In fact, I love him so much it . . . well, my heart *aches* when I think about how much I love him.'

Alexander blinked. 'I see. In that case, I don't quite understand your tears, Meggy.'

Meggy grasped his hands. 'You don't comprehend my internal conflict? I thought, perhaps, as a scientist, you might.'

The physician frowned. 'I confess, I don't. I've long wondered if you returned Nick's sentiments in kind, but now that you've so clearly indicated you do, I don't see where the conflict resides. You love him, he loves you. You want to marry him, he wants to marry you. Sounds like the happiest possible situation, from my perspective.'

'But I don't know if I want to marry him. My head doesn't agree with my heart.'

'Ah.' Alexander tilted his head. 'Now what do you mean by that?'

'My mind won't permit me to accept his proposal,' Meggy said. 'After how I've suffered from my brother's poor choices, I simply cannot believe people change their ways. Not forever, anyway. Therefore, my mind tells me that Nicky is impulsive and will continue to be so for the rest of his life. When he faces overwhelming challenge – and all lives have overwhelming challenge – Nicky slips into vice. Overall, his behaviour lately has been very good, but that cannot last forever. Why, even this morning, after our quarrel, Nicky was riding with . . . with a courtesan in Hyde Park.'

'I say, Meggy!' The physician's brows shot up. 'Who told you such a thing?'

'Mr Carow.'

'Bah!'

Meggy's hopes rose. 'Nicky *wasn't* riding with Kitty Preece?'

Alexander's cheeks pinked. 'Er, I can't say *that* . . .'

Meggy inhaled sharply.

'But Meggy,' Alexander said, smiling, 'it wasn't at all what it seems to a fool like Carow, who knows nothing about Nick. Nick was riding with *me* in the park – with me and the rest of our group. You know: John Tyrold, Edward Matlock and Sidney Wakefield. And, also with Kitty Preece, but Kit wasn't there because of Nick. She's Sidney's friend.'

Meggy's eyes stretched so wide her eyelids hurt. 'Kitty Preece is Reverend Wakefield's mistress?' she asked, gasping. Did that gorgeous, sensual woman and the handsome golden-haired curate, who seemed as noble as an angel, do with each other what Meggy had done with Nicholas in the gazebo?

357

Alexander shook his head. 'Oh no, not his mistress. Kitty's most definitely above Sid's touch. He says she's his writing muse, but it's all quite platonic and innocent, I assure you. She's only a friend to any of us, even Sid.'

'What did you mean when you said she's above his touch?'

Alexander reddened. 'I shouldn't have said that to you. Forgive me.'

'I despise it when men act as if ladies are too delicate to comprehend such matters.'

The physician smiled. 'Be fair, Meggy. Remember my line of work. *I* know ladies aren't delicate.'

'Then tell me what you meant when you said she's above Sidney's touch.'

Alexander stuck a finger under his shirt collar and tugged. 'A man needs a certain . . . income for someone like Kitty. Sidney will continue to be as poor as a church mouse until he gets his uncle's parish one day, and Kit's always been kept by dukes and . . .'

Meggy's heart pounded. 'And what?'

'And such.'

'Marquesses.'

Alexander sighed. 'Yes, but not Nick. He'd never touch Sidney's dearest friend, and, besides, even before you, he didn't keep mistresses.'

'Because he never maintains his interest in the same women. He told me so himself, and you only prove that point.'

'But, Meggy . . .'

'Can you guarantee Nicky will never break my heart?'

'I believe he won't, but you know I cannot guarantee it.'

Meggy sighed. 'Then what should I do?'

Alexander lifted his palms. 'All I can do is listen. You must decide for yourself.'

More tears streamed from the corners of Meggy's eyes. Alexander held out his arms, and she rested her cheek on his shoulder. She was no closer to a decision, but it was pleasant to unburden herself to a friend. He stroked her back; she closed her eyes.

Nicholas's voice shattered her peace. 'Goddammit, Alexander!'

The physician's arms went rigid.

Meggy turned. She hadn't heard Nicholas's boots on the brick walk, but he glowered under an arching arbour laden with yellow roses.

'Nick.' Alexander's tone was tense.

'On your feet *right now*.'

'Calm down first.'

'Absolutely not, you Scottish bastard. Stand up.'

'Nicky,' Meggy said. 'Please stop.'

Nicholas's eyes glinted. 'This is between me and Alexander. He knows what he has coming to him.'

Alexander stood, chin tilted, nostrils flaring, jaw clenched. 'You had better think about what you have coming to *you*.' He flexed his fingers. 'I warned you I wouldn't take this nonsense from you again.'

Nicky removed his coat and threw it to the ground. 'Damn you to call this nonsense.'

The two men glared at each other, their breath quick, their chests out.

Meggy rolled her eyes. They were like two stags preparing to lock antlers over a misunderstanding. She placed herself between them. 'Stop it, both of you. Alexander, thank you for our conversation, but you should go home. Nicky, put your coat on.'

Nicholas glared at the physician. 'I shall call on you later.'

'I look forward to it.' And, with his narrowed eyes locked with Nicholas's, Alexander pressed Meggy's hand to his lips. '*Adieu, ma chérie.* I enjoyed our time together *immensely.*' His voice was honeyed, but he sneered at his friend.

Nicholas lunged at Alexander, who strolled out of the rose garden with his hands clasped behind his back, but Meggy grasped Nicholas's arm. 'Stop it, Nicky, he's only teasing you because you're being nonsensical.'

She paused, gathering her breath to explain her conversation with Alexander.

But Nicholas's eyes blazed. 'I don't much mind Carow, Webb and Harrison – I still don't think you give serious consideration to any of them – but that snake in the grass has been waiting for me to fail. He wants you for himself.'

'No, he doesn't, Nicky,' Meggy said calmly. 'Alexander is merely my friend.' Her cathartic cry had calmed her and confessing her conflict to Alexander had strengthened her. She wanted to tell Nicholas everything and explain why she needed patience and support from him. She inhaled, readying her words.

But Nicholas scoffed, his lip curled, his expression horrid. 'Your *friend* – so you term me as well, Meggy. And we both know what you did with me last night.'

Anger as black as night rose inside Meggy. Her jaw dropped; her breast heaved. 'You . . . you beastly man!' How dare Nicholas take something so precious and drag it through the muck?

Nicholas glared. 'Don't play innocent. You were embracing him – he kissed you.'

Was he doubting Meggy's virtue? 'Nicky, he kissed my *hand*.'

'Yes, and he intended to kiss your lips when I came upon you both.'

'You imagined that.'

Nicholas shook his head, his lips turned down. 'And why the devil wouldn't he kiss you? He's only a man, and you were making yourself available to him. God knows I've fallen for your trap several times. I foolishly thought I was unique, but apparently that's how you behave with your *friends*.'

Meggy gasped, horror-struck. 'What's that supposed to mean, Nicky?' she asked, dangerously. He'd better dig himself out of this hole with an apology at once, or . . .

'It means precisely what you think it means.' Nicholas's voice cracked. 'You play with men's feelings the way a cat plays with a mouse. Harrison, Webb, Carow, Alexander, and *me*.' His face crumpled. 'You rip apart my love – my heart is *nothing* to you. You're crueller than Arabella.'

Meggy's smouldering rage exploded like lava. 'If I hadn't heard those words with my own ears, I never would've believed you capable of saying such a thing, Nicholas Burton! But at least now I have a definitive answer to your proposal. I will *never* marry you. Never, ever, ever!'

Meggy turned on her heel and stormed inside.

27

Nicholas collapsed upon the marble bench as Meggy, the embodiment of his hopes and dreams, stormed to the house. And then he *bawled*. Ragged, terrible tears as he gripped fistfuls of hair.

A footfall on the brick made him whip around, longing for Meggy, but it was only a wide-eyed gardener grasping a pair of pruning shears. 'Begging your lordship's pardon . . .' The man backed away.

'Stop – please. Send to the house for a bottle of brandy.' Nicholas smeared the tears off his cheeks with the back of his hands. Although he'd not touched brandy in months, he needed to drown his sorrows.

'Aye, m'lord.'

Five minutes later, a footman delivered a tiny decanter and a cut-crystal glass on a silver platter.

'I asked for a *bottle*.'

'L–Lady Rose suggested this instead, my lord.'

Nicholas's shoulders slumped. Damnably less poetic and romantic than what he'd had in mind, but drunkenness hadn't ever helped him, as Rosy had said for years. 'Very well. Fill the glass and take the rest inside.'

Dejected, Nicholas carried his drink to the middle of the maze – to the last place he'd been happy. In the gazebo, he sprawled upon a bench with one arm behind his head and nursed his brandy, resting the glass upon his waistcoat-clad chest between sips. He breathed the floral-laced air, spiced with his pungent drink as the skylarks began their evening love songs – undoubtedly singing to their mates over a cluster of eggs in their grass-lined nests. The lowering sun shone amber rays through the clematis vines on the west side of the gazebo, and the prismatic etching on Nicholas's crystal glass cast rainbows against the domed marble ceiling.

This *was* a magical spot – and now, forevermore imprinted with the heartbreaking memory of his love-making with Meggy. Those precious moments when he'd thought himself loved.

Nicholas's heart ached. He'd crossed an unfair – and untrue – line by mentioning Arabella, and he deserved Meggy's vitriol. He was as abusive as his mother, *and* as pathetic as his father. No wonder she sought solace in the arms of someone reasonable. Someone composed and self-possessed.

Nicholas's fingers tightened on his glass.

Someone who needed a beating.

The sun sat low in the sky when Nicholas left to settle his score with his friend. Because he was still hatless, the brightness glared as he plodded west along Piccadilly. He shielded his eyes with his hand, and his thumb brushed the stubble on his cheek.

He was a dishevelled, unshaven muddle.

Appropriate.

The sunlight no longer plagued him when he turned north on Half Moon Street, for the contiguous tall brick townhouses shadowed the cobbled road. Nicholas considered calling on John Tyrold or one of his other friends to mediate as he passed their residence. But he dismissed the idea.

After all, boxing had always improved Nicholas's mental functioning. It cleared his mind, focused his thoughts. Once he'd smashed his fist into Alexander's smug face, *then* he'd be able to accept the horrible fact that the physician was more worthy of Meggy's love.

The Mayfair Maternity Hospital, on a corner across from the Chesterfield Gate to Hyde Park, was a stone building with flowering window boxes and a daffodil-coloured door. Alexander's trim three-storey brick house adjoined its east side.

Nicholas banged the brass knocker.

The butler answered. 'Good evening, Lord Holbrook. Dr Mitchell is with his patients, but if your lordship cares to wait inside, I shall send him word of your arrival.'

'No, I shan't come in. Tell Dr Mitchell to meet me by the Serpentine when he's available.'

Nicholas entered the park through the wrought-iron entrance across Park Lane. A gravel footpath passed through an avenue of lime trees and traversed open green lawn towards the Serpentine. On the north side of the lake, Nicholas crossed a bridle path, scant of traffic at this time, and watched the sunset as he waited under the arching trees at the waterway's banks.

Alexander's voice drew Nicholas's attention. 'I expect you're here to apologise.'

'Not bloody likely. I'm here to settle a score with you.'

'What score is that?'

'You know how dearly I love Meggy. After everything you and I have shared over the years, I'd think my sentiments would matter to you at least a little. I know you're the better man, but I've *tried*. And to take her from me now—'

'Stop!' Alexander threw off his coat. 'I told you some months ago if you ever again accused me of attempting to steal Meggy's affections, I'd give you a trimming. And, by George, so I shall.'

Nicholas's coat joined Alexander's on the grass.

'Excellent.'

They squared off, but Nicholas wasted little time strutting. He recalled his friend's smug '*ma chérie*', and he led with a punch to the physician's stomach. But Alexander grabbed his arm and twisted him round with surprising agility. He planted a boot against his bottom, and Nicholas thudded onto the grass.

'Belly-go-firster, eh? Damn, Nick. What a predictable attack. I thought you'd be more imaginative.'

Nicholas jumped to his feet and swung at Alexander's face.

Only to end on the ground again.

Alexander laughed. 'Followed by a pathetic attempt at a facer. What poor sport this is. Have you had enough yet?'

But Nicholas saw red. 'I'll have enough when you eat dirt, you dog.' He attacked with an uppercut to the chin which knocked his friend back, combined with a left hook to the abdomen. Alexander struggled briefly to regain his breath, but Nicholas's victory was short-lived because Alexander's next punch was a solid facer that sent him reeling to the ground again.

Alexander flexed and shook his right hand. 'If you make me injure my hands, I'll meet you with swords next. These are my livelihood.' He grinned when Nicholas rose. 'Tapped your claret, I see.'

Nicholas put his fingers to his aching lip. They came away with blood.

'Not much you didn't. I didn't know you'd be this good.'

Alexander scoffed. 'Ye didnae ken ah'd be guid, eh? I'm Scottish, Nick. Of course I can fight, although I generally choose not to. These hands' – he waggled his eyebrows and flexed his fingers – 'are precious. Now, enough talking. I have patients to attend to.'

They attacked with equal zeal, and ended in a double headlock, each pummelling the other's back. Nicholas hooked Alexander's leg in a successful attempt to bring him to the ground, but Alexander returned in kind. They both ended in the grass, rolling on each other.

Alexander gained the advantage and pushed Nicholas's face into the ground. 'Apologise.'

Nicholas's left arm wasn't pinned. After a quick thrust, he was the one on top and straddling his friend's back. Alexander lay belly-down, and Nicholas pressed the physician's cheek into the dirt. Triumph swelled his chest. '*You* apologise.'

'What do I have to apologise for? Meggy's her own woman, Nick. She's free to make her own choices, and you can't control her.'

Nicholas's fist was poised for a blow, but Alexander's words paralysed him.

You can't control her.

His heart thudded; his ears rang. 'I'm not *controlling* her.'

'Are you so damned certain?'

The weight of his recent actions hit Nicholas like a boulder. Pressuring Meggy to marry him, demanding she account for her actions, mocking her need for time, disparaging her desire for physical love without commitment.

'Good God,' he said, aghast. 'No, I'm not certain at all, as a matter of fact.'

'Those are the first reasonable words I've heard from you in a while. Now get off me, you lump.' Alexander shoved Nicholas's chest.

Nicholas stood, although the world churned and his mind swirled.

Alexander rose and brushed dirt and grass off his trousers. His loose shirtsleeves were green-stained, his waistcoat dusty. 'Now, my friend, what would you do if I told you Meggy loves me?'

Nicholas's stomach knotted. '*Does* she love you?'

Alexander shook his index finger. 'I asked my question first. What would you do? Would you despise her? Would you flee to another woman to make her jealous?'

'No. No, I wouldn't. I wouldn't do either of those things.' Nicholas inhaled deeply, and his shoulders loosened as he exhaled. 'I shan't ever stop loving Meggy, and I wouldn't hurt her.'

Swans, matched in pairs, glided along the lake's glassy surface, and a weight lifted from Nicholas's chest. Papa hadn't been *weak* when he loved Nicholas's mother; he'd demonstrated the inexplicable power of unconditional love.

The recipient of such love doesn't earn it. The bearer bestows it as a gift.

Even if it makes him vulnerable to hurt.

Nicholas ran his fingers through his hair. 'If Meggy loves me and needs me, she'll come to me, in time. And even if she never wishes to marry me, I shall be her constant friend.'

'Good man! Took you long enough.' Alexander brushed grass off Nicholas's sleeve and then clasped him in a one-arm embrace. He whispered in his ear. 'By the way, Meggy and I spoke of *you* in the rose garden, you daft fool. You're a damned fortunate dog with good reason to hope.'

Nicholas's heart raced. His eyes cut to his friend. 'Truly?'

Alexander nodded and ruffled Nicholas's hair, and then pushed him away with a laugh. 'Aye, ye eejit.' He stuck his hands in his trouser pockets and looked over the water. 'Although it's what Edwin always knew, of course.'

'What the devil do you mean?' Nicholas asked, surprised.

369

Alexander shrugged. 'Edwin thought you and Meggy were perfect for each other. Told me so the last time I saw him. Asked me to help you both along on the path to everlasting happiness.'

'*Edwin* said that?'

'Yes. He adored Meggy. His first sibling, his little blue-eyed, freckled sister. So clever and capable, so selfless and darling, ever a spark of joy in his bleak life – those were his words.'

Nicholas blinked. 'Then why did he desert her?'

'Nick, Edwin's addictions ruled his life. He lost control, even to help the one he cherished the most. But he hoped you and she would love each other. He was damned fond of you; something you told him years ago convinced him that despite your best efforts to pretend otherwise, you're a noble sort of man. Edwin said if his death could unite you and Meggy, his life wouldn't have been in vain.'

'So his demand that I help Meggy find a husband was a ruse?'

Alexander lifted his brows. 'Depends on how you look at it. What did he ask of you?'

'He told me to find her a man of means and honour. Someone who will love the scamps and be kind to Meg . . . Oh, I see.' Nicholas's bruised lip ached when he smiled. 'I did have to look about a bit before I found him, didn't I? What a damned good scheme – and you were his accomplice all along. Were you never serious about courting Meggy?'

Alexander chuckled. 'I wouldn't say that. I doubted the hell out of the plan at first. How could Edwin

Fairchild's sister breach the impenetrable heart of Nicholas Burton? But then I saw Meggy and spoke to her – and I must confess, for several minutes, I thought to consign you and Edwin both to the devil, if I could. But you were already in love with her, and so I joined into the spirit of things again, much to Rose's relief.'

'Rose knew Edwin's scheme?'

'Yes, we amused ourselves planning how we'd play Cupid before you and Meggy arrived at Alton Park. We assumed you'd be the more difficult one to convince. But you were a lovesick mooncalf from the moment of your arrival – although as tormented as the very devil about it – whereas Meggy was as cool as a cucumber.' Alexander picked up their coats from the grass. He tossed Nicholas his and put on his own. 'She's less cool about you now, my friend. Be patient. Be worthy.'

Nicholas struggled into the tight garment. 'She's decidedly the opposite of cool now. She's furious with me, and rightly so.'

'Well, you know what to do.'

'Apologise. Grovel.'

Alexander nodded. 'An excellent start.'

They stood together at the shore as a cooling breeze rippled the water. A sliver of the setting sun perched upon the treeline, and the sky flamed. Alexander patted Nicholas on the back. 'I ought to return to my patients, but before I do, I want to give you one solid clout for causing me so much trouble this year and for bruising my hand with your impossibly hard head. The two complaints are related, you foolish and stubborn bastard – and you know you deserve it.'

Nicholas held up his hands. 'Do your worst, my friend. I shan't resist.'

Alexander grinned, and Nicholas braced his abdomen for the expected gut punch.

But instead, Alexander grabbed him by the shoulders and pushed him backwards.

And Nicholas fell, bottom first, into the Serpentine with a resounding splash.

28

Meggy hurried inside from the rose garden and removed her bonnet and gloves in the back vestibule overlooking the lawn. She took three deep breaths to release her smouldering rage, pursed her lips, and considered.

After longing for solitude all day, she was alone at last. But she didn't need to ponder Nicholas's proposal anymore. Meggy wouldn't marry a man who hurtled horrid accusations when she embraced a friend.

Dreadful, baseless accusations.

Fleeting images of Mr Webb's furrowed brow – *'if you decide you could marry me, I shan't mind that you are in love with Lord Holbrook'* – and Nicholas's sorrowful grey eyes – *'you play with men's feelings like a cat plays with a mouse'* – were swept aside.

Only to be replaced by Nicholas kneeling in the moonlight. *'You belittle our love . . . since the beginning of our acquaintance, you've been hot one moment and cold the next . . .'* and *'You know how desperately I love you, Meggy, and yet you dash my hopes again. I've tried so hard to be a better man.'*

She bit her lip.

'You rip apart my love – my heart is nothing to you.'

Meggy shook her head. No, she was selfless, doing what was best for her siblings, and Nicholas was a fool not to understand.

A beastly, horrid fool.

Meggy needed to free herself from Nicholas's hold on her.

She crossed her arms and chewed her bottom lip. Tomorrow she'd call upon John Tyrold and rethink financial matters. With a few hundred pounds a year, perhaps she could maintain a small cottage for the children and Miss Kimberley. Yes, it would take longer to pay off the mortgage on Berksleigh Hall, but it would be just *them* again, like in the old days. Before they knew Nicky and Rose and the girls.

Meggy pushed away a sudden painful longing. Her heart was sentimental, but her mind was pragmatic. With time away, she'd recover from this impractical love.

She bounded up the stairs. A sweet cottage . . . it would be stone, of course, perhaps with a thatched roof. Wisteria would blossom upon the weathered grey sides and rose bushes would bloom beside the wooden door. Copper would dash about in a wee garden behind a mossy stone wall. Meggy would devote herself solely to the children, as she'd always done . . .

And Nicholas would see they didn't need him in the *least*. He could sulk and pout and feel sorry for himself, as he was wont to do, but it would make no difference to Meggy because she wouldn't be there to see it.

She ignored the lump in her throat as she strode down a corridor on the top floor and burst into the children's chambers. Much like at Alton Park, these sun-soaked rooms overflowed with toys and games: rocking horses, tin soldiers, dolls, atlases and puzzles. Meggy smothered all the children in kisses but squeezed Harry and Sophy until they wriggled. She'd tell them of her cottage plan the moment she'd spoken to Mr Tyrold.

Meggy refused to think about how much Harry and Sophy would miss Rose and her daughters.

And Nicky.

By eight o'clock, an hour before sunset, the children were ready for bed. Reading to Harry and Sophy in the evenings had always been a joy to Meggy, but because of the busy social season in London, she and Rose had often missed doing so in the last two months.

Meggy delighted in it this evening.

Children after their baths were children at their sweetest. They smelled clean and soapy, dressed in cotton night-clothes fresh from the day's airing. Tired from play and full of dinner, they sought snuggly story-time adventures.

Sophy requested *Much Ado About Nothing* from the children's book adaptation of Shakespeare.

'One of my favourites.' Rose opened the volume, and the girls clustered about her. 'Let us see if true love will prevail against the odds, shall we?'

Meggy's stomach dropped, and for a moment, she couldn't attend to Rose's sweet cadence. When she did, the words made her heart drop.

'. . . *so it was with Benedick and Beatrice; these two sharp wits never met but a perfect war of raillery was kept*

375

up between them, and they always parted mutually displeased with each other . . .'

Meggy stared at her hands. So it was with Nicholas and Margaret – they always parted mutually displeased with each other.

Harry tapped her shoulder. 'I don't like these love stories,' he whispered. 'Will you read to me from my pirate book instead?'

Meggy smiled, relieved. 'Certainly, squirrel.'

Harry placed a large, leather-bound volume in her lap.

Meggy read the title aloud. '*A General History of the Pyrates*.' She flipped through the pages. Woodcut illustrations of pirates fluttered between tales of their lives. Charts and diagrams of ships were dispersed throughout the text. 'Where did you get this lovely book, Harry?'

'Nicky gave it to me.'

Of course.

Harry opened to a page marked by a folded piece of paper. 'Nicky and I stopped reading here last night before he left to dress for the ball.'

The folded paper bore Nicholas's seal. 'Is that a letter, Harry?'

'Yes. My special letter from Nicky.'

Meggy raised an eyebrow. 'Why is it special?'

Harry rubbed his nose with the back of his hand. 'Because it teaches me to be the best I can be, even when it's difficult. One day at a time, Nicky always says. Sometimes two steps forward and one step back, but always with an eye on the goal.'

376

'Nicky says that?' It was a lovely sentiment—and so practical.

Harry nodded so hard his round cheeks jiggled.

Meggy's palms prickled. 'D-Does Nicky share what *his* goal is?'

'Yes. Nicky's goal is to be a sturdy ship.'

Meggy blinked. She hadn't expected *that*. 'A sturdy ship? What does he mean?'

Harry pointed at the folded letter. 'Read, and you'll understand.'

Meggy opened the single page covered in Nicholas's sloping hand. Her heart hammered harder and harder as she read, and her eyes lingered over the last paragraph: *And whatever happens, I shall be there when you need me, whatever mistakes you make, whatever accidents befall you, whatever joys and successes you experience. Our friendship, Harry, is like a sturdy ship such as we saw in Ipswich. Whatever tempests the seas churn, we shall work together to stay afloat.*

Meggy's eyes widened as realisation washed over her like waves.

Whatever tempests the seas churn . . .

. . . we shall work together to stay afloat.

She gasped – *she* was the fool. She was the beastly, horrid fool who'd not recognised that she, Rose, Nicholas and the children had long since become a family. A group of people bound by love who resided together in a sturdy ship.

A sturdy ship they *worked* to keep afloat, no matter what tempests the seas churned.

Meggy stood. The book slipped from her hands, thudded onto the floorboards, and the letter fluttered after it.

Everyone looked at her.

'Something the matter, dearest?' Rose asked.

Meggy clasped her hands to her breast. 'I've just realised something.'

'What?'

'There *are* no guarantees.'

'No guarantees about what, dearest?'

'In life. There are no guarantees in life.' Meggy shook her head. 'No, that's not what I mean. That sounds silly. I always knew there were no guarantees in life. I mean there are no guarantees in *love*. No absolutes. No assurances. Love makes us vulnerable, therefore loving someone is *always* a risk.'

Rose smiled. 'Yes.'

Meggy pointed at the letter. 'Working together to build a boat to weather any storm reduces the risk, but there are still no guarantees. I simply must decide if I love him well enough to take that risk. If I love him well enough to be vulnerable.'

'And do you?'

Meggy's heart filled her chest. 'Yes, Rose. I do. He's the centre of my world.'

Rose's smile broadened. 'Well then.'

Harry tugged at her skirt. 'But *who*, Meggy? Not one of those rapscallions who drive you around Hyde Park, I hope.'

'No,' Rose said. 'She means Nicky, of course.'

Harry's eyes sparkled. 'Do you, Meggy? *Do* you mean Nicky?'

Meggy crinkled her nose. 'Yes, Harry, I mean Nicky.'

A chorus of squeals erupted from the girls.

Meggy knelt before her brother. 'Harry, I'm very sorry, dearest, but may I read your pirate book to you tomorrow night?'

'Because you want to find Nicky and tell him you'll marry him?'

Meggy nodded.

Harry beamed. 'Then *yes*. Love's a scaly thing, but not if it means Nicky will be my big brother.'

Meggy held her hand to Rose. 'Will you help me find him?'

Rose put down the book, kissed the girls, and grinned. 'I'd be delighted.'

Three quarters of an hour later, after a search of the gardens and a dash to Alexander's house, Rose and Meggy walked arm-in-arm along the gravel footpath from Cumberland Gate towards the Serpentine. And just as the last bit of the setting sun slipped past the treeline, a silhouetted Nicholas fell back into the water with a resounding splash.

Meggy gasped.

Nicholas had given in to his despair.

She dropped Rose's arm and sprinted to save her love.

29

Meggy would have jumped into the lake to save Nicholas from his watery death, but Alexander caught her arm.

Nicholas treaded water in the evening glow, not the least bit like someone who'd attempted to kill himself. 'Did you come to rescue me, Meggy?'

She nodded, and Alexander released her.

Nicholas crawled out of the Serpentine. Rivulets streamed from his clothes, and water squished over the tops of his boots. 'I don't understand how you suddenly appeared, but as you did, please allow me to apologise at once.'

Meggy crossed her arms. 'Because you spoke to Alexander and *now* you realise my innocence?'

'In fairness,' Alexander said, 'he realised on his own before I told him anything.'

Nicholas shook his head. 'That's not perfectly true. Meggy, I realised it doesn't matter. You're free to feel however you wish about Alexander, just as you are free to take as much time as you need to consider your future. Forgive me for pressuring you.'

Tension eased in Meggy's shoulders. 'Thank you, Nicky. Thank you for saying those words. That's what

I wanted from you last night – I needed comfort and understanding and patience. And . . . and reassurance.'

Nicholas closed his eyes. 'Meggy, I'm so terribly sorry I didn't understand last night, but I do now. Next time I shall remember to *ask* how I can help you—'

'You *never* remember to ask, Nicky.'

He nodded. 'At any rate, I promise to do better, but you may need to remind me on occasion. And I shall provide what you need, no matter what you decide about us.' He put a hand to his heart. 'Forgive me, please. For last night and for my inexcusable behaviour today. If you can.'

'I *can* forgive you, Nicky. Even for what you said in the rose garden, but don't *ever* say such a thing again.'

'I shan't. I can promise that with conviction, because the truth is, I give you my love with no conditions. It will always be yours to command, yours to treasure or throw away as you wish.'

Warmth infused Meggy from head to toe. Despite trembling legs and weak knees, as if her muscles had melted, she stepped forward and put her hand to Nicholas's wet cheek.

But rather than say the words she'd long held back, she gasped. 'Why! What happened to your lip? You're bleeding.'

He sniffled as he leaned his head into her palm. 'Alexander cuffed me.'

Meggy whipped her head around, her brows drawn together. 'What did you hit Nicky for, you horrid man?'

Alexander lifted his hands. 'I was trying to knock some sense into him.'

She scowled. 'You didn't need to do that. He knocked sense into himself.'

'He did indeed, and I heartily apologise to *you*, Meggy, for my boorish behaviour.' The physician placed his hat on his head with a smile. 'My dear Rose, it's an enchanting evening. Would you object to a stroll with me? A promenade along Rotten Row, and then I shall see you safely home?'

Rose put her hand on his elbow. 'It would be a pleasure. There's something divine about the park at twilight.'

'Romantic, I would say.'

'Just so. The scent of love everywhere.'

Alexander sniffed the air. 'I smell only a sort of foul fishy stench coming from your brother, but I shall take your word for it. Good night, Nick. *Adieu*, Meggy. Should you require my professional services in, say, nine or ten m—'

Rose clapped her hand over his mouth as she pealed in laughter. They doubled over in a half-embrace and staggered away, but their merriment floated back for some time.

Meggy and Nicholas gazed at each other in the dusk, her hand still on his cheek.

Nicholas cleared his throat. 'Alexander is damnably impudent. I didn't beat him soundly enough.'

Meggy stepped closer and brushed Nicholas's bruised mouth with her thumb. 'This must've hurt terribly.'

His eyes twinkled. 'Not so very badly. Alexander didn't loosen any teeth, after all – although I wish he had. It would bring me closer to your toothless ideal husband.'

Meggy's hand dropped, but she stepped closer and fiddled with the buttons on his sodden waistcoat. 'Nicky, would you . . . would you be horribly disappointed in me if I prefer a *young* husband *with* teeth, after all?'

He inhaled sharply, his chest swelling under his waistcoat. 'But what shall we do about our partnership to find you an old man?'

She cast a glance through her lashes. 'I fancy changing the terms of our partnership. I'd like something more . . . lasting. Something forever.'

'My sweet, sweet love.' Nicholas grasped Meggy's hands and pressed them against his heart. '*Truly*? What changed your mind?'

'I realised *some* things are worth the risk. And true love is one of those things.'

His eyes softened into grey pools. 'True love? Do you love me?'

Meggy rose on her tiptoes to whisper into his ear. 'Nicholas Burton, I love you with my whole heart.'

He drew in a ragged breath and clasped her to him. And although the front of her gown dampened, the embrace was warm. 'Will you marry me, then, Meggy?'

Meggy pulled away. 'About that . . .'

His smile vanished. 'Yes?'

'You *do* need to kneel. You've never proposed *properly*.'

Nicholas beamed. 'I shall remedy that now.' Water sloshed from one boot as he knelt on the ground.

He retained her right hand, and the last light of dusk reflected off his tear-damp eyes. 'Margaret Fairchild' – his voice broke, and he laughed – 'I *hope* I can speak without sobbing. Margaret Fairchild, my love for you is strong enough to withstand the challenges of life – and it grows greater every moment I'm with you. Share my life with me, please, and allow me to care for you and the scamps. To provide for you and protect you. I have a thousand faults, I know, and I've made many mistakes – and I shan't ever be perfect – but I swear I shall always love you, and I shall be true to my marriage vows. Meggy, will you do me the honour of becoming my wife?'

The rest of the world receded into the background. Meggy was weightless, and, as her heart lifted like a cloud, a warm surge spread to the tip of every extremity.

Yes, yes, yes. But first . . .

She trailed her fingers along his cheek. 'My darling Nicky, before I give you my answer, I need to say something. As we pledge our unconditional love, we must also give each other our complete trust. No more jealousy. There's only us, faithful to each other, in the ship we work together to keep safe, united as we weather every storm. Do you agree?'

Nicholas nodded. 'Always and forever.'

'Then, *yes*, Nicky. I shall marry you.'

He closed his eyes and squeezed her hand. 'Oh, my dearest love. Other men have said it to other women, but none with such heartfelt sentiment – you've *truly* made me the happiest of men.'

Meggy gasped as he pulled her onto his knee, her bottom on his thigh, and held her in a tight embrace. Her gown soaked up more water from his saturated coat, and she nestled her face into his sodden neck. And they both laughed.

'I'm getting you thoroughly wet, Meggy.'

She giggled into his ear. 'Not *yet*, but soon, I hope.'

Nicholas threw his head back and roared, and Meggy caught the infectious joy. They gripped each other until their tears streamed. 'My joke wasn't *that* amusing,' Meggy gasped. 'I think we're both giddy.'

Nicholas held her face between his hands. 'We have good reason to be. May I kiss you, my love?'

In answer, Meggy leaned forward and pressed her lips against his bruised mouth. His tongue slipped into her, her own answered back. Nicholas's embrace was warm protection, safety and security. But it was also smouldering heat and rising passion.

It was love. Romantic, fervent, everlasting love.

Meggy kissed him harder, and he winced. 'Did I hurt you?'

'A little. But please continue.'

She touched his mouth. 'My poor, wounded Nicky.'

'I shall be well again, at some point.'

'I shall care for you until you are.' She kissed his forehead. 'And you must be cold and uncomfortable in these beastly, sodden clothes.'

He sniffled and nodded. 'I am, a little.'

'You need a warm bath.'

'That would be nice.' He twisted a curl that lay

upon her shoulder. 'And after *that* . . .' He trailed the tip of his finger along the neckline of her dress, and his eyes twinkled with playfulness. 'Meggy, once you mentioned a hot posset – brandy and milk, if I recall correctly. For your husband when he's feeling poorly. To be spoon-fed as he lies upon your breast. Do you remember?'

She smiled. 'Yes.'

'Might *I* – he twisted the curl again – 'have a warm brandy posset tonight?'

Meggy pushed wet curls off his forehead. 'No, Nicky.'

'But why not, my love?'

'Because you already drank brandy today. I tasted it when you kissed me.' She pressed her lips to his forehead. 'So, no more brandy, but you *may* have a posset of boiled milk with honey and nutmeg.'

'Spoon-fed to me as I lie upon your breast?'

'Naturally.'

'Then that's perfect.' He grinned and stood, helping her to her feet. 'Shall we go home? To *our* home?'

Meggy snuggled against his sodden arm. 'Yes, Nicky.'

Dusk had deepened into darkness as they strolled onto Knightsbridge from the south-eastern exit of the park. Meggy leaned against Nicholas's shoulder. His boots squelched with every step, and the night air was cool against her damp gown.

As they walked together under the gas streetlamps, Meggy pressed her mouth to Nicholas's coat and chuckled.

'What's amusing?'

'We must look ridiculous.'

He laughed. 'Likely so. Do you mind?'

'No, my darling Nicky. We are in our safe ship, after all.'

'We are indeed.' Nicholas patted her hands. 'My love, I want to tell you something about Edwin . . .'

30

At Alton Park on a warm afternoon in early July, Meggy dressed for her bridal trip with the aid of her new sister Rose, in the gilded and ornate chambers known as the Marchioness's Rooms.

Meggy laughed as her snowy silk net and glistening satin wedding gown slipped to the ground, for Rose had just relayed a tale. After the wedding breakfast, Eliza had admitted to her mother that *she* was the reason Harry had blackcurrant juice smeared upon his snub nose when he handed her new Aunt Meggy to Uncle Nicky in marriage.

'To tell the truth,' Meggy admitted, 'I didn't notice Harry's dirty nose.'

Rose's smile glowed. 'You and Nicky had eyes only for each other.'

Meggy didn't even attempt to deny it.

Rose assisted Meggy into a cool summer frock for her journey.

'Mark my words,' Meggy said. 'Eliza and Harry will end up married.'

Rose sobered as she laced the gown. 'I wouldn't presume, of course. Harry's an earl, and with *my* background . . .'

Meggy wagged a finger. 'None of that nonsense.'

'You know what I mean. I'm only being practical.'

'But you know Harry's not one of *those* sorts, Rose. None of us are. Family and friendships are stronger than that. Family like ours and *certain* friendships, I mean.'

Rose fastened the clasp of Meggy's pearl necklace and arranged a dainty lace cap – signifying that Meggy was a married woman – on her curls. She assisted Meggy into her light green spencer jacket and green-trimmed straw bonnet.

She kissed Meggy's cheek. 'Sweetest sister.'

Meggy kissed her back. 'Cherished sister.'

They embraced.

Then Rose waved her hand at the room. 'These chambers are hideous and look nothing like *you*, dearest. The decoration was my mother's choice, and she was as ridiculous about gold as I am about pink. I shall do them over whilst you and Nicky are away in the Lake District, so please tell me now what colours you want.'

Meggy shrugged. 'I'm certain whatever you decide will be lovely – except, if you don't mind, I'd rather not have pink.'

Rose laughed. 'I don't mind in the least. But what *is* your favourite colour?'

'I don't think I ever had one until recently, but now I'd have to say grey.'

'*Grey*? Grey's not a colour – it's a drab shade.'

'I disagree. The soft grey of a dove's wing *is* a colour. Neither blue nor lavender, but something between them which surpasses both in loveliness. Look in the mirror, and I shall show you.'

Rose's laughter chimed. 'You mean the colour of Nicky's eyes.'

'And yours, my dear sister.'

Rose smiled and then surveyed the space through narrowed eyes. 'I *shan't* do this room in grey. Not *only* in grey, at any rate. But lavender and a soft blue *and* grey . . . perhaps.' She nodded. 'Yes, it would be an interesting project.'

Meggy kissed her cheek. 'I shall love whatever you do, Rose.'

Nicholas was waiting in the white marble entrance hall when Meggy emerged. He wore a blue tailcoat, light trousers, gleaming Hessian boots, and crisp linen, and he stood within a rectangle of sunlight streaming from the tall window.

When their gazes locked, he grinned his impossibly beautiful smile and his eyes shone with love.

And Meggy's heart soared.

He offered his arm. 'Shall we, Lady Holbrook?'

She tucked her gloved hand into the crook of her husband's elbow, and they descended the wide front steps of Alton Park with the children and Rose following. The crested travelling carriage awaited them.

'I'm reminded, my love, of your leaving Berksleigh Hall with me ten months ago. You didn't allow me to assist you into the carriage then, but may I now?'

She smiled. 'Please do.'

Rather than offering a hand, Nicholas swept Meggy off her feet and carried her up the carriage steps as the girls giggled. He plopped her onto the upholstered seat and kissed her forehead.

Then he leaned his head out the door. 'Harry, my boy. Hand up Caesar, please.'

'Is your pug coming with us, Nicky?' Meggy asked.

Nicholas sat beside her, Caesar in his arms. 'Edwin's dog? Absolutely.'

And Meggy's heart filled her chest. 'Yes.' She scratched Caesar's head. 'I'm glad he is.'

'But Caesar, you must sit with your back to the horses, because I want my wife all to myself.' Nicholas placed the pug on the opposite seat. Caesar turned three times on the silk cushion and collapsed with a sigh.

The team lurched forward, and they began their journey north. Nicholas and Meggy embraced during their first precious moments of solitude as husband and wife. The carriage swayed as Caesar snored.

Nicholas's hand rubbed Meggy's back, kneading away tension. Her arms encircled his waist under his coat, and her cheek pressed against his shoulder.

Nicholas's hand stilled. He placed his finger under Meggy's chin. 'Edwin saved my life *twice*.'

Meggy raised an eyebrow. 'Did he?'

'Yes. Once literally and once figuratively. He helped me find my purpose again.'

'Which is?'

'To be the man I always longed to be. To be my father's son.'

Meggy smiled. 'You *are* your father's son. But you're also more than that. You're *my* Nicky.' They kissed. 'You don't doubt it anymore, do you, my darling? That you *are* his son?'

Nicholas shrugged. 'Rosy is correct. I'm his son because he called me his son, and he was my father because . . . because he loved me unconditionally and wholeheartedly.'

Meggy crinkled her nose. 'And you clearly have his smile.'

'A smile's only a smile. It could be anyone's.'

'No, not yours and your father's. You both have a distinctive little tilt to the corners of your lips, so you look as if you're smiling even when you aren't. It's a certain something that proclaims your inherent good-ness, even when you're being a scoundrel. I noticed at once, of course – the moment you stepped from your carriage by the brambles at Berksleigh Hall. I told you so as we walked together in the gardens. But I thought I mistook myself.'

'You *did* mistake yourself. The good man inside me had been hiding so long you couldn't possibly have noticed him.'

'I don't know about that, but I shan't argue. He's here with me now, and that's what matters.'

They snuggled closer, and Nicholas played with a curl upon her shoulder. 'Do you know I fell in love with you in a carriage, Meggy?'

'Did you indeed? When, precisely?'

'Not fifteen minutes after we'd left Berksleigh Hall. You were exhausted – I perceived it in your expression, although you tried to hide it – but you'd brought food and travelling games for the children, and you distributed them with kisses and hugs and endearments, and answered all the scamps' questions with loving patience. I didn't realise at the time, but that was the moment when I gave you my heart.'

She smiled. 'Truly?'

'Yes.'

She played with the buttons on his waistcoat. 'That's *very* interesting, because I *also* fell in love with you in a carriage.'

'Really? I can't imagine when. Unless . . . was it on the way home from Lady Frampton's ball in London?'

'No, not then. Not whilst we were in London at all.'

'We've rarely been in a carriage together – you *can't* mean that terrible drive from Ipswich in my curricle.'

She laughed. 'No, not then either. It was when you played a little game with the children about Sir Knight rescuing Dolly from Pugius Caesar and the sleeping dragon. Do you recall?'

Nicholas's hand stilled on her shoulder. Meggy grinned up at him, but he didn't smile back. He blinked, his mouth ajar. 'You *cannot* be serious.'

'But I am.'

'You've loved me since *then*? Since the same morning when I fell in love with you?'

She scrunched her nose. 'Yes. Ever since then, even though you were a reprehensible rake.'

He frowned. 'I'll be damned.'

Meggy rested her head against him. Some minutes passed before Nicholas again broke the silence. 'I'm still a reprehensible rake.'

'*Are* you?'

'Yes indeed. But there is only one woman this rake wants.'

'Who's that?'

He lowered his voice as if telling a secret. 'A grand lady indeed. Margaret Burton, the Marchioness of Holbrook.'

Meggy glanced through her lashes. 'Fortunately Lady Holbrook is a bit rakish herself.'

'*Is* she?'

'She's an extremely lusty lady.' And Meggy placed her hand over Nicholas's trousers. He was erect in a moment, and his face fell into heavy-lidded passion. It was an expression that did impossible things to Meggy's body: flutters and tingles and urgent desire.

Nicholas whipped the curtains closed around them. The sunbeams filtering through the green velvet cast a muted light like a shady forest. Meggy unbuttoned his trousers and released his cock. He moaned. 'Show me how lusty a lady my wife is.'

Meggy straddled him, and her white skirts – embroidered with lilies-of-the-valley – fell between them in a frothy muslin pile. She was wet and ready, as she always was, and she closed her eyes as she slid onto him. Ah, the exquisite pleasure of having the man she loved inside of her. She squeezed him, and he groaned, lost already to passion. She leaned forward and whispered from the depths of her heart those words he cherished more than any others in the world. 'I love you, Nicky, you wonderful, wonderful man.'

'Oh, Meggy. My heart, my joy, my wife.'

Acknowledgements

I love stories. History, novels, fairy tales, plays and musicals, anecdotes about daily life told over lattes at a steamy-windowed coffee house on a snowy day. Old photographs speak to me, as does art. I crave stories when I travel: tell me about this place, what it's like to live here, your history, your culture.

Stories are at the core of everything. Sometimes amusing, sometimes heart-wrenching, always testaments to life.

Imaginative tales have lived inside me since my child-hood, writhing to escape. When the pandemic abruptly halted my creative lifeline – teaching drama – I pursued a life goal: writing a novel.

I hoped to write a book that paid homage to two of my favourite storytellers of all time: the incomparable Jane Austen and the marvellously fun Georgette Heyer. These magnificent icons influence all Regency romance writers directly or indirectly; I am no different. Thanks to a lifetime fascination with the long eighteenth-century, I knew the history – how difficult could the rest be?

Turns out, it's incredibly difficult to write a novel, and I could not have done so without the support and guidance of many people. I've dedicated *A Lady's Risk* to my first two cheerleaders, my dear friends and fellow drama teachers, Jessica Riley and Julie Stanley. Amanda Dinscore and Olivia Marsh were my initial readers, zipping through the flawed first draft of this novel in sections and encouraging me to keep going. Their early advice strengthened Meggy and Nicholas's story greatly. My beloved critique partner (also, apparently, the British twin from whom I was separated at birth) Jessica Bull – a fellow Janeite and long eighteenth-century historical fiction writer – was my rock. We make the Atlantic Ocean as small as possible by our frequent virtual chats – I with my coffee and Jessica with her tea – in which we dissect each other's writing. Because of Jessica, the loneliness of my writing life (and it can be lonely indeed) is very much reduced.

I believe in chasing one's dreams, but chasing this dream required a teacher, and I am immensely grateful to my mentor and first editor, Suzy Vadori, who took me under her wing after a mutual friend introduced us on a most auspicious day. Suzy teaches the best virtual creative writing course available – and at tremendously good value. Suzy, thank you a million times over for sharing your wealth of expertise.

I owe many thanks to my sisters-in-law Kristen Hassmiller and SaraLynn Welke, who read early drafts and cheered me every step of the way. My everlasting gratitude also goes to my dear friend Kim Williams.

To these nine women collectively: although I dedicated *A Lady's Risk* to Jessica R and Julie, I dedicate the series to all of you, because you each played a pivotal part (or several pivotal parts) in my writing journey. Stay tuned for your upcoming novels.

Several other readers perused bits and pieces of this novel in various draft forms. To all of you, especially fellow Canadian romance writer C.J. Banks, thank you. And to Paula Joiner, for being a much-needed pair of fresh eyes at the end – thanks, buddy.

And to brilliant Regency Romance author Mary Balogh, for offering valued advice: thank you so much for sharing your expertise.

To my publisher and editor, Rhea Kurien: I cannot thank you enough for seeing potential in a manuscript that still needed much work, and for your amazing editing suggestions which nudged me into developing a stronger novel.

To everyone at Orion Dash and Hachette UK who helped, especially Sanah Ahmed – thank you.

To my agent, Kate Nash, and to Saskia Leach – thanks for your support!

My thanks go to my brother and mother, who took the news of my steamy novel surprisingly well, and to the rest of my extended family for not scoffing when I told you I wanted to be a writer. To all friends and family who offered encouragement, thank you. It meant a great deal.

Thank you to my children, Benjamin and Susannah. During the writing of this book, my young teens learned to wash clothes, make meals, and master the Toronto transit system because their father worked impossibly long hours as a frontline worker during a pandemic, and their mother used lockdown to write novels.

And how much less pleasant my days in front of a computer monitor would've been without the presence of my dog Scout and my cat ChiChi, who curl into little sleeping furballs beside me as I write. Thanks, floofs.

Lastly, a quick note on my historical sources. I owe a debt of gratitude to the Twitter long-eighteenth-century community, social historians, reenactors and fashion historians, especially Chris McKay, Kitty Pridden, Paul Couchman, Catherine Curzon and A Stitch in Time.

I am a social historian by education, and the vast majority of my historical research comes from primary sources: paintings; letters; memoirs; eighteenth-century cookbooks, servants' manuals, travel guidebooks and dictionaries; also maps and drawings. These primary sources are too innumerable to name individually.

I also relied on several invaluable (and fascinating) secondary sources, which I list in no particular order: *Georgian London: Into the Streets* by Lucy Inglis; Peter Ackroyd's *Revolution*; Robert Morrison's *The Regency Years*; *Jane Austen's England* by Roy and Leslie Adkins; Roy Porter's *English Society in the Eighteenth Century*; Amanda Vickery's *Behind Closed Doors: At Home in Georgian England*; and Ian Mortimer's *The Time Traveller's Guide to Regency Britain*. My heartfelt gratitude to these brilliant historians.

I've saved my biggest thanks for last: thank you, Tim, for supporting my crazy dreams and for challenging me to be my best self.

Printed in Great Britain
by Amazon